WHY WAIT FOR THE WIND?

P P Leonard

CONTENTS

Cordula's Tale

Cover Art by: Gill Gill Illustration

Why Wait for the Wind? is a thorough re-working of my earlier award-winning book about Ursula and her 'army of women' *Ursula's Maiden Army* which was published in the USA, Germany, Italy and Russia (see below).

The story has now been re-written with greater historical detail; and additional episodes have been added, especially to the later sections accounting for the women's tragic demise.

Publishing history of the earlier version:

USA   *Ursula's Maiden Army** - Beagle Bay Books 2006

Germany   *Das Heer der Jungfrauen*** - Rowohlt Taschenbuch 2004

Italy   *L'esercito della Fanciulle* - Mondadori/Harliquin 2006

Russia   *Королева легионов Афины* - AST 2008

Awards:

* USA 2006: winner of Independent Publisher (IPPY) Book Award in the Historical Fiction category.

** Germany 2004: "recommended read" in *Die Welt* newspaper.

I dedicate this book to the many thousands of women who met a violent death outside the gates of the Roman city of Cologne sometime in late-Antiquity and whose heroic deeds sowed the seeds in peoples' minds that would eventually develop into the legend of St Ursula and her 11,000 'virgin martyrs'.

Who these women really were and whether or not they regarded themselves as an "army" we can only speculate*. All we know for certain is that a very large number of them were killed in some sort of mass killing and their remains are still to be found to this day both within and beneath the Basilica of St. Ursula in modern-day Cologne.

If you examine their skeletons and study the evidence still visible of their wounds, I'm confident that, like me, you will conclude we cannot rule out theirs being a death worthy of great warriors.

*See "Historical Note" p 334

CORDULA'S TALE

I

'*AAA-YYY-EEE!*'

A young girl's high-pitched scream filled the villa's main reception room, making Cordula and her visitor jump. The visitor, a tall man in fine regalia, had been carefully unwrapping the precious object that was the purpose of his visit and had just exposed some braids of vivid red hair that were obviously part of a dead woman's head.

Startled by the shriek, the visitor let go of the sackcloth that had protected the gruesome object on its long journey from Germania. The cloth fell away revealing a face; and the dark caverns of its sunken eyes stared with a cold penetrating gaze directly at the gap in the curtains through which the young girl was peeping.

'*AYY-EEE!*' squealed the girl again, grabbing her brother for protection.

'Come here *at once* young lady!' commanded Cordula. 'You too young man; I know you're also there.' She glared at the curtains. 'I thought the pair of you were out feeding the animals. How long have you been listening? What have you heard?'

The girl burst from her hiding place and ran into her mother's arms sobbing. Sheepishly, her older brother followed, mouth agape and unable to take his eyes from the monstrosity upon the table.

'And who might these young folk be?' asked the visitor after the girl's sobs died down. His voice was heavily accented, but cultivated with a warm and friendly tone.

'Oh, I beg your pardon Your Grace.' Cordula turned her children round to present them, twisting their shoulders to stop them gazing at the head. 'Children, this is Bishop Clematius of Colonia. Your Grace, this is— '

'A very special young man,' interrupted Clematius. 'One of only two living Britannic witnesses of the martyrdom of the province's best, though a mere babe in arms at the time.'

The boy bowed politely. Clematius responded with a deferential nod before bending forward and looking deeply into the boy's eyes.

'Tell me young man, I'm curious. Do you have any memories of that day; any recollection at all?'

The boy looked questioningly at his mother. Cordula was staring at them intently, her expression tense and guarded. Reluctantly, she nodded permission for her son to answer.

'I ... I'm not sure Your Grace. I don't remember exactly, but I do have a dream sometimes; I dream of something white and beautiful slowly being smothered by something black and ugly as if ... as if the black thing is eating the white thing ... '

He glanced up at his mother, and the Bishop did the same. They both saw her sudden look of anguish and her eyes welling with tears. She swallowed hard and gave another nod for her son to continue.

'Go on,' said Clematius gently.

'In my dream there are people wailing all around me and I can hear Mother's voice shouting. Then there's a long silence with just the sound of a bird far up on high; a lone hawk of some kind. It is screeching out its call as it circles overhead.'

'*Incredible!*' The bishop stood up and addressed the heavens. 'God be praised for giving this child such a wondrous gift!' He looked back at the boy and smiled. 'God gave your infant's mind such powers my son, so that you would truly remember that which should never be forgotten.'

Still smiling, the bishop turned to the girl.

'And you must be the lovely Brittola, named after one of the most revered of the martyrs.'

Brittola needed no further bidding. She stepped boldly forward and thrust out her hand to the visitor, who took it and kissed it politely.

'I apologise if this—*ahem* – if our item of business scared you little one. I know how horrid and fearsome it must look; I assure you there really is nothing for you to fear.'

'There are many worse sights in life than that Your Grace,' said Cordula firmly. 'They will need to get used to them sooner or later.' She pulled her children round to face her. 'Now that you are here, you can stay while we conclude our business, but I want you to be good and keep quiet. The bishop has little time and we have much to discuss. Is that clear?'

'Yes Mother,' they replied.

Obeying their mother's silent command, the boy then took his sister to the far side of the table. Satisfied they were settled, Cordula looked at the bishop and they both nodded sombrely. The moment had finally come. She approached the head and began to scrutinise it, studying it closely – first one side, then the other – all the while with Clematius watching her intently, looking grave and solemn. Eventually, after what felt like an eternity to the children, their mother reached forward to pick up the grisly object. Just as she was about to touch it, Brittola let out a whine of revulsion, but a fleeting sideways glance from her mother soon hushed her quiet.

With her hands poised in readiness to grab the head, Cordula then closed her eyes. She could feel her scalp tingling and the hairs on her neck standing on end as fears and memories long-forgotten, nightmares long-vanquished, suddenly rushed to the fore, flooding her mind and filling it … memories of army life; being out on patrol forever on the march; making camp then breaking it; securing supplies and building fires; skirmishes and tactics; frantic rides both daytime and night as well as long, long journeys; a vast fleet of galleys out in the open sea caught by a monstrous storm; the relentless pounding *BAROOM-BAROOM-BOOM* of a thousand approaching war drums; then the greatest nightmare and worst fear of all … the terrifying Huns!

The sound of her daughter shuffling impatiently snapped Cordula back to reality. She opened her eyes, clasped the head firmly and lifted it up to eye level. The neck had been set in tar and placed on a dark wooden plinth. This must have been done recently because the tar was still soft to the touch. Being crudely embalmed, the skin was shrivelled and crinkled like a dried fruit, grey all over except for yellowish patches where the flesh was loose from the bone. In places, the skin was brittle and flakes fell away as Cordula examined it. The most striking part of the head, however, was not the face but the hair. Arranged in Britannic braids about the ears, it was easy to imagine how the distinctive mix of golds, reds, yellows and oranges must have blazed like a burning beacon when let loose to fly in the wind. Now, however, it was dull, dank ... and completely lifeless.

'It could be her,' she said quietly. 'The cheeks are in the right proportion to the forehead and jaw; and the hair *is* how she was wearing it that day.' She stroked the braids. 'But then many of the women wore it that way and hair can easily be re-arranged after death.'

'I must admit there is some merit to the owner's claim that it has an officer's bearing.' Clematius leaned forward to peer closely at the face.

'Well, there is only one way to be sure.' Cordula cupped the head firmly in one hand and thrust the forefinger of her other through the slightly parted lips. Clematius was visibly shocked and the children gasped as she proceeded to close her eyes and feel around the inside of the mouth. While she was probing, the head made hollow eerie crackling noises like a damp fire in the cold. Eventually, she opened her eyes, pulled her finger out and wiped it on the crumpled sacking, before carefully placing the head back down.

'That's not Pinnosa,' she declared decisively.

'B-but how do you know?' spluttered the bishop. 'How can you be so certain?

Cordula smiled and moved over to the small glass window that overlooked the inner courtyard.

'This woman has all her teeth. Pinnosa had one missing.'

'Which one?' he blurted.

Cordula turned to face him.

'I think I'd rather keep that to myself Your Grace. Just in case any more of these, these poor women ... ' she nodded at the head, 'come in search of being put to much-needed rest. Now, would you please see to it, Your Grace, that she is buried amongst her own ... with honour?'

'Yes, yes, of course, of course; I assure you I will *personally* ensure she is laid to rest with all the dignity she deserves.' Clematius looked awkward. 'But I would very much like to know—*ahem* – what I mean is ... may I ask how you came to know which of Pinnosa's teeth was missing? I do not wish to imply, of course—well, I hope you understand ... it's just that I *am* accountable to others in this matter and ... '

'There is no need for you to feel uncomfortable about asking Your Grace. I shall be more than happy to tell you.'

Cordula looked at her children brimming with eagerness to hear what she had to say ... which made her smile.

'This was once her home you know; Pinnosa's family used to live here. Her father built it and named it the "Villa Flavius". She and her two younger brothers were—'

She had to pause. A sudden rush of memories had made her lip quiver and her voice alter. Swallowing hard, she forced herself to continue.

'But all that was long, long ago ... '

To hide her tears, she returned to the window and looked back out at the courtyard where it was snowing again. She stared at the shapes and forms now rapidly turning to mere lumps and bumps beneath the deepening blanket of white; and when next she spoke it was more to herself than the others.

'I remember the day Pinnosa lost her tooth so vividly. Can it really be that long ago? It seems like only yesterday. We – that's Ursula, Pinnosa and I; Martha and Saula weren't there; they were probably off with some of the young officers as usual – we had just returned to Glevum after our first ever hunt and Brittola, who was too young to hunt at that time, ran up to join us as we entered the gate. I was only seventeen which means Ursula and Pinnosa must have been eighteen and Brittola no more than fifteen. We were so full of ourselves as we paraded around the forum arm in arm. Pinnosa had two deer tails and a hare's paw strung in her hair, Ursula had another deer tail and a foxtail in hers and I had a couple of hare paws in mine. Brittola grabbed Pinnosa's bow to give it a twang and we all started singing '*Off We Go*' at the tops of our voices— '

She glanced across the courtyard at the opposite door of the west room. As she did so, Clematius saw her give an almost imperceptible nod as if someone had just given her permission to continue.

'We were laughing at being shooed away by a beggar, a funny old woman with a missing ear; she's still there to this day I believe, when suddenly Pinnosa cried "*Dammit!*" She was clasping her jaw and wincing with pain. "What is it?" I asked. "Wait here," she said. "I shan't be long." She ran over to where a surgeon was washing his kit in the water trough and spoke to him briefly. He reached down into the water and produced his tooth-puller. Pinnosa helped him to work it into position and then knelt before him. They both gripped the handle and started pulling *hard!* It was a tough struggle and she seemed to be doing most of the pulling. The next thing I knew he was polishing a new silver denarius and she was splashing her face with water.' Cordula laughed. '*Ha – typical Pinnosa!* When she came back, she tried to carry on with the singing as if nothing had happened. It was only at Ursula's insistence that she opened her mouth wide and showed us the bloody hole.'

'*Incredible!*' cried Clematius. 'She pulled the tooth herself. Most *men* couldn't do such a thing.'

'Come now Your Grace. Our job is to dispel fanciful myths not add to them. I only said it *seemed* that way. The forum was crowded that day and we were several stalls away; I couldn't see clearly what happened. On the other hand, as you well know, Pinnosa, God rest her soul, was capable of many things well beyond the reach of many others, including most men.'

'She truly had a man's heart and spirit; and yet … ' Clematius joined Cordula to stare out of the window. 'I found her surprisingly feminine at times. I vividly recall her taking her vow of chastity. When she bowed her head forward to take my blessing, her hair – which was loose for once – fell across her face and, for a brief moment, I saw before me a vision of pure womanhood. She was looking at the chalice and her eyes – eyes that had seen so much – had an expression of such innocence, such purity … ' He tailed-off as a thought occurred to him and turned to face Cordula, looking troubled. 'You – *um* – you just mentioned Martha and Saula being—*ahem* "with the officers as usual." They were … weren't they? Oh, how in God's name can I broach such a sensitive point? They were— '

'"Worthy of their vows"?' Cordula laughed a shallow empty laugh. 'Oh, you need have no fear of that Your Grace. It was because Martha and Saula enjoyed the company of men so much that they valued their chastity more highly than any of us.'

She returned to the table, placed the woman's head back inside its sackcloth and started to draw the cord. As she did so, her eyes once more filled with tears.

'Believe me Your Grace, I can attest to the purity of *all* my fellow officers as well as the women in the ranks for, as you know, that is why I am not with them in Heaven.'

'Forgive me! I did not mean to— '

'There is nothing to forgive Your Grace,' struggling to quell the tremor in her voice, Cordula drew a deep breath and looked back up at Clematius. 'There is nothing *left* to forgive.'

She glanced across at her children who were standing completely still and staring at her wide-eyed with concern.

'Now, much as it is an honour and a pleasure to see you Your Grace, the snow is getting worse and the sun is getting low; and you need to be back in Magnis before dark.'

II

'Why didn't he stay Mother?' asked Brittola as the children worked together bolting the doors and shutters in readiness for the night. 'He was a nice man; I liked him.'

'Yes, he is a nice man,' said Cordula while fanning the fire for the fish pan and giving it a stir. 'Your father and I are very lucky to count Bishop Clematius as a close friend and it would have been nice if he'd stayed for your father's return. Unfortunately, he was in haste to return to Colonia where he is much needed.'

'What a horse he was riding!' exclaimed her son. 'Are all Batavian horses as big as that Mother?'

'They're not all as big as the bishop's, but they are generally of a good size.'

She uncorked the garum jar, filling the kitchen with the rich pungent aroma of fish essence, and added a few drops of the dark liquid into the simmering broth.

'Your grandfather used to have some Batavian mares in his stock, but no stallions. He found the stallions too thickset in the shoulder and he was breeding for speed.'

She plucked some bay leaves and dried hyssop from bundles that were hanging nearby and dropped them in the broth, before turning her attention to the freshly-caught barbel on her marble slab. As she set about gutting and filleting it, she smiled to herself.

'I can still recall your old granddad's favourite motto, the one he used whenever he was talking to a potential buyer; "Moving fast is better than holding fast when danger comes a-calling." It worked like a charm every time.'

'I love it when you tell us about the past Mother. Oh, *do* tell us more,' pleaded Brittola. 'Please tell us about— '

'*Aunt Ursula!*' cried her brother. 'You *never* talk about her!'

Cordula froze and Brittola gasped. Any mention of Aunt Ursula was strictly forbidden at home. The children saw their mother visibly tense and braced themselves for a tongue-lashing. But then, instead of an outburst of anger, she slowly relaxed and turned to face them.

'Aunt Ursula? Let me think; what can I tell you about her? Well, your Aunt Ursula was—*OW!*'

She snatched her hand from the fish as if it had bitten her; one of the bones had nicked the tip of her finger. She held it over the pan to let the broth catch the drips before rummaging in her sewing basket for an oddment of cloth to wrap the wound. While she was tying a knot using her teeth, she glanced at her children and smiled to herself.

'Aunt Ursula was my cousin, just like Docilina's children are your cousins. Her mother Daria and my mother were— '

'Yes Mother, we *know* all that, but what was she really *like?*' said her son impatiently.

'Yes Mother; please tell us!' pleaded Brittola.

'What was she like? Well, to me … ' Cordula's voice took on a quality her children had not heard before; wispish and dreamlike. 'To me she was life itself. In a way she gave me my life just as assuredly as I gave you yours. But she did far more than just give me life, she moulded it, shaped it, defined it. Not only mine, there were many others, hundreds, thousands, for whom it was the same. And then— '

'You mean she was like a big sister?' Brittola looked puzzled.

Cordula looked down at her daughter's quizzical expression and started to laugh.

'Yes, my little darling, just like a big sister.'

Brittola smiled and Cordula gave her a hug.

'Did I ever tell you she had the same eyebrows as us?'

'No.'

'Well she did; and whenever she was concentrating hard on something, she used to crease them up, just like you and I do.'

'That must mean she was funny sometimes, and not all serious like they say at school?' Brittola giggled and clapped her hands excitedly. 'What about Aunt Martha and Aunt Saula? They were funny too, weren't they?'

'Oh, they were the funniest! I could tell you a thousand stories about those two!'

'Oh, *yes* Mother, please *do* tell us,' cried her son, also getting excited. 'Please tell us—*ple-eee-ase!*'

'All right you two, I'll tell you the story of the First Athena— '

'*Hooray, hooray!*' The children joined hands and began jumping with joy.

'But not right at this moment; after we've eaten.' She turned back to the fish pan to give the broth another stir. 'We'll have our meal first and then we'll clear away; and *the-eee-en*, if you're not too tired, we'll go to bed and I'll tell you all about Ursula and Pinnosa and— '

'And Aunt Martha and Aunt Saula?' cried Brittola.

'And the Franks and the Huns, and their big fierce warrior chieftains?' added her brother.

'*And Aunt Brittola!*' shouted Brittola, getting over-excited.

'*And Emperor Constantine*— ' cried her brother, tugging Cordula's sleeve, ' *—and the Great Expedition!*'

'And, that's *enough* you two!' Cordula clapped her hands for silence. 'I am now going to finish cooking our meal. While I'm doing that, you young lady can prepare the fruit, and you young man can lay the table and pour the wine.'

'Yes Mother.'

Cordula looked on as the children hurriedly set about their errands, then with a smile she retuned her attention to the barbel. A few moments later, just as she was laying the fish in the broth and adding a squeeze of lemon, she heard Brittola humming a tune. She recognised it instantly and her smile froze.

It was an old hymn that people often sang while they worked, but Cordula had forbidden it being sung it at the villa; nobody, not even her husband, was allowed to sing it. She span round and snapped angrily.

'What is *that* you are humming?'

Brittola fell silent and looked at her mother anxiously.

'It's "Praise the Lord" Mother.'

'I know that! Where did you learn it?'

'At school.'

Cordula glared at her daughter. She could see the sudden rush of redness in her cheeks, the look of fear in her eyes and her quivering lips. Her anger abated and she smiled.

'It is a beautiful song. Do you know the words?'

'Yes Mother.'

'Then please sing it properly. Don't just hum it.'

Brittola began to sing the opening lines and her brother quickly joined in. By the end of the first verse they were both in full voice.

Praise Him
Praise Him
Praise Him
Praise the Lord

Christ our Lord
Teach us
Teach us to be right

Christ our Lord
Lead us
Lead us to the light

Jesus
Take us
Feed us
Make – us good
Oh Lord!

You came
You saw
You knew
You un–derstood

Oh Lord!

Your love
gives power
like
no o–ther could

Oh Lord!
Praise our Lord!

Cordula was about to return her attention to cooking the barbel when a flicker outside the narrow kitchen window caught her eye. She moved closer to see what it was. The tiny opening offered a clear view of the villa's inner courtyard and she could see there was a fresh flurry of snow. The return of the snow had caused the sky to darken, robbing the courtyard of its remaining daylight. As she watched the falling flakes, a trick of the fading light made the courtyard seem alive with fast-moving shadows of cold blue and grey. The shapes were ever changing; jumping here, racing there, disappearing and reappearing. Although they took no specific form, she knew exactly what they were.

At that moment, the old hymn reached her favourite verse and the sound of her children's voices seemed to fill the entire villa. She looked upward into the falling snow and, as she did so, a familiar voice spoke into her ear.

Less than ten years from now, they'll be as old as we were when we first came to this place. And in a further four years they'll outlive us.

'I shouldn't be telling them the story,' she replied out loud. 'They are not yet of an age to fully comprehend it all.'

Oh, I wouldn't let that bother you, said the voice with a gentle laugh. *Neither were we when it all began.*

Suddenly, there it was in the whirling white, the stark image of Pinnosa's face rendered hideous with anguish and fear.

And there was her piercing cry, echoing and reverberating throughout all eternity, shrill with urgency.

'*URSULA-AAA-AAA!*'

The face rose up through the falling snow and the cry became fainter and fainter until it was engulfed by her children's singing. At that moment, they commenced another verse and Cordula wiped away her tears.

III

'When I was young, long before you were born, things looked very bleak for Rome … even bleaker than it does today.'

Their meal was complete, the dishes had been cleaned and they'd retired to the cubiculum for the night. They were all seated on Cordula's bed with an oil lamp burning on a nearby shelf to provide light. Because it was a cold night, the children had woollen blankets covering their legs. Cordula was reclining on her favourite silk cushions wearing her winter stola with big folds of its combed wool plumped-up about her neck, shoulders and arms. Having made themselves comfortable, the three of them were finally ready for the telling of a story.

'The whole of the Empire was in turmoil. Hordes of the fearsome Goths were on the rampage, even threatening the great mother city of Roma itself. They forced the Emperor, Honorius, to take refuge in fortress at Ravenna where, together with his army commander, Stilicho, he plotted and schemed against his enemies.

'At the same time, much further to the north on the far side of the Alps beyond the Empire's borders, tribal warfare was raging amongst Rome's neighbours. Whole peoples were being driven from their native lands and forced to migrate in search of new homes. Many of them headed for the safety of Roman territory where the already over-stretched armies were unable to contain them or keep them at bay.

'At about this time, when I was still in my eighteenth year, a host of Germanic tribes led by Suevi and Burgundians, broke through the frontier between the Rhenus and Danubius rivers to ravage the cities and estates of Germania and Galliae.

'Britannia wasn't safe either. The Saxon landings had just started, adding to the threat of Hibernian and Pict raiding parties and stretching our defences to their limit. And yet, it was just at this time that our men were summoned to the Continent to aid Honorius in dealing with the invading Germanic tribes.

'As if all that wasn't enough, little did we know that a new enemy was also heading our way. From distant lands far to the east there was fast approaching a foe more fearsome and terrible than the rest, a fierce war-like tribe who posed a truly formidable threat to all that stood in their way, a foe more terrifying than any other ... *the Huns!'*

Brittola shrieked at the sound of their dreaded name. Both children were sitting upright and staring at their mother, their faces full of alarm. Cordula smiled and held out her arms. They needed no further bidding and dived for her protective embrace.

'There, there,' she said soothingly. 'There are no Huns here, there are no Huns in the whole of Britannia. Have no fear little ones; you are safe here.'

'What about Ursula?' The muffled voice of her son came from somewhere beneath her sleeve.

'Yes Mummy, what about Aunt Ursula?' Brittola's face peeped out from the bundle of blanket she had gathered. 'When did *her* story begin?'

Cordula couldn't help laughing at the look on her daughter's face, and the sound of her laughter made all three relax.

'When did Ursula's story begin? Now, that *is* a good question. Hmmm, let me see ... '

The children could sense that the real story was about to commence and they shuffled into more comfortable positions; Brittola snuggled under her mother's arm and her brother lay next to her with his head resting on his hands.

'I suppose it all *really* started one hot day in May in Corinium ... '

PART ONE

BRITANNIA

Chapter One

THE MEN DEPART

I

The relentless pounding of the legionaries' feet as they entered Corinium, the capital city of the Dobunni tribe in the southwest of Britannia, and paraded past the royal palace was so strong it shook the small figurines of the house gods, the lares, in the corner of the ladies' chamber on the upper floor, causing one of them to topple over.

The sound of the marching combined with the general roar of the excited crowd in the street below forced Princess Ursula, her cousin Cordula and three other young noblewomen gathered in the chamber to shout at the tops of their voices in order to be heard.

Martha and Saula were together beside the balcony, eagerly awaiting the highlight of the parade; the arrival of the commanders. They were peeping out from behind a large silk tapestry that depicted Cuda and the three Matres or Earth Mothers, stretching their necks in their efforts to see the view outside without being spotted by the people in the street below. Being lean and willowy with long straight mousy brown hair, they looked like a pair of herons.

Cordula, with her dark brown locks pulled back in a ponytail, was on the other side of the balcony, looking over the rooftops to the view beyond the city walls where she could see the Londinium road and would be the first to spot if a messenger should appear; one in particular, her beloved Morgan riding his powerful black horse Hermes.

Attendants and other slaves were constantly going to-and-fro, all a-buzz and busy making preparations for the great feast. Some were collecting the various ornamentation's that were to adorn the feasting tables, while others were relaying important orders for the kitchen from their mistress.

Ursula was at the heart of all the bustle, issuing her instructions and, in between giving directives, she was carefully

1

selecting her attire for the evening. She was seated on the other side of the room from Cordula, Martha and Saula, with her back to the window, picking through her large oak chest of stolas and togas, while her old attendant, Oleander, combed out her hair, readying it to be arranged.

Brittola was hovering at Ursula's side, eager to be involved in things but anxious not to get in the way. Her wild naturally curly black hair had already been tamed into plaits about her ears, exposing her youthful face and allowing her bright hazel, almost green, eyes to be seen clearly for once, rather than being lost behind her usual tangle of curls.

'How will you wear your hair tonight Ursula; loose and tied back or braided to the sides?'

'I haven't decided yet, but I think ... ' She paused and glanced up at the younger woman with a teasing look.

'Yes?' Brittola leaned forward eagerly.

'I think I'll wear it to the sides which means I won't be needing this.' She produced an ornate gold and onyx hairpin from her accessory casket and turned to face Brittola. 'Would you like to borrow it by any chance?'

'Oh yes—could I?' cried Brittola excitedly, before quickly restraining herself. 'That is, if none of the others would like to wear it?'

'Oh, I shouldn't think they'll want it. Besides it'll look far more effective in your dark curls than in their horses' manes.'

Ursula handed the hairpin to Brittola who took it with the wide-eyed wonder of a child receiving a gift. At sixteen, Brittola was the youngest of their group a full three years younger than Ursula. They shared a private grin. Like everyone else at the palace, they were both highly excited at the return of the legion. At that moment, there was a momentary lull in the cacophony of shouts and cries from the crowd outside.

'Oh, where are the Vanguard and the senior officers?' groaned Saula. 'Where's Constantine? Why does he have the army pass first? Why doesn't he lead the parade like other Roman commanders?'

Ursula called out in reply over her shoulder.

'The men are his glory, so they share his glory. He says, "Those who work hardest should rest soonest." It's his way; his men always come first; the only time he goes ahead of them is when they march into battle; and besides Saula … ' she turned and stared pointedly at her friend, 'he's a *Britannic* Roman commander.'

'It's not really Constantine she's so eager to see Ursula,' said Martha. 'It's the Vanguard she's anxious about and a certain young officer called— '

'*Mar-tha!*'

Saula tugged Martha's sleeve to shut her up. Martha retaliated by ruffling Saula's hair which prompted Saula to attempt to smother her best friend with the silk wall hanging. Their loud giggles and boisterous play forced Ursula to stand up and give the two of them a censorial look, glancing pointedly at the slaves and attendants. Duly scolded, the pair reluctantly contained their excitement and returned their attention to the scene outside. After a while, with a sly glance to check that Ursula wasn't watching, Martha leaned surreptitiously toward Saula and spoke quietly into her ear.

'I *love* watching the men on the march, don't you? See how handsome and smart they all are. Is there a sight to be more proud of in the entire empire?'

'Especially as most of them are single and extremely eligible.' Saula nudged Martha in the ribs. 'And I'm not the *only* one with a specific young officer in mind.'

They both giggled and Martha peered over her shoulder to see if Ursula was watching. Seeing that she was busy with Oleander, she cupped her hand to Saula's ear.

'I wish I was a bathhouse slave tonight.'

They both burst out giggling.

'Will you two please be quiet?' snapped Cordula.

Martha and Saula both poked their tongues out at her before returning their attention to the street below.

'*Look!*' cried Saula. '*The commanders' standards!*'

'Is Constans … ' Ursula leapt to her feet.

Cordula glanced across at her cousin and knew instantly that the word on her lips was "there?" But then, she saw Ursula constrain herself and say something different instead.

' … the leader?'

'*Oh yes,*' cried out Brittola excitedly. 'Is it Constans, or Constantine or someone else who has the position of honour?'

She ran past Ursula to the back of the balcony where she could be seen by the crowd below. Meanwhile, Martha and Saula were straining to look down the side of the palace. It was Martha who spotted them first.

'I can see the leading horse's head. It's … it's … '

'*Gerontius!*' They both groaned as a huge thickset man came into view.

'The ugly fat bull!' hissed Saula.

'But wait, there're two of them abreast,' cried Brittola. 'No, three! All three are leading together. And the one in the centre is … *Constans!* Constans has the greatest honour!'

Ursula closed her eyes with relief. At that moment, the crowd below the palace balcony caught sight of the commanders and gave an almighty cheer.

'Oh Ursula, *do* come and look!' pleaded Brittola. 'Constans and Constantine are riding side by side, father and son, great heroes both like Philip and Alexander; and it is your Constans at the heart of the glory. Oh, *do* look Ursula—*please!* You'll be so proud!'

'*Ursula!*'

A rich clear voice rang out from the street below; the familiar and welcome sound of their great protector Constantine.

'Come out on the balcony Princess, and let your people see you—*come!* And all you other young ladies too; I know you're up there keeping discreetly out of sight. Cast aside undue decorum! Come now—*come!* Come forward and greet us with your majesty! Let Constans see his beloved bride-to-be and let the men know that we are truly home!'

Martha and Saula needed no more asking; they threw aside the tapestry they were hiding behind, grabbed Cordula and Brittola by the hand and led them both out on to the balcony where they were met by rapturous cries from the crowd. The legionaries too let out a great cheer at the sight of the four fine-looking young noblewomen which made Brittola squirm with embarrassment. The cheers then died down and an expectant hush gripped everyone, city dweller and legionary alike, as all eyes fixed their gaze upon the balcony with many raising their hands to shade their eyes against the bright May sunshine.

Slowly, Ursula emerged from the shadows. Being taller than the others, and with her long white hair falling loosely over her shoulders, she filled the window with her presence. Having reached the full-bloom of womanhood since the army left on its expedition almost a year before, she looked a picture of serenity; and with her commanding dark blue eyes she carried all the dignity and authority of her fondly-remembered mother, the late Queen Daria. Upon her appearance, the crowd redoubled its cheers. Ursula smiled in acknowledgement and briefly took in the scene before fixing her gaze upon Constans.

He too had matured since they had last met; the final residue of boyhood had left him. His hands held the horse's reins with a firm grip and his wispy beard had filled out into the same thick black gorse as his father's; his skin had the weather-worn look of a seasoned campaigner and had lost its supple shine; and his smile was now a knowing one, not so full of questions.

While the whole assembly witnessed the look of love that passed between their handsome young commander and their beautiful princess, Constantine slowly reached up, removed his helmet and bowed. Constans followed his father's lead and so too did Gerontius, but reluctantly and with a sullen smile.

'*Behold, good people of Corinium! Behold all the folk of Britannia!*' Constantine grabbed his son's arm and raised it high in triumph. '*Behold ... your future! Behold ... Constans and Ursula!*'

'*Constans and Ursula! Constans and Ursula! Constans and Ursula!*'

The cry was picked up by the rest of the crowds filling the city streets and seemed to fill the whole of Corinium. At the height of the chanting, the commanders gave a further graceful bow, replaced their helmets and urged their horses on, resuming the parade. Just as the commanders' standards were disappearing from sight, Cordula grabbed Ursula by the arm.

'Look Ursula—*look!*'

She pointed to the hilltop beyond the city walls. Even at such a distance, there was no mistaking Pinnosa. She was riding her black mare Artemis and dressed in hunting clothes. Her red

5

hair was tied back so that it wouldn't get in her way; a string of game was slung over her shoulder and a deer was draped across Artemis. Her bow was across her back and she held a hunting spear in her hand. As her friends watched her, she turned the great horse and rode away.

'She must have heard the noise and known the army was on parade.' Brittola's voice was heavy with disappointment. 'Why didn't she come to join us?'

'She was probably too busy with that deer,' said Martha. 'You know how nothing can keep her from the hunt, especially once the chase is on.'

'I think you're right Martha, but I wish she would change her ways.' Ursula sighed. 'She can't keep avoiding her responsibilities; she needs to be here performing her duties just like us and not keep shunning "the world of men".'

'The truth is she envies men and their world,' said Saula jokingly to Martha as they turned to go back inside. 'She's like a fox obsessed with joining the wolves.'

They all chuckled as they left the balcony and even Ursula smiled as she returned to making preparations for the great feast.

II

Ursula turned to Brittola who was seated beside her at the ladies' head table and murmured in her ear.

'Where are all the men?'

The great feast had already started even though most of the men had yet to arrive; this was due to the presence of some important Roman dignitaries from Londinium. The officials were at the head table with King Deonotus, Morgan the messenger who had just arrived from Londinium, Bishop Patroclus and a handful of other local noblemen, but there were still many empty seats reserved for Constantine, Constans, Gerontius, Brittola's grandfather Conanus and all the other senior commanders. The lower tables, which were supposed to be a pleasant mix of men and women, were also still half-empty; the wives, mothers and sisters were there, but the junior army officers themselves were conspicuously absent. Most of the women at the ladies' head

6

table were present with the wives of the Roman officials seated alongside Ursula, Brittola, Cordula, Martha and Saula; the only important woman missing was Pinnosa.

The food was lavishly presented and smelled tantalising; there were calves and pigs on spits; huge mounds of game plus shellfish and fruit on great silver platters. The aromatic mulled wine with herbs was beginning to whet everyone's appetites. Indeed, the ample-framed Bishop Patroclus, after breaking the bread and blessing the feast, had already given full rein to his hunger and accumulated quite a pile of debris from his ravenous indulgences. Meanwhile, the entertainment had begun. A fire-eater, clad in a striped animal skin of some kind which Cordula thought might be called "zebra", was keeping the women so well amused by his acrobatics they did not seem too perturbed by the absence of the men. Ursula took advantage of the diversion to slip over to her father.

'Where *are* they Father? Where can they be?' she said quietly into his ear. 'They should have been here long ago.'

'Don't fret my dear; have patience.'

'But Father, their baths should be complete by now. What can they be doing? Surely they are hungry and thirsty.'

Her father glanced at her awkwardly.

'Don't trouble yourself so my dear. Your work is done. The feast is magnificent. Be patient; they'll be here soon. I'm sure you— '

'They're at the *altar*, aren't they?' she said with disgust, raising her voice.

'*Hush!*' Deonotus turned her away from Bishop Patroclus even though the portly old priest was fully-engrossed with the juicier parts of a succulent young partridge. 'It is not easy for commanders to leave their men, especially the junior officers. Let them complete their work.'

'Well, I'm going to put a stop to their "work" and fetch them here.'

'*No, you mustn't!* These are men's matters my dear; you shouldn't concern yourself with them.'

'Anything that concerns men is of great concern to women, as well you know Father.'

He looked at her and smiled.

7

'You are just like your beloved mother. I know there's nothing I can do or say to stop you once your blood is up.'

She returned his smile then left.

At that moment, with a flash and a crackling sound, the fire-eater made a white dove appear from a flaming hoop and fly across the gathering, causing several of the women to gasp in amazement. Cordula also shrieked with surprise and even Bishop Patroclus put down his partridge to join in the applause.

Brittola, however, wasn't clapping. She'd been keenly watching Ursula with her father and, as soon as she saw her cousin slip away, she quietly followed after her. At the same time, Oleander also left the feasting hall, determined as ever not to allow her mistress out of her sight, just as she'd done ever since she was old enough to walk.

Back at the ladies' head table, Cordula took advantage of Brittola's departure to make herself more comfortable. She stretched her legs, reached for a clutch of succulent fully-ripened grapes and proceeded to consume them with delight.

III

Outside, a bright sunset flooded the shadow-filled streets with a warm pink glow. A brisk evening breeze was agitating some of the farm animals; geese grumbled and half-honked, pigs shuffled and snorted, and somewhere nearby a dog was yapping. Adding to these sounds was the *flap-clap-flap* of sandals on stone paving as Ursula strode briskly down the main street heading for the Officers' Hall.

'Wait for me,' cried Brittola breathlessly, running to catch up.

'Brittola?' Ursula stopped and turned. 'You shouldn't be out here. Go back to the feast. I shan't be long. I'm just going to fetch Constans and his father. They've probably been caught up with something and forgotten the time.'

'And I'm going to fetch Grandfather. He's probably been caught up too.'

'I'll make sure he comes with them. Now please go back.'

'I'm coming with you. They're up to something, aren't they?'

'If they're up to what I think they're up to, then you must stay behind. Your grandfather would most certainly not wish you to see it. It's not for young eyes like yours.'

'How can you say that to me Ursula? When our mothers died, you were the same age as I am now. Wouldn't you have been just as determined as I am to check on your father and, if needs be, put him straight?'

'You're right, I would,' replied Ursula. 'When my mother died, my father was my life even though Constans was my love.'

'And I don't even have a love. Grandfather is all I have.' Ursula smiled.

'Very well; you may come,' she said. 'But be prepared. This ... '

Brittola knew what she was going to say next. It was a phrase they always used when bracing themselves to face any difficult or unpleasant task; and they completed it in unison.

' ... may not be easy!'

They laughed, put their arms round each other and set off together.

IV

The front of the Officers' Hall faced outward from the city centre which meant Ursula and Brittola approached it from behind. They were just passing the rear of the building when the sound of chanting caught their ears. It seemed to be coming from the alley behind the hall, and as they listened it crescendo'd with a loud guttural roar.

'Come on; let's catch them at it!'

Brittola ran off down the alley to investigate.

'*Brittola! Come back! Come back, I tell you!*' shouted Ursula, but she was too late; Brittola had already disappeared.

The alley opened into an old courtyard, and the rear wall of the Officers' Hall formed one complete side of the yard. It had no openings of any kind except for a small window high up in the centre well beyond reach. Immediately outside the window was a large old lime tree that Ursula and Brittola had known since childhood. It was rumoured that the window looked down into the room where dead soldiers' souls and shadows lived; and it had always been a big dare among the city's children to climb the tree's creaking old boughs to see if the shadows could be seen moving.

Ursula caught up with Brittola at the base of the old lime. The sound of chanting had resumed and was definitely coming from the window.

'Come on. Let's see what they're up to.' Brittola leapt upward, grabbed the lowest bough and starting to climb.

'Come back down Brittola,' cried Ursula. 'We're not children now you know.'

Ignoring her cousin's plea, Brittola continued climbing and, with a sigh of resignation, Ursula reluctantly followed her. While she was making her way up to the bough with the view through the window, the chanting once again climaxed with a loud roar like the one they'd heard earlier.

'*Brittola!*' she cried. '*Come down! It's not safe!*'

But Brittola was already on the bough and could see what was happening inside the hall. By the time Ursula caught up with her, she was transfixed with one hand gripping a branch overhead and the other clasping the large silver cross she always wore, brandishing it before her to ward off evil. Ursula joined her and together they looked down into the room.

There was a hooded figure with its back to her swathed in black cloth, wearing a red and gold headband. The figure was bent forward as if preparing something and it was surrounded by many others in similar attire. Standing in front of the figure and facing the window was Gerontius, clean-shaven and naked to the waist. As they watched, the figure straightened-up and thrust a great jewel-encrusted gold goblet into the air, causing a red liquid to splash upon its cloak. Gerontius then took hold of the vessel and held it in the air for the duration of the guttural roar the gesture elicited from the congregation. As the noise abated, the bull-necked commander then lowered it to his lips and drank. His draught complete, Gerontius then placed the goblet on the altar and moved out of view. As he did so, the men resumed their murmurous chant. The hooded figure lifted the head of a calf into the air by its ears and refilled the goblet with its dripping blood. At that moment Brittola's grandfather Conanus, who was also freshly shaven and naked to the waist, came into view and stood before the altar.

Brittola gasped and looked as if she was about to faint.

'Come on. We've seen enough.' Ursula raised her hand in an attempt to shield Brittola from the awful sight. 'Let's get back down now.'

'*Oh, dear sweet God!*' Brittola brushed Ursula's hand aside. 'What *is* he doing? He isn't even wearing his cross! *Oh God, oh God, oh God!*'

'*Shhh Brittola!*' said Ursula as Brittola threw back her head and screamed at the top of her voice.

'*AAAAH, GOD! MAKE IT STOP! MAKE IT STOP! ... PLE-EEE-EASE!*'

Ursula grabbed Brittola to lead her back down the tree. As she did so, she caught a glimpse of the scene inside the hall. All the men, including the hooded figure, were looking up at the window. The hood on the robed figure fell away, revealing the stern face of Constantine; and next in line for the ceremonial rite, also cleanly shaven and naked to the waist, was Constans.

V

Ursula was still helping Brittola down the tree when the men – now fully-dressed in their togas and carrying torches – emerged from the alley and surrounded the gnarled old lime.

'Come down here at once you hysterical young wench! I'll give you something to scream about!' shouted Gerontius.

'*Hold your tongue Gerontius!*' Constantine made his way through the men accompanied by Constans. 'Can't you see it's Princess Ursula?'

As he spoke, Ursula was easing Brittola onto the bottom-most bough. Constans reached up to help her down and the moment he let her go, she fell to the ground weeping.

'We are truly sorry to have disturbed you, gentlemen,' said Ursula, leaping from the tree. Although she addressed the entire gathering, she kept her eyes firmly on Constantine and

11

Constans. 'We simply came to remind you that the great feast being held in your honour at the palace awaits your presence.'

She bent down beside a sobbing Brittola and began rocking her gently to-and-fro.

'There-there Brittola; don't cry. It's all over.'

Her grandfather, Conanus, forced his way to the front. He was the army's most senior statesman and was much older than the other commanders.

'Come my dear; pull yourself together. You've made enough of a spectacle of yourself this evening and we've got a wonderful feast to attend yet.' He stepped forward and, smiling kindly at Ursula, grabbed his granddaughter by her arm.

'*Let me go! Let me go!*'

Brittola waved her grandfather away and scrambled to her feet.

'How *could* you Granddad? I noticed you took off your cross. Why was that? Because you thought you could hide your shame from God?'

Conanus tried to reach out and take hold of her, but she pushed him away again.

'I don't understand *them* doing such a thing— ' she made a sweeping gesture to signify the surrounding men, 'but why *you* should do it is beyond me. You don't need to prove anything to anybody other than to God. You of all people who was blessed as a baby by the great Emperor Constantine himself. How could you do such a thing Granddad? Where is your faith?'

'Come, my dear. There are better times and places to have such discussions.' He tried to lead her away, but again she resisted.

'*No-no-no!* I want to know why you and all these other Christian men can't keep faith with the *true* God!'

'We keep faith with whichever God, or gods, we please young lady.' Constantine stepped forward and took hold of her arm. 'It's one of the freedoms we fight for and part of the glory of Rome. Only Rome is powerful enough to embrace more than one religion and any number of gods. All gods yield to Rome's superior power.'

Though Constantine was addressing the entire gathering, his gaze was firmly upon Ursula.

'The freedom you enjoy, which gives you the luxury of having such discussions about whether we are ruled by God or the gods, or about whether "faith" or "fate" weighs heaviest in the balance ... ' He'd allowed a hint of mockery to enter his voice and the men sniggered. 'This freedom is hard won and needs to be constantly defended against a whole multitude of hostile forces. So, before all else, before God, before faith or fate, before even freedom itself, must come ... *duty!*'

Constantine shifted his gaze to his son.

'It is every Roman's duty to defend Rome and *all* that she stands for; and, it is only after he has performed his duty that a man can retire to the company of his family and friends and— '

Sensing his grip relax, Brittola wrestled herself from Constantine's grasp, grabbed her silver cross with both hands and thrust it high into the air.

'*No!*' she cried. 'That's not right! You must be clear in your mind, and your heart, that your only real duty is to God. The *one* God! The *true* God! What kind of "hard won freedom" is it that makes you free to drink the blood of the beasts? Seek to live in a good world too. And you can only do that by rejecting these false gods and by ceasing to act like-like ... *like animals!*'

Constantine visibly bristled, but before he could say anything Ursula stepped in between them.

'As your grandfather rightly says this is neither the time nor the place for such discussions.' She turned and addressed Conanus. 'I think you should take her to the feast where such topics are more appropriate.'

'Come, my dear.' The old man gingerly placed his arm around Brittola's shoulders and led her away. As they entered the alley, she pulled free and span round.

'*Your first duty is to God, not Rome!*' she cried. '*You are a Christian army first and a Roman army second!*'

The men all stared at her; none of them spoke and not one of them stirred. She glared at them defiantly then reluctantly turned away. Her sobs could still be heard, echoing in the dark alley, well after she disappeared from view. As the sound faded, Constantine gave a firm and deliberate nod. His silent order was instantly obeyed and the men dispersed, leaving him alone with his son and soon-to-be daughter-in-law. It was Ursula who eventually broke the awkward silence.

'She does have a point; you do face a dilemma when you're both a Christian and a Roman army. Tell me I'm curious; when you're out on a campaign, waging war and fighting battles, deep in your heart what exactly is it that are you fighting for; the ancient gods or the one true God? Rome or Christ?'

'It is often knowing what we are fighting *against* that is the most vexing question,' Constantine returned her fierce gaze. 'The important thing is we *do* our duty. We don't need to know *why* we're doing it.'

'But what about your personal reasons? Surely you have a duty to yourself,' she persisted. 'What exactly do you fight for when you go into battle Constantine? Do you put your belief in your "faith" or your "fate"?'

They stared at each other silently for a long moment, making Constans feel awkward.

'I thank goodness you're a woman,' said Constantine, 'That means you'll never have to go into battle. Even though I'm a man of war and I have seen both God and the gods in action, I can't answer your question Ursula. Is it "faith" or "fate" that wins battles? Who can tell? Both make excellent weapons and both make excellent shields.'

He turned to Constans and slapped him on the shoulder.

'I believe we have far better things to be getting on with apart from playing games with words. Will you please escort our beautiful princess back to her palace and the grand feast where she belongs? I'll be along shortly.'

Constans took Ursula by the hand and led her away. As they left, Constantine placed his torch on one of the old tree's boughs, clasped his hands behind his back and stared up at the now dark window of the Officers' Hall.

'*Ursula!*' he called out after her. 'If ever I do make a decision about whether it is God or the gods, Faith or Fate, I truly believe in, I'll make a point of letting you know.'

VI

Constans and Ursula walked the length of the alley in silence hand-in-hand. As they entered the deserted street they stopped and turned to face each other.

Finally, at long last, they were alone and looking into each other's eyes. The rest of the world with its burning issues and its constant demands was completely forgotten. All that mattered, all that existed, was their love for each other. But, as she pressed up against him and offered herself for his embrace, he hesitated and pulled back.

'How could you allow such a scene like that in front of Gerontius and the others? Couldn't you control Brittola? Please remember you are soon going to be my wife. One day they will be our subjects and we will need their respect.'

'Brittola had good reason to be upset at what you were doing … *and so did I!*' He tried to say something, but she cut him off. 'I don't want to be the wife of a blood-thirsty pagan! You were just about to drink from the chalice too—don't deny it; I saw you with my own eyes! Where, oh where, is my Constans, the *Christian* Constans I was baptised with? What kind of man are you becoming?'

'A man shaped by his work! See these hands that you love to feel so tender upon your soft skin? Oh, how you would admire their skill; thrusting a spear into a man's gut; slashing at an enemy's throat with a sword; carrying a comrade from the gore and yanking arrows from his flesh. That is my true place of work, my trade, my craft, the battlefield; and in battle, believe me when the arrows fly or the enemy charges each man prays to the only gods that count; those who control fortune and destiny, not the holy god within. It is Fate—not Faith that works wild in the fray!'

'What you speak of has nothing to do with Faith or-or God, and everything to do with luck. How can you say that the battlefield is your place of work? Your true place of work is in the hearts of men as their leader, their commander; and one day, as their king. Your hands weren't meant for maiming and killing, but for signing decrees and greeting visiting dignitaries, and— '

He started to laugh.

'*Ha ha ha* – and holding my wife, and caressing my children. Oh, how I love you when you're full of ideas. Your forehead becomes furrowed and your face always says far more than your voice.'

He tried to pull her close, but she resisted and pushed him away.

'Don't *distract* me so Constans! This is important. I mean what I say; I will *not* marry a pagan! Brittola is right; you must be as true to God as you are to me … or our children.'

He stopped laughing and grabbed her by the shoulders.

'Ursula, you must listen to me. You know yourself how strong this new army is. With my father at its head we are truly the most powerful in all Rome. The emperor couldn't wish for a mightier hand to do his work, and I think our time has come … '

He stared deep into her eyes and as he did so a sudden cold fear gripped her heart.

'We're on full alert; we've mobilised all the reserves. Things are looking bad in Germania and Gallia … ' He took a deep breath and swallowed awkwardly. 'I think we will be setting forth any day now.'

She flinched at his news and tried to step back, but he held her firm in his grip, forcing her to look downward to hide her tears.

'Do you remember the last time our army went away to the Continent, when your father was a centurion, and you and I were just children? Do you remember how splendid and proud the legions looked when they departed? We were with all our mothers on top of the white cliffs at Dubris, and we watched them leave … remember? Their weapons gleamed and glistened in the sunlight as galley after galley slid quietly away, heading for Gesoriacum … and we were all *so* proud … and *so* excited.'

She raised her head; her lips were quivering and her cheeks were wet.

'And they were so full of shame when they returned years later; only a handful of men, virtually weaponless with their uniforms in tatters. There were barely enough of them left to rebuild the army; but rebuild they did. And now look at you … the best army this province has ever had.'

She looked upward to the heavens.

'Why, oh why are we cursed on this island? Why is it that every time we manage to build a strong army, an army that we can truly be proud of, it is taken away from us? Why must Rome, with all its twisted politics and trickery ... why must Mother Rome always reap our harvest?'

He pulled her close and held her tight in his arms.

'We won't fall prey to the power politics of Rome my love. We are more than a match for this task. We will be decisive in our campaign; the frontier will be stronger than ever before. They say that some of these northern peoples can be made into useful federal allies. We will settle them along the Rhenus to act as guardians against further invading tribes. Once this is done, our homes will finally be safe, a place where a man can give up war and retire to be with those he loves.'

She nestled her head against his shoulder; as he spoke, she could feel his heart beating.

'When this time comes my love, when my duty is finally done, I shall devote myself to you and to our life together. And, I shall put all gods aside but the one true God we share in our hearts; forever and ever ... I promise.'

They kissed a long gentle kiss, holding each other tight, breathing as one; then slowly they moved apart.

'What God would not forgive a little blood-drinking idolatry after such a speech? You always could charm the wind from the trees with your words Constans!' She laughed. 'And such noble words they were for a fighting man!' She punched him playfully in the ribs. 'Come on; let's join the feast!'

She grabbed his arm and they walked off briskly towards the palace, filling Corinium's main street with the sound of their laughter. As they rounded the corner, Oleander emerged from the shadows and hurried after them.

'Hearing them like this, they could be children all over again,' she muttered to herself. 'You wouldn't think she is now a beautiful princess fit for entertaining kings and emperors, or that he is a handsome high-ranking officer who can command a legion.' She smiled. 'Oh, how happy she is whenever he's here.'

VII

The feast was going well; everyone was settled, reclining and relaxed, and enjoying themselves … apart from Gerontius.

Constantine, Constans and King Deonotus were grilling Morgan for news from Londinium or the Continent. They were listening intently and only interrupting occasionally with the odd comment or quip that caused an outburst of laughter. Gerontius, however, had been placed on the other side of the head table with some of the visiting Roman officials where he looked distinctly awkward and uncomfortable. Ursula, who was with the officials' wives on the adjacent table, smiled to herself as she watched him straining to hear what Constantine and the other commanders were saying.

'He's like a pig wondering what the spit iron's for,' whispered Brittola with a giggle; her earlier outburst behind the Officers' Hall now completely forgotten.

Just then, the sounds of a scuffle broke out behind the dining screens and attendants could be heard making protests.

'Out of my way! *Out of my way, I say!* Get back into the kitchen and stoke up the fire!'

Pinnosa appeared in front of the head tables. She was still in her hunting clothes; a young deer was across her back complete with its first growth of antlers. The general merriment and laughter ceased, and everyone stared. Some of the Roman officials and their wives were open-mouthed with astonishment.

'I'm sorry I'm late My Lord,' she called across the room, addressing King Deonotus. 'Only it crossed my mind you might need some more meat for such a magnificent feast. At first, I thought I'd get a big fat and ugly boar, but then I remembered you already had Gerontius.'

Everyone laughed except Gerontius who scowled into his drink. Pinnosa unloaded the deer into the hands of two nearby attendants. Then, pulling out her hunting knife, she grabbed hold of one of the deer's antlers and hacked it off.

'Here Gerontius!' she cried, strolling over to the heavily built man who had his back to her. 'This is for you. From what the bathhouse slaves tell me, you need all the help you can get!'

The entire gathering burst into laughter, but then – as Pinnosa threw the antler into Gerontius' lap; her eyes glaring with naked aggression – the laughing petered out and the great hall fell into an uneasy silence. Without warning, Gerontius suddenly stabbed his knife *'thunk!'* into the table top, making everyone jump. The jolt knocked several drinking vessels over and caused a dish full of oysters to topple, spilling its contents across the floor. Slowly, he stood up, turned around and snarled in his strong guttural northern accent.

'I'll not let good company and the need for manners stop me from thrashing an impudent young brat, whatever the sex.'

'You? Thrash me?' Pinnosa laughed then leaned forward mockingly, puffing out her cheeks and pulling a comical face which caused a ripple of nervous laughter. 'You're a big man in the army Gerontius where you can get others to fight for you. But on your own ... you're just mouth and flab.'

'Why, you ... ' He dived forward and tried to grab her. She ducked nimbly to one side, avoiding his clutches with ease; then she rounded on him, brandishing her hunting knife, poised ready to strike and leering at him with a look of disgust mixed with raw hatred.

'That's enough, you two!' ordered Constantine, standing up. 'Remember our guests. Save your petty squabbles for the street and don't bring them in here.'

'Come and join the ladies!' Ursula hurried across the room to grab Pinnosa, calling out to the attendants. *'Bring her a dining robe!'*

'I'm not an impudent young brat now Gerontius,' snapped Pinnosa before Ursula could reach her. 'I'm full grown and more than capable of shifting your bulk which is more than you did for my father! Furthermore, I intend to prove it ... ' She addressed the company. *'I hereby challenge you to a contest!'*

'What?' cried Gerontius. 'A contest ... with you?'

'Come and sit down Pinnosa,' pleaded Ursula.

'What's the matter Gerontius?' Pinnosa sheathed her knife then moved forward to sneer directly into his face. 'Not man enough to test your strength against a mere woman? *Pah!*' She spat at his feet. 'Just as I said ... all mouth and flab.'

Gerontius glanced across at Constantine who simply raised a questioning eyebrow and shrugged; then he turned back to face Pinnosa.

'If it's a lesson you want, then a lesson I'm happy to give you.' He forced a strained polite smile, bowed to the ladies' table and sat down, once more turning his back on his adversary.

'Tomorrow morning in the south meadows after morning bells,' she snarled, still glaring at the back of his head.

Not bothering to turn around, Gerontius nodded.

Pinnosa bowed gracefully to the two head tables and allowed Ursula to lead her to place amongst the ladies, smiling politely as she went and saying repeatedly 'Hello, how nice to see you' whilst grabbing handfuls of food and a goblet of wine.

VIII

News of the contest spread rapidly. By the time Ursula arrived at the south meadows, she found herself surrounded by officers and legionaries as well as scores of townsfolk. Her friends were with the visiting Roman officials and their wives beneath a large elm by the river where they were enjoying some dainties – fruit and nuts, honey cakes and cheese – that Oleander had prepared.

A few minutes later Constantine and Constans arrived, along with slaves and attendants carrying flasks of the finest wine from the palace's well-stocked cellars. Ursula loved the palace wine. As she drank, its tangy aroma always awakened her taste buds. Draining her goblet, she looked upward. The morning sun was glistening in the dew-laden treetops, making their fresh May foliage sparkle.

'It's a perfect morning for a contest,' said Constantine, raising his drinking vessel. 'Come, let us drink to Gerontius and to his bane, the dutiful daughter Pinnosa who would avenge her poor father's maiming.'

'*May the best fighter win!*' cried Constans and everyone cheered.

A hunting horn sounded from the upper branches of a huge oak tree by the entrance to the meadows. Ursula smiled to herself as she heard Brittola say excitedly 'It's Pinnosa! She's up in the tree!' The horn sounded again, a long shrill note repeated three times; the signal that game had been spotted. The branches rustled and Pinnosa emerged, sliding down a rope to land on one of the lower boughs. She blew her horn three more times and sprang to the ground.

'*I can see my prey!*' she called out. '*The hunt is on! I'm coming to get you!*'

Pinnosa made her way through the assembly with purposeful strides, forcing people to move aside. As the crowd parted, Gerontius became visible at the opposite end of the meadow. He'd just arrived with some junior officers on a small boat and they were still disembarking. Pinnosa reached the centre of the newly cleared space and came to a halt. Gerontius stared at her for a while like a bear sizing up its opponent, then he adjusted his helmet, straightened his sword and slowly walked toward her.

Just then, King Deonotus stepped forward to address the gathering.

'Pinnosa of the House of Flavius. You have the honour today of having your challenge accepted by the great centurion and high commander of the Britannic legions, Gerontius. Speak young woman, so that we might know your cause.'

'I am here, Your Majesty, to avenge the tragedy of my father, the great commander Marcus Flavius. He was not only abandoned by this man in his moment of need in the midst of battle, but was reduced to great shame by being made lame and crippled for the rest of his life by his wounds, wounds that could have been avoided had it not been for Gerontius who ran from the fray in blind terror like the scurrying bloated rat that he is!'

Pinnosa caught sight of Ursula in the crowd and they exchanged a quick nod of acknowledgement.

'My cause, Your Majesty, is to give my father, who now lives the life of a helpless invalid, the satisfaction of knowing that the cause of his shame and suffering, this loathsome coward, Gerontius, was bettered by a mere woman.' She took several steps toward Gerontius and glared at him fiercely. 'For it was *Gerontius* who should have mustered the men shoulder-to-shoulder around my father when the first arrow struck; it was *Gerontius* who chose instead to withdraw to the safety of the

21

main line and it was Gerontius *again* who left my poor dear father to almost drown in his own blood!'

She turned away from the king to address the gathering.

'I hereby swear by all that is holy and true that I shall finally give my father satisfaction.' She raised her voice and shouted her cause for the heavens to hear. '*The honour of the House of Marcus Flavius!*'

'*Marcus Flavius! Marcus Flavius!*' The cry was quickly picked up by all present, including several of the junior officers. Gerontius glared at them but, with Constans leading the chant, they felt emboldened enough to ignore his threatening gaze.

'And now you, Gerontius, commander of legions.' The king had to raise his voice in order to be heard. 'What is your reply? Speak forth so that we may hear your response to this slight upon your honour!'

The crowd fell silent and for a brief moment only the morning birds could be heard.

'I've got nothing to say that hasn't already been said. I just want to teach this young wench a lesson she's long had coming to her and put her back in her place. Oh aye, her father were a great man all right and I feel sorry for him, or what's left of him but, on the day that she's talking about, the fighting took me one way and him another; and that's all there is to it. If she can't face up to the truth then that's her tragedy, not her father's plight.' He fidgeted impatiently with his sword. 'Now, let's get on with it! I've got more important things to do with my time than teaching a young wench about men's work!'

'Very well,' said the king. 'The contest shall commence! As the challenged, Gerontius, it falls to you to nominate the first round.'

'*Horses, shields and spears!*'

Pinnosa's horse, Artemis, and Gerontius' brown stallion were both brought onto the field without any trappings and the protagonists were handed identical weapons and shields. While the preparations were underway, Ursula led Constans a little away from Constantine and the others.

'Trust Gerontius to choose spears,' she said. 'Swords would have been fairer.'

'Gerontius isn't concerned with playing fair. He's only concerned with winning, and winning by whatever means. He's very good at it which is why he is where he is.'

'Do you ever have to fight alongside him?'

'Not under normal circumstances, no; our contingents have completely different places in the formation Father uses. Only if we had to come around in a wide sweep, or if he was pinned down and driven to the right, would we find ourselves fighting side by side.'

Constans became engrossed in the preparations for the contest and Ursula stared at him full of concern. At that moment, Pinnosa got up onto Artemis and everyone, including Constans, gave a loud cheer. Suddenly, a gnawing fear gripped her again. It felt as if her insides were tying themselves in knots.

'Don't trust him Constans,' she murmured; her voice tense. 'Don't ever trust him.'

'Hmm?' Constans turned and smiled at her distractedly. 'Don't trust who?'

Another cheer came from the crowd as Gerontius mounted his steed.

'Gerontius, of course. You're his greatest rival now. As you say, he'll do anything to win, use whatever means. I'm warning you my love, no matter how closely you work with him on campaign, never, ever trust him, especially if— '

'If what, my love?' He lowered his head so that his ear was by her mouth.

'Especially if your father should die,' she whispered.

He looked at her and was about to say something when yet another cheer from the crowd drew his attention back to events.

'They're ready to make the first pass,' he cried excitedly.

Gerontius had taken off his commander's helmet and plumage. Like Pinnosa, he wore only a tunic with a leather belt about his girth. They each had a single spear and a small circular shield.

'This will be a test of their horsemanship,' explained Constans, knowing that Ursula had never seen such a contest before.

23

'In what way?' she asked, putting her arm through his and pulling him close.

'They're riding bareback and aren't allowed to grasp, or even touch, their steeds with their hands. I didn't know Pinnosa could ride like that; did you?'

Ursula did not reply; instead, she simply smiled.

Pinnosa and Gerontius were in position at opposite ends of the clearing. Simultaneously, they urged their horses forward and began their charges. The crowd roared in anticipation of the clash and the cry '*Marcus Flavius!*' reached new heights.

Iron struck leather and Artemis reared.

'If she falls off, it's all over,' cried Constans as the crowd gasped.

'*Stay on Pinnosa!*' shouted Ursula. '*You must stay on!*'

Pinnosa managed to remain mounted, but only just. It was all she could do not to grip Artemis' mane, especially as she had dropped her spear which she'd been using to keep herself steady. Gerontius rode on, waving his spear in triumph as he urged his horse round for a second pass. Artemis had barely settled when Gerontius was upon Pinnosa again, attacking her exposed shield-less side. At the last moment, Artemis responded to Pinnosa's will and back-stepped, leaving Gerontius thrusting into mid-air. While he was off-balance his horse reared. Seizing her chance, Pinnosa urged Artemis forward and lunged at him with her shield. He lurched forward and gashed his cheek on his own shield. The sight of blood excited the crowd and their cries intensified as the two combatants pulled apart and positioned themselves for another pass.

'A third pass!' exclaimed Constans. 'I've never seen one of these go to three.'

Pinnosa and Gerontius rushed headlong at each other. She swerved at the last moment, forcing him to pass on the spear side. As Gerontius made his thrust, she managed to grab hold of his spear. In tugging hard to get free from her grip, he lost his balance which caused his horse to sidestep. While he struggled to stay on, Pinnosa wheeled Artemis around and made another play for his spear. Just as she reached for it, his horse reared and she gripped his arm instead. Both riders toppled and fell.

'*A draw!*' shouted Constans, clenching Ursula's arm.

Badly winded and gasping for breath, Pinnosa was the slower of the two to pick herself up. Gerontius came up behind her and struck her hard across the back with his shield, pushing her face down into the trampled earth. The crowd booed and Constantine called out.

'*Play fair Gerontius, play fair! Remember she's only a wench!*'

Pinnosa pulled herself to her feet, spitting out dirt.

'I'll get you now Gerontius; let's have a real fight!' She turned and yelled her challenge. '*Long swords and shields!*'

There was so much excitement at the prospect of a sword fight, and the gathering was so preoccupied with the preparations, no one took any notice of a messenger who, at that moment, rode into the clearing at full gallop, dismounted and headed straight for Constantine. Ursula spotted him though and she freed herself from Constans' grip in order to watch as the messenger delivered his message. It was clear from his manner that the news he bore was of great importance; and there was no mistaking the effect his message was having on Constantine whose smile dissolved and shoulders drooped.

Constans was totally engrossed in the contest and unaware of what was happening but, like Ursula, the king had noticed the messenger's arrival. The moment he saw look on Constantine's face, he rushed over to join him ... and Ursula followed. While the messenger dutifully repeated his dispatch for the king's benefit, Ursula felt her dark fear return, freezing her insides in its icy grip.

'Germania is in complete turmoil, Your Majesty. Three whole tribes of Burgundians and two of the Suebi that are even larger have broken through the frontier defences and crossed the Rhenus at several points between Mogontiacum and Argentorate. The imperial court had fled for the safety of Arelate, and what was left of the Colonia, Mogontiacum and Treveris auxiliaries has scattered to the four winds. The Germans are pouring in and all the cities can do is shut their gates; the whole of Germania and northern Gallia are vulnerable to attack.'

Constantine and Deonotus shared solemn nods of agreement before the king finally spoke.

'The time has come. We cannot wait for the emperor's orders a day longer. We must put our plans into operation at once.'

'We leave tomorrow,' declared Constantine. 'Constans will depart at morning bells with the First Horse. They'll need to ride hard to the coast and cross the Oceanus Britannicus as quickly as possible. That way they can make a good start in rallying whatever forces are left in Germania and Gallia before the rest of us arrive. The legion will commence its march around mid-morning. We'll head for Londinium and make the necessary arrangements with the Governor before heading for the Oceanus Britannicus and undertaking the main crossing.'

'*Marcus Flavius!*' Pinnosa's cry signalled she was ready for the second bout of the contest; and the crowd roared.

'We need to begin making preparations at once, but first my dear friends … ' With a warm smile, Constantine placed his arms around Deonotus and Ursula to lead them back to the contest. ' … let us enjoy our sport.'

Screaming a wild battle cry, Pinnosa's onslaught caught Gerontius by surprise; she was able to hack at his shield several times before he responded and their swords clashed. Still she came at him, her sword flashing from left to right, merciless in her blows, clash upon clash upon clash; and she succeeded in forcing him back four or five steps before he regained sufficient footing to make a stand.

His counter-attack was almost overpowering in its brute force. He struck her shield so hard with such a relentless barrage of powerful downward hacks that it began to crack and break apart; but then, just as he was about to deal the decisive blow, Pinnosa managed a fierce upward swipe. Even though it was partly deflected by his shield, it made a deep gash under his arm; and the sight of Gerontius' blood whipped the crowd into a frenzy.

They broke apart and began circling each other, both desperate to regain their breath. As soon as her lungs were full, Pinnosa screamed her fiercest battle cry yet, full of rage. She lunged forward, her sword flashing in a swirling blur and seeming to come at Gerontius from every direction. Despite his frantic left-to-right sweeps, she landed three powerful blows in quick succession upon his shield, forcing him to his knees. She threw aside her shield and, using both hands to grip her sword, hit him so hard with a side swipe that his shield split in two. The blow also opened up a third wound on his forearm, making the crowd cheer. His defensive upward thrust met thin air as she leapt to one side. He lost his balance, his sword slipped from his grasp and he fell at her feet; the fight was over.

Pinnosa put her blade to his throat and forced him to lift up his sweaty head so that they were eye-to-eye. They were so close she could feel the stench of his foul breath in her throat which almost made her gag.

'I call upon all those present to bear witness to this contest and declare that the house of Marcus Flavius has been avenged upon this vile and loathsome man, Gerontius. Let it be known wherever he goes that though he might achieve some measure of fame and glory on campaign with the army amongst strangers in far distant lands … ' She looked down at Gerontius who was beginning to dribble over her blade. ' … here amongst his own where he is well-known by all he shall only ever know the eternal shame of being bettered … by a mere wench!'

The crowd began cheering '*Pinnosa! Pinnosa!*' and Ursula started to make her way back to Constans. Seeing her approach, he put down a flask of wine so that he could embrace her. She was only a few steps from him when a group of Roman officials' wives rushed up to her, bursting with questions.

'Can all you young Britannic women fight like that?'

'How old is Pinnosa and where does she come from?'

'Who is this Marcus Flavius?'

While Ursula was doing her best to answer them, she could only watch as Constantine shouted orders for all officers present to assemble at the Officers' Hall without delay. All she could do was look on as her beloved gave a slight shrug and smiled; then he walked away to join his father.

'Do all you young noble women ride bareback?'

'What do you wear when you go hunting?'

The questions kept coming. As if from far away, she could hear herself sounding calm and giving polite answers. But deep within, her fear was tearing her apart and her inner voice was screaming '*Don't go Constans! Please don't go!*'

IX

The rest of that day saw Corinium abuzz with activity. Every single man, woman and child was busy helping with some aspect of the army's preparations; wheelwrights and carpenters repaired wagons; cobblers, tailors and tanners worked through the night preparing uniforms while blacksmiths repaired weapons and armour. Slaves busily cleaned things and children ran errands; fetching water, relaying messages and carrying goods of every description; meanwhile ordnance crews scoured the whole city, procuring this, checking that and storing everything.

Doctors attended to any ailment or injury, ensuring no condition was left untreated and no wound, not even the most minor, was left undressed. Horse doctors did the same for the horses and even the guard dogs were checked. The barbers pulled over five hundred teeth that day. A special box for them was later made out of bone and placed in the basilica at the base of the statue of Claudius, the Emperor who'd made Britannia part of Rome.

Messengers and ordnance crews were sent ahead to secure provisions, clear camps and barracks, and get the huge transport galleys and their crews ready for the mass Oceanus Britannicus crossing. This last task was Morgan's responsibility as head messenger which meant he was the very first to leave.

Ursula just happened to be looking out of the window from the ladies' chamber with its clear view of the Londinium road when the moment came for him to depart. A horn sounded a long shrill note followed by three short ones; then she heard a loud cheer go up from the messengers' yard just inside the gate. Morgan then came into view outside the city walls. Hermes was already at full gallop as the messenger headed up the gentle rise away from the city, commencing his long ride to Londinium.

As Ursula watched, she saw Cordula leap out from behind a tree half way up the rise to flag Morgan down; and she could clearly see her cousin pleading with the handsome young messenger. He was the son of a horse breeder from the wild frontier country who'd been killed when his farmstead was attacked by Hibernian raiders and burnt to the ground. Morgan had returned home to find his entire family dead and his farm completely destroyed. All he'd had left was the strong young black stallion he had been riding, Hermes, and the two of them had been in the army's service ever since.

In that time, the steadfast, intelligent and well-spoken young man, along with his amazingly fast steed, had not only rapidly won a reputation in Constantine's eyes as the best messenger in Britannia, he had also ridden into Cordula's life like the wild lion winds of March.

Being still within sight of the city, Ursula knew that Morgan couldn't dismount; to do so would have been a bad omen for the many eyes that were still watching at the city gate. Instead, he leant forward as far as he could toward Cordula who was straining to reach up for a farewell kiss. Ursula saw them embrace; then Morgan broke free, gave Hermes a slap and rode off up the rise heading for Londinium. Just before he crested the ridge, he turned one last time and waved at Cordula.

She was wearing a bright red shawl which she untied and used to wave back, continuing to do so after he disappeared. Eventually, long after the dust from Hermes' hooves had wafted away on the May breeze, she stopped waving. The shawl flopped against her arm, slipped from her grasp and fell to the ground. Then, she too fell, crumpling into a sobbing heap.

Ursula knew full well that until the moment came when Morgan reappeared over the horizon, every minute of every hour would be torture for her cousin; endless anxious hours lay ahead of her day and night until she could hold him in her arms once more, run her fingers through his hair and look deep into his eyes. Ursula knew all this because that was precisely how she felt about Constans.

The thought suddenly occurred to her that, like her cousin, she too desperately needed to speak to her beloved before he too disappeared over the horizon.

'Oleander!' she cried. 'Quickly run over to the Officers' Hall and take a message to Constans. Tell him I'd like to see him when they pause to eat.'

'I'm sorry Mistress; I've just heard that the commanders and your father have asked for hot morsels and titbits to be prepared. They won't be stopping for a meal.'

'Then tell him I'll wait for him in the palace garden around midnight.'

'Very well Mistress.'

Ursula returned her attention to the scene outside. She could still see the figure of her cousin lying by the side of the road, weeping. Taking a deep breath, she wiped her eyes and resumed work on the small trinket that lay in her lap.

X

Midnight found Ursula dressed in her finest summer toga seated on a stool in the palace garden and staring up at the stars. There was Ursa Minor, her namesake, doing its eternal dance with Ursa Major around the Pole Star.

All through the night she sat until the pre-dawn glow awakened a cockerel and its call snapped her from her thoughts. Oleander was a little way off under a small ornamental willow, snoring gently. The cockerel's cry meant the start of the day and the attendants' quarters soon began to bustle with activity which finally prompted Ursula to stir.

'Come on Oleander.' She eased her stiff joints into a standing position, heaved a long sigh and headed back inside. 'We need to get ready for the farewell parade.'

Yawning, the old attendant rose slowly to her feet and set off after Ursula. As she crossed the garden, she spotted a small object lying next to Ursula's abandoned stool and stooped to pick it up.

'Mistress,' she called out, 'you dropped your picture.'

XI

Constans looked magnificent in his full regalia. His uniform and equipment had been well-burnished and it glistened in the bright morning light. Moreover, he was freshly-shaven which did much to disguise his tiredness after having been up all night with his father and the rest of the legion's commanders, poring over maps and making plans. His men in the First Horse, a full contingent of two hundred cavalry on horseback, were mounted. They were arranged in ranks of twenty – five abreast and four deep – in

Corinium's forum which was just big enough for such a force to assemble, complete a circuit and depart. Later that day, only Constantine's Vanguard would be turning out in dress uniform for the formal farewell speeches and a parade through the town. The main body of the legion were due to assemble in a large clearing by the road to Londinium two miles from the city before commencing their march.

For the formal farewell ceremonies, King Deonotus' throne was placed on a platform in the centre of a large purple carpet at the end of the forum. The royal party consisted of King Deonotus himself, Princess Ursula, the visiting Roman officials plus their wives and members of other local noble families, including Brittola, Martha, Saula and Cordula. Pinnosa was also there and dressed in her finery for once, a pure white toga with gold trim. Her long red hair was braided with yellow and orange ribbons. Constans stood at full attention at the base of the steps before the platform, one hand on his hilt, the other holding his helmet and plumage correctly against his right shoulder plate. Constantine and Gerontius were standing to attention beside their horses and positioned on either side of the royal party as guards of honour. Both mounts were wearing ceremonial masks that were so heavy and cumbersome they had to be removed before the horses could be ridden anywhere. Gerontius had a dressing on his arm, covering the wound he had received in the contest. Spotting this, Ursula's friends made their way surreptitiously to the edge of the platform immediately above his head.

'Fancy a big important army commander being beaten by a simple frontier country wench!' said Martha in a loud voice.

Gerontius went bright red, but continued to stare straight ahead as the young women began to giggle.

'You know what they say, don't you? "Even young roses have thorns",' said Pinnosa, leaning over him. 'And there are plenty more thorns on *this* young rose Gerontius!'

Her friends' laughter gave rise to frowns and mutterings of disapproval from the rest of the royal party, forcing Ursula to slip from her father's side in order to 'shush' them quiet. She was just tugging Cordula's toga when a fanfare of horns sounded and the king stepped forward to deliver his address.

'People of Corinium, most noble visitors, and men of the legion Britannia; I stand before you humbled by this magnificent display. Men of the First Horse … *I salute you!*'

Deonotus raised his hands high above his head. His palms had been coated with a special mixture of gold dust and ground glass; and as they opened, they sparkled in the morning sunlight. The crowd gasped with amazement and delight at such a dazzling effect.

'*Go forth men of Britannia!* Go forth to the rescue of Germania and Gallia and perform your great deeds. Become victors, heroes and conquerors of all … *a legion of legend!*'

He was forced to pause by the raucous noise and applause that erupted. When he resumed his speech, he adopted a more sombre tone.

'Remember these words men of Britannia. As you depart this beloved island province that we call home, remember that no matter how honoured and exalted you become on the Continent, you will always be strangers to them. Only to us, only here, will you ever be sons, cousins, family and true friends. So, return home heroes, return home with riches in triumph and in glory, but above all … *RETURN HOME! Return home safe … and return home soon!*'

The king paused and, after the cheers died down, for a long moment there was silence as many of the cavalrymen exchanged glances with loved ones in the crowd. Ursula too wanted to look into her beloved Constans' eyes. She'd been watching him while her father was speaking. Even though he was standing rigidly to attention and facing forward, she knew he could see her out of the corner of his eye and, as her father's speech had come to its close a tear had run down his cheek.

'See his tears?' she whispered to Cordula. 'I wish I could wipe them away.'

Cordula sneaked a swift sideways glance at Ursula and saw her tear-filled eyes. Ursula saw her cousin looking and gave her a fleeting wink; then she raised her hands and starting to clap. The whole assembly followed her lead and erupted into rapturous cheers and applause. The cavalry men on their steeds responded by banging their shields with their spears at which point Constantine unsheathed his long sword and waved it through the air in a wide arc to command silence.

'Good people of Corinium, distinguished nobles and honoured guests … and our brave, brave men of the First Horse; I humbly bow in honour of our great king … *King Deonotus!*'

As he bowed the crowd cheered.

'I also humble myself to the greater honour of serving truly the bravest and most noble people in all Rome … *the proud people of Britannia!*'

He bowed again and the cheers intensified.

'Men of the First Horse … *I salute you!* Britannia's Bravest, Britannia's Finest … *and Britannia's Best!*'

As the cheers died down, he slowly and deliberately pointed his sword at Constans.

'I say to you my son: do as your king tells you; return home, return home safe and return home soon. But in addition, and most importantly of all … *return home to your future!* To your beautiful bride-to-be … *Princess Ursula!*'

Ursula bowed to acknowledge the crowd's cheers then, in a sudden move, she lifted her arms high above her head and a white dove flew out from each of her sleeves. As the crowd's applause intensified, she winked at Pinnosa who'd helped her to devise the trick. She then strode boldly over to Constans, clasped his face in her hands and kissed him full on the lips. The hoots and shouts for "*More!*" were almost deafening. She needed no further bidding and did as the crowd demanded. This time he wrapped his arms around her and held her tight in his embrace.

With the crowd still chanting "*More!*" she pulled back and handed him the small trinket she had been working on.

'*What is it?*' he was forced to shout.

'It's a tiny portrait of me that Brittola painted. I had it set in a silver frame and encased in wood. I decorated it myself. It's something for you to remember me by.'

While she was speaking, she placed it around his neck. For a moment, it dangled awkwardly against his breastplate on its black cord. She smiled and tucked it inside against his chest.

'I shall never take it off even when I'm bathing.'

He took her firmly by the shoulders and looked deep into her eyes.

33

'Always remember this. Only in your voice … I hear family. Only in your eyes … I see home.'

There were so many things she wanted to say, so many things she needed to say, but all she could manage was 'Come home soon.' They kissed a third time, taking the crowd's cheers to new heights.

'*ATTENTION!*' bellowed Constantine.

Constans let her go, stood to attention and spun round to face his men. As he did so, Ursula whispered just loud enough for him to hear.

'Please let our eyes meet, just one more time.'

She watched him put on his helmet and straighten his cloak then looked on helplessly as the ceremonial mask was removed from his horse's head and he mounted in readiness to ride. His attendant handed him the standard of the First Horse and he urged his horse forward to take up position at the front. When he raised the standard high it produced the loudest roar yet from the crowd.

'*Commander! Lead your men out!*'

'*Yes, Sir! Men of the First Horse … FORWARD!*'

Constans wheeled his horse round and, as he made his parting salute to the royal party, his eyes did, indeed, meet hers. They only had a fleeting instant to look at each other, and in that moment they both strained to say so many things: 'Take care of yourself and be ever mindful of your enemies.' 'Remember me.' 'I'll always be here waiting for you.' and 'I'll always be true to you.' but then his salute was complete and the moment was over. He placed his hand on his lips and blew her a farewell kiss. She barely managed one in reply before his horse turned and he was off. The men circled the forum and exited down the main street towards the main gate, Londinium and the Continent.

To Ursula, the cheers from the crowd now seemed to be coming from another time and place … somewhere far, far away. The standard of the First Horse was now all that was visible of him and his officers; and it appeared to be floating away upon a blurred haze of bobbing plumage.

Her friends, along with the rest of the crowd, ran across the forum after the men, crying their farewells; and she could hear Brittola's shrill voice above all the others, shouting '*God goes with you!*'

Pinnosa, however, remained behind. She walked over to stand beside Ursula on the royal platform and gently put her arm around her.

'Come, you're tired. You should go back to your room and have a little sleep before Constantine's departure. By the time that's over it'll be around midday and we'll still have the whole afternoon ahead of us. I say we go for a ride up into the hills to get away from all this and leave the city behind. You and the others can find a nice quiet spot to rest, and I ... ' she smiled, 'I might just do a little hunting.'

Ursula didn't say anything; instead she gave a slight nod and smiled. As they stepped down off the platform and started heading back to the palace, the others caught them up to form a group of six young noblewomen linked arm in arm, each one looking their finest ... and all heading in the same direction.

Chapter Two

DEFENCELESS?

I

Later that day, soon after Constantine and the Britannic legion had departed, Pinnosa, Ursula and the others, accompanied by their attendants, slipped out through Corinium's North Gate and set off towards the rolling hills that lay between Corinium and Glevum intent on enjoying a couple of days' hunting on King Deonotus' vast estate.

Two days later – feeling duly refreshed and invigorated with a cart full of catches – the six young noblewomen and their entourage emerged from the forest onto the Corinium road a few miles south of Glevum. It was just past midday when they joined the road along with their entourage. Almost immediately, they spotted an over-loaded farm wagon just ahead of them; and they could tell at once that something was wrong.

Sharing a look of concern, Pinnosa and Ursula told the others to hold back and went ahead on Artemis and Ursula's grey mare Swift to investigate. As they drew close, they could see that the wagon was being pulled by a pair of mules; and, urging them on with loud cracks of his whip, was an old man. Seated next to him was a young woman desperately trying to comfort two small children who were both wailing and crying. Three older children were perched upon the belongings in the rear of the wagon and two slaves were following behind bent forward with heavy loads upon their backs; bundles of cloth, flagons and urns, even items of furniture.

As they neared the front of the rickety old farm cart, Pinnosa suddenly recognised the family.

'*Aelwines Galicus? Heulwen?*' she called out. 'What's happened? Where are you going?'

The woman, Heulwen, looked anxiously back over her shoulder.

'Pinnosa? Is that you; is that really you?' She held her children close as Pinnosa and Ursula drew up alongside. 'Hush-hush little ones; have no fear, these women are friends.'

While the women were speaking, the old man Aelwines ignored them, preferring instead to keep his eyes fixed firmly upon the road ahead while continuing to crack his whip, his whole demeanour tense and full of urgency.

'They came down the valley two days ago from the direction of the coast,' said Heulwen. 'Hibernian raiders over a score, maybe three dozen, in number. They were on the rampage, murdering and pillaging everywhere they went; and anything they couldn't carry they burned. We were lucky to get away. Father here was fishing upstream when he heard the terrifying screams of Gynreth the potter as they tormented the poor man to his death. Father ran as fast as he could back to the farm. We just had enough time to throw our belongings in the cart before they were upon us. When we got to the top of Old Witch's Hill and looked back, we could see smoke and realised it was ... it was the fire of our burning home ... '

She had to pause; the memories were still too painful and raw. The children started to whine again, and she coddled them to quieten them down. Then she took a deep breath and forced herself to continue.

'By the time we got to Magnis it was already full with people fleeing from the menace. We didn't feel safe there, so we continued on to Glevum and got there just before dawn. As soon as we arrived, we went straight to the centurion and pleaded with him to send a force to go after the murdering swine. He couldn't do anything though. He only has fifty men, and they're needed to guard the city. The only real help we got from him was when he told us that the field army was at Corinium. So we're on our way there now to find our Gildred and— '

'He's gone,' interrupted Pinnosa. 'They've all gone. The army left for the Continent two days ago.' She leaned forward and stared intently at the woman. 'What of my family Heulwen? Did you see them? Are they all right?'

Heulwen returned her fierce gaze and shook her head.

'I'm sorry ... '

Sensing her mistress's tension, Artemis came to a halt. As Pinnosa dropped back, Ursula saw her stiffen like game before the chase, her eyes staring wide and wild. She turned back to Heulwen and spoke with urgency.

'Please listen carefully Heulwen; I am Princess Ursula, daughter of King Deonotus and good friend of Pinnosa. I must ask you to take our attendants with you to Corinium. Will you do that?' Heulwen nodded. 'Thank you. You will be well rewarded. Now, when you get there, I want you to go directly to the palace and make sure the king himself hears your story. Tell him you met Pinnosa and I on the road, and that we have gone to Glevum. Is that clear?' Heulwen nodded again.

Seeing that the others has almost caught Pinnosa up, Ursula quickly rode back to them to explain things.

'It sounds like Pinnosa's family might have been attacked by Hibernian raiders.'

'*No!*' exclaimed Brittola. 'How do you— '

'*WE RIDE!*' Pinnosa's powerful voice filled the air as she wheeled Artemis round and set off at a full gallop towards Glevum. '*COME ON! RIDE, DAMN YOU—RIDE!*'

The others hesitated for a moment unsure what to do.

'*Hells teeth! Don't just stand there—go after her for goodness' sake!*' shouted Ursula. '*Follow her and try not to lose her! Now—GO! I'll catch up with you shortly!*'

Oleander came scurrying up to Ursula with her old donkey Toby in tow.

'*Mistress! What's happening Mistress?*'

Keen to be with her stablemates, Swift had become highly agitated and it took all of Ursula's strength to rein her in while she addressed her attendant.

'We have to go to Glevum, and most probably into frontier country, to make sure Pinnosa's family is safe. I want you to go with these poor folk to Corinium. Tell Father I shall return home in a few days and that I will bring the others back with me safe and sound.' She pointed to the supplies on Toby's back. 'I'll need some of that food and those water flasks.'

Oleander hastily unpacked the provisions and began tying them to Swift's straps, all the while muttering to herself.

'It's all very well you making sure *they're* safe, but who's going to be making sure *you're* safe?' When she'd finished, she grabbed Ursula's leg. 'Please take good care of yourself Mistress, as well as them.'

Ursula glanced down at Oleander and smiled; then she looked back up at the road to Glevum and urged Swift forward.

The young grey mare needed no further bidding. She set off after her stablemates and was quickly at a full gallop, living up to the name she'd gained as a filly.

II

Riding hard, they reached Glevum in less than an hour. As soon as they entered the city gate, Pinnosa and Ursula dismounted and ran to the guard station to find out what was happening, leaving the others to take care of the horses in the messengers' yard.

They found the garrison centurion, Leonius, in the commanders' room at the Officers' Hall. He was the gruff no-nonsense sort; a well-seasoned old campaigner.

'News of the raiders first reached us last night, Your Highness. A messenger rode in from Magnis just before evening bells. He said some travellers had seen the raiders coming over the mountains from the coast two days earlier. From what they told him, he reckoned it was probably a three-boat group about twenty-five to thirty in number. It's obvious they're here to plunder the Vaga Valley and they're probably making for Magnis itself. Then, just this morning, two families – the Galicuses and the Valenses – arrived, looking for— '

'What about my family; the Flavius household?' interrupted Pinnosa. 'Any news of them?'

Leonius shook his head.

'We met the Galicuses on the road to Corinium,' said Ursula. 'Do you know the whereabouts of the Valenses? They might know something about Pinnosa's family. Are they here?'

'Oh yes, they are still here in Glevum Your Highness. They've been taken in by— '

'And, what exactly have you done about the situation in the valley?' snapped Pinnosa. 'Have you sent out a patrol or sent reinforcements to Magnis?'

'Not exactly, no Mistress. We— '

'Why *not?*' Pinnosa began pacing up and down.

'Give the good man a chance to answer you properly Pinnosa,' said Ursula.

'Thank you, Your Highness,' said Leonius. 'There are only fifty of us and we are needed here to— '

'So, what *have* you done? You must've done *something* for goodness' sake!'

Pinnosa lunged forward and tried to grab Leonius by his arm. Ursula too dived forward to hold Pinnosa back as he instinctively reached for his sword.

'Of course, we've done something,' he snarled through gritted teeth. 'We sent six Vaga Valley men to the main garrison at Viroconium to muster a fifty-strong cavalry unit who are to ride to Magnis in haste. We need proper numbers if we're to deal with so many of these swine.' He turned to Ursula and continued in a calmer tone. 'The reinforcements should be setting off from Viroconium first thing in the morning Your Highness. They'll be at Magnis by mid-afternoon at the latest.'

'That's *far* too late,' said Pinnosa. 'You're giving those Hibernian scum a whole day to do as they please. They could attack another dozen homesteads in that time, torturing, raping, and murdering each and every family. Worse still, they might even find their way back to their boats and escape with all their rich pickings before any legionaries *finally* show up!'

'Don't you think my men with families in that valley wanted to go to their rescue?' snapped Leonius, still gripping the hilt of his sword. 'Of course, they did! But they obeyed their orders rather than their instincts and went to Viroconium instead, because they knew it was the wise thing to do. We are desperate for good fighting soldiers here now that our army has left for the continent. I can't go losing units of my men every time there's a raiding party. If I let that happen, within a year, we'd have no men left!'

Pinnosa looked at Ursula then back at Leonius.

'Then maybe it's time for the *women* to do some of the fighting!' She span round and headed for the door. 'We're off to Magnis right now. If my friends and I meet up with any of these raiders on the way – even though we are only carrying hunting

weapons – I'm sure we wouldn't be afraid of taking them on.'
She glanced at Ursula and added, 'and there's only *six* of us.'

Leonius looked alarmed.

'I cannot order you not to go to Magnis Mistress but, with all due respect, there's a big difference between hunting game and tackling murderous Hibernian thugs.' He turned to Ursula. 'I implore you Your Highness, don't do anything rash. The men from Viroconium will arrive in the valley tomorrow and they will deal with the problem properly. I understand how Mistress Pinnosa must feel but I wouldn't be doing my duty if I didn't strongly advise you to stay here in Glevum tonight. If you do decide to proceed to Magnis tomorrow, I'll happily provide you with an armed escort, indeed, I'll escort you there myself.'

Leonius paused for Ursula to say something, but she remained silent, staring hard at Pinnosa.

'In any case Your Highness,' he added, 'you will never make it to Magnis before dusk; it's well over thirty miles.'

'He has a point, Pinnosa.' Ursula spoke without taking her eyes off her old friend. 'If it were only you and I on Artemis and Swift we might make it, but think of Brittola and— '

'*Hell's teeth—think of my family!*' cried Pinnosa.

Ursula turned to face Leonius.

'Thank you for your information and for your kind offer. I assure you we will give the matter much careful thought and, if we do decide to continue on to Magnis, we'll proceed with the utmost caution.'

Pinnosa and Leonius both tried to say something, but Ursula cut them off.

'Now would you be so kind as to tell us where we can find the Valenses?'

'In a fishmongers' of the same name by Fisherman's Quay Your Highness.'

'Thank you.' Ursula moved over to the door and was about to leave when she remembered something. 'Oh, by the way, I wanted to ask; what's happened to the coastal galley patrols that are supposed to be preventing these raiding parties from landing?'

Leonius looked awkward.

'*Er* – well you see Your Highness, the thing is I – *er* – I think I may have heard something recently about some of them being in dock in Maridunum, being refitted and repaired … and – *um* – cleaned.'

'Oh? And do we know how many, exactly, are in dock, being refitted and "cleaned"?'

'I – *er* – I think it might be around ten or so; even, possibly as many as – *um* – twelve, I believe.'

'I see. And how many are there in total?'

'How many galleys?'

'Yes, how many patrol galleys are there in total … exactly?'

'Oh, about – *um* – about fourteen or fifteen.'

'*Hah!*' barked Pinnosa. 'What good are "clean" galleys, when it's *fighting* ones that we need?'

'That's enough,' said Ursula sharply, leading Pinnosa away.

The Valenses had no news of Pinnosa's family and could tell them nothing about the situation in the valley that Ursula and Pinnosa did not know already. Like the Galicuses, all they could do was recount with terror their narrow escape. Having thus gleaned all the possible information Glevum had to offer, they rushed back to re-join the others.

The sun was already low in the sky when, with a face like thunder and without uttering a word, Pinnosa stormed across the messengers' yard, leapt up onto Artemis, wheeled her round and galloped out of the gate.

'Don't just stand there—*go after her!*' shouted Ursula, leaping up onto Swift.

'What's happening?' cried Brittola as she scrambled to get on her young mare Feather. 'Why are we leaving? Where are we going?'

'*We're heading for Magnis, and we need to move fast!*' cried Ursula as she disappeared through the gate.

'*Magnis? In frontier country? On country tracks with no proper roads?*' yelled Saula. '*There's no way we can make it to Magnis before dark!*'

42

III

The first part of their journey through the gentle hills between the Rivers Sabrina and Vaga was easy going and they were able to make good progress. Pinnosa led with Ursula and the others, none of whom had ventured beyond Glevum before, strung out in a line behind.

Along the way, through a faint haze to their south, they could sometimes make out the odd flash of fire coming from the huge smelting yards where iron was produced for the army and the West Country cities. Even though the fires were miles distant, they could still smell their foul acrid smoke.

The sun was getting very low by the time they passed through the main settlement of metal workers called Ariconium. For over a mile, the road was flanked either side by waggoners' yards where iron smiths, wheelwrights and carpenters built, or repaired, wagons, carts and chariots, alongside workshops where armour or household goods were made. All of the yards and workshops were quiet and still as the women galloped through with only the occasional slave or child cleaning up.

Continuing to ride hard, they managed to reach the valley of the River Vaga and traverse several of its winding bends before the sun finally disappeared. Finding themselves on rough frontier country roads in rapidly fading light, they slowed down and formed tight a group which gave them their first chance to speak since leaving Glevum.

'So, this is the wild frontier country, eh Pinnosa?' said Martha. 'Is it true what they say, that the mountains have voices and the trees have eyes?'

'Mother Nature is in her glory in those mountains,' replied Pinnosa over her shoulder. 'One day, I'll take you up into those peaks so that you can experience their magic. I promise they'll weave the same spell on you that they did on my father many years ago when he was a young legionary ... and ... '

An awkward silence fell; it was Ursula who finally spoke.

'Tell us more about these frontier lands Pinnosa, and why your father chose to make it his home.'

'Where shall I begin? Well, Magnis I suppose,' She heaved a long sigh. 'Magnis is a very small and basic town, not much more than an army outpost really. There are few of the pleasures of city life there; no busy forum, no shops selling fine robes or jewellery. The food is plain and the town's store only stocks one type of oil and one type of wine, though old Saenus likes to give them a different name each month!' She gave a little chuckle. 'When you get beyond Magnis the frontier lands really start. Hardly any families live there; apart from a few hill folk, the only people you meet in the mountains are army patrols, and there are lots of those – though nowhere near as many as there used to be. Its excellent training country for legionaries; perfect for encampment practice, forced marching and— '

'But it's not just *training* for the legionaries, is it?' interrupted Brittola. 'They see plenty of *action* too, don't they?'

'Against the Hibernian raiding parties, you mean?' said Pinnosa. 'Oh yes, they come across in boatloads in the summer months. The galleys usually stop most of them and those that get through are usually caught by the mountain patrols.' She looked up at the distant peaks that were rapidly becoming invisible in the gathering murk. 'These days there are fewer patrols which means more and more of the Hibernian scum are managing to cross the mountains … and come down into the valleys … '

The awkward silence returned. Ursula was about to say something when Pinnosa continued.

'My father first came to these mountains when he was a young legionary on a training march. He fell in love with them and swore to himself that he would one day make them his home. As the years passed, he rose in rank to become a great commander, one of the main builders of Constantine's new army, and the time came for him to build a home for his family. The Vaga valley was still mostly wilderness with just a handful of small homesteads like the Galicus one. When he announced his plans to clear the land and build a complete villa estate, the people of Magnis and Glevum thought he was mad. "Why live here," they said "when you could have your pick of the choicest properties in Britannia or Gallia, or even Roma itself?" But at that time the mountain patrols were keeping the raiders at bay and anyway his heart was set. I remember him saying to my

44

mother who was reluctant to follow him at first "I know those mountains and they know me. They're as much a part of me as you and the children. They'll allow me to tame their wild spirit; and in return I'll allow them to tame mine."'

'How about you Pinnosa?' said Ursula.

'Me?'

'These mountains are your home too, aren't they?'

'Oh yes,' said Brittola. '*Do* tell us about your life out here.'

'There's not much to tell really. Most of my childhood was spent in Glevum, not out here. Our villa wasn't completed until I was quite old. These— ' she slapped her breasts, 'were almost full-grown by then. I remember my father coming home from a campaign in Africa and he was determined to enjoy some good autumn hunting up in the mountains. I was the only one of us three children old enough to join him. Julius was eight and Titus was only six.' She smiled. 'We spent four glorious weeks together; riding, hunting, fishing, building camp. He taught me so much. I'm sure he knew such time with me was precious. He said to me one night as we sat under the stars eating fish and boar by the camp fire "What a strange family we are; a girl who knows all about horses and weapons and the thrill of the hunt, and boys who know only farm animals and kitchen gardens. If I died tomorrow, it would fall to you to bring Julius and Titus up properly into manhood. You know that, don't you?" Then, just two days later, he was called away to serve on the big campaign against the Pict and Hibernian Grand Alliance.' She fell silent and stared up at the early evening stars.

'Why don't we talk about something else?' suggested Cordula, but Pinnosa forced herself to continue, fighting back her tears.

'He came back six months later in a wagon; he was in constant pain and unable to walk without crutches. Mother was wonderful; she nursed him day and night, and never let him out of her sight. Just as he'd predicted, it fell to me to prepare the boys for life in the legion; horse training, survival skills, hunting techniques, blade craft … everything.'

'They must be about the same age as me,' said Brittola. 'Did you train them well Pinnosa? Are they ready for the army?'

45

'*A-ha!* Looking for a possible husband, eh?' Pinnosa turned to Brittola and smiled. 'Well I think they're both very handsome. Julius, the older one, is tall and has brown hair. Titus is shorter but very strong with red hair like Father and I. He's the one for you Brittola. He loves riding and—*oh*, that reminds me Cordula?'

'Yes?'

'Did you know Artemis was from Morgan's father's stables?'

'*No!* Really? But, of course, come to think of it, that would make sense. Morgan's father always named his stock after the god that best matched the nature of the new owner.'

'That's right "Artemis the huntress". Because I needed to train the boys well, when he returned home, Father gave me some gold from his invalid purse and told me to go and buy "the best horse in the mountains" and here she is!' She patted Artemis on the neck and the large black mare responded with a shake of her mane. 'She's from the same sire as Morgan's horse Hermes. She was only two years old when I got her. We've grown up together, haven't we Artemis?' She leant forward and nuzzled her neck, 'My lovely, lovely Artemis.'

'Pinnosa?' said Saula.

'Hmm?'

'Wasn't it about three years ago that the mountain patrols were drawn down to make up the field army?'

'Uh-huh,' said Pinnosa, continuing to make a fuss of Artemis.

'And, didn't the Hibernian raiders start penetrating more deeply inland soon after that?'

'That's right!' exclaimed Cordula. 'It was one of the early raids that killed Morgan's family and destroyed their stud farm. I suppose I owe the Hibernians my gratitude for forcing Morgan to become a messenger!'

'So, with the increased danger Pinnosa,' pressed Saula, 'why didn't your family move back to the safety of Magnis or Glevum?'

Pinnosa froze and visibly bristled.

'My father *loves* these mountains!' she snapped. 'In his torment, they are his one great joy. It'll take much more than some drunken Hibernian louts to tear him away. He may be feeble but he's no coward!'

'I-I-I didn't mean— '

Saula winced at Pinnosa's sharp rebuke and looked to Martha for help, but before Martha could think of anything to say, Ursula beat her to it.

'It's almost dark Pinnosa! How much further is it?'

Her outburst forgotten, Pinnosa peered into the growing shadows of twilight. It took her a moment to get her bearings.

'*A-hah!*' she said eventually. 'There's the burnt oak coming up. That means there's only another five miles to go.'

'We'd better stop talking and concentrate on the road,' said Ursula. 'We'll switch to single file from here on. You and Artemis take the lead Pinnosa, and I'll take the rear.'

IV

'*HALT!*' A night sentry called out from the palisade as he heard movement on the wooden ramp. '*WHO GOES THERE?*'

Apart from a couple of stone buildings, Magnis was mostly made from timber, including the town's single gatehouse. Encircling the town was not one but two deep ditches in parallel, each well over twenty cubits deep and with steep banks that were almost vertical, making it impregnable to all but the most well-equipped and determined of invaders. The only way in or out was to use the extended ramp that traversed the ditches and, as the horses of the six companions moved onto it, the sharp '*clip-clop*'s of their hooves echoed loudly on its wooden planks, announcing their arrival.

'*Pinnosa, daughter of Maximus Flavius! I bring with me Princess Ursula, daughter of King Deonotus, and four friends!*'

'*Come forward to the gate to be identified Pinnosa, daughter of Maximus Flavius! All you others stay on the ramp!*'

As soon as they were safely inside, the town's centurion Calixtus gave orders for baths and hot food to be prepared for the young noblewomen before leading them to their quarters, a small dormitory adjacent to the Officers' Hall. While the others were

47

being undressed, washed and groomed by slaves, Ursula and Pinnosa took Calixtus aside and asked for the latest information.

'We have over twenty families from the valley taking shelter here, Your Highness. We know the Galicuses and Valenses have moved on to Glevum. That leaves your family Mistress and four others unaccounted for. Flavia Lucilla isn't here because her villa was spared. She has a staff of over thirty, and they put up a spirited resistance with just farm implements and hunting weapons when the murderous mob came their way. They managed to kill two of the raiders and turn the rest back. That was late this afternoon. We haven't received any more reports since.'

'Why haven't you responded?' cried Pinnosa. 'Why haven't you even sent out a patrol to check on the missing families?'

The elderly Calixtus, a kind-hearted man who Pinnosa had known since childhood, looked awkward and embarrassed.

'As you well know Mistress, there are only fifteen of us here. We have to be capable of defending the town if necessary. We sent a rider to Glevum yesterday, asking for reinforcements, but none came today. In fact, when we heard your horses, we thought you might be them.'

'Six Vaga Valley men have been sent from Glevum to Viroconium,' said Ursula. 'You should expect about thirty reinforcements tomorrow.'

'That's good to hear.' Calixtus looked relieved. 'A bit late, but good. Then at last we'll be able to go out there and deal with the murdering swine!'

'A *bit* late?' Pinnosa was about to say more, but was stopped by a glare from Ursula.

'Thank you, Centurion.' Ursula nodded courteously. 'You've been most informative and most kind. Now, if you'll excuse us, we've had a long day.'

She was about to walk away when Calixtus coughed politely and spoke again.

'Your Highness?'

'Yes?'

He shifted uncomfortably from side to side.

'You are not thinking of going up the valley to the
Flavius villa by yourselves unescorted, I hope?'

'Pinnosa is understandably concerned about her family.'

'Yes, of course, but you mustn't do anything foolish,
Your Highness. These Hibernians are extremely dangerous. The
cavalry unit is on its way from Viroconium. I'd rest much easier
if you and the other ladies would at least wait until they get here,
and we can provide you with a proper escort.'

Ursula smiled.

'I appreciate your concern Centurion. I assure you, we
do not intend to do anything that will add to the burden of your
responsibilities.'

'Thank you, Your Highness.' He saluted and made to
leave, pausing to add, 'I bid you a pleasant night's sleep.'

The women were so exhausted, they ate their meals in silence,
after which Martha, Saula, Brittola and Cordula went straight to
their beds. As soon as the others were settled, Pinnosa leaned
over to Ursula and whispered in her ear.

'Before we go to bed, I want you to come outside with
me to check on the horses.'

Ursula reluctantly followed her even though all she
really wanted was to curl up in her bedroll and sleep.

Outside the night was still. Their horses were tethered to
a rail by their quarters. They had been watered, fed and covered
with blankets. Swift and Artemis were nearest the door with their
necks nestled against each other. A night sentry patrolled past on
the nearby palisade silhouetted stark against the bright yellow
disc of the moon.

Ursula found Pinnosa standing completely still on a
walkway beside the horses, watching the sentry doing his circuit.

'You mustn't worry' she said quietly. 'I'm sure we'll
find them tomorrow. I bet Titus and Julius managed to hide your
parents somewhere safe from the raiders.'

'I ... I had a terrible dream last night.'

'Oh?'

'I dreamt we – Father and I – were out in the mountains
on our horses just like when I was young. He was his old self
again ... ' She smiled. 'We were having great fun, hunting deer

49

and splashing our way along a fresh mountain stream, when suddenly the sky turned from blue to silver and the water in the stream dried up. We looked up and rushing towards us from out of the sky were four riders in black robes and hoods, riding four powerful black horses and galloping hard, coming directly at us. Then, there were more black riders, dozens and dozens of them. More, and then more, until the sky was full. Hundreds of black riders … thousands.'

She paused and shivered.

'Go on,' said Ursula as she too shivered. While Pinnosa had been speaking she'd felt the icy tentacles of her dark fear rising from deep within.

'Just as the black riders were about to overwhelm us, they disappeared. There in their place, standing absolutely still, facing away from us as if they were about to depart, were four lone white riders. They were in white robes with hoods and sat astride white horses.' Her voice became choked and tight with emotion. 'I don't know why but I became so terrified of their leaving. "Don't go!" I shouted and they turned around to face me. It was then that I saw their faces.'

She looked at Ursula with tears down her cheeks.

'It was Father and Mother, Julius and Titus.'

Ursula rushed up to Pinnosa and gave her a hug. They held each other tight as if holding onto life itself. After a while, Pinnosa continued.

'They each gave me loving smiles and waved goodbye, then they turned away and began heading into the bright white light which now filled the sky. Just as they were disappearing from view, Father turned around once more. I heard him cry, "We shall be waiting for you Pinnosa! We shall be waiting!"'

She had to stop, unable to control her tears.

'Have you ever had such a dream before?'

'No, never.'

Pinnosa wiped her nose with her sleeve to stop herself crying. As she did so she pulled back to look Ursula in the eye.

'That wasn't the end of my dream. There was more.'

The hair on the back of Ursula's neck rose. Somehow, she knew exactly what Pinnosa was about to say next.

'I turned around and the person next to me, the companion I'd been hunting with, the person who had once been my father ... was now you.'

Ursula felt as if she was going to faint and had to grab hold of a nearby rail to steady herself.

'Next to you were Martha, and Saula, and Brittola ... though curiously I don't recall seeing Cordula. All of us were dressed as white riders, and— '

'*Don't!* Please don't say any more!'

'But Ursula, the nightmare was over. It had become a beautiful dream. The white light was now all around us. It felt so warm, so beckoning. We all held hands and started to laugh. We were so free and happy together. In some strange way, we had become liberated from the nightmare, so that we could finally be happy. Stranger still, the happiness wasn't limited to our friends and ourselves. We were sharing it with a whole *host* of white riders ... hundreds of them ... thousands. And the strangest thing was – all the white riders were women. There wasn't one man amongst us.'

A sudden loud cracking sound made them both look down; Ursula's grip on the rail had become so tight it had come apart at one of the joints.

'I'm sorry, but I'm too tired to think about what this means,' said Ursula. 'I-I desperately need some sleep.'

With her head reeling, Ursula carefully made her way back towards the door. She was just about to go inside when Pinnosa spoke again.

'It was a dream about death, wasn't it?'

'Yes ... ' Ursula's voice was flat and matter-of-fact. 'Yes, it was.'

'My parents and brothers are dead, aren't they?'

'*No!* That's not true. They were in your dream; we were in your dream. We're not dead ... why should they be?'

'They were killed by those Hibernian scum yesterday.'

Ursula looked back and saw Pinnosa staring up at the moon with her face etched stark in its cold pale light.

'We'll find out one way or another tomorrow,' she said wearily, then went inside and gently closed the door behind her.

V

'*Wake up!* Come on, come on; we've got work to do—*wake up!*'

Pinnosa went from bunk to bunk, shaking her friends awake. It was still dark, but through the open window the eastern horizon was beginning to glow.

'Why have you woken us up so early?' Cordula sat up, rubbing her eyes. 'Are the men from Viroconium here already?'

'We're not waiting for the reinforcements,' said Pinnosa, dragging a heavy sack in through the door which made metallic rattles and clanking sounds.

'Why aren't we waiting for the reinforcements?' said Martha, biting into an apple. 'You're not suggesting we go up the valley *alone* I hope?'

'I'm leaving before the cock crows.' Pinnosa let the sack drop with a loud clatter and stood up straight. 'Those of you who wish can stay here and wait for the men from Viroconium. If, on the other hand, you decide to come with me … ' she pointed to the sack ' … there are your weapons.'

Martha, Saula, Brittola and Cordula exchanged looks; then they all turned to Ursula.

'I thought I heard you say to the centurion last night that we wouldn't be a worry to him?' said Brittola.

'What I told him was we wouldn't add to the burden of *his* responsibilities.' Ursula moved over to Pinnosa beside the door. 'But we can't stop Pinnosa from going and I, for one, am not letting her go alone.' She looked back at the others. 'And *I* take full responsibility for that.'

'Oh, silly me; I forgot,' said Martha, winking at Saula. 'Didn't you mention yesterday something about there not being any good shops here in Magnis Pinnosa? Nowhere I can find fine clothes or jewellery?' Pinnosa nodded and Martha stood up. 'Well, in that case, if there's nothing better to do around here, I'd love to come with you for a ride deep into wild frontier country. How about you Saula?'

'You don't expect me to miss out on all that brisk early morning fresh mountain air, do you?' Saula rose to her feet. 'They say it's good for heart, mind, body *and* soul.'

'I'm with you Pinnosa.' Brittola leapt from her bunk. 'All we're doing is riding up the valley to Pinnosa's home and visiting her family. It's not as if we're actively seeking the raiders or anything like that, is it?'

'Precisely,' said Ursula.

They all looked at Cordula … who broke into a smile.

'Well, don't expect me to be the only one left behind full of worry. Besides, I'd rather fight the Hibernians than have to explain to our friend the centurion what you lot are up to.'

While they were getting dressed and snatching morsels of food from a platter left out for them by Calixtus' attendant, Pinnosa distributed the equipment she'd gathered from the armoury while they were asleep. They were each given a small round shield, a hunting bow with a full quiver of arrows, a hunting spear and a short legionary's sword. When they were almost ready, she reached round behind the door, produced a long officer's sword in an ornate scabbard and proceeded to strap it about her waist.

'Where did you get *that* from Pinnosa?' asked Brittola.

Pinnosa smiled and tapped her nose.

'Don't forget I know this town well.'

'What do think you'll need it for?' asked Ursula.

'Extra protection,' replied Pinnosa as she strolled out the door. 'Shall we be off?'

Outside, they found their horses lined up ready for them to depart along with an elderly slave holding an oil lamp. The instant they were all mounted, at a nod from Pinnosa he scurried off to open the town gate.

The eastern horizon shed just enough light to show the way as the six young women set off. The sound of their horses' hooves reverberated like thunder as they galloped across the long wooden ramp. The noise woke the whole of Magnis, causing dogs to bark and cattle to moo. With Pinnosa in the lead and Ursula once more guarding the rear, they headed straight for the river where they picked up the rough valley road that took them upstream towards the Flavius villa. Soon, they left the safety of Magnis far behind as they headed further into frontier lands … and whatever the wild hills had in store.

VI

They reached the last bend in the river before the Flavius villa just as the fiery bright rim of the sun became visible above the mountain tops. Pinnosa led them to a glade by the riverbank where their horses could be left safely tethered, then took them along a deer path into the woodland adjacent to the villa grounds.

'Wait here,' she whispered as the first glimpses of the villa's outbuildings became visible through the trees. 'I'm going to take a look around; I'll be back soon.'

Before any of them could say anything, she disappeared into the undergrowth. They waited for several long minutes, listening intently for any sign of Pinnosa's return until Ursula decided they should wait no longer. Following her lead, they crept slowly and gingerly through the trees and undergrowth toward the villa's outer buildings, taking every care not to make a noise. As the trees thinned, they spotted the broad gravel track that led to the villa from the river. Just a few more steps and they would be out in the open and fully exposed to view.

They carefully scoured the landscape for any sign of activity. All they could see was the peaceful serenity of a sleepy Roman estate languishing in the morning light of what promised to be a glorious summer's day. The woodland was alive with the noises of busy birds and animals. Everything was a picture of tranquillity; a country idyll like in a tapestry or a villa wall painting; there was certainly no sign of any Hibernian raiders.

Ursula cautiously led them with shields raised and weapons drawn out from the cover of the undergrowth into the open space of the villa's grounds. As soon as they emerged from the woods, there in plain view for all to see was a truly horrific sight. In the middle of the road, hanging upside down from the branch of a large oak tree like a piece of carrion, was a mutilated and naked body; and kneeling before it was Pinnosa. The corpse was that of a young boy; his entrails and strands of congealed blood were dangling from huge gashes slashed across his front, covering his face. Even though they couldn't see his features, they all knew it had to be Pinnosa's youngest brother Titus, because of the red hair still visible through the gore.

Casting caution aside, Ursula ran up to Pinnosa, knelt beside her, put her arm around her shoulders and bowed her head forward. Martha, Saula and Cordula followed. They also briefly hugged Pinnosa, but then quickly adopted crouching positions with their shields raised and weapons poised, on the alert against attack. Brittola was the last to join the group. She walked slowly up to the others and stood immediately behind Pinnosa, staring open-mouthed at the corpse. Suddenly, she dropped her weapons with a loud clatter, grasped the silver cross that she wore around her neck and started to recite a prayer out loud.

'*Hush!*'

Pinnosa span round and glared hard at Brittola, causing her to burst into tears.

While Cordula comforted Brittola, Pinnosa turned her fierce gaze on the main villa buildings and set off determinedly towards them. Ursula and the others quickly followed; Cordula with her arm around Brittola; Martha and Saula keeping a watchful eye to their rear. They caught up with her in the shade of a large stone corn store that flanked the main villa complex; and, as they drew near, she shushed them quiet. Pinnosa and Ursula then peered round the corner of the building.

There, across a broad ornate courtyard full of statues and fountains, was the villa's grand entrance with its ornate wooden door. It was eerily silent, not even the homely cluck of a chicken could be heard.

Pinnosa pointed toward the far side of the courtyard which was bathed in bright warm sunshine and indicated that she – and she alone – was to approach from that side. Ursula nodded to agree the plan. Pinnosa returned the nod, then stepped boldly out of the protection of the shadows and dashed across the courtyard, completely exposed in the bright sunshine, readily visible to anyone who might be watching from one of the villa buildings.

With Pinnosa acting as decoy, Ursula led the others up the near side of the courtyard that was shrouded in shadow. They met up with Pinnosa again in the portico outside the villa's main entrance. The large wooden door with its bright highly-polished brass fittings was slightly ajar. Pinnosa put her finger to her lips to shush the others quiet, then, as they all held their breath in case it creaked, she slowly and carefully eased it open far enough for them to slip through.

As soon as they entered the villa, their senses were assaulted by a gut-wrenching stench. They all had to cover their mouths and noses with their hands, and Cordula had to fight hard to stop herself from gagging. Despite the dreadful smell, Pinnosa signalled they should keep absolutely still while she listened out for the slightest sound. Content it was safe, she then indicated they should follow her.

The moment they took their first steps, Cordula slipped and had to grab Saula to prevent herself from falling. The rattle of her weapons caused the others to spin round and shush her quiet. They all looked down to see what had made her slip and saw a huge pool of blood that had spread out from beneath a wooden stair. Pinnosa went carefully over to the alcove and peered inside. She then turned back to the others and mouthed 'Mother's attendant'. All they could see of the poor woman was one sandal-clad foot sticking out from the shadows.

Brittola uttered a hushed blessing and crossed herself as Pinnosa led them down the passage to the west room, the large chamber that her parents had made their private room ever since her father had retired. It extended out from the main building to the rear and had an open terrace that overlooked the inner courtyard and the mountain peaks beyond.

As they entered the west room another terrible sight met their eyes. At the far end of the chamber were two dead bodies; both fully robed in their finest togas, lying close together. The morning sunshine pouring in through the terrace illuminated them, highlighting the folds in their robes and making them look like a pair of alabaster statues. One was seated on the floor with its back against the wall; the other was hunched in a ball and slumped forward in a heap. The seated figure was Pinnosa's father Marcus Flavius. His eyes were wide open, staring out at his beloved mountains. A long sword had been thrust through his heart. He looked calm and serene as if all his pain and suffering had been lifted. The other body was that of Pinnosa's mother Patricia impaled on another long sword. They had obviously opted for the dignity of killing themselves in a manner of their own choosing rather than succumb to the nightmarish death that had come pounding on their villa door.

'*Look!*' hissed Brittola, pointing outside.

The others turned to see what she was pointing at and instantly leapt for the safety of the shadows. Pinnosa and Ursula darted behind the open door that led out onto the portico, the others scurried either side of the chamber's window. As one, they then all carefully took a peek at the scene outside.

The courtyard was full of Hibernian raiders and they were all sound asleep. Scattered about them were dozens of empty wine urns. Not one of the louts stirred; each one remained motionless where he had collapsed in a drunken stupor the night before. The chief, a grotesque beast of a man with a broad bearded face, was flopped across a stone chair in the centre of the yard. He was wearing a large grimy leather cloak beneath which they could see several blades, including a huge sword strapped across his bloated belly. His bodyguards, two huge thick-necked dolts, were stretched out on the paving at his feet.

Some men were lying in clusters against the walls of the yard as if they had been heaped together; others were sleeping on the ornamental borders with their heads in amongst the herbs and shrubs. The yard was littered with weapons; bludgeons, swords, knives and axes; and stacked against the walls were sacks of plunder, each one filled to the brim with looted goods.

At a signal from Pinnosa, they all quickly withdrew to the passageway where they could talk in muted whispers and come up with a plan of action.

Plan agreed, Pinnosa and Martha made their way round to the east room on the opposite side of the courtyard and Ursula led the others back to the west room, all with arrows drawn at the ready. As soon as they were all in position, Pinnosa raised her hunting horn which she always wore around her neck, and gave a single short high-pitched '*toot*'.

Six arrows flew. All six hit their targets and went in deep. Five of the men, including the chief and one of his bodyguards, screamed themselves awake in terrible agony. The other bodyguard couldn't scream because an arrow had pierced his neck.

Pinnosa's horn sounded again and six more arrows flew. This time the bodyguards were hit a second time and they both fell to the ground. A further three raiders were hit and began squealing in pain like tormented pigs. The courtyard was now in complete pandemonium with men scrambling about for weapons and loot like crazed beasts. In the middle of the chaos, the horn sounded a third time, then a fourth; and yet more men fell each time. The wounded now outnumbered those left unscathed.

'*Drop your weapons!*' yelled Pinnosa from the shadows of the east room. '*You are surrounded!*'

She repeated the order in their own tongue which she'd learned as a child from some of the Hibernian merchants who occasionally visited Magnis. All the men, including most of the wounded, turned to where the woman's voice had come from; some started shouting abuse and brandishing their weapons. The horn sounded again and six more arrows flew.

'*I said drop your weapons!*' Pinnosa's voice was firm and she repeated herself again in Hibernian. Several clatters and thuds sounded around the courtyard.

'*Drop ALL your weapons!*' This time it was Ursula who shouted as she let fly another arrow. It ran through the arm of an older man who was holding a huge iron axe behind his back. It fell with a heavy thud onto the paving stones, rapidly followed by the sound of more yet weapons being hastily dropped.

Pinnosa finally emerged from the east room and strode boldly into the centre of the yard. She had discarded her bow. Instead, she wielded her short sword in her left hand and the long one in her right. Martha also entered the courtyard, but remained in the shadows with her bow drawn and poised ready to fire. At the same time, Ursula and Saula emerged from the west room, followed by Cordula and Brittola; all with their bows drawn. Pinnosa then used her long sword to point to the wall at the far end of the courtyard.

'All of you that can still move, go over there and lie down flat on your stomachs; and no talking! Anyone that talks will get an arrow in the throat.'

Slowly … reluctantly … the men obeyed the instructions of the wild-looking woman with a mane of red hair, including several of the wounded; and the chief, who had just yanked an arrow from his thigh, started to follow them.

'*NOT YOU!*' Pinnosa ordered. '*You stay right there!*'

She strolled over to one of the bodyguards who was ashen white and shaking in agony. Covered in sweat, he was desperately trying to pull an arrow from his side. She bent over him and, without hesitation, slit his throat from ear to ear.

'That's for Titus.'

She turned to face the chief and pointed to his sword that was lying near his feet.

'*Pick it up!*'

'We ain't got no trouble to be making with you Mistress.'

'I *said* ... pick it up!'

'You wouldn't be harming a wounded man now would you Mistress?' He winced with pain as he bent down. 'Now, that wouldn't be a fair thing to be doing.'

'*Enough! Be quiet!*'

Pinnosa sheathed her short sword and started slowly circling him with her long sword held in both hands.

'How dare you! How *dare* you come here ... to my beloved home ... and-and-and *desecrate* all that I hold dear? How *dare* you ... you loathsome miserable pile of *dung!*'

'Now listen here Mistress; I'm beggin' you. I can see how you're all upset like, but to be fair now, how was we supposed to know that this here Roman house was— '

'*Silence!* I don't want to hear any more of your foul voice, you filthy murdering swine!'

Still circling him, she started dragging the tip of the blade across the stone paving, sending up a shower of sparks.

He raised his sword in readiness for her attack.

'I never want to hear your *disgusting* voice ever again, and ... ' She tossed her sword from one hand to the other. 'I *never* ... ever ... want to *see* ... your ... vile ... hideous ... ugly ... face ... ever ... ' She gripped the hilt firmly with both hands. ' ... *again!*'

She raised her sword and ran at him. He brought his blade up to counter her attack. They clashed blades and she flicked his aside. His weapon flew from his grip and slid across the paving with a jangling clatter. He went for one of his knives, but was too slow.

She threw herself forward against his body – chest to chest and face to face – thrusting her sword deep into his huge pot belly.

His eyes bulged wide and he started to gag.

'*That* is for my mother … and *this* … ' She took a deep breath, grimaced and pushed the hilt again even harder. There was an audible cracking sound as her blade cut through his spine; then, piercing his rank and tattered cloak, it emerged out of his back like a pike staff, completely drenched in blood. ' … is for my father!'

She stepped back, put her foot on his chest and, using both hands, yanked her long sword free, tearing his bowel wide open as she did so, allowing his bloated guts to spill forth. His quivering bulk flopped to its knees and toppled forward. It landed flat on its face, lying motionless in a rapidly spreading pool of its own blood and fowl-smelling body fluids. One of his gaping eyes was still visible, full of hate and evil intent … even in death.

Pinnosa calmly wiped her blade clean on the dead man's cloak and left the courtyard, returning to her parents' chamber.

The rest of the raiders were clearly terrified of the ferocious redheaded Roman woman and her band of huntress friends; and not one of them moved. With Cordula by her side, Ursula did a quick circuit of the courtyard to make an assessment of the situation, all the while keeping their blades drawn. In one of the herb beds they found a man very near to death. He lay on his back with an arrow through his stomach. He was bleeding badly and twitching violently. Ursula put the tip of her sword to his throat and pressed down hard; there was a muffled crack and his suffering was over. She then continued with her assessment calmly and methodically and, once her circuit was complete, she called Martha over.

'You're our fastest rider. I want you to go back to Magnis and fetch help. You'd better bring leg irons for twenty— no, make it twenty-five; and try to secure enough wagons for the wounded.'

VII

The incessant rattling and clanking of the prisoners' chains had quickly become a source of irritation for Ursula and the others, so much so they had set up a rota, taking turns to switch between escorting the able-bodied shuffling on foot and the wounded who'd been loaded onto in carts.

It was mid-afternoon on the third day of their long trek across the mountains towards the coast and time for a change over. Martha fell back from the lead riders where she'd been chatting to Calixtus from Magnis, allowing Ursula to peel away from the rattling shackles. She joined Cordula who was riding at the rear a little behind Brittola and Saula who, in turn, were closely following the wagons with the wounded.

'Oh, what a relief it is to get away from that dreadful noise,' she said to her cousin as Swift settled in beside Cordula's horse Lucia. 'I can hear it in my sleep.'

'Sleep?' said Cordula. 'I can't remember what sleep feels like. We haven't slept properly for days.'

'I know. It's the same for the men too. They've been on the go as long as we have, especially the Vaga Valley men from Glevum. One of them was saying to me earlier that— '

'*Look!*'

Interrupting her cousin, Cordula pointed straight ahead. Pinnosa had suddenly appeared in the distance ahead of them, emerging on Artemis from behind a rock at the side of the trail. She had been shadowing the deportation party ever since they began their long trek. Sometimes she would disappear for hours at a time; then they would spot her up high on a bluff, motionless like a sentinel, or galloping pell-mell along a nearby stream. As Ursula and Cordula watched her, she crossed the path in front of them and headed off down a narrow track beneath a rocky bluff which took her out of sight.

'She needs to be alone,' said Ursula. 'She's not the type to express her feelings, not even to us her closest friends.'

'I can't imagine how I'd be if such horror came into my life.' Cordula sighed and lowered her head. 'I wish Morgan was here. The same questions keep going round and round in my mind: "Where is he now?" "What is he doing?" "What dangers is he encountering?" "Is he all right?"'

'You should try to put such thoughts to rest.'

'Oh, I try—believe me, I *do* try, but I ... I can't.'

'I know you can't.' Ursula reached out and touched her cousin's arm. 'I can't either.'

They lapsed into silence, both deep in thought. After a long while Cordula spoke again.

'Poor Pinnosa; she's trapped in such torment and grief, a grief that no person should have to bear, not even one as strong as her.'

'You're right,' said Ursula. 'Losing your whole family like that is a horror that I do not want to contemplate. It was bad enough when I lost my dear mother; imagine losing everyone you hold dear all at once. Thank goodness we're here for her; without us she would have no-one to help her.' Ursula shivered as her own fears stirred deep within; and she thought back to the events at the Flavius villa two days earlier.

The hours while Martha was away had been extremely tense and difficult. Ursula, Saula, Brittola and Cordula had moved fast to bind the hands of all the prisoners, wounded or otherwise, whilst at the same time search them for weapons. Luckily, the raiders had been so terrified by the fearsome onslaught of the redheaded Hibernian-speaking woman not one of them had resisted.

All the while Ursula and the others had been busy with the prisoners, Pinnosa had frantically searched the villa and its grounds for her other brother Julius. They'd heard her constantly yelling his name at the top of her voice which had reverberated in the courtyard like the haunting wail of a banshee. Sometimes it had come from the buildings nearby in the villa complex and at other times it had been far off like a lost echo. Eventually, she'd fallen ominously quiet and a short while later she'd suddenly reappeared in the courtyard, bursting forth from the east room with both her swords drawn and screeching in a high cackling voice made hoarse and shrill by her shouting.

'Where is he you filthy sons of whores? What have you murdering swine done with him?' Not waiting for an answer, she'd grabbed a nearby prisoner, pinned him to the floor and cut his hands free, before forcing him to outstretch the fingers of his right hand and placing her blade across his knuckles.

'Tell me right now,' she'd hissed, 'or you won't even be able to count your blessings.'

The man had been too frightened to speak and he'd lost three of his fingers before Ursula could reach Pinnosa to pull her away. At that point, a young lad barely out of boyhood had bravely risen to his knees and spoken out in clear Britannic.

'Excuse me Mistress. Are you looking for the other young Roman boy who defended this house?'

Pinnosa had wheeled round to face the red-haired youth. As she did so, Ursula had noticed something astonishing; he was brandishing a simple wooden cross that was on a plain length of string tied around his neck.

Brittola was riding next to him now, talking about God and occasionally breaking into a psalm or hymn together with him whenever they discovered they knew one in common.

'Don't you think it's strange?' said Ursula to her cousin. 'We think of these Hibernians as uncivilised primitives, yet we have one here who knows the scriptures. I wonder how many more there are like him beyond Rome's borders. I wonder if he can sense the presence of God in the same way we do.'

'I imagine they're some of the questions she's asking.' Cordula nodded toward Brittola and smiled. 'After all, he is a very talkative young man with a lot to say for himself.'

Ursula laughed for the first time in three days and looked at the Hibernian lad afresh. He was quite handsome in a farm-boyish kind of way with a mop of long red hair falling in loose ringlets rather like Brittola's did when it wasn't properly braided and tied.

She gasped with surprise.

'What is it? asked Cordula.

'Can you believe it? All this time riding with her, sharing camp with her; and I've not noticed before now.'

'What? What are you talking about Ursula?'

'Look at Brittola's hair. Can you see what I can see?'

Cordula peered at Brittola's head and her eyes widened with surprise.

'Oh yes, she is still wearing your gold and onyx hair clip— '

' —the one I loaned her for the great feast.'

'Oh, Ursula; doesn't that seem a long time ago?'

'Yes ... yes, it does ... it feels like another lifetime, the life we see in our reflections.'

'It'll take a good mirror to show you how to get that clip free from that wild mane of a tangle.'

They shared a chuckle.

'It'll be quite a time before the next great feast; I don't think I'll be needing it for a while. Anyway, it looks good in her hair. I'll let her keep it. It goes well with her cross—*hold on* ... it was *him* ... and he must have been going for his cross!'

'What are you talking about Ursula?'

Ursula grasped Cordula's arm.

'I've just realised that's the lad I spotted fumbling in his tunic during our attack at the villa. I thought he was going for a hidden weapon, but he was simply reaching for his cross just like Brittola does when she's frightened or upset. It's lucky my arrow missed him.'

'It's dangerous to conceal your cross under your tunic,' said Cordula. 'People are bound to think you're going for a weapon when you reach for it.'

The two cousins continued chatting, but after a while their tiredness overcame them and they lapsed once more into silence, content to ride side by side lost in their thoughts.

Ursula's attention drifted back to Brittola and her newfound friend. They'd just begun reciting another psalm together and she was staring idly at the back of Brittola's head. Her eyes widened as an idea occurred to her.

'Cordula?'

'Hmmm?'

'What if you *wanted* to conceal a weapon? Do you think— '

A splashing sound and a loud whinny from Swift interrupted her. They were fording a sizeable stream and the great mare, whose temperament was normally calm and placid, seemed to be enjoying the cool sensation upon her legs and lower body. At that moment, Pinnosa reappeared off to their left upon Artemis. She was galloping hard away from them up the same stream with splashes of sparkling water flying in every direction. The boy's words came rushing back to Ursula.

'He's dead Mistress. He was killed like the other boy but, instead of hanging him from a tree, they … ' He'd nodded toward the dead chief's bodyguards. ' … threw him in the river.'

Pinnosa had gone deadly quiet at the news; then, slowly, she'd lowered her head and walked back into the west room to be with her parents.

Shortly afterwards, Martha had returned accompanied by the contingent of men on horseback from Viroconium. With their help, the prisoners had been properly shackled with those unfit to walk being loaded into wagons. Their preparations complete, they'd then assembled outside the villa's main entrance in readiness for their departure to Magnis.

They had just been about to set off, when the villa's ornate wooden door had slowly opened to reveal Pinnosa with her sword in one hand and her other hand pulling at her hair. The change in her appearance was dramatic; her eyes were bloodshot and puffy from her weeping and her hair was tangled in a matted mess where she'd been tearing at it in her grief.

'Where are you taking them?' she'd cried as she walked out into the open, her voice still hoarse from her wailing.

'To the cells in Magnis Mistress,' Calixtus had replied.

'*Oh, no you are NOT!*'

She'd wrenched her hand free from her head – pulling out a big clump of hair which she threw to the ground – then she'd used both hands to lift her sword.

'They're going back to where they came from, back where they belong. I'll not rest until this land is rid of this … *this pestilence!*'

'But Mistress— '

'Or … ' she'd pointed her sword at the prisoners, 'I run them through with this here and now! I swear I will cleanse these hallowed stones made foul by their cruel deeds by washing it good and proper … with their vile and evil blood!'

Her eyes had blazed with such fury Calixtus had been completely at a loss for words.

'What is it to be centurion; a blood bath of these steps …
or a cleansing of the land?'

'I-I would need special orders Mistress.'

'You would obey orders from Princess Ursula, daughter
of King Deonotus, would you not?'

He'd nodded.

Pinnosa had then slowly turned her wild gaze upon
Ursula.

'Well … Your Highness?'

For the longest of moments, the two women had stared
at each other. Eventually, without taking her eyes from Pinnosa's
and speaking in a loud clear voice, Ursula had issued her
instruction.

'Commander, you are to use half of your men to escort
these prisoners back to their boats. The rest are to assist with
cleaning up the valley and helping the other families return to
their homes. Oh, and one more thing … ' She'd glanced across at
the others who were gathered near the wagons. 'All six of us will
accompany the prisoner escort.'

Calixtus had at first frowned a stern frown and looked as
if he was about to say something, but then he'd bitten his tongue
and bowed his head graciously in compliance.

'As you wish, Your Highness.'

The moment Calixtus began issuing his orders, Pinnosa
had heaved a long sigh, sheathed her sword and wandered off
down the gravel path to the river. Brittola had started to go after
her, but Pinnosa had waved her away at which point Ursula had
walked over to her friends, put her arm round a dejected Brittola
and explained her decision.

'Pinnosa is in deep torment and if we don't follow her at
least some way into her madness, we won't be able to pull her
back from the awful abyss that has opened before her.'

Loud shouts of excitement from the front of the line of prisoners
interrupted Ursula and she urged Swift forward, leaving Cordula
behind with the wagons for the wounded.

She reached the head of the line at the same time as
Calixtus. The Hibernians began explaining excitedly in broken

Britannic that they had spotted the rock formation which marked the track to the cove where their boats were hidden.

VIII

'See over there, Your Highness?' Calixtus nodded to indicate a nearby headland. 'If you ride to that bluff yonder, the one that looks like a bear's head, you'll see an old temple complex directly below you. Some say it was built by the Druids. Not long ago a group of Christian monks from Viroconium and Glevum cleaned it up and started using it as a retreat, but they had to abandon it when the frontier garrisons were reduced; we could no longer guarantee their safety. I think you'll find it is still in good repair, and it is a suitable place for you and your companions to rest and clean yourselves up.'

'Thank you. I don't think we're needed here any longer,' Ursula glanced back at the others who were tending to the horses at the rear of the beach. 'We'd best be going before the darkness beats us.'

'Very wise, Your Highness.'

She looked round the rim of the cove for some sign of Pinnosa, then turned back to the commander.

'If Pinnosa appears, would you please inform her where we have made camp?'

'Of course, Your Highness.'

Calixtus looked awkward and hesitated as if deciding whether to say something. After checking that none of his men could hear, he leaned forward and spoke to her in hushed tones.

'I'd just like to say, Your Highness, that Britannia owes you and these other fine young ladies a great debt. You did the work of twenty men back there. And what's more, if a small group of six men had done what you did, they would be heroes worthy of the greatest honours.'

'Thank you, Commander.' She smiled. 'Coming from you, that is indeed a compliment.'

'One more thing, Your Highness. The lady Pinnosa's had a terrible shock. I've seen grown men twice her age go the same way after a battle, including officers of the highest rank. She's strong though, I'm certain she'll get through it; and when

67

she does, she'll be tougher than ever. I've seen it work that way many a time.'

'I think you are probably right.'

Ursula had come to respect the old officer a great deal over the past few days. She briefly cast her eye over his men and was struck yet again by their age; not one was under forty years of age and many were well over fifty. She took Calixtus' hand and shook it firmly.

'Thank you for your help Commander. I assure you I will highly commend you and your men to my father when we return to Corinium.'

As she turned to walk away, he stood to attention and bellowed a proclamation for all to hear.

'*On behalf of our garrison, our legion and of the people of Britannia ... Your Highness, I salute you and your brave companions!*'

IX

The sun was close to the horizon by the time Ursula and the others reached the old temple ... and they were in for a very pleasant surprise.

Set in a large cave overlooking the sea, it was a well-sheltered spot that was perfect for enjoying sunsets. A number of well-established vines graced the entrance, and their countless dangling tendrils gave the cave the feel of a secluded grotto. Inside the cave behind the veil of creepers, a fire pit with a large cauldron for heating water had been built to feed a nearby shallow pool used for bathing. Outside was a natural open and flat 'terrace' with a large rock in the centre upon which a plain altar had been erected along with a simple wooden cross.

It was a warm evening and the sea was calm, so they decided to make their beds in the open on the 'terrace' where they could enjoy the sound of the waves on the rocks below. After they had bathed, they prepared some food and sat upon their bedrolls in a circle around a fire to enjoy a quiet supper. They were just clearing away and getting ready for some much-needed sleep when they heard someone approaching down the coastal path. It was Pinnosa.

She strode purposefully across the terrace and came to a halt beside the altar. Silhouetted against the blood red sky, she cut a dramatic figure with her cloak billowing in the evening breeze and the hilt of her sword glinting gold and silver against the glow of the sunset. She had in her grasp a small sack which looked shiny in the twilight as if it were damp.

'Where have you been Pinnosa?' Ursula stood up to greet her. 'We've been worried about you.'

When Pinnosa finally spoke, her voice was subdued, flat and lifeless.

'It's all over ... all over and done with.'

She walked slowly across to Ursula and held the sack out for her to take.

'Here ... do with this what you will.'

'What is it?'

Ursula tentatively took hold of the unpleasant dank object.

Pinnosa looked awkward. She turned and spoke quietly to Brittola.

'Don't worry; I spared your young red-haired friend.'

'What have you done Pinnosa?' said Brittola, looking anxiously at the sack.

'I've made sure that they – and all their kind – will think twice before joining any more raiding parties and setting forth for these shores. Such vile and evil filth will not blight this land ever again.'

'What have you *done* Pinnosa?' cried Saula. 'What, in God's name, have you done?'

'With the help of Calixtus, I ... I cut off their thumbs.'

Brittola squealed and the others gasped.

Grim-faced and speechless with rage, Ursula strode to the edge of the terrace and flung the sack as far as she could out into the sea. Then she turned to address Pinnosa.

'You're right, it is over!' She said, glaring hard at her old friend. 'I hope that you're happy now that you've had your "revenge"!'

She turned away and went back to her bed roll.

'I think we *all* ought to get some sleep. Tomorrow we head back to Corinium ... and civilization.'

Once Ursula had laid down, the others, including Pinnosa, quickly followed suit and within moments they were settled. Then, just as they were beginning to drift into slumber, Brittola stirred. She clambered out of her bedroll, walked over to the altar and knelt down to pray.

'Dear Lord and Merciful God. Terrible deeds have been committed in recent days in the name of revenge. We have seen, Lord, how sin begets sin and how those who are sinned against, in wanting to redress the sin, become sinners themselves. For this, Dear Lord, we ask—nay, we beg … your forgiveness … '

She lifted her head.

'Amen.'

They all repeated her "Amen" … and the loudest voice was Pinnosa's.

X

Ursula was awakened by the sound of seagulls squawking and squealing as they swooped down to rummage through the rich pickings left by the departing tide. She rose quietly and walked over to the edge of the terrace. The sea was almost calm but a gentle breeze was catching the few waves there were, making them shimmer in the dawn's light. Wrapping a blanket around her shoulders, she made her way across the rocks toward a large outcrop that jutted out into the sea, where some of the bigger waves were breaking and splashing.

Settling down on the tip of the outcrop, she tilted her head back and let the breeze take her hair, then sat motionless, taking in the scene and enjoying the sensation of sea spray upon her legs and feet. After a while, something caught her eye. About fifty cubits out a turbulent eddy was causing some of the waves to crest prematurely.

It's probably a hidden rock or some quirk of the undertow, she thought and, deep inside, her dark fear began to stir. *Those hidden currents are just like events on the Continent. I hope Constans isn't becoming ensnared by some sly hidden menace or engulfed in a convoluted and twisted mire of trickery and treachery. I've seen for myself these past few days how easy it is to be distracted from—*

70

'Looking for a fish for breakfast?' Pinnosa's voice made Ursula jump. 'The others are all still asleep. I spotted you out here and thought I'd join you ... or would you rather be left alone with Constans?'

Ursula moved over so that Pinnosa could sit down.

'I was thinking about our Hibernian friends actually,' she said. 'In fact, I think I owe you an apology.'

'An apology?' Pinnosa looked at her quizzically.

'Yes, an apology. I can see now that you were right to do what you did last night and cut off their thumbs.'

'Well, I'm not so sure about that.' Pinnosa frowned. 'I was acting in anger and not really thinking.'

'Whether you were thinking or not; thank goodness your thirst for revenge got the better of you.' Ursula stared into the far distance. 'These are truly dangerous times Pinnosa. We've seen for ourselves how overstretched the garrisons are. Barely enough men in Glevum, and old ones at that; only a handful in Magnis, also old; and, worst of all, hardly any galleons in active service for goodness' sake! How on earth are they supposed to keep the Hibernian raiders at bay with just a handful of galleys?'

'I'd wager it is the same story all over the province,' said Pinnosa, nodding slowly as Ursula continued.

'I have a horrible fear that the men's departure has left Britannia virtually defenceless. Both here in the West Country as well as up north in Wall Country, I bet the frontier defences are virtually unmanned. If my fears are true, we might as well issue an invite saying, "Come east Mister Hibernian, come and do your worst; and you too Mister Pict, come south and help yourself to some nice easy Roman pickings."'

They both instinctively stared at the distant horizon on the lookout for a raiding party.

'Every potential raider, Hibernian or Pict, is going to try his luck sometime in the coming months Pinnosa; you mark my words. We simply can't afford the luxury of deporting prisoners who are capable of returning here to wreak more havoc.' She frowned. 'In fact, I think I should speak to Father and ask him to declare a "no prisoners" policy, at least until the men return.'

Pinnosa sighed.

'Actually, if you think about it, there are even greater dangers than just the risk of freed prisoners returning to make further raids. When they get home, they'll tell stories of a weak Britannia, of empty army camps, of very few legionaries and of Roman estates only being able to defend themselves with mere slaves and women. The rumour will quickly spread across all of Hibernia and probably north to the Picts as well. We could easily see them forming another Grand Alliance; then they'll attack us on two fronts at the same time and in large numbers. Without a proper Britannic field army here to tackle the thieving swine, hundreds, if not thousands, of our people will end up like my family.' She looked at Ursula. 'What is it?'

Ursula was looking Pinnosa her with a curious expression upon her face.

'"Only able to defend ourselves with mere slaves and women" eh?' She punched Pinnosa playfully on the arm. 'I think we gave a pretty good account of ourselves back there. You with your little toots on your horn and the rest of us with our arrows flying *and* finding their targets … many of which were *moving* targets I hasten to add.'

They both smiled … then sniggered … then started giggling like Martha and Saula. Pinnosa put her hand to her mouth and started making little '*toot*' noises and Ursula began firing make-believe arrows with comical '*twang*' sounds. Soon they were laughing out loud and making as much noise as a pair of squawking seagulls.

'Hey! I've just had an interesting thought,' said Pinnosa as their laughter abated.

'What's that?' said Ursula, still giggling to herself.

'A proper contingent of hunting women like ourselves would make quite a formidable force, don't you think? If there were a number of us patrolling the coast, we'd easily catch any raiders before they could wreak any more havoc. We certainly wouldn't be defenceless then; *and* that would really give the Hibernians, as well as the old guards, something to think about.'

Ursula sat up straight.

'Do you know, I quite like the sound of that. Just imagine it; a group of us hunting women, fully-armed and patrolling the coast. That might make a lot of sense.'

72

She gripped Pinnosa's arm.

'Do you think there are enough huntswomen like us to bolster our defences while the men are away?'

'*Why, of course there are!*' said Pinnosa emphatically. 'Think of some of the big hunts we've been on. Remember that Baetica from Lindinis? She could handle a horse better than most men, including her husband; and he's in Constans' vanguard! I can think of many others who can fire an arrow or throw a spear as well as any man. I see no reason why we couldn't easily raise a force—oh, I don't know, say fifty strong.'

'Yes, you might be right about that,' said Ursula. 'Remember all those women from Lindinis who joined last summer's hunt on Father's estate? I reckon we could easily find fifty women from Corinium alone; and if we had some of the Glevum women too ... you know, I think we could easily muster over a hundred if we were to issue an invitation throughout the entire West Country.'

A noise from behind made them both glance back at the temple. The others were beginning to stir; Cordula and Saula were already rolling up their beds.

Ursula looked at Pinnosa.

'You're serious about this, aren't you?'

'Yes, I am,' said Pinnosa. 'And why not? The more I think about it, the more I'm certain it would work. For instance, we could bring them here to do their training rather than in Corinium. That way, they would be on station and ready to deal with any raiders who came trying their luck.'

'Keep talking,' said Ursula, smiling. 'Tell me more.'

'Well, let's see ... ' said Pinnosa, ' ... it would probably take about a month or so to issue invitations and get the numbers we need.' She counted on her fingers. 'By then it would be high summer. We could organise ourselves into infantry and cavalry units just like a regular mobile field army. Once they were fully trained and actively out on patrol, the men could take to sea in the entire fleet of galleys and make a show of force along the Hibernian coast; and then— '

'Couldn't the women take some of the galleys out?'

Pinnosa shook her head.

73

'No, the extra training would take too long; though, mind you, the galleys themselves *could* be refitted to accommodate three per—*but wait!*'

Pinnosa sat bolt upright.

'What is it?'

'I have an even better idea! Forget the galleys; you're right, the men could take care of those. What if, after we put on a show of force here on the western coast … we then turn our attention north to the Picts?'

'The Picts? In Wall Country?'

'Yes, those horrid rat-eating Picts! Bear with me, hear me out.'

'Go on.'

'Well, come harvest time, us women could go on a proper campaign north into Wall Country. We could send patrols into the Pict homelands to deter them from— '

'No, that's too much Pinnosa; it's a leap too far! We've got more than enough to do here, dealing with the Hiber— '

'It'll work, I tell you! Word travels very quickly over there … ' She nodded towards Hibernia. 'Their raiding parties will soon stop once they realise the coast patrols are back to full strength; and that will allow us to turn our attention north, to those foul scabby, smelly and rotten, Picts.'

'But Wall Country is so far from here; it's one hell of a long march Pinnosa.'

'Nah, it's not that far! I reckon there would still be enough of the campaign season left for us to march north and complete a full series of patrols. In fact, I'd wager we'd be able to muster in Eboracum by the end of the harvest and we'd be back in our homes in time for the hunter's moon. The borders, both west and north, would be secure; *and* we'll have given our men folk plenty of food for thought!'

Ursula looked hard at Pinnosa, then slowly began to nod.

'*We'll do it!*' she exclaimed. 'As soon as we get home, I'll get Father's permission and then we'll issue invitations throughout the West Country, announcing that we are mustering any women of the hunt who wish to embark on a summer patrol of the frontier lands, both west and north.'

'"A muster of women of the hunt",' repeated Pinnosa, savouring every word. 'Sounds good to me – "*toot, toot!*"'

'Sounds good to me too – "*twang, twang!*"'

'Think of it Ursula; a force of women like the Amazons of old,' said Pinnosa, 'fighting side by side with our men against the enemies of Rome, and— '

'No, *not* the enemies of Rome Pinnosa. The *men* are fighting the enemies of Rome; that's why they've had to go away, and we must never, *never* forget that. We, the women, shall be fighting for something much more important … the enemies of our *home* … the enemies of Britannia!'

Just then, a cheery '*Hallo-ooo you two!*' sounded from the terrace. They both looked and saw Brittola waving.

'Shall it be me who tells the others about the plans we've devised or you … ' said Ursula, returning Brittola's wave while glancing at Pinnosa. ' … Commander?'

XI

'An army of women, eh?' said Martha. 'Well, I'm all for it; count me in. We'll show the men a trick or two, won't we Saula?' The two of them giggled.

'Have you really thought this through you two?' said Cordula, looking worried. 'I mean, it's not just the fighting units is it? What about things like messengers and provisions, and-and all sorts of practical things that I can't even think of right now.'

'You can't think of such things right now Cordula, but you will do soon enough.' Ursula glanced at Pinnosa. 'We're putting you in charge of the ordnance crews.'

'And the messengers,' added Pinnosa.

'Yes—*and* the messengers,' said Ursula, nodding her agreement.

'Me? In charge of the messengers?' Cordula beamed with delight as Ursula and Pinnosa shared a smile.

The only one not giggling or smiling was Brittola. She had lowered her head while the others were talking, and now she raised it again, her eyes full of tears.

'Oh, no—oh, Dear God, *plee-eee-ease no-ooo-ooo!*' she wailed, then ran into the cave, sobbing.

'I'll take care of this.'

Signalling to the others to stay on the terrace, Ursula ran into the cave after her.

Ursula caught up with Brittola at the back of the cave in a small recess almost devoid of light that was intended for private prayer and contemplation. She was kneeling before a simple altar made from beach pebbles topped with a plain wooden cross.

'What's the matter Brittola? Don't you like the idea of us huntswomen forming an army?'

Brittola stopped crying, sniffed and wiped her face with her hands, then looked up at Ursula.

'You're all so keen on this-this "army of women" idea, but armies mean *war* Ursula, and war means fighting and killing. Isn't enough blood being spilled by the men? I don't think us women should be adding to all the killing and maiming; it's just not right, it's *wrong*, plain wrong! Don't you think it's wrong Ursula?'

Ursula stared long and hard at Brittola, then smiled and reached out to give her a hug.

'Do you know something?' she said, stroking Brittola's hair. 'I think you might be right.'

Brittola pulled back to stare questioningly at her older cousin.

'You do?'

'Yes, I think you have raised a very important point. An army of women doesn't have to be the same as an army of men, does it? At least, not in every respect. For instance … '

They began talking in earnest, and they stayed in the cave for quite a while before, eventually, heading back to join the others.

'Ahoy, everyone!' Ursula clapped her hands to command attention as the two of them emerged with their eyes squinting from the darkness of the cave into the bright daylight on the terrace. 'Brittola has an important announcement to make!'

The others stopped chatting and turned towards Brittola. Their expectant stares, especially Pinnosa's, made her hesitate. Ursula smiled encouragingly, but still she hesitated, forcing

Ursula to give her a hefty shove. Eventually, reluctantly, she stepped forward to speak.

'There'll be no killing,' she said quietly.

'Did you just say "no killing"?'

Pinnosa looked surprised and bemused.

'Yes, I did say there will be … no … killing,' repeated Brittola. 'We will only use our weapons as a last resort; and even then, only to wound and disarm. We won't aim to kill unless it's absolutely necessary in self-defence.'

Brittola glanced at Ursula who nodded, indicating she should continue.

'It won't be our mission to add to all the misery and pain in the world. Instead we'll concentrate on being a show of force, a magnificent show of force, acting as a deterrent to would-be attackers, and nothing more. In this way, we will show the world the true power and goodness of God. We'll be a Christian force acting purely in His name … a force for good!'

'Is that all right with everyone?' Ursula looked pointedly at Pinnosa who glared hard at them both, her eyes steely cold.

Then she smiled.

'Is it all right? Why, it's perfect!'

She strode over to Brittola with her arms outstretched.

'Without you acting as my Christian conscience Brittola, I'd be nothing more than a bloodthirsty red-haired, wild and untameable, barbarian frontierswoman.'

Towering over her young friend by more than half a cubit, Pinnosa gave Brittola an enormous hug … and all the others rushed to join in.

Chapter Three

A CLARION CALL

I

Ursula, Pinnosa and the others were completely unprepared for the reception that awaited them upon their return. News of their exploits had spread far afield. Their first taste of the excitement they'd created came at Magnis. When they appeared on the road from the river, a loud cheer went up from the palisade. Then, as they crossed the long ramp and entered the gate, they were engulfed by a large crowd.

'All hail, Princess Ursula, royal huntress of Hibernian scum!'

'Well done Pinnosa! You beat off over thirty of the murderous swine!'

'More like sixty!'

'What are you talking about? There was over a hundred of the thieving bastards!'

Everyone wanted to see, and thank, the six young noblewomen, the fearless heroines, who had beaten off one of the more dangerous raiding parties seen in the wild frontier lands in recent years. They were showered with flowers and had so many gifts of food, cloth and wine thrust upon them they later had to arrange for a four-wheeled wagon to take it to Corinium. The following day, when they passed through the metal workers' yards at Ariconium on the road to Glevum, the street was again filled with people calling out blessings and praise and cheering at the top of their voices.

'If ever you go fighting raiders again, and if you need good, women's body armour, which is as strong as a man's, but light ... remember the name Balig!' cried a large man with a big booming voice.

'*I'll give you a better price than he will,*' shouted another. '*Remember the name Haleseth!*'

'*I have three daughters. You only have sons Haleseth. Mine's sure to be the better fit!*' retorted Balig, and the whole crowd laughed.

In Glevum, they were met at the city gate by a mounted guard of honour. It was led by Leonius, the gruff old centurion who, several days earlier had tried to dissuade them from riding unescorted to Magnis. He saluted the young noblewomen formally as they approached.

'Your Highness. Your safe return to our city brings us great joy and cause, indeed, for celebration. I fear I must offer you, Your Highness, and your companions my fullest and most humble apologies for wrongly underestimating your zeal and courageousness which are clearly matched only by your prowess.'

Ursula smiled and bowed courteously. The others did the same apart from Pinnosa who remained completely impassive and contented herself with patting Artemis.

Leonius continued, looking more than a little uncomfortable.

'In addition, Mistress Pinnosa, I would like to express my deepest sympathy for the loss of your family which must— '

'Save your flowery words,' said Pinnosa. 'They're wasted on me.'

Leonius coughed and bowed awkwardly, then resumed his well-rehearsed welcome speech.

'It now gives me great pleasure, on behalf of all Glevum, to welcome you back safe and sound, and to greet you … *in triumph!*' He gestured towards the open gate. 'Your Highness … Ladies … *GLEVUM SALUTES YOU!*'

Escorted by a guard of honour, Ursula and her friends paraded down the main street through cheering crowds to the forum where a delegation of city nobles dressed in their finest robes was waiting for them. Once again, they were showered with gifts, this time including fine silks, embroideries and tapestries; even some pieces of jewellery.

Their biggest and warmest welcome, however, was at Corinium. When they reached the point where the forest ended and farmland began, they were amazed to find the road already full of people even though they were still a few of miles from the city; and there, right at the very forefront of the well-wishers, was Oleander.

'*Mistress! Mistress!*' she cried, running up to Ursula. 'Thank goodness you're back safe and sound; your father *will* be relieved. We've been so worried. The messengers said you were safe, but they didn't say whether those foul creatures had done you any harm. Are you all right? Were you or any of the other young ladies wounded?

'Not a scratch Oleander,' said Pinnosa before Ursula could reply, 'apart from scars that never heal.'

'What does she mean Mistress?' The old attendant looked worried. 'Are you hurt, or aren't you?'

'We're all *fine* Oleander,' Ursula leaned forward to allow the old woman to kiss her hand. 'But Pinnosa's family were all killed by the raiders along with many other poor souls from a valley that was not forewarned, totally unprepared and, worst of all, completely unprotected.'

II

So many of Corinium's people wanted to praise, bless or simply touch them, it took Ursula and the others a long time to complete the final stretch of their journey home. As they rounded the last bend in the road, the city's northern gate came into view and they saw the king himself waiting outside the gate to escort them into the city.

Deonotus was dressed in full royal regalia, including his bejewelled gold crown which sparkled in the sunlight; and he was surrounded by a smaller than usual contingent of the Royal Guard in ceremonial dress. Ursula learnt later that the twelve men present were the unit's entire strength – less than a quarter their usual number; the rest had left with Constantine to act as his personal bodyguard.

Even from afar, the king's anger was tangible and, as Ursula and the others approached him, their smiles quickly withered against his relentless cold stare. He waited until they had pulled up in front of him before speaking.

'You could have all been killed.'

When he spoke his voice was muted and sombre, and the coldness of his gaze was severe.

'But Father— '

'*I said* you could have *all* been killed for goodness' sake. What demon, what madness, possessed you to take on a gang of cold-blooded killers hell bent on murder or worse, hmm? What would we, your families, be doing now if the raiders hadn't been in a drunken stupor, hmm? What would we be doing now if it had been *them* with the upper hand in a deserted villa instead of you? Did you pause to think about that before rushing headlong … and headstrong … into your appointment with Fate? … Well? … Hmm?'

He deliberately looked them each in the eye. Only Ursula and Pinnosa could return his gaze; the others were forced to look down in shame.

'It was I who— ' said Pinnosa.

'Father, we— ' said Ursula.

'*Hush, both of you! Save it for later!*'

The king's fierce expression of disapproval gave way to a broad smile.

'As it turns out, God, in his wisdom, has seen fit to reward us with cause for celebration rather than punish us with cause for mourning and despair.'

He raised his hand for silence and in full voice cried out his proclamation.

'*Good people of Corinium! Upon this glorious day, my dearest daughter, Princess Ursula and her friends have not only returned home safe and sound; God be praised, they have also returned home … IN TRIUMPH!*'

At the king's signal, ceremonial trumpets gave an ear-splitting fanfare from the battlements, heralding Ursula's parade through the city. As the king and his guards led his daughter and her friends through the gate, from high above on the city wall, dozens of children threw handfuls of coloured feathers and petals up into the air which then showered down upon the procession like multicoloured snow.

Once they were inside the city, the sound of the trumpets was lost in a cacophony of horns, pipes, drums and bells, along with loud cheers, shouts and cries. There were so many people intent upon touching them, it took almost an hour before they could make their way through to the forum where their formal reception awaited.

At the entrance to the forum, they tried to dismount and proceed on foot, but the moment they alighted from their horses they were hoisted on the shoulders of excited townsfolk to be carried on shoulders the full length of the great square to a high wooden dais that had been erected especially for them on the steps of the Basilica.

King Deonotus himself had gone ahead and was already in position in front of the dais, patiently waiting to receive his daughter and her friends. He was seated astride his mount which was now fully adorned in the same heavy ornamental regalia that it had worn the day the Constans and Constantine had departed.

'*People of Corinium!*' he cried as soon as Ursula and the others were up on the platform above him. The crowd's cheers were so loud and persistent it took several blasts on the royal horns before the king could continue. '*Good people of Corinium! They have come home at last!*'

A deafening outburst of cries, drums and whistles prevented him from saying more. While the horns were trying to quell the noise, he lifted himself up on his mount and shouted across to his daughter.

'They're not going to let me say much; they want to hear from you!'

Eventually, the uproar subsided, allowing the king to complete his address.

'*On behalf of all Corinium, I just want to say ...
WELCOME HOME AND WELL DONE! ... Brittola ... Cordula
... Martha ... Saula ... Pinnosa ... and of course my wonderful,
wonderful daughter Ursula ... WE SALUTE YOU!*'

Ursula and the others all waved their arms in response to
the tumultuous roar of the crowd. They were still wearing their
riding cloaks and they each had long swords strapped round their
waists. Led by Pinnosa, they formed a line and simultaneously
bowed in acknowledgement of the cheers. Then Ursula stepped
forward to the edge of the platform and raised her hands for
silence, but the townsfolk were far too excited to be quiet.

'*You showed those ugly Hibernian swine Princess
Ursula!*' shouted a young girl. '*Their brawn was no match for
your brains!*'

'*When are you going to go raider-hunting again
Pinnosa?*' cried an old man beside her. '*How many are you
going to kill next time? A couple of dozen? A hundred?*'

'*People of Corinium! People of Corinium! We are truly
humbled by your—* ' began Ursula, but the cries from the crowd
persisted, forcing her to wait. She glanced back at the others, her
eyebrows raised in exasperation. Then she looked down at her
father who mouthed 'Be patient!'

'*God be praised!*' shouted the old gatekeeper, '*that six
young ladies should do the work of thirty men and escape
unharmed!*'

'*Where were the men?*' bellowed a large woman near the
front. She was the miller's wife. '*It's not right that our young
noblewomen had to do the men's work! Where were the guards
from Magnis? Or from Glevum, for that matter?*'

'*There aren't any fighting men left! Constantine lied!*'
boomed the loud deep voice of a market vendor. '*They're down
to fifty at Glevum and less than a hundred at both Deva and
Viroconium! We're defenceless I tell you! We don't stand a
chance if the Hibernians and Picts form another alliance!*'

Ursula shared an anxious glance with her father.

'*That's right!*' cried the miller's wife. '*We are totally
defenceless! Where are the fighting men, the cavalry units and*

83

the archers, we need to keep back the murdering Hibernian swine? We can't defend ourselves with young women!'

'That's where you are WRONG!'

Pinnosa's powerful voice forced the crowd to fall silent. She cast her fierce gaze around the forum before glaring hard at the miller's wife and addressing her individually.

'There are plenty of women who are capable of fighting and keeping the invaders at bay!'

'Pah!' The huge red-faced woman sneered. 'The best of our fighting men have gone and now some soft-handed women with horses think they can take their place.'

' "Soft-handed women with horses?!" ' Pinnosa's face blushed red with anger. 'Just what are you— '

Martha rushed forward and grabbed Pinnosa by the arm.

'Might it be a good idea if we reminded people of what "soft-handed women with horses" can do?'

She nodded to indicate the far end of the forum. Pinnosa looked puzzled for a moment; then, realising what Martha had in mind, nodded in reply.

'Move back and make room!' Pinnosa drew her long sword from its scabbard and thrust it high into the air. Then, keeping her arm outstretched, she slowly lowered it to eye level and pointed down the centreline of the forum. *'Move back and make room I say!'*

The crowd obeyed her command and an open space began to appear down the length of the great square. Pinnosa then put her fingers to her lips and gave a long shrill whistle. From the far end of the forum, Artemis neighed in reply. The townsfolk turned to see the great mare rearing and punching the air with her powerful hooves. Pinnosa then gave another whistle and Artemis thundered through the clearing toward her mistress, forcing any stragglers to leap out of her way.

'You are right to say that there aren't enough men to keep the Hibernian and the Picts at bay,' shouted Pinnosa, as Artemis came to a halt immediately beneath her. *'There aren't enough men who can do this!'*

84

She sheathed her sword and leapt from the platform onto Artemis' back; to which the crowd gave a small cheer and began to applaud.

'*And there aren't enough men who can do this!*'

She grabbed her hunting bow and quiver from Artemis' flanks, slung the quiver across her shoulder and readied an arrow to fire. She then wheeled Artemis around and they broke into a full gallop. Halfway down the forum, she took aim and let the arrow fly. It hit a leather flagon hanging from a shop awning, making it spin and spray water in every direction. The crowd cheered loudly and began chanting her name as Pinnosa and Artemis turned to commence a second run.

'*And where are the men who can do this?*' she cried, letting a second arrow fly. It struck the spinning and swaying flagon so hard the strap broke and it fell to the floor with a loud *splat!* As wild cheers filled the forum, Pinnosa halted Artemis at the base of the podium and leapt back up to where she'd been standing. She raised her hand for quiet, but before she could address the crowd, she was interrupted by the miller's wife.

'*We all know what you can do Pinnosa,*' cried the woman, '*but you're special; you were raised on a horse!*' She turned and shouted to the crowd. '*There aren't many women like her who can fight like a man! Without more men, I still say we're defenceless!*'

'*That's right!*' boomed the market vendor. '*We're defenceless against the invaders!*'

'*YOU ARE WRONG!*' roared Pinnosa, glaring at them both. '*There are plenty of women who are capable of dealing with these invaders.*'

'What women?' sneered the miller's wife with a dismissive wave of her hand. 'Who?'

'Hunting women of course,' snapped Pinnosa.

'There are hundreds of hunting women in Corinium and Glevum,' Brittola rushed forward to stand at Pinnosa's side. 'Certainly, enough to form a field army of women, a *Christian* army of women, that can patrol the western coast while the men are away; and even go north to Wall Country if necessary.'

85

'*WHAT!*' exclaimed King Deonotus, looking aghast at his daughter.

'Brittola and Pinnosa are right!' returning her father's fierce gaze, Ursula stepped forward. 'If there aren't enough able-bodied men left in the province to defend us against invasion … we women will have to do it!'

She raised her hand for silence and this time the crowd obeyed. Still staring at her father, she continued.

'We are going to send out a call across the entire West Country for hunting women to muster here in Corinium in order to patrol the western coast and deter any more Hibernian raids.'

'"A patrol of women?" Did she just say "a patrol of women"?'

Ursula's words were picked up by the deep-voiced vendor as well as the young girl, then quickly spread throughout the crowd, filling the forum. Meanwhile, Ursula and the others remained completely still, waiting for the murmur to die down; and, when it did, Ursula glanced at her friends.

'Are you ready ladies?'

In a prepared and rehearsed move, they moved forward to the edge of the raised platform and stood in a straight line; six young noblewomen in a neat row, each one cloaked with a long sword sheathed by their side.

An expectant hush gripped the crowd as Ursula very deliberately placed her hand on the hilt of her sword. In response to her silent command, the others drew their weapons and held them low, pointing them to the ground.

Following Pinnosa's lead, apart from Ursula, they all then raised their blades and thrust them high into the air. Being highly burnished, they shone with golden sparkles as if ablaze with fire, eliciting gasps of amazement from the crowd. Ursula, kept her head bowed waiting for the noise to die down, and when, eventually, it did … she looked up.

'Out of love for our realm, our people and our beloved home … for the defence of our province … and to the glory of God … '

She unsheathed her sword and raised it high to join the others pointing upward to the heavens.

'The women of Britannia shall fight!'

III

'Any news of Constantine Father?' asked Ursula.

'Don't you really mean "of Constans"?'

Deonotus glanced teasingly at his daughter with a playful smile as he settled onto his recliner for the welcome home feast. Even though it was a small informal gathering of close family and friends, the king had nevertheless insisted on a lavish spread; and the rich aromas wafting from the impressive array of dishes were mouth-wateringly tantalising.

Included among the guests were three children: Martha's brother Uricalus and Cordula's sister Docilina who were both ten-year-olds, as well as Saula's little sister Trifosa who was barely six. Cordula had persuaded the king to give them the honour of attending the feast and serving the guests. He reached for his favourite drinking vessel, an elaborately carved onyx goblet with gold trim, and held it out for wine as he answered Ursula's question.

'All we know for certain is that the legion's departure went well. By all reports, Constantine's fleet was a magnificent sight; over one hundred galleys in full sail, heading for the beaches of Gallia. We haven't received any news yet from the other side of the Oceanus Britannicus, just the odd rumour from merchants; and you know how unreliable they can be.' He raised his goblet. 'To the success of Constantine's campaign! May they all return home safe … and soon!'

'May they all return home safe and soon,' echoed the women, raising their wine glasses and goblets in salute.

'Why did all the men have to go Your Majesty?' asked Docilina as she held out a bowl for Deonotus full of prepared figs and pomegranates.

'To fight off the German tribes stupid,' sneered Uricalus, pushing Docilina aside and thrusting a platter of oysters at the king. 'Where will the first big battle be Your Majesty? Treveris? Mogontiacum?'

'Ah, the battle-lust of young boys; where would we be without it?' The king smiled as he took a fig and an oyster. 'You are right Uricalus. In a way, they have gone to fight the German tribes but, unfortunately, it's not quite as simple as that. Let me try to explain it as simply as I can to you ... '

The king sat up and beckoned the children to huddle round him.

'Now, I want you to close your eyes and imagine your villa estate at home in the country with all its beautiful gardens; flower gardens, kitchen gardens, even hanging gardens. Are you with me?' The children all nodded and the king continued. 'In addition to your beautiful gardens that are the envy of your friends, you have your fields for growing crops, your grazing land for livestock, your yards for poultry and your stables for horses. Can you picture all that?'

The children nodded again.

'Now, expand the picture in your mind to include the wilderness and wild forests beyond your estate along with all the wild creatures that roam there. What kind of beasts are they?'

All three children opened their eyes and began calling out excitedly.

'*Bears!*' cried Uricalus. 'Big bears and-and-and *wolves!*'

'And foxes,' said Docilina.

'And the monsters of the night,' said Trifosa, 'like dragons and big snakes.'

'Well, let's not worry too much about monsters for now.' The king gave her a reassuring smile. 'Let's think about the foxes and the wolves. What do they want from your estate? What are they always trying to grab?'

'*Lambs!*' shouted Uricalus getting over-excited and provoking a 'shush' from Cordula.

'And calves and foals,' said Docilina.

'And baby birds,' added Trifosa, also becoming over-excited, 'and-and even *big* birds!'

'That's right. The foxes and the wolves are always trying to sneak into your estate and steal tasty morsels; and so it is with Rome herself. The provinces are like large estates in a way, and the great cities, including our magnificent city, Corinium, are the villas. The creatures of the wilderness are the barbaric tribes beyond our borders. Just like wolves or bears, they can be very fearsome and dangerous, and they constantly lurk in wait for a chance to take advantage of a breach in our defences and rush in to grab their plunder. Here in Britannia, the Hibernians and the Picts are the creatures of the wilderness. In Germania and Gallia, it's the German tribes. In Italia, and elsewhere, it's the Goths— '

'"*The Go-o-oths*"!' cried Uricalus in a silly voice. He pulled a funny face and leered at Docilina to which she frowned, as if to say 'don't be so childish', and turned away dismissively in a 'huff'. Watching them with a smile, the king glanced across the table at Ursula.

'The problem we have right now, children, is that in recent years the garrison armies in Germania who normally patrol the frontier keeping the wild creatures of the wilderness, the barbarians, at bay have been busy elsewhere, distracted from their task. This has meant that the Empire's defences have been weakened just at a time when the number of raiders, or 'wild creatures', has been on the increase; and, as a result, raids and incursions by these barbaric tribes have risen tenfold, including some wholesale large-scale invasions. Worse still, they have tried to cross into Imperial territory at different points along the frontier, from Gallia in the west to Thracia in the east, stretching our already weakened defensive forces well beyond their limit.'

'So, Constantine's gone to put them all to the sword!' Uricalus started miming swordplay. '*Take that, slimy Goth! And that, verminous German! And that-and that-and that!*'

'*Uricalus!*' snapped Cordula. 'Be quiet; your king is talking—sorry, Your Majesty.'

'*Ho*—I wish it were so simple Uricalus!'

Deonotus looked pointedly at Ursula.

'You see these raiders are not really raiders any more. They're no longer content to merely sneak in and make off with plunder back into the forest from where they came. Now they are coming in large numbers and bringing their families with them; children like yourselves, and grandparents too, on wagons and carts. They are even bringing their livestock with them. From Germania to Thracia, whole peoples are on the move. They're breaking into Roman territory in order to make it their home and enjoy the protection of Roman law. They want to make *our* homeland *their* homeland.'

'Why do they want to take our homes?' asked Docilina. 'Because they're so beautiful?'

The king smiled.

'I'm sure that's one of the reasons, but the main reason they want to make their home inside Roman-controlled territory is because they think they will be safe here, well-guarded and protected. And, *that's* because they themselves are afraid of other, more barbaric, tribes beyond the frontier; the new "monsters in the wilderness".'

'Wh-wh-what kind of monsters?' asked Trifosa, looking frightened.

'Well, no one knows for sure little one, but I keep hearing the same name being mentioned more and more often, especially in reports from the far east, of a warlike and godless tribe with big heads and long hideous faces called … ' He leaned forward and opened his eyes wide for emphasis. ' *"The Huns"!*'

Trifosa burst into tears.

'That's enough for now Father!' Ursula had shivered as he'd uttered the name, feeling a chill run down her spine.

'*Woo-ooo-ooo—the Huns, the monster, monster Huns!*' Uricalus pulled an ugly face and put on another silly voice as he once more leered at Docilina, this time with his hands curled like talons. She punched him on the arm to make him stop. Taken aback, he clasped his arm and gave her a retaliatory punch.

'*Ow!*' she cried and started pulling his hair.

In an instant, they were rolling on the floor in a scrap; forcing Cordula and Martha to scramble forward and try to pull them apart.

'*Ha ha ha* – the boy's got spirit!' said the king, laughing out loud. 'He'll be a good fighter when he grows up!'

'So too will she!' said Pinnosa pointedly. 'Anyway, Your Majesty, how do you imagine things are actually going over there?'

'As I say, we haven't received a proper report from Morgan yet.' He glanced at Cordula. 'Constans will have his work cut out mustering men in Germania and Gallia. When the imperial court abandoned Treveris and headed for the safety of Arelate in the south they left in haste and would've taken the garrison legion with them as well as any other readily available units of fighting men. Constans' only hope will be to scour the smaller provincial towns and to lure as many of the retired old campaigners off their estates as he can. I imagine he will have some success, but it'll take time. Nevertheless, he should be able to please his father with a reasonable show of force when they eventually converge on Treveris.'

'What about Colonia and Mogontiacum?' asked Pinnosa. 'They both have huge barracks and stables. Why haven't they managed to contain these invaders?'

'Now that is a good question Pinnosa, a very good question indeed. I fear they have both been severely depleted in order to help Stilicho with the Goths in Italia. We've had reports recently that Mogontiacum is down to less than a half a legion, with barely a dozen centurions. In my day there would have been well over ten times that number. We're not sure how many men there are in Colonia, but we do know they're sending a sizeable force to meet up with Constantine at Treveris. That includes the all-important cavalry units he'll need if he is to rein in the tribes that have already broken through and are wandering all over Germania and Gallia wreaking havoc.'

'How long will my daddy be away Your Majesty?' asked Trifosa, stepping forward with a tray of honey cakes shaped like birds' eggs and arranged as if in a nest.

'We hope they'll be back before the winter sweetheart.' The king gave a courteous bow and helped himself to a cake. 'But it may take them longer to accomplish their mission than they – or we – would like. Hopefully, little one, your father will be back in time for next year's harvest.'

'"Next year's harvest!" But, that's more than a whole year!' Trifosa burst into tears. *'He can't go away and leave us a whole year!'*

'Why so long Your Majesty?' asked Saula as she comforted her sister.

'I fear the legion might have to go south after they've secured the border against the Germans. Firstly, they may need to escort some of the Germanic tribes across the mountains to Hispania where there is more land for them to settle on. And secondly ... ' He looked very deliberately at Ursula who was listening intently. 'They may have to cross the Alps to help the Emperor against the Goths.'

'Not to Italia! Not them too!' groaned Pinnosa. 'Hasn't that blasted Stilicho got enough men?'

Ursula remained silent.

'I met Stilicho many years ago in Roma,' said the king. 'Without doubt he is Honorius' best hope against the Goths, but there was also something in his eye I couldn't trust. He's ... he's ambitious ... ' He looked around the gathering. '*Bah!*' He shook his head and held his goblet up for more wine. 'Let's just say there are many possible reasons why Constantine and his men may be drawn across the Alps.'

'But maybe Your Majesty— ' began Cordula.

'Perhaps Constantine will— ' began Pinnosa.

The king raised his hand for silence.

'Enough about such weighty matters abroad! Let us talk about things closer to home. What is this "woman's army" that you all seem to be so set upon? When do you intend to execute these bold plans of yours?'

'We start tomorrow,' said Pinnosa. 'We will send out a call to all able-bodied women in the West Country— '

'All able-bodied *Christian* women,' insisted Brittola.

92

Pinnosa smiled at the correction and continued.

'All able-bodied *Christian* women will be invited to join us. We're going to form a field army, including cavalry units, to go on patrol along the western coast as well as up north to Wall Country all throughout the campaign season. We'll train in the frontier lands beyond Magnis. Then, around harvest time, we'll embark on a full campaign up to the Wall and on to Eboracum. We should be home before the hunter's moon.'

'As she says Father,' Ursula glanced at her friends, before looking sheepishly at the king, 'we'd – *um* – we'd like to dispatch the first messengers tomorrow.' She hesitated. 'I know we haven't – *um* – we haven't consulted with you Father, but could we ... possibly ... *please* ... use your seal?'

For a long moment, Deonotus held his daughter's questioning gaze.

'*Hmmm*—tomorrow, you say?'

She nodded tentatively and then smiled as she spotted the flicker of a smile flit across his features.

'I do wish your mother was here to see such enthusiasm. You get it from her, you know.'

He turned to look pointedly at his hunting tapestry and scratched his chin, feigning deep thought.

'Actually, I was thinking of going hunting tomorrow with my guards. That means my seal will be out on my writing table from dawn till dusk with no-one to keep an eye on it.'

Ursula clambered around the table and gave him a great big hug.

'Oh, *Father!* Thank you, thank you, thank ... *you!*'

'Thank you, Your Majesty.' Pinnosa reached across to take the king's hand and kiss it. The others echoed her thanks and bowed. The king then broke free from his daughter's embrace and reached for his onyx and gold drinking vessel.

'It would seem a measure of these vexing times that our women are having to do the work of the men. But I can feel a strong wind of change blowing us in a new direction. We must do things differently if we are to prevail; and if that means an "army of women" ... *so be it!*'

93

He stood up and raised his drink.

'I salute you, my daughter, and you, her trusted friends, as well as to all the other fine women of Britannia who will help guard our tomorrows while the men are away.'

He clinked his goblet with Ursula's.

'To tomorrow; to all our tomorrows; and to whatever our tomorrows will bring.'

They all raised their drinks.

'*To tomorrow!*'

IV

'Wake up Mistress, wake up!' Oleander sounded agitated as she shook Ursula from her sleep. 'I'm sorry to wake you when you must be very tired after last night's feast, and I know it's barely dawn, but you are needed urgently downstairs. Mistress Pinnosa sent me for you. She is already there with Mistresses Cordula and Brittola. Mistresses Martha and Saula have also been sent for. They need you as soon as possible; the street outside is full to bursting.'

Ursula could hear the sounds of a crowd outside. She rushed to the window and was astounded at the scene below. Oleander was right; the street was crammed with women. Yet, it had only been the previous evening when they'd dispatched the messengers with proclamations from the king, complete with his great seal.

She hurriedly got dressed and arrived in the palace courtyard at the same time as Martha and Saula. Pinnosa already had things organised. The women were entering the courtyard one at a time and being taken to a table to be interviewed. Pinnosa, Cordula and Brittola were seated on a bench on one side of the table with a scribe, and opposite them was another bench for the women to use.

'Ah, there you are!' Pinnosa waved to indicate the other end of the courtyard where a second table was waiting, complete with benches and a scribe. 'Don't stand there, get stuck in! Many of these women have been waiting all night. Isn't it incredible? Word must have spread like wildfire.'

'What do we have to do?' asked Martha.

'Make a note of their names and where they're from,' said Pinnosa.

'Find out whether they're married and have children,' said Cordula.

'And don't forget to ask them whether they're practicing Christians,' added Brittola. 'That's important.'

'Then ask them why they want to join us,' said Pinnosa. 'Don't tell them now whether they're in or not, make a discreet note after they're dismissed; we'll put up lists later. Now, come on you three—*get to it!*'

V

'Good morning, Your Majestoy.' Martha put on a thick country accent and shuffled oafishly toward Ursula. 'Oy'd like to joyn the oymy please.'

The others laughed while Brittola yawned. It had been a very long day; they hadn't managed to clear the street till late-afternoon. Even though they'd interviewed over three hundred women in that time, less than a hundred had been suitable and of those only a handful had been strong candidates. After the last woman had left, Ursula and the others had retired to the ladies' chamber in the palace to enjoy a well-earned hearty supper and reflect upon the day's events.

'What's that?' continued Martha. 'Am Oy pregnant? Nah, o'course Oy'm not.' She acted puzzled. 'Well actualloy, come to think of it, what toyme of the year is it?' She scratched her head and rubbed her stomach. 'Oh – *whoops* – I moyght be!'

They all shrieked with laughter.

'What about that one with the pigs?' cried Saula with a giggle, and the others roared at the memory. "I'm a-taking all my pigs with me Mistress. If *they* don't go, *I* don't go!"'

'I had one … ' said Cordula, 'who would only go if she could take her husband with her.'

'That's funny,' said Saula, 'because I had one who would only go if she could leave her husband behind!'

'There were several like that,' said Pinnosa, laughing. 'Good God in Heaven we had all sorts, didn't we? There were those that were too old; the oldest was sixty-three, I think. Then, there were those who were too young; remember the girl who said she was sixteen? She couldn't have been a day over eleven.'

'Don't forget the ones who were too fat,' said Cordula. Remember the miller's daughters?'

The rest giggled as Martha pulled Saula and Cordula to their feet and the three of them play-acted the miller's plump girls as they squeezed through the courtyard door and waddled over to the interview table. Then, throughout their interview, one would slip off her end of the bench, nudge her way back on and, in doing so, push the other off the other end. It had been torture for them not to laugh at the time, but now they could give full vent to their mirth; and Brittola fell to the floor, laughing hysterically.

'Oh, I almost forgot,' said Saula, 'I had one strange woman who was obsessed with hunting down all the honey makers. She said she wanted to join our army so she could rid Britannia of them.' She pulled a funny face. '"It's the cause of all evil y'know, and them's that makes it are the Devil's own!"'

'Oh, talking of "the Devil"!' Martha suddenly became serious. 'Did you see that strange woman who came in toward the end; the one with the evil eye?'

'Ooh, yes-sss!' hissed Brittola in a hushed whisper. 'She really was evil; and a complete stranger too. I've never seen her before. Who was she?'

'Well, she gave her name as Rune and this is what she told me.' Martha adopted a twisted crooked pose and spoke with a thin sinister voice. 'I would very much like to join your army. I'm no stranger to the blade you know; and I have the scars to prove it, see. There's people who would vouch for my skills with a blade, if they could, but they can't because … well, because

I've had to deal with them, see. And when I deals with people they— '

'It sounds like she's had a tough and sad life.' Ursula cut Martha short because she could see Brittola getting scared. 'I had one woman whose story really touched me.'

'Who was that?' asked Pinnosa.

'She was about forty I'd say,' said Ursula once they'd grabbed their drinks and settled back into reclining positions. 'The first thing she said was "I want to join your women's army so that I can be with my husband." When I asked her what she meant, she said he was dead and waiting for her in heaven. It turned out he'd died on the last campaign to the Continent. Her two sons were also on that campaign and they too went missing. Unlike when her husband died, the poor woman never received confirmation that they were killed, official or otherwise. All she knew was that they never returned home; and that was more than five years ago. She'd lost her father many years before and, being an only child, her mother was all she'd had left. Then her mother had died in the same plague that took our mothers … ' She looked at Brittola and Saula. 'Since then she's been living alone, desperately lonely and tormented by the hope that her lost sons might yet return. She told me she'd reached her limit; that she was about to kill herself rather than continue enduring the torment of her misery. Then yesterday, when she'd heard about our woman's army, she finally woke from her nightmare; she felt something existed that she could be a part of; something that could give her a sense of purpose. It didn't matter, she said, if she died in the doing. All that mattered was that she was doing something … was part of something that— '

'Will she join us?' interrupted a very tired-looking Brittola, stifling yet another yawn.

'I think there might be a place for her in the ordnance crews, but she was too old for active duty, too tired out and drained—rather like you lot; you all look completely worn out!'

'It's time we were in bed,' said Pinnosa, yawning and stretching. 'It's been a long day and we need a good night's rest. I have a feeling tomorrow is going to be just as hectic as today.'

They all got up, said their goodnights and left Ursula alone in the ladies' chamber. Pinnosa was the last to depart and she paused in the doorway.

'I'll be down in the courtyard before dawn. Will you be up in time to join me?'

'Join you?' replied Ursula with a weary yawn and a smile. 'I'll wake you!'

Pinnosa smiled, nodded and left, heading after the others. As the '*flip-flap*' of her sandaled feet echoed down the stone corridor and receded into the night, Ursula's smile faded. Slowly, she stood up and wandered over to the writing desk at the back of the chamber. There, she picked up an oil lamp and held it so close to her cheek she could hear its faint crackling hisses and feel its heat against her skin. She peered into the bronze mirror on the wall nearby; the woman staring back at her looked tired … far too tired.

'I'm here Constans my love. I'm here for you wherever you are.' She looked into the lamp's yellow flame and watched the constantly moving shapes ever-changing in form. 'Where are *you* I wonder my love? What are you doing? What dangers are you facing, what threats, what hidden menaces?' She closed her eyes. 'I wonder if you are thinking of me? I am here my love, I'm here for you. Can you hear me?'

She strained every sinew of her being to sense some message in reply but, despite the warmth of the lamp, all she could feel was a cold empty nothingness.

'Oh, God; please don't let him die! Please don't let my life be like that poor woman's; once so full and now … so, so empty. Please find it in your grace, Dear God, to bring him back home to me safe and sound. I give you my life and I give you my soul. Just have the mercy to keep him alive and bring us back together. Please, God … please bring him home to— '

A gentle cough from the doorway interrupted her.

'Are you all right Mistress?'

Ursula span round to see Oleander standing in the doorway, looking at her with an anxious expression.

'I'm fine,' she replied.

'Nugget's here as you requested Mistress. He's waiting outside.'

'Then bring him in, bring him in. Don't keep the poor man waiting.'

Oleander led into the room a short, stocky and bald old man. He was wearing his leather work apron which covered his body from his neck to his knees. His hands were badly scarred and permanently blackened; and two of his fingertips were missing. He was Corinium's master metalworker and jewellery maker; his family had been making the royal jewellery and metalwork for five generations. He looked the same as he had done for as long as Ursula could remember; and he reeked of his work. Like everyone else she knew him simply as Nugget.

'Evening, Y'Highness,' he growled in a deep phlegmy voice. 'How can I be of service?'

'Has Oleander explained what I'm looking for Nugget?'

'Yes, Y'Highness. An alloy what looks like gold but's as hard as iron. Here you go, Y'Highness … ' He rummaged in his apron pouch and as he did, she could hear the rattle of metallic clutter. 'I brought you this.'

He produced a small trinket box and offered it to her. She took it from him and held it up to the lamp for scrutiny. In the soft light, it gleamed with a yellowy glow.

'It's more or less the right colour … and it's certainly heavy,' she spoke quietly as she examined the object, turning it over and over, looking at it from every side. 'But is it strong?'

'Oh yes, Y'Highness. It's the strongest alloy I've got what'll pass for gold at a glance.'

He took it back from her and placed it in the centre of the writing table. Then he grabbed a hammer from the rear of his belt and brought it down hard upon the box with a heavy *'Thud!'* Ursula picked it up and re-examined it; the surface was marked but its shape was intact.

'Perfect,' she said. 'Can it be fashioned into a thin blade? A razor-sharp thin blade?'

'It's poor man's gold, Y'Highness,' replied the old man with a toothless smile. 'It can be made into anything you like.'

'Very well; here's what I want you to do.' She produced a drawing on parchment from a small drawer under the writing table and started to explain what she had in mind.

VI

The following morning the first women started to arrive from nearby estates and townships; they were mostly able-bodied unmarried women and they all professed to being Christians.

Some of them came alone with just a slave or attendant, but the majority came in pairs or small groups. Many of them were on foot, though a fair number came on horseback; and most of the horses were suitable for military duties.

For the first few days, the numbers were manageable; then on the fifth day, something incredible occurred. Not long after morning bells, the sound of many trumpets could be heard coming from the road to the south-east. Ursula, Pinnosa and the others rushed to the parapet where a magnificent sight met their eyes. Heading toward them and filling the road were scores of women, over two hundred in number, all marching in disciplined ranks. Cordula was the first to read the standards and shouted excitedly that they were a combined force from the Calleva Atrebatum and Venta Belgarum areas.

Barely had the women from the south-east entered the city to be formally greeted by Ursula and Pinnosa when more trumpets sounded, this time from the south-west. Once again, Ursula and the others rushed to the parapet and saw a cohort of women on horseback, again well over a hundred in number, approaching the city, carrying weapons and shields; but this time they were following the colours of Lindinis.

They now had more than enough women for what they wanted to accomplish, so later that same day, Ursula issued a second proclamation announcing that volunteers were no longer needed … but the message didn't work, as yet more and more women continued to arrive in Corinium.

Within less than a week, they had an infantry seven hundred strong and a cavalry unit almost three hundred in number. Moreover, they'd also secured sufficient additional women to act as ordnance crews. They were using Corinium's west barracks as a base for the volunteer army and by the end of the week the complex was heaving with women of all classes and ages as well as horses, mules, hunting hounds and other beasts of burden.

Ursula and her friends, meanwhile, were still staying at the palace. Even though they weren't billeted with the rest of the women, they had nevertheless quickly settled into a military routine. Every morning, they rose well before dawn and spent the morning in the Officers' Hall, making plans and organising the women into cohesive units complete with commanders and other officer ranks. Then, in the afternoons, they went their separate ways in order to attend to the various duties they'd assigned themselves.

Pinnosa oversaw all the fighting drills, both infantry and cavalry, including defence, battle formations and manoeuvres. The main field trials of the cavalry units were led by Martha and Baetica from Lindinis who was, indeed, an exceptionally good horsewoman; and most afternoons they were out and about in the hills surrounding Corinium, practising various cavalry tactics.

Saula worked mainly with the cavalry too; her role was to concentrate on their self-defence; shield work, sword fighting and spear techniques. She also supervised the women's training in using signal codes and developing their semaphore skills.

Brittola had taken responsibility for overseeing the basic infantry marching drill for new recruits as well as maintenance of the infantry's kit; and this latter duty meant she had to work closely with Cordula who spent most of her time working with the messenger corps and ordnance crews.

Ursula worked mostly with the senior officers to develop systems for the effective relaying of orders and messages; plus, disciplinary procedures and appropriate codes of honour and behaviour for the women both on and off duty.

Just before dusk, each day ended with a full turnout on the parade ground at the heart of the barracks for an inspection. Pinnosa would check the women's uniforms, weapons and equipment, whereas Ursula would concentrate on their overall bearing and morale. In the evenings, the commanders would join Ursula and her friends to work with the king in planning their campaign's overall strategy and operational requirements, often well into the night. As high summer approached, their basic training was finally complete and, thanks to Corinium's hard-working crafts folk, they were fully uniformed and equipped.

Eventually, on Alban Heruin, the summer solstice, the only men involved in the operation, the messengers, were dispatched to key cities such as Viroconium, Luguvalium and Eboracum to announce the women's mission and initiate the necessary preparations. Soon afterwards, advance parties of ordnance crews set off with accompanying guard detachments. The 'army of women' was ready.

VII

It was a clear bright summer's morning with just a slight breeze from the west and barely a cloud in the sky. A loud fanfare of trumpets sounded from the parapets of Corinium's tall and proud city walls; then the north gate slowly opened.

Outside the gate, standing rigidly to attention in rows beside the road to Glevum and dressed in their newly-designated livery consisting of cloaks dyed a deep royal blue with matching plumage on their helmets, were the neatly-marshalled ranks of the field army. They awaited the appearance of the Vanguard as they made their ceremonial departure from the city, followed by the commanding officers who would be leading the legion on its first campaign.

Grouped into ten divisions, each with a cavalry escort, the women remained completely motionless except for the odd flutter of a cloak or some plumage as it caught the gentle breeze. Their disciplined display was so impressive; the townsfolk who came running through the gate ahead of the Vanguard all stared open-mouthed in astonishment.

Then, following a second fanfare, from out of the gate came the formal procession itself. The drum players were the first to emerge, playing drum rolls to mark the marching beat. These were followed by the horn players who would later be presaging the legion on their march accompanied by the legion's mascot, a woman wearing a bear skin. Next came the standard bearers, proudly carrying the legion's insignia; three white lilies on a field of royal blue and capped by a small golden bear. Only moments earlier in the forum, King Deonotus, in one of his eloquent and stirring speeches, had presented the commanders with their standards and bequeathed upon the legion its official name ... "The First Athena".

Behind the legion's banners came the local standard bearers carrying the symbols of: Corinium, Glevum, Calleva Atrebatum, Venta Belgarum and Lindinis. Then came the eagerly-awaited Vanguard, the elite women of the legion's cavalry. They all looked magnificent in their blue cloaks with white trim and matching helmet plumage. Beneath their cloaks their highly-burnished body armour glistened in the sunlight.

True to Britannic tradition, the last to appear were the commanders. Martha, Saula, Brittola and Cordula came first; sitting proud upon their horses, they emerged through the tall wooden gate in single file. Their uniforms were similar to the Vanguard, but their horses were conspicuously adorned from nose to tail with elaborate and highly-worked blue and white livery, matching that of their riders.

Then, finally, Pinnosa and Ursula emerged side by side. Their cloaks were the same blue as the others' but the trim was much more ornate, being a rich mixture of gold and white braid. There was nothing to distinguish between their two uniforms or their horse's apparel, apart from a streak of imperial purple that had been added to Ursula's helmet plumage.

Behind the commanders, and acknowledging the crowd's loud cheers with graceful bows and waves of his hand, came King Deonotus accompanied by six of his royal guards on horseback. As they emerged from the shadow of the city gate, they formed a line across the gateway. Then the king drew his sword and raised it for silence. Three short-but-loud trumpet blasts from the parapets not only quietened the onlookers, they also acted as a signal for the Vanguard to come to a halt.

'*COMMAN – DERS!*' bellowed the king.

Maintaining their formal straight-backed decorum, Ursula and Pinnosa slowly turned Swift and Artemis around to face the king and, as soon as they were in position, he issued them his orders.

'*On behalf of the good people of Corinium, and of Glevum, and of ALL Britannia … Commanders of the First Athena … prepare to lead your legion on a patrol of Britannia's frontiers!*'

A roar of cheers from the crowd forced him to pause.

'*Prepare also to add a glorious new chapter to the annuls of Rome itself!*'

He took a moment to look once more with great pride upon his daughter dressed in all her fine regalia.

'*Women of the First Athena … GO FORTH!*'

Ursula and Pinnosa formally saluted the king who solemnly nodded in acknowledgement and turned their horses once more to face the assembled ranks. Then, calling out in a formidable voice that could be heard well inside the city walls, Pinnosa issued the first command of the campaign.

'*LEGION FIRST ATHENA … FOR – WARD!*'

VIII

The women spent a full month in the mountains, patrolling the western coast on constant alert for Hibernian raiding parties.

As planned, their presence freed the few remaining men to take a fleet the galleys from Maridunum across the Hibernian Sea in order to make a show of force. Even though there were barely enough men to crew five vessels, the exercise had the desired effect and not a single raiding party was seen.

Despite their growing frustration at not seeing any action, the women grew very fond of the wild mountainous frontier lands. Catching the westerly winds fresh off the great ocean, they were prone to sudden rain-filled squalls followed immediately by blue skies and bright sunshine. The resulting bounty of rainbows filled the women with wonder and they quickly dubbed their patrols their "rainbow patrols" in the "Rainbow Mountains".

While they were abroad in the mountains, the women made the best use of their time, repairing several of the outpost forts and improving many of the encampment sites. Whenever Brittola was supervising the work, she ordered a small Christian chapel to be built. Each one was painted with a coat of limewash to make it pure white both inside and out, and it was equipped with a rudimentary altar along with simple benches for prayer. When the women later handed the installations back to the men, they were in a much better condition than before; and their male counterparts were duly impressed.

The men eventually ended their coastal patrols just in time for Lughnasadh, the start of the harvest season; and their return to the mountain encampments meant it was time for the women to commence their long march north to Wall Country ... and Pict territory.

IX

The legion arrived in Wall Country at the end of August and were surprised at what they found. The landscape was similar to that of the Rainbow Mountains – rugged and mountainous – but where the frontier lands were mostly wild and untamed, Wall Country was a highly-developed military zone. The forest had been cleared for well over a mile on either side of the Wall to give a clear view of any movement, and a sophisticated network of roads, forts and military facilities extended its entire length.

Then, of course, there was the mighty Wall itself. Straddling the province from coast-to-coast, its fortifications had a truly awesome presence, forcing into submission anyone who dared approach it. The seemingly endless line of impregnable high parapets completely dominated and controlled the entire area as it snaked its way across the landscape.

There was another important difference between Wall Country and the Rainbow Mountains that the women quickly became acutely aware of. From atop the wall's high parapets you looked directly out over enemy territory. Those were *his* wooded hills, *his* valleys, and *his* meadows and streams. His presence was everywhere; he was there facing you and not safely tucked away beyond the horizon across open sea. Ursula and the other commanders quickly became concerned about the effect this was having on the women's morale. They weren't singing as much as usual, being constantly on the alert; they resisted being sent on patrol in small units; and they were often heard to mutter 'The trees have eyes I tell you.'

As the legion made its way eastward along the Wall, they discovered that the situation was actually much worse than anticipated. Only the main fortresses had contingents of guards, and most of them were old retired auxiliaries whose fighting days were behind them. There was only one unit that was at proper strength, a contingent of around a hundred able-bodied legionaries at Luguvalium, the garrison town at the western end of the Wall; but even their cavalry unit was reduced owing to a shortage of horses. Away from the forts on the Wall itself, the women were dismayed to find that only a handful of the sentry towers were occupied. Long stretches of the fortifications, mile after mile, were completely unmanned and vulnerable to attack. Even when the occasional tower was manned, it never had more than a handful of men. They encountered just one cavalry unit, only five strong, who were based at one of the more remote mile forts. Horses were in even shorter supply than men, so much so that messengers were using donkeys or even going on foot.

When they reached Cilurnum, the large military complex in the middle section of the Wall, they were astonished to find it virtually deserted with only a caretaker guard unit of auxiliaries and commanded by an aged centurion who had retired and taken his pension twenty years earlier. Not only were the baths closed, the kitchens had also been shut down because the few men that were on station were living with their families in the nearby villages and had no need of such facilities.

Having got full measure of the seriousness of the situation, Ursula and the other commanders decided to deploy the legion immediately so that the women could commence frontier patrols without further delay. They divided the Wall into three sections: west, centre and east, and the commanders drew lots to see who would take responsibility for each. Pinnosa took command of the western section and, because her women had the furthest to travel, she set off that same afternoon, heading back the way they had come and taking a third of the legion with her. Her main objective was to make a show of force in the unruly lands that flanked the coast to the north-west of the Wall. The following morning, Ursula and Saula departed for the eastern section of the Wall, heading for its main town, Segedunum, which left Martha and Brittola in Cilurnum with the contingent of women assigned to the central section—the stretch of Wall Country that was most prone to attacks by the Picts.

X

It wasn't long before Martha and Brittola's women were required to go in action; indeed, the incident occurred barely an hour after Ursula and Saula had set off, marching east.

The dust had barely settled from Ursula's departure when a cavalry patrol came galloping back from a section of the Wall just three miles to the west to report a broken gate and clear signs of a raiding party. Martha and Brittola were still inside the commanders' building along with the other officers, organising the barracking arrangements as well as the recommissioning of the bathhouse and kitchens, when the news arrived.

While the riders were delivering their message, Martha could tell that Brittola was feeling apprehensive. As soon as the other officers hurriedly began to don their helmets and swords and set about issuing orders, Martha grabbed her firmly by the arm led her to one side.

'What is it Martha?' snapped Brittola, clearly agitated.

'It looks as if all our well-rehearsed preparations and plans are about to be put to the test … ' She checked nobody was listening then leaned forward to whisper into Brittola's ear.

'This … '

Brittola looked at her old friend quizzically, then suddenly realised what she was saying and smiled.

' … may not be easy,' they said together in hushed tones and the two old friends shared a warm smile.

All their strategic planning and training now came into play. Martha's officers summoned thirty of her horsewomen while Brittola's mustered a fifty-strong infantry unit. As soon as they were ready, both units set off to intercept the Pict raiding party.

The infantry took a detour to the south so that they could quickly march along the broad military road that followed the Wall in parallel, thereby avoiding some of the rougher terrain. The cavalry, on the other hand, were able to take a more direct route across the high rock-strewn heathland between the road and the Wall. They quickly reached the broken gate and picked up the raiders' trail which led across the military zone into some farmland beyond. From the freshness of the tracks they knew they were close; and it wasn't long before they were spotted.

The Picts, about twenty in number, were all on foot. They were roving in a loose group on the lookout for pickings and were scattered across the open hillside in small bands of three or four. They had already managed to grab three head of cattle which they'd roped together, and when Martha's women caught up with them, they were making their way toward a small settlement in the valley below.

Sounding their horns, Martha's cavalry immediately gave chase. By splintering into two groups they managed to surround the Picts and force them into a tight huddle; however, the women quickly realised they would be no match for the fearsome looking men, so they contented themselves with circling the raiders and keeping them contained while they waited for the infantry to arrive.

Not knowing that more Roman women were on their way, the Picts, who had formed a defensive cluster using the livestock as a shield, started making threatening gestures with their primitive weaponry, all the while shouting bloodcurdling war cries and issuing gruesome-sounding threats, very little of which, fortunately, the women could understand. The only Pict weapons that were visible were some long hunting spears, a few primitive bows and the odd vicious-looking bludgeon, but it was reasonable to assume that they also had plenty of blades of one kind or another hidden beneath their long grey woollen cloaks.

Luckily for Martha's women, it didn't take Brittola's contingent long to arrive; and the instant that they appeared the raiders went ominously quiet.

Martha, Brittola and the other officers made a quick assessment of the situation and decided on their plan of action. Brittola's women quickly got into formation and began their advance. The Picts immediately resumed their chorus of fierce war cries as well as issuing their foul guttural threats. As soon as the women were within range, the they let fly a volley of arrows, but the women were grouped in close formation and had formed 'tortoise shells' with their shields which meant that any missiles on target were deflected.

Still the infantry pressed on and the Picts fired a second volley of arrows, but once again the 'tortoise shells' did their job and not one of them hit home. The front row of women was now within hailing distance and Brittola, who was in the forefront of the centre group, lowered her shield to address the raiders.

'*You are completely outnumbered!*' she shouted. '*Throw down your weapons and we will escort you back to the Wall! You will not be harmed or punished because you have yet to commit any serious crimes!*'

The Picts' reply was a stream of foul abuse followed by another wave of arrows. This time one of the women was hit in the ankle, making her shriek with pain. Despite her wound, she was still able to stand and she even managed to pull the arrow out unaided, but she couldn't continue in action and had to be rescued by one of the cavalry; all of which gave the Picts cause to yell their war cries even more loudly and fiercely.

After their cries had died down, Brittola tried once more to reason with them.

'*You must surrender now and throw down your weapons! You will not be harmed; I repeat, you will not be harmed! We will escort you to the Wall and let you go! Now, throw down your weapons … please!*'

'"Please"?' murmured one of the women behind her.

'Shush!' hissed Brittola; then she gave the order to advance ten more paces, this time with swords drawn.

'Drawn swords' was the signal that Martha had been waiting for and Brittola's women had barely taken another step when the cavalry charged at the men from all sides at once.

Riding hard towards the Picts at a full gallop, Martha's women each fired their arrows aiming low. They thudded into the ground at the men's feet like hail, forcing them to hop and leap to avoid being hit. Only three of the raiders were injured; one was pierced in the knee, another in the calf and a third had an arrow go right through his foot, but it was enough to reduce the Picts to submission. They released the livestock and threw down their spears and bows.

'*Drop all your weapons!*' ordered Martha, riding to the fore. '*Throw your weapons down – now!*'

Several blades, including some Roman swords, were pulled out from beneath cloaks and discarded.

'*Take off your cloaks, too, so that we can see what else you've got hidden!*'

They didn't understand Martha's command at first, but after she mimed what she wanted, they complied; and when they did, the women were astonished at what they saw.

Without exception, each tribesman was completely covered with tattoos. From neck to ankle, their skin was smothered with swirling blue and brown lines surrounding images of birds, animals or fantastical creatures. Some of the older men had even more of the curling and swirling lines on their faces, accentuating their facial features.

XI

'I was so astounded,' said Brittola, breaking into a giggle, 'I didn't notice that they were completely naked until we were about to set them free at the Wall and we gave them back their cloaks.'

The whole company laughed. It was three weeks later and the entire legion was mustered at Cilurnum. Ursula and her friends were enjoying a reunion along with the rest of the senior officers. They had all just bathed in the newly-refurbished baths and were now feasting in the dining chamber reserved for senior officers, as was their right, being fully commissioned officers in the service of King Deonotus. Their decision to use the officers' facilities had actually caused consternation among the attendants, because it had meant them having to hide, or disguise, many items of equipment and decor that were never intended for the use, or eyes, of young noblewomen. Indeed, it was such a serious problem, Oleander had been nominated by the others to have a quiet word with Ursula.

'Mistress, I was once a married woman, yet some of these-these "male facilities" make me blush,' she had said in disgust. 'I don't think it's fitting or proper for noble ladies such as yourselves to see them. Please, Mistress, please think of young Mistress Brittola.'

The laughter at Brittola's admission died down, and it was time for another tale.

'The trickiest moments we had were when we were doing house-to-house searches in their villages,' said Pinnosa.

'"House-to-house" you say?—*per-lease!*' said Martha. '"Sewage pit-to-sewage pit" more like—*phewwwee-eee!*' She pulled a face and pinched her nose then took a swig of wine.

'We learnt early on that it's best to do the searches in groups no smaller than ten,' continued Pinnosa. 'Our very first detail worked only in fives and one group inadvertently entered the chief's hut. He was ready for them with two of his men; and they were armed with those huge blades of theirs— '

'What happened?' asked one of Ursula's officers.

'Luckily, they all got out alive, but two of them were wounded and had to be taken to Luguvalium for treatment; one lost an eye I believe.' Pinnosa leaned forward for emphasis. 'The thing is—whenever you go into one of these Pictish hovels, you must enter in fours! Entering in twos, even back to back, isn't safe enough; you're still exposed on both sides. You need to make sure you are in fours; that way your sides are covered.'

'I can give you another important tip … ' said Saula, 'Don't trust the children no matter how innocent they might look. On our very first search one of our women decided to ignore three "little angels" she saw cowering in the corner and concentrated on the adults. Before she knew it, she had three huge gashes on her legs and had to be carried out. She couldn't walk or ride; and we had to commandeer a cart to get her back here to Cilurnum.'

'*Ladies! Ladies!* Gather round; I have important news!' Ursula came rushing back into the room, having been called out to receive a messenger a few moments earlier. 'As you know, in addition to sending reports to my father in Corinium, I have also been sending them to King Aurelius at Eboracum; and we've just received our first reply.' She smiled at the raft of expectant faces about her. 'He congratulates us on the success of our campaign and informs us he has managed to muster a force of five hundred cavalry and seven hundred infantry which he is sending at once to relieve us!'

The women let out a loud cheer and Ursula had to wait for them to settle down again before she could continue.

'They should be arriving the day after tomorrow. That means we can look forward to a well-earned rest, enjoying the delights of Eboracum—*a full two weeks ahead of schedule!*'

A couple of the women shrieked with excitement and they all cheered again.

112

'By the time we return home to the West Country, the campaign season will almost be over and our last remaining duty will be to stand on station at Glevum and Viroconium for a few weeks, sending out routine patrols. Ladies ...' She reached for a goblet of wine and raised it. *'Congratulations! Our campaign has been a complete success. Let us salute ... the First Athena!'*

They all raised their glasses and echoed her cry.

'The First Athena!'

'Oh, just one more thing ... ' Ursula glanced at Pinnosa with a wry smile. 'The relief unit from Eboracum is comprised solely of women, including the commanders.'

XII

The women from Eboracum had a livery as red as the Corinium women's was blue. Their standard was three white lilies on a deep red field and, to represent their allegiance to the same commander-in-chief, it too was capped by a small golden bear. They were officially named "The Second Cohort of the Legion First Athena", and their leader was Princess Julia, a distant cousin of Ursula's who she'd only ever met once before when they were both young children and her family was on a royal tour of the province. She was the daughter of Deonotus' older half-brother King Aurelius.

Ursula received Julia just outside Cilurnum in a large open space beside a great bridge across the River Vedra. The cohorts of both regiments were drawn up in formation on the opposite sides of a long sloping field in full dress uniform. As Julia and her officers entered the area, Ursula and her senior commanders were all assembled in the centre of the clearing ready to greet them and formally complete the handover.

'All hail, Princess Julia of Eboracum!' cried Pinnosa as Julia and her contingent drew close. *'We salute you and the women of the Legion First Athena, Second Cohort!'*

'Greetings, all!' cried Julia in reply, but instead of continuing with the usual ceremonial acknowledgements, she

113

leapt from her horse, strode over to stand immediately in front of Artemis and Swift, and scrutinised the two commanders-in-chief with her hands on her hips and a broad grin.

'You must be the renowned Pinnosa; am I right? How could you not be; you're just as the reports describe, a real red-headed firebrand! Which means you must be Cousin Ursula. I know I should say out of politeness that you haven't changed a bit since the last time we met, but that would be a barefaced lie, would it not? I think we have both changed a great deal more than either of us would care to admit!'

Ursula and Pinnosa leapt from their horses and embraced Julia. She was about the same age as them and a similar height to Pinnosa, but she was more slender in build, a tall thin woman with a long face. The senior officers of the two cohorts quickly formed a close huddle, surrounded by their horses, to exchange intelligence and discuss plans. While they were thus engaged, the ranks of the two regiments eyed each other across the large clearing with a mixture of awe, admiration and, it has to be said, more than a little rivalry. The two groups of officers eventually broke apart and returned to their respective ranks. Formal salutes were exchanged and Pinnosa gave the order for the women from Corinium to commence their march to Eboracum. The Vanguard of the Second Cohort lined the approach to the grand bridge over the river in order to give the commanders from Corinium a special salute as they passed by in pairs.

'Quite a sight, isn't it?' said Cordula to Brittola as they exited the bridge.

'Quite a sight, indeed,' replied Brittola. 'A sight to warm the weary and ease exhaustion; a sight to put a spring back in— '

'That's certainly true,' interrupted Ursula, speaking over her shoulder in front of them. 'But our women really *do* need a good rest; I know I certainly do; and I fully intend to enjoy every minute of our stay in Eboracum. I know neither of you has been there before. You are both in for a well-earned treat; there is no better place in the whole of Britannia; Eboracum has it all!'

XIII

Their reception at Eboracum was spectacular; surpassing all hope and expectation, even Ursula was impressed.

To begin with, King Aurelius insisted that the entire legion parade through the city in triumph, not just Ursula's officers and the Vanguard; and when they did, the streets were crammed full with excited townsfolk and children, all waving and cheering. Next, the women were told that one of the large imperial barracks just outside the city walls had been prepared for them and was well-stocked with generous amounts of food and clean clothes. Ursula and the other commanders, however, were to be guests of honour in the magnificent royal palace. In addition, that evening, the king hosted a huge feast to welcome all the officers, senior and others, in the palace's Great Hall.

Being late summer, the food was both plentiful and varied; and the wine as well as the oils were wonderfully fresh. The entertainment surpassed anything to be seen in Corinium. There were African dancers accompanied by musicians playing unusual music on bizarre instruments. There were magicians wearing exotic costumes and performing exciting new tricks that none of the Corinium women had ever witnessed, as well as wild beasts from Africa they'd only ever seen in mosaics.

'*Look!*' Brittola clapped enthusiastically as a huge long-necked creature was led into the hall and paraded around for all to touch and stroke. 'It's one of those creatures on that tapestry in the Officers' Hall at home. Can you remember its name?'

'I think it's a "Zarraf" or some such thing,' replied Cordula. 'I preferred the one earlier with the humps on its back— '

'*Oh, ye-eee-ess!* What was that now? A "gammel" or "camelus" or something— '

'Oh yuck, wasn't that ugly! And those hideous noises it kept making. You know who it reminded me of don't you?

They looked at each other and burst out giggling.

115

The following day, King Aurelius set off with Ursula and her fellow commanders on a hunting trip. Around the middle of the afternoon, they stopped beside a stream for a short break and while the others were tending to their horses the king took Ursula to one side.

'Your father must be very proud of you,' he said once they were alone. 'You and your "army of women" have certainly achieved great things and earned considerable respect even from a tired old man like myself who thought he'd seen everything and had little left to learn.'

Ursula smiled and looked up at the king who was quite tall and still a very handsome man despite his advancing years.

'That, Sire, is a true compliment, especially coming from you.'

'You know what many are saying about the First Athena, don't you?'

'No, Sire?'

'They are saying "What has the world come to?" and "Why are our womenfolk having to do the work of our men? It is our men who should be protecting our province and defending us against barbarian raids. It's not right that our women are having to do it." "Bring the men home," they cry, "and let our women stick to what they do best; bringing up our sons and daughters; protecting our future."'

Ursula bristled and made to speak but before she could say anything the king continued.

'Whenever I hear such ideas being voiced, I am quick to remind people that our men are the best and most disciplined fighters in all Rome, and it is precisely because they are so good at what they do that their skills needed elsewhere. I then point out that if it weren't for our brave women getting themselves organised and putting on a show of force where it is desperately needed, this province would now be on its knees and begging for mercy from the likes of the Picts and their Hibernian allies.'

Again, Ursula attempted reply, but once more the king pressed on.

116

'It truly is incredible what you and your fellow women from the West Country have accomplished, and in such a short time too. Deonotus has much to be proud of.' He hesitated and suddenly looked awkward. 'Those friends of yours, your fellow "commanders", really are a remarkable bunch, especially that Pinnosa. Now that I've met her, I can see for myself she is every bit as formidable as people say; her reputation is well-deserved. I imagine the tales I'm hearing are barely half the story. And that Brittola is quite something too. Is it true she is not yet eighteen?'

Ursula nodded and allowed the king to continue. She could sense he was about to broach the matter he really wanted to raise.

'I – *um* – I hope my Jul – *cough* – I hope my daughter proves herself worthy of being called Commander-in-Chief of the Second Cohort of the Legion First Athena.'

'Oh, have no fear of that, Your Majesty,' said Ursula with a broad reassuring smile. 'I'm sure she will; she seems a very capable leader. Tell me; did she organise the Eboracum contingent herself, or was it really all your doing?'

'*Ha!* Straight to the point, eh? I like that in a woman!' The king laughed. 'No, I can take no credit for the creation of the Eboracum cohort, none whatsoever. If only you'd seen the look in Julia's eyes whenever you and your endeavours in the West Country were mentioned, you'd soon understand why she ... ' He tailed off and looked into the distance. 'She's been hunting with me since before she was ten, you know. Like you, she's no stranger to horsemanship, the chase and the kill. She also knows how to use of a variety of weapons as well as follow a trail and, like you and your Pinnosa there, she is far happier in the wild outdoors than within the stifling confines of the city. There's nothing she hates more than petty court gossip.'

'I know how she feels, Your Majesty,' said Ursula, slowly nodding.

'So, when she heard you were out in the mountains on patrol, chasing raiders, on the march—oh, you should've seen her! She was like a caged wolf, pacing up and down, looking for a way to join the pack. The day I received your father's message telling me that the Hibernian coast was safe and that you were heading for Wall Country, I said to her "That's not right! Our cousins are coming up here doing our work for us just because we're short of men. What do you think we should do about it?"'

He looked at Ursula and grinned.

'Do you know what? I haven't had a kiss that big since I asked her mother to marry me.' They both laughed. 'She had it all organised in under a month. The palace was a-buzz I tell you; messengers were sent out and within hours the first volunteers started knocking on the palace gate. I've never seen anything like it; orders for the livery and weaponry, and armour fittings, and horse selections, and training regimes—oh, and maps, maps and more maps; briefing after briefing with her officers— '

'I – *um* – I know, Your Majesty,' said Ursula, politely interrupting him. 'I know exactly what Julia has had to do.'

XIV

The day after they returned from the hunt, Ursula and her old friends decided they would discard their uniforms and spend a day enjoying the delights of Eboracum.

Immediately after morning bells had sounded, they left the palace and set off to explore the magnificent city, the largest by far in Britannia outside Londinium. Between its grand and renowned public buildings of great splendour, they found a myriad of bustling streets full of interesting shops and stalls selling all manner of things; pottery, jewellery, food and clothes, that they'd never seen before in either Corinium or Glevum.

As midday bells sounded, they were seated by a large fountain not far from the south gate, enjoying a curious local hot dainty, a blood sausage cooked in a wine and mushroom sauce, and wrapped in a crust of butter-rich pastry. Pinnosa and Martha loved it, but Brittola most certainly did not. Ursula, Cordula and Saula hadn't made up their minds and were discussing how it might be made more palatable for West Country taste when, suddenly, they heard the shrill note of a horn coming from the

Londinium Road outside the city's south gate. Recognising the sound immediately, Cordula dropped her pie and ran to the gate.

As soon as it opened, Morgan came galloping through on Hermes. He had crossed the Oceanus Britannicus five days earlier bringing with him the first full report of Constantine's expedition. Following the official Britannic circuit, he had first gone directly to the governor in Londinium before heading up the Great North Road to Lindum and then on to Eboracum. He still had to go to three more major towns, including Corinium, before his circuit was complete; and then, little over a week later, he would be making a return crossing of the Oceanus Britannicus with a head full of fresh messages and a bag full of documents.

He'd barely dismounted when Cordula ran up to him.

'*Morgan! Morgan! It's me!*'

'Cordula? What are you doing here?' He exclaimed as he brushed away a heavy coating of road dust from his cloak.

'It's a long, long story; it'll take me at least a walk in the moonlight to tell it to you.'

She laughed as they hugged. Then, they looked deeply into each other's eyes ... and kissed.

Watching from the nearby fountain, Ursula imagined it was Constans who had ridden in through the gate; Constans who had returned safe and sound; and Constans who had leapt from his horse to embrace his love, his one true love. His voice suddenly filled her mind.

Always remember this. Only in your voice ... I hear family. Only in your eyes ... I see—

'Ahem!'

The king's attendant, a lanky sour-looking old man with a long neck and a hooked nose, gave a loud cough of disapproval as he approached the embracing couple. He'd just glided past Ursula and the others by the fountain like a wraith on a breeze.

Morgan opened his eyes and glared at the haughty courtier. He was about to berate him for his rudeness when he noticed Princess Ursula standing nearby, and he hastily extricated himself from Cordula's embrace.

'Y-Your Highness,' he spluttered, adjusting his cloak and bowing awkwardly.

'Ahem!'

The long-necked courtier turned to face Ursula and her companions and also gave her a cursory bow.

'His Majesty, King Aurelius, awaits the messenger's dispatch in his private chambers. He also graciously invites Princess Ursula and her – *ahem* – 'senior officers' to join him.'

XV

'Refreshments are on their way Morgan. Now, we're in no rush. Take us through things slowly and tell us everything, each little detail, no matter how trivial—*and* … ' the king raised his bushy grey eyebrows for emphasis 'whatever you do, do *not* on any account, leave out *anything* you told the governor in Londinium. Understood?'

'Yes, Your Majesty,' said Morgan.

Ursula could barely contain herself.

'What luck to be here for this!' she whispered to her friends. 'Father won't receive this news for a couple of days at least.'

She was sitting on a long bench beneath a window with her friends on either side. Morgan was seated directly in front of them, facing the king who sat opposite on a stone chair that was positioned to enjoy the view through the window.

Cordula's very lucky, she thought, looking at the dark-haired messenger's profile. *Morgan really is quite handsome.*

'Are you ready ladies?' asked the king.

They all looked at Ursula, and she nodded.

The king, in turn, nodded to Morgan.

'Then, please begin.'

'His Lordship, the Supreme Commander of the armed forces of Britannia, Constantine, sends you all his loyal and heartfelt greetings and humbly craves … '

Ursula felt exasperated with the formalities and wished they could get on with it. There had been a time not long ago when she'd enjoyed such things; they were to be savoured as some of the pleasures and pleasantries of civilised life, but now they were just tiresome and irrelevant. Fortunately for Ursula, Morgan was very adept at speeding up the formalities without appearing brusque, and he soon started recounting his news. Indeed, he was an excellent messenger in many respects. He could describe scenes and events with such precision and clarity that his listeners felt they had actually been with him to witness and experience them. He also had an uncanny skill, whereby he allowed just a touch of the sender's characteristics to enter into his voice and manner, enabling him, without degenerating into a vulgar impersonation, to create the feeling that the sender was addressing the audience in person.

'The crossings went very well, Your Majesty. Both Constans and Constantine successfully landed in Gallia without any difficulty; but, as you and the other kings had feared, they did experience considerable problems when it came to rallying local forces.

'The Seine valley was much more severely depleted of legionaries than they'd anticipated. What few remaining able-bodied men there were simply refused to leave their towns and estates because of the threat from the wandering German tribes. As a result, Constans had to ride further south than originally planned to the Liger valley where the level of depletion wasn't so great and the fear of the Germans less.

'He eventually managed to raise a force of over three thousand, mostly infantry; but this success came at a heavy cost in terms of it being many days—weeks even, before Constans was able to head north to re-unite with his father which was much later than they'd hoped or anticipated.

'Unfortunately, things did not go according to plan for Constantine either. Instead of heading straight for Treveris as intended, they were greeted at the coast with news that the men from both the Colonia and Mogontiacum garrisons had been deployed to deal with a large group of Germans who'd been spotted coming down the River Moenus.

'That meant long stretches of the frontier east of Colonia were left virtually unmanned; moreover, following the breaches made by the Germanic tribes last winter, in many places it was also in dire need of repair. Constantine had no choice other than to march directly to the area to shore up the defences before he could revert to his original plans and head for Treveris.

'The result of all this was that Constantine and Constans did not succeed in reuniting and combining their forces until after Alban Heruin, well into the summer and almost a month later than planned. It then took them a further two weeks before they were finally able to meet up with the remnants of the Colonia regiments at Mogontiacum. But … eventually … '

Morgan smiled and proudly straightened his back.

'I am pleased to report that the combined numbers of the Britannic, Colonia and Liger veterans amounted to almost thirty-three thousand!'

The women gasped and King Aurelius breathed a huge sigh of relief.

'*Ha! Thirty-three thousand, eh? Well, thank goodness for that!*' exclaimed the king. 'From what you were saying Morgan, I was expecting to hear he'd only mustered a measly few thousand, but now he has more than enough men to— '

'That's not all, Your Majesty.' Morgan's smile broadened. 'Their cavalry is over *ten* thousand strong!'

Ursula and her friends leapt from their bench, applauding and cheering.

'*Those damned and blasted Batavians!*' The king was jubilant with delight. 'Thanks be to God for those wonderful blasted Batavians and their love of horses!'

'Now they can *really* get down to work,' said Pinnosa. 'With numbers like that, Constantine should have no difficulty rebuilding the frontier defences and getting Mogontiacum back into shape.'

'As well as rounding up most of the German tribes that are now wandering all over Germania and Gallia,' added Ursula. 'Morgan? What news do you have of that situation?'

Morgan's smile froze.

'It appears that the situation there is far more serious than we thought. In just the Sequana valley alone, people have been forced to abandon their estates and withdraw to their walled cities. Constans actually came across one tribe that was on the move while he was passing through ... '

He looked down at his feet; his smile had gone completely.

The Germanic tribes! A stark and ominous thought suddenly filled Ursula's mind. *That is where the true danger lies!* She visibly shuddered as if she'd been slapped; and her friends all turned to look as she hurriedly sat back down.

'Please go on,' she forced a smile of encouragement.

The others returned their attention to Morgan as they resumed their seats, apart from Pinnosa who continued to watch Ursula out of the corner of her eye.

'Constans was completely astonished at the sheer number of people on the move; he estimated it was many tens—possibly *hundreds* of thousands. They were spread far apart in loose-but-large groups comprising of men, women, children, old folk and babies, as well as all their livestock and belongings.

'Even though he had a full cohort of cavalry with him, he was powerless to do anything. They did actually ride through some of the outer groups but then quickly withdrew to safety. There are bands of warriors roaming amongst the wandering tribes, ex-Roman auxiliaries who are known to be fast moving and formidable foes – it wasn't worth the risk. He estimated he would need a force of at least two thousand cavalry to tackle the fighting men and subdue them, plus two thousand infantry, or more, to escort the tribes to whatever lands they were allocated. The last time he and Constantine spoke to me about the matter, they were seriously thinking of creating two special units of five thousand men – half cavalry and half infantry – to dispatch on these missions.'

'Only two units?' interrupted Pinnosa. 'But I thought there were at least five of these tribes on the rampage!'

Morgan could only look at her and shrug his shoulders; and the gathering fell silent as the immensity of the task facing the men became clear in their minds.

'I think it all depends on how quickly they can secure the frontier,' he continued. 'East of Mogontiacum there are complete sections – sometimes more than a day's march in length – with no guards whatsoever. What they face isn't simply the rebuilding of those defences; they have to redesign them too, so that they can be manned very sparsely by cavalry patrols. I think that task alone is going to take the rest of this year and much of next. But, remember, each time a new tribe approaches them intent on invasion, they lose a whole month … or more.'

'Do you know what I'd been naïvely thinking?'

It was Martha who broke the long silence that ensued.

'I had actually started to think that our women were doing similar work to the men. I was beginning to feel proud of the First Athena for succeeding in doing the men's work for them. I was even intending to tease them about it when they returned home.' She sighed and slowly shook her head. 'But what is chasing down a dozen Picts or dealing with a score of Hibernians compared to rounding-up tens of thousands of Germans and escorting them to new lands? How can repairing a gate in a wall or rebuilding a chapel compare to reconstructing an entire stretch of the frontier a day's march in length?'

Ursula looked at the others. Cordula, Saula, and Brittola were nodding in grim agreement with Martha; and Pinnosa was staring intently at King Aurelius with an expression of fierce determination upon her face.

She then turned to look out the window and her thoughts drifted far, far away. Something high up caught her eye. There, circling far above the city, was the unmistakable silhouette of a hawk. As she watched, she thought she could hear it give a faint and forlorn cry as it disappeared into the blazing disc of the sun.

XVI

Throughout the winter of AD 407 and 408 the army of Britannia stayed on the Germanic frontier, rebuilding and restructuring the defences. By the spring, the invading tribes of Burgundians in central and eastern Gallia and Suebi in the west were wreaking so much havoc that Constantine was forced to redeploy his men, and the frontier work had to be left temporarily unfinished.

He split his force into five divisions. There were two large mobile units, each five thousand strong: one comprised legionaries from Gallia under the command of Gerontius; the other, consisting of Britannic and Batavian men, was placed under Constans. It was their task to round up the two large wandering Suebi tribes that were creating the biggest problems in the west of Gallia, and escort them across the mountains to Hispania where there was more open land for them to settle on. A third unit of cavalry, mostly natives of the Germanic frontier lands, was stationed along the newly rebuilt defences under the command of Britannic centurions. The fourth contingent was assigned the extremely difficult task of settling the Burgundians, a collection of small tribes constantly at war with each other, along the more southerly reaches of the Rhenus.

Finally, Constantine himself led the fifth contingent to the south of Gallia in response to an urgent request from the imperial court in Arelate for reinforcements against the threat of further menaces that might come across the Alps from Italia at any moment.

The overall strategy worked well at first. Constans and Gerontius both succeeded in subduing the Suebi warriors and were able to escort their assigned tribes south toward Hispania. In addition, the internecine warfare of the Burgundians almost ceased and the new defences on the Germanic frontier, though incomplete, appeared to be keeping other German tribes at bay.

But then, in the middle of AD 408, things started to go wrong. At the height of summer, while festivities were under way to celebrate Lughnasadh, Stilicho died unexpectedly in suspicious circumstances, creating a dangerous power vacuum in Italia which made things especially perilous for Constantine in Arelate. Prior to his death, Stilicho had made no secret of the fact that he perceived Constantine's success in Germania and Gallia to be a threat to his authority over the Roman armed forces in the region; and he'd managed to convince Emperor Honorius of the need to take measures to stem Constantine's rise in influence in the region.

Upon the emperor's orders, units in the Vindobona area who were not under Constantine's control, were withdrawn from the northern frontiers and sent elsewhere. This left the empire's defences severely weakened on Constantine's eastern flank and had the desired effect of stretching his newly-created mobile forces beyond their limit. Almost immediately, more roaming tribes of Burgundians, Suebi and Franks began pouring across the frontier, laying waste to areas that had barely started to recover from the previous devastation. With his hard-earned prestige and authority successfully undermined, Constantine was forced to redeploy the main contingent of his men from Arelate to try and cope with the new invaders. This left him dangerously vulnerable to attack from any would be successors to Stilicho's crown who wished to attempt an opportunistic foray into Gallia to prove their worthiness.

While all these events were unfolding, the mission to relocate the two large Suebi tribes to Hispania also ran into major problems. Constans was taking a coastal route, intending to cross the mountains far to the west then head south into a sparsely-populated part of north-west Hispania. Gerontius, however, had followed the main trade route directly south to the powerful city of Cesaraugusta where the imperial court had been none too pleased at having Gallia's invaders foisted upon them. Just as Gerontius' rather feeble diplomatic skills were being put to the test, a local Hispanian cavalry unit had joined forces with some of the men under his command and, in a night of brute terror, massacred thousands of the Suebi women and children. Having thus compromised the dim-witted Britannic commander, the court found themselves with a useful puppet. They had then begun to use him in their power plays with their neighbouring provinces, as well as with the emperor himself, who always had to 'earn' Hispanian co-operation in whatever schemes he was pursuing.

Meanwhile, back in Britannia, the campaign season of AD 408 was turning into another great success for the First Athena. The First Cohort had already beaten off more than thirty Hibernian raiding parties and the Second had kept the Wall Country so quiet they'd been able to send a four hundred strong force north to the Antonine Wall where they made basic repairs to some of the long-neglected mile forts and sentry towers.

Then, toward the end of July, something completely unforeseen and totally unexpected happened.

Ursula and Pinnosa's detachments had just returned to Corinium for a much-needed rest, having completed an exercise at the northern end of the western coast. They were settling into their quarters when they heard the sound of trumpets coming from the east. Rushing to the city's high parapets, they saw a force of over fifteen hundred women, including five hundred cavalry, in dark green livery came down the Fosse Way and entered Corinium's eastern barracks. They were led by a very fierce-looking woman riding a chariot and from their standards, they could tell they were from far-away Lindum.

The Third Cohort of the Legion First Athena was led by Princess Faustina, the daughter of King Regulus of Lindum which, along with Eboracum and Corinium, was one of the most important cities in Britannia outside Londinium. Their addition to the legion meant that the First Athena's numbers had nearly doubled to around four thousand in total.

XVII

'Enter!'

King Deonotus was alone in his private chamber which was full of maps and parchments. The heavy oak door creaked open, revealing Ursula. For once, she wasn't in uniform; instead, she was wrapped in a heavy woollen toga, because the palace was unseasonably cold even though it was not yet autumn.

'You sent for me Father?'

He turned to face her, smiled and opened his arms in greeting. She rushed over to give him a firm hug. It had been a few months since they'd last seen each other. She happened to be in Corinium procuring weapons and supplies for the legion and he'd just returned from attending a hastily convened meeting of the three provincial kings with the governor in Londinium.

'Sit down my dear,' he said after they'd embraced. 'I'm afraid I have a very serious matter to discuss with you.'

'What is it Father?'

She sat on the edge of the couch beside the fire, looking at him with concern. He seemed agitated and began pacing up and down.

'It seems the governor and you share something in common; you both wish the men would return home soon.'

She said nothing and waited for father to continue, knowing full well that anything involving the governor was never as simple and straightforward as it first sounded. What started as good news invariably ended as bad.

'But that's as far as you and he agree; your reasons for wanting them home couldn't be more different.'

He stopped pacing, sat down beside her and took her hands in his.

'What I'm about to tell you Regulus will also be telling Faustina and Aurelius will be telling Julia.'

His manner reminded her of when he had broken the news to her that her mother had died. She shivered as he continued, but not with the cold.

'The problem my dear is that Britannia simply can't afford to finance two armies any longer. You know about the recent tax riots in Londinium and the southern towns?' She nodded. 'The whole province is thankful for what you and your women are doing. People know they need the First Athena out on patrol, protecting them from invasion, but … ' he looked her in the eye, ' … they don't want to pay too high a price for it.'

'Does the governor want us to disband?' she asked.

He resumed pacing and spoke more to himself than her.

'Aurelius and I knew this would happen. We knew that crafty old rogue Regulus wouldn't be content to sit back and let his daughter be outshone by you and Julia. We knew he would encourage her to match your efforts; but at the same time, we knew that there was a limit to how much the people of Britannia were willing to pay—*Bah!*'

He spun around and kicked the embers of the fire in exasperation, raising a cascade of sparks.

'We warned Regulus not to try and match the Corinium and Eboracum numbers. "Send Faustina to join with Julia," we said. "Let her wear the red or the blue," we said. "Oh no!" says he. "If my Faustina is to fight for Britannia, she fights in the green." The next thing we knew the First Athena had doubled in numbers—and it doesn't stop there does it? With the number of volunteers you're getting, the First Athena could well reach six thousand in strength next year – seven even – and we will *still* be paying for the twenty thousand men on the Continent.'

'What have you and the governor decided to do?' Ursula did her best to remain calm and hide the raging turmoil of fear and emotion churning inside of her.

'Well, there were only three possible courses of action open to us. The first option was to disband the First Athena … '

Struggling to take in what he was saying, Ursula took in a deep breath and stared at her father who, in turn, was staring into the fire with his back to her.

'The second option was for Gallia to pay for our men, but the court in Arelate is still financing their own units in Italia. We received their governor's reply last week—a very emphatic "*No!*" That left only one further possibility … and was the reason I had to go to Londinium.'

The king turned to face her and smiled.

'It's one more patrol in the Rainbow Mountains for you my dear; Constantine is going to mint his own coins and pay his men with his own money.'

Ursula gasped.

'You mean— '

'Yes, my dear. He is going to take the laurels and put on the purple.'

He went over to a small pile of sealed parchments and handed one to her.

'Here,' he said, smiling. 'Read your first ever personal letter from an emperor … and prepare yourself to become a future empress.'

XVIII

"I hereby salute you and your fellow officers. Well done on your magnificent work protecting the good people of Britannia. Your deeds give the men and me great cheer and make us wish for the genteel rigors of the "Rainbow Mountains"! Are you aware that your fame has spread far and wide; that tales of your exploits are being told and recounted throughout the empire? Why, even Honorius on his high throne in Ravenna has heard of you; of the terrifying Pinnosa, the bane of the Hibernians; and the fearless Brittola, the scourge of the Picts!"

They all laughed. Even though each one of Ursula's friends had read it a dozen times, Constantine's letter never failed to raise their spirits, especially when Martha read it out loud adopting his mannerisms.

'Now go ahead to the part about finances,' said Ursula.

They were reading it for the benefit of Julia who had just arrived. She'd ridden hard from Wall Country accompanied by three of her senior officers in order to relieve Ursula, Pinnosa, Martha and Baetica, so that they, in turn, could rush to Lindum where Faustina was desperately trying to cope with a new, and very worrying, menace; Saxon raiding parties.

It was September, the day before Alban Elued, the autumn equinox, and Julia caught up with Ursula and her fellow officers in the old Christian temple by the sea where, a year-and-a-half earlier, she and Pinnosa had conceived the idea for the First Athena. All the commanders were seated in the grotto area round the bathing pool, drinking wine and catching up on news.

Martha found the relevant passage and continued.

"*I assure you the First Athena will not be restrained or disbanded because of petty squabbles between governors over finances. I hereby give you my solemn pledge as your emperor that the legion will only disband when you hand your standards to me personally upon my return to Britannia, a day we all hope to see soon. Until that day comes, carry on with the good work you are doing, work that the province now relies upon, and do not give money matters a moment's thought. Leave such things to us old men as we rummage through our vaults, rattling boxes and arguing over how much blood we can squeeze from stones.*"

'He must have suspected that he would have problems with Hispania when he wrote that letter,' said Julia. 'By all accounts, the governor of Hispania is the only one in the West with substantial reserves. Father received word he has refused to make any payments to Constantine for what he called a "Gallo-Britannic" army which he says has no bearing, or claim, upon Hispanian interests. In fact, he has gone much further than simply refusing to recognise Constantine; he has raised a little-known nobleman from Cesaraugusta, Maximus, to the purple and created a rival Hispanian emperor.'

'What of our armies in Hispania?' asked Pinnosa, 'Aren't they in a precarious position if the province has raised its own emperor?'

'I was coming to that,' said Julia. 'According to the report, Gerontius has declared his allegiance to the new imperial house in Cesaraugusta. In return for his "loyalty", he has been made Commander-in-Chief of all Hispanian armed forces.'

'Hell's teeth!' snapped Pinnosa. 'I should have cut that traitor's throat while I had the chance.'

131

'Any news of Constans?' asked Ursula, looking intently at Julia.

'The report merely mentioned that Constans was still in the far west of Hispania, in Emerita Augusta; but that's all the news I have of him I'm afraid.'

Julia frowned and looked grim.

'We can only assume the lack of reports from Constans is because he's surrounded by hostile forces and the messengers can't get through. We think he's having to protect the Suebi against the Emerita Augustans who have risen in anger against having the German's foisted on them. He certainly has a fight on his hands whichever way he turns.'

'I see.' Ursula quickly changed the subject. 'Please tell me more about Constantine; do we know if he is still planning to take his men into Italia to help Honorius against the Goths?'

Before Julia could answer, Pinnosa stood up and suggested that they move outside to the terrace to enjoy the sunset over the Hibernian Sea. She'd spotted Ursula's sudden unease and hoped that once they were out on the rocky platform, they'd all become too engrossed in enjoying the view to notice her old friend's disquiet.

'So, what news do you have of Constantine's march into Italia?' Pinnosa asked Julia once they had settled.

They were all now sitting in a row on the edge of the terrace, dangling their legs over the waves lapping gently below.

'Well, now the old schemer Stilicho is no more,' replied Julia. 'Constantine is the only hope Honorius has left if he is to defeat the Goths. That's why he should really be taking his army into Italia, but with these recent developments in Hispania he'll have to strengthen his position in Arelate before attempting a campaign into unfamiliar territory; which means he *still* has to wait for Constans to return. He can't just go marching into Italia, leaving Arelate undefended and vulnerable to attack.' She leaned back and tried to catch Ursula's eye. 'I hate to say it but, until father and son manage to reunite their forces, in a way they are both trapped.'

For a long moment, the women remained silent, each pondering the enormity of the situation; then, suddenly, Saula leapt to her feet.

'*Dear God in Heaven!*' she cried. 'Why couldn't the men simply repair the frontier defences, escort the Germans out of Gallia and return home? When will this *endless* expedition of theirs be over? Won't they *ever* come home?'

She started pacing up and down behind the others.

'I'm about to see my twenty-first winter! How much longer are we women going to be doing *this*, doing the men's work for them? Aren't we *ever* going to have normal lives? Aren't we *ever* going to marry and have children? And, with all the men gone, who are we going to marry and have children *with*, for goodness' sake?'

'Lady Saula has a point, Ma'am,' said Baetica, who was sitting beside Ursula. 'If you don't mind me saying so, Ma'am, I'm a little older than the majority of the women, including yourselves, and I'm the only one here who's married. A lot of the women have been speaking like Lady Saula, Ma'am. They say the men will never come home because they're mostly unmarried, and we all know unmarried men like to make their home where they are well paid.'

'"An army of spinsters"!' Martha stood up to join Saula. 'That's how one of my women put it; she said we'll *still* be doing this work when we're thirty and too old to have children.'

'And if we fail to have children,' said Saula, 'who will take over our work in twenty years' time when we're too old to fight? Hell's teeth—we need to be meeting our husbands and marrying them soon, otherwise Britannia will— '

'All right you two, you've made you point,' interrupted Ursula, leaping to her feet and spinning round to glare at Saula and Martha. 'You are both right to ask such things, and so are all the other women. Where *are* the worthy husbands and where *are* our children, our future, going to come from? These *are*, indeed, the burning questions, but do either of you actually have any answers? Well do you? … Hmm?'

Martha and Saula looked at each other then shook their heads.

Ursula turned her fierce gaze upon Pinnosa.

'Do you have any answers?'

Pinnosa too shook her head.

Ursula looked down the line to Julia, Baetica, Brittola and the other officers; and they all shook their heads.

'Well then, it's a good thing that *I* do!'

Stunned into silence, they all stared at Ursula as she stood on the very edge of the rock platform and fixed her gaze upon the setting sun.

'There's something very special about this place. I don't know why, but I seem to be able to see matters much more clearly whenever I'm here.'

She pointed to some nearby rocks.

'It was over there that the idea of creating an army of women first came to Pinnosa and me, and now I think I know what we need to do next.'

She turned back to face them.

'There *is* a way we can set things on a different course; but, before I share it with you, I need to ask a simple question of Baetica?'

'Yes, Ma'am?'

'I imagine your husband is the kind of legionary who, though a loyal home-loving husband, nevertheless, whenever he *is* home, yearns for the next campaign season, to be with his comrades in his cavalry unit, out on patrol and looking for action. Am I correct?'

'That's correct, Ma'am.'

'Under normal circumstances, when a man like your husband, a good man and a loyal legionary, goes off on a campaign, what is the most effective way of ensuring that he returns home as soon as the campaign is over and doesn't volunteer for extra duties?'

'Send word that he's a father,' said Baetica without hesitation. 'Let him know there's an addition to the family at home—preferably a boy.'

'But Ursula, most of the men with Constantine and Constans are unmarried,' protested Martha.

'And these are most certainly *not* "normal circumstances",' added Saula.

'You are absolutely right, but think for a moment on what Baetica has just said about the best way to lure a good man back to his home.'

Ursula looked pointedly at Pinnosa and Julia.

'I propose we expand the First Athena to equal the number of Britannic men under Constantine and Constans' command; and— '

'But that's over twenty thousand!' exclaimed Martha.

Ursula pressed on, ignoring her outburst.

' —and we ensure that this enlarged First Athena matches Constantine's army not only in number but also in composition, being comprised mostly of *unmarried* personnel. At the same time, we create a reserve legion, the Second Athena, with approximately the same number of women as we had this season, around five thousand. This will take almost a year to accomplish which means the next stage of the plan couldn't be put into operation until the end of the next campaign season; but *then* ... '

She paused and looked at the others one-by-one.

'Then, with the Second Athena remaining behind to maintain Britannia's defences, we'll take the First Athena to the Continent, catch up with Constantine and hold a grand wedding, marrying all the men and women together.'

'"A grand wedding"?' Cordula clapped her hands with delight.

'Two entire armies?' cried one of Julia's officers.

'Equal numbers; just think of that ... ' said Martha.

'A woman for each man ... ' Saula slapped Martha on the back. ' ... and a man for every woman!'

Several of the women started talking excitedly.

'There's one more very important stage to this plan … '
Ursula had to raise her voice to be heard.

'The women will need to stay with the men for however long it takes for them to become pregnant. Then, as soon as they are with child, they will return to Britannia, carrying the babies that will ensure their husbands' return; the babies we need to secure Britannia's future.'

There was a long stunned silence.

'I think that is an *outrageous* plan … ' Cordula leapt to her feet and stood beside Ursula. ' … and a tremendous one too! There will be many problems to overcome *but*— ' She put her hand on Ursula's shoulder and was surprised to find it was shaking. 'It's a logical and natural extension of the legion's mission to defend Britannia and I for one support it … ' she then added with a smile, ' … though I have no idea how to organise the training and equipment for the final part!'

They all laughed.

Julia patiently waited for the laughter to die down before speaking.

'I think you're absolutely right cousin; our situation does warrant drastic action. As far as I can see, there is no other way. Not only does this plan ensure that in less than twenty years Britannia has a new generation of strong young legionaries, it will also lure many, if not most, of our best men back to their home where they know they have a family waiting for them.'

'More than that,' said Ursula. 'If, for whatever reason, the men fail to return, the mothers, being the highly-trained and capable women that they are, will ensure that our young stock of legionaries receives the best of training.'

While the others began to talk excitedly about the prospect of training young sons in the arts of soldiery and the crafts of war, Pinnosa moved away from the group and stared thoughtfully out to sea. After a while, she took Ursula aside and spoke to her quietly.

'It's a good plan, one of your better ideas I have to say, though I'd like to make one minor adjustment.'

'What's that?' asked Ursula.

'You have your Constans, Cordula has her Morgan and almost everyone here has her mind on some handsome officer who is currently serving far from home, but I really can't think of any particular fine young man I would care to marry and bear the child of, and—well, let's just say you're not the only one prone to having good ideas in this special place.'

Before Ursula could do anything, Pinnosa span round and clapped her hands for attention. The others fell silent and turned to look at her.

'I wholeheartedly support this bold venture, and I solemnly swear that I will play my part to the best of my ability; but I hereby exempt myself from any marriage or childbearing. This will enable me stay in active command and maintain the readiness of the First and Second Athena's while you're all busy with your new families, making your new homes and rearing your young legionaries.'

'*I'll second that Pinnosa; and I'll be joining you!*'

Brittola's raised voice came from the old altar. She was holding her cross out in front of her and staring at them wildly, as if warding off something evil.

'You're all talking about marriage as if you were breeding horses … "making a new generation of high-quality leaders and fighters" "all getting pregnant at the same time" "restocking our army". May I remind you that marriage is a holy estate; the blessed union of a man and a woman in their service to God? True marriages are built upon love, not-not breeding potential!'

She lowered her eyes and the cross, her anger spent.

'I will go with you on this desperate mission because I am one of you, I am proud of you and I love you all as if you were my sisters. But I cannot, and I will not, take part in this … this cattle market marriage.'

The women all stood still, staring at her in silence as an evening breeze lifted their hair and ruffled their cloaks.

'There's something else … '

Brittola looked back up and fixed her gaze upon Ursula.

137

'You say you don't know why this place makes you have these special ideas of yours. Well I do know why … '

She knelt down in front of the altar and began to pray.

'Dear Lord and Merciful God. You have chosen this holy place to seal our fate. You have shown us how it is through Ursula that you exert your will, and through her that you reveal to us our true mission in this life. We will follow your bidding, oh Lord, and succumb to your will. We will obey your wishes with true love and devotion, though we know not yet where our mission, your mission, is leading us.'

She began to sing an old Christian hymn they all knew from their childhoods called 'Praise the Lord'. One by one, the others joined in and by the end of the first verse they were all singing at the top of their voices.

Chapter Four

THE STORM

I

It was a year later and the banks of the river Tamesis were crowded with training detachments. Some cavalry units were practising river crossings; one group was in midstream battling against the current while another was galloping along the river's shoreline in formation. In the shallows, women were discarding their uniforms and learning to swim, wearing just their tunics. All three of the training galleys were in use with several crews lined up on a nearby jetty awaiting their turn.

Overlooking the scene was a vantage point where the Londinium Road passed alongside the banks of the Tamesis and it was here that Ursula had brought Swift to a halt in order to allow the others to catch up.

Swift had enjoyed being given full rein on the ride upriver from Londinium and, as a result, Ursula had left Pinnosa and Julia, as well as their cavalry escort, far behind. She needed to wait for the others to re-join her so they could complete their urgent ride together as one troupe, thereby making just one crossing on the large horse-carrying barge to Holy Island.

Holy Island was a large island in the middle of the Tamesis where the Athenas had made their new base. Just a day's journey upstream from Londinium, it was called "Holy Island" because it had a pool in its centre renowned for its healing properties beside which stood an ancient Druid temple dedicated to the Lady of the Lake; and it was an important place of pagan pilgrimage and worship, drawing folk from all over the province; something that Brittola heartily disapproved of.

Being an island, it was the perfect place for the Athenas to use, providing natural protection from the kind of unwanted attention that large numbers of healthy young women inevitably attracted; and the fact that it was so well-known made it an ideal assembly point for the seemingly never-ending stream of volunteers arriving daily from every corner of Britannia.

It had not been women from far afield, however, who had caused the most dramatic increase in the legions' numbers. The constant comings and goings in and out of Londinium of the various cohorts and their commanders had finally roused the interest of the people of the province's capital, and one day in late-April just before Beltane, the festival to mark the beginning of summer, at the break of dawn, the lookouts on Holy Island had rushed to fetch the officers to witness an extraordinary sight.

Both banks of the Tamesis, as far as they could see in either direction, had been flanked with women, all standing silent and still in their new Londinium livery, bright orange with a blue and white trim. They were led by a group of young noblewomen from the capital's merchant aristocracy and they were five thousand in number, including a cavalry contingent over a thousand strong.

Just then, one of the training galleys splashed past with its oars in chaotic disarray. It was full of frantic shouts from the trainer accompanied by the strained grunts and groans from the crew in reply. Because they were below deck, their voices echoed in the vessel's bowels, becoming amplified and distorted, and sounding from the outside like the honking of a goose followed by some braying donkeys in a barrel. Immediately below Ursula, a group of new recruits were on the riverbank drying themselves down after their swim and the sounds coming from the galley caused them to have fits of giggles.

She smiled at the comical scene but the smile quickly faded as her mind returned to the vexing issue that was troubling her. Earlier that day in the Imperial Palace in Londinium, they had received an extremely worrying report from Faustina. They knew they had to do something about the very serious situation unfolding in Lindum, but what precisely?

Deonotus, Aurelius and Regulus' initial reaction to the idea of a Great Expedition and the Wedding of the Legions had been swift and unanimous; a firm and unequivocal 'No!'. But gradually, over the course of a long cold winter, after listening to their daughters' relentless badgering, their resolve had weakened and early in AD 409 the three provincial kings had reluctantly agreed to convene a special meeting to discuss the matter.

The meeting was due to be held in Lindum immediately prior to their regular visit to the governor in Londinium to mark Alban Eiler, the spring equinox. However, even as Deonotus' and Aurelius' entourages were wending their way through the gentle Lindum vales and converging on the city, grave news reached Regulus of a dramatic turn of events on the Continent.

An urgent dispatch from Constantine told of how he'd been forced to abandon his mission to help Honorius in Italia because his army had been too small to tackle the huge roving horde of Goths led by the treacherous Alaric; and he'd not been able to make his numbers up with local legionaries as he'd been greeted with nothing but hostile suspicion from the moment he'd crossed the Alps. While he'd been in Italia, however, he'd unearthed yet another devious plot by the old schemer Stilicho, involving the governors of both Britannia and Hispania who, it transpired, had long been in league with him.

The following day, instead of heading to Londinium in ornate procession along with their entourages to try and persuade the governor to finance a larger women's legion, the kings had been forced to set forth on war horses accompanied by a large cavalry contingent composed of the Corinium, Eboracum and Lindum royal guards to depose and arrest him.

When they'd arrived in Londinium it came as little surprise to discover that the governor and his court had fled, taking with him the imperial guard as well as the entire contents of the treasury. Fortunately, the kings had suspected something like this might happen and as a precaution had kept payments to the Roman coffers to a minimum. As a result, well over three-quarters of Britannia's wealth remained in the province, safe in the keeps of Corinium, Eboracum and Lindum.

The kings had then taken the decision to remain in Londinium throughout AD 409 so that they could work more closely together. This had helped Constantine's cause immensely by making communications between Arelate and Britannia much easier which meant he was able to devote his best messengers to maintaining essential links with Constans across the mountains in northern Hispania, a task fraught with treachery, danger and death at every turn … and a task that Morgan excelled at.

With the corrupt governor out of the way and good communication firmly established with Constantine, the kings had determined the time was right for Ursula's ambitious plans to be enacted; and in June of AD 409, on the eve of Alban Heruin, the summer solstice, they had issued a rapid series of royal proclamations to be read aloud in forums and basilicas the length and breadth of Britannia, as well as across the Oceanus Britannicus in the neighbouring provinces on the Continent.

The first had announced the Great Expedition of the First Athena across Gallia to join the Britannic Emperor Constantine in Arelate; the second had announced the Wedding of the Legions which Constantine himself would officiate over; the third had announced the creation of the Second Athena to defend Britannia while the First were away; and the final one had proclaimed that the official base of both the First and the Second Athena's would henceforth be at Holy Island on the Tamesis.

The whole province had been full of excitement at such important announcements, and as the various units of the First Athena had converged on Holy Island, they'd sometimes been mobbed in the street by supporters and admirers, particularly if one of the renowned commanders had been present such as the formidable Pinnosa or the extravert and entertaining Martha and Saula. The greatest excitement, however, had been generated whenever one of the royal commanders-in-chief was on the move; whether it was Faustina, Julia or Ursula herself.

The entire province had gotten behind the Athenas and Ursula's plans worked well. The legion successfully relocated without any significant disruption to their frontier patrols on the west coast or along the Wall, and the enrolment of fresh recruits surpassed expectations both of single women for the First Athena and married women for the Second.

But then, barely a month after the move to Holy Island was complete, a dramatic development had changed everything … a large Saxon invasion of the east coast, the biggest yet.

Ursula and her fellow commanders already knew what a formidable foe they faced in these Saxon raiders, having dealt with a number of their incursions the previous year. Physically,

142

they were of a larger build than most Hibernians or Picts, and were also more fearsome fighters, being better equipped with superior shields and weaponry as well as having greater skill in the use of both. More importantly, they were led by chiefs who, having served in Roman armies as auxiliaries, knew how to fight in formation and use tactics. Even with the reinforcements from Corinium and Eboracum, Faustina's women had still been hard-pressed to defeat them and send them back across the Oceanus Germanicus ... minus their thumbs.

Ursula had been in the Imperial Palace in Londinium with Pinnosa and Julia when Faustina's urgent message had arrived from Lindum. Her report told of fresh Saxon raids at several points along the east coast, involving many dozens of sea-going vessels and thousands of men. Faustina's women had found themselves outnumbered, overstretched and badly in need of urgent assistance.

Whereas the previous year, the total number of Saxon raiders throughout the campaign season as a whole had barely exceeded a thousand; this year, it appeared that well over two thousand were ashore already and still more were landing.

More worryingly, the Saxons had brought with them cavalry units for the first time; and there had also been a detail mentioned at the end of the report which had particularly irked Ursula and given her cause to worry. Apparently, these new raiders were crying out a challenge in both Latin and Britannic for the 'feeble thumb-stealing women' to come out and fight.

'I've been thinking things through,' said Ursula as Pinnosa drew up beside her on Artemis accompanied by Julia on her fine grey mare Amethyst. 'We have no choice; we must send as many of our best and most experienced cavalry to Lindum as we can spare, and do so as quickly as possible.'

'I agree,' said Pinnosa. 'It has to be the entire cavalry division from both the Corinium and Eboracum cohorts. To send anything less than that will not be sufficient.'

'But surely they're needed in the Rainbow Mountains, and along the Wall,' said Julia with alarm.

'Not if we activate the Second and send them to relieve the First,' replied Ursula.

'The Second? Are you sure? Do you think they are ready?' said Julia.

'They're as ready as we were two years ago,' said Pinnosa with a wry smile.

Julia hesitated, then slowly nodded in agreement.

'Good,' said Ursula. 'That's settled. As soon as we get back to camp, we can start making preparations. I want both contingents of the Second on the march soon after dawn.'

She looked pointedly at Pinnosa.

'While Julia and I are getting the Second ready, I want you to round up all the experienced cavalrywomen, including Baetica and Martha and the rest of the trainers, and set off for Lindum straight away; don't wait till dawn. Faustina needs reinforcements urgently, the best we can spare as quickly as possible.'

'Take care, Pinnosa,' said Julia. 'Even with Faustina's chariots and cavalry you still won't have enough women to match two thousand Saxons hell-bent on a fight.'

'The numbers don't bother me,' said Pinnosa. 'We'll whittle away at them whenever they break off into smaller groups.'

'*No!*' Ursula gave Pinnosa a fierce look. 'I *don't* want you to engage them in a fight until Julia and I arrive—and *that's* an order! Limit yourself to monitoring their whereabouts and evacuating any settlements that lie in their path. We don't need any 'heroic' skirmishes which might incur heavy losses. I want you, Faustina and the First Athena intact for the expedition. You are to *wait* until Julia and I arrive—is that fully understood?'

'Yes, Ma'am!' Pinnosa saluted with an exaggerated flourish.

'I mean it Pinnosa—no adventures!'

'Don't worry. We'll play it safe until the pair of you arrive.' Pinnosa smiled. 'Which of you will make it to Lindum first, do you think?'

Before Ursula or Julia could reply, horns sounded and their cavalry escort came into view. All three commanders hauled their mounts round and set off at full gallop, resuming their urgent ride to Holy Island.

II

Pinnosa did as ordered and avoided any confrontations with the Saxons, despite considerable provocation. Whenever the Saxons spotted a unit of the First Athena, their horsemen would leap on their mounts and give chase, all the while emitting terrifying war cries and shouting out the names of the commanders, especially the head of the cavalry.

'*Pinnosa Blood Hair!*' they would shriek in crude Britannic at the top of their voices. '*We want Pinnosa blood!*'

Fortunately, the women had one great advantage over their enemy; their horses were better bred, making them both bigger and faster, and whenever the enemy gave chase, they could easily lose them.

The Saxons were in three main groups, one large and two small, and were systematically working their way through the area between the Great North Road and the Fosse Way which was home to countless tiny hamlets, many with pottery kilns or metalworking pits. This made the women's task of evacuating the local inhabitants extremely difficult. Even though Pinnosa's units were doing their best, dozens were being attacked, robbed and slaughtered daily.

The trail of blood and devastation left by the invaders was so horrific, Ursula decided to act as soon as she arrived with the women from Corinium and not wait for Julia with the women form Eboracum who were still a full two days' march away.

Around noon the following day, at a point on the Great North Road an hour's ride south of Lindum, Ursula and Faustina's units finally converged, forming a force that was large enough to take on the Saxons. They knew from Faustina's scouts that the main group of raiders was only a few miles away, ransacking a small town called Causennae which, fortunately, had been evacuated by one of Pinnosa's patrols the previous evening.

While the officers from the newly-converged cohorts were hastily erecting a field camp tent and laying out maps, Pinnosa and Ursula took Brittola to one side. She looked at them questioningly and, following a nod from Ursula, it was Pinnosa who spoke first.

'Listen to me carefully, Brittola. We're about to have our first proper encounter with these Saxons and there's something very important that you need to understand. They are far more dangerous than the Hibernians or Picts and we have no choice other than to put the women's safety first. You know what that means don't you?'

'Of course,' said Brittola. 'We aim to kill.'

'You understand, don't you Brittola?' added Ursula. 'We have to keep the First Athena intact for the Great Expedition.'

'Do you take me for an idiot?' she snapped. 'These Saxons are the most dangerous beasts on God's earth! An arrow or a spear through the foot wouldn't be enough to stop one of them from breaking a woman's neck!'

The three old friends shared a smile, then Pinnosa turned to address the rest of the officers which included Faustina, Martha and Cordula, but not Saula who was with Julia and the Eboracum cohort.

'Ladies; we have an extremely serious problem on our hands. The tactics we've used up till now simply won't work against these Saxons. Even though we have superior numbers, an attack in close quarters is out of the question; much as I hate to admit it, we wouldn't stand a chance, they'd tear us to pieces. Worse still, there are about three hundred of them on horseback. We need to devise a new strategy.' She looked questioningly around the gathering, one by one. 'Any ideas?'

'If only there was a way to shower them in a rain of arrows,' said Cordula. 'But how could we do that? How could we get them to line up for us in the open … down field and an easy target?'

'I know just the place!' exclaimed Faustina, stepping forward. 'Not far from here is the river Witham. If we lure them down into the valley, there's a point below a long ridge where the woods open out into a huge meadow. It's the ideal place for an ambush; we could hide whole cohorts of archers in the trees; they would be completely invisible.'

'*HA!*' Pinnosa gave the tent pole a hefty slap with her hand, making the tent wobble. 'That sounds perfect! And I know exactly how we could lay the bait … '

While the commanders were busy formulating their plans, the skies grew ominously dark and it started to rain, and by the time the women set off to hunt down the raiders the rain had turned into a torrential downpour.

Nevertheless, despite the terrible weather, the early stages of the operation all went according to plan. Pinnosa's "bait" – a 'dummy' cavalry patrol, consisting of their most fleet-footed horses, including Artemis, Swift and Feather as well as Martha and Cordula's mounts – deliberately broke cover in a clearing west of Causennae, making themselves visible to the Saxons. As soon as the invaders saw the women, their horsemen rushed for their horses shouting *"Pinnosa Blood Hair!"*; and the chase was on.

With their knowledge of the area, Pinnosa and two of Faustina's officers led the others, opening a lead over the rest of the women who followed in a tight pack two or three abreast. Then, about half a mile behind and galloping as fast their horses could manage, came over a hundred Saxons, yelling war cries at the top of their voices.

After a short chase at full gallop through some dense forest, leaping over fallen logs and bursting through clearings with woodcutter huts, they finally crested a ridge and headed downward through some dense thicket into the Witham Valley where, sure enough as Faustina had said, the woodland suddenly gave way to a long broad area of open meadow.

Even through the driving rain, Ursula and the others were quick to spot two broken boughs arranged in a cross which was the marker indicating where the archers were lying in wait. The bait had worked and the trap was about to be sprung.

At that moment, a scouting party of a dozen Saxons on horseback emerged from the trees at the far end of the open meadow directly up ahead. They spotted the Roman cavalry galloping directly for them at the same time as the women saw them; and without hesitation, issuing loud piercing war cries, they drew their weapons and charged.

Ursula immediately saw the dilemma facing Faustina and her women who were hiding in the trees. If they let fly a volley of arrows to fend off the scouting party, the main force of Saxons following behind would be alerted to the trap. There was nothing she or anyone else could do to avert the inevitable hand-to-hand clash that the scouts were intent upon, especially as they had now seen the rest of their cavalry in the distance, emerging from the woods at the base of the ridge.

'*Dear God, we're caught in our own trap!*' she cried out as the pouring rain lashing her face. '*What are we going to do?*'

The answer to her question unfolded before her, filling her rain-drenched vision like a living nightmare.

Upon recognising Pinnosa, the scouts began to bellow out their taunting battle cries.

'*Pinnosa Blood Hair!*'

'*We want Pinnosa blood!*'

Pinnosa and the two Lindum officers were now well-ahead of the rest of the women and halfway between the two groups, having pushed Feather hard, was Brittola, riding all on her own. Ursula, Martha and Cordula were far behind both of their old friends, riding in amongst the main group of women and, despite being at full gallop, they were several crucial moments away from being able to help them.

As she watched, she saw the Saxons converge on the three lead riders; and she could hear their maniacal yells as they charged. Both of Faustina's officers fell as soon as the Saxons attacked, though one of them did manage to drag her attacker down with her. Their riderless horses then whinnied and ran away, leaving Pinnosa and Artemis completely exposed.

Matching the yells of the men with her own great war cry, Pinnosa discarded her shield and drew both her swords just as two of the Saxons came at her at once, one on each side. She clashed swords with the one on her right, but as she did so, the other managed to duck beneath her wide sideswipes and hack at her thigh with his blade, opening up a long and gaping wound. She arched in pain and her long sword slipped from her grasp. At that moment, a third raider wielding a broad axe rode up behind her and dealt her a vicious blow in the middle of her back which knocked her off Artemis. She fell to the ground where she lay on her side, crumpled in a heap and completely motionless.

It was then that Brittola arrived.

Screaming in wild fury and leaping from Feather, she rushed to Pinnosa's side and, staving off enemy blows with her shield, did whatever she could to prevent her fallen friend from being slashed by the Saxon blades. Sensing her mistress' danger, Artemis too joined the fray, kicking ferociously at the Saxons with her hind legs. Feather did the same; and if it hadn't been for the two horses' combined frenzy, those few fateful seconds would have seen both women cut to pieces.

For the longest of tortuous moments, all Ursula and the others could do was look on helplessly through the torrential rain as Brittola took blow upon blow upon her shield, desperately protecting Pinnosa, but then—

—they were upon the mêlée!

'*Martha! Cordula! Grab Artemis and Feather!*' shouted Ursula over her shoulder. '*The rest of you keep going! Don't fight and don't stop!*'

Most of the Saxon scouts had veered to one side and were readying themselves to attack the main body of women, but their leader was still harassing Brittola along with Artemis and Feather. Ursula didn't hesitate and went straight for him. He saw her coming and spun round so that he could slash at her with his long sword. She brought her sword up in defence and somehow managed to deflect his blade away. As the weapons clashed, her arm was badly jarred; she felt her grip weaken and knew at once that she wouldn't be capable of deflecting another heavy blow. He swerved his horse around and raised his sword for a second strike, aiming for her thigh as he had done with Pinnosa. Just at that moment, Swift neighed loudly and sank her teeth deep into his horse's neck. His mount reared and, with blood streaming from its wound, veered away out of control.

Ursula leapt down to join Brittola by Pinnosa's side. The rest of the women had already ridden past; and now the war cries of the main group of Saxons could be heard rapidly approaching. Pinnosa was bleeding badly and barely conscious. She managed to raise her rain-soaked head and saw that, despite Martha's best efforts, Artemis was refusing to budge. With her last vestige of strength, she managed to raise her arm and wave the great mare away, crying out '*Go away! Shoo!*'; then she glanced at Ursula and added 'you too' before losing consciousness.

Ursula knew there was only one thing they could do with the Saxons almost upon them.

'*Brittola! Get up onto Swift quick!*'

'*But what about Pinnosa?*'

'*Do as I say—NOW!*'

Brittola obeyed and climbed up onto Swift. Ursula laid her shield over Pinnosa to protect her from the arrows that were about to fill the air, but then stared aghast because her legs were still exposed; and now the Saxon cavalry were just strides away. Looking desperately around, Ursula spotted the tattered remains of Brittola's shied lying nearby and just beyond it was Pinnosa's still intact. She dived for the good shield, grabbed it and laid it over Pinnosa's legs; then she hauled herself up onto Swift behind Brittola, took the reins and urged the great mare to fly.

The Saxons were only a few lengths from galloping over Pinnosa, when the relentless pelting rain became thick with a barrage of sharp, pointed and deadly missiles.

Pinnosa did not need the shields after all. The First Athena had trained well; all their arrows found their mark in the midst of the enemy pack and not one raider came close to the legion's seriously wounded commander-in-chief.

III

'It's too soon to tell,' said Ursula, dabbing a wet cloth gently on Pinnosa's brow, 'but she should pull through.'

Thanks to her rain-sodden woollen cloak, the axe wound on Pinnosa's back was mostly bruising; the actual cut was only skin deep. The gash in her leg was a much more serious matter; though long and deep, the cut was clean and the palace surgeon didn't want to amputate the limb. The main problem, however, was not her wounds, but the terrible fever that had gripped her while she was being transported to Lindum. The surgeon had stayed by her side, administering various medicines and tonics, but the fever had stubbornly refused to abate. Eventually, he'd been forced to attend to other patients and leave Pinnosa in the care of her friends. As he'd departed, he implored them to find a way to make her drink if they wanted to be sure she would make it through the night.

Ursula turned to face the others who were sitting in a row on the opposite bed in the officers' hospital, looking on anxiously.

'Please go all of you; it's getting late. There's nothing more any of you can do here. Go and tend to your own needs; I'll stay with her for now.'

'B-b-but Ursula— ' said Brittola, shivering badly. They were all still wearing their rain-soaked uniforms, the rain having persisted relentlessly ever since their defeat of the Saxons and return to Lindum. Only Ursula was warm and dry, having been tended to and wrapped in a clean toga by Oleander the moment she'd entered the palace.

'That's an *order* Brittola,' snapped Ursula. 'Now *go!* Get out of those wet clothes, have a hot bath and sleep.'

Reluctantly, her old friends obeyed her and rose wearily to their feet. As they made their way to the door, Ursula thought of something.

'Cordula? Could you come and relieve me at midnight?'

'Of course,' Cordula smiled then ushered the others out. 'Come on everyone. We won't be any use to Pinnosa if we fall ill too?'

Brittola was the last to depart.

'Don't let her die Ursula, please don't let her die. You won't let her die, will you?'

Ursula gave her a reassuring look and mouthed an emphatic '*Go!*'

Brittola left, closing the door behind her; but then, her voice came back from the corridor outside loud and clear.

'*Get well Pinnosa! God is with you! He won't let you die; you still have plenty of work to do!*'

Ursula smiled to herself as she heard the others 'shush' Brittola quiet and lead her away. Within moments, the small chamber was quiet with only the occasional murmur from the delirious wounded commander interrupting the gentle hiss of the oil lamps. She reached for the beaker of spiced medicinal wine that the doctor had prepared and lifted Pinnosa's head to make her drink. The thick brown fluid went in between her lips, but she was still too unconscious to swallow, so it trickled out of her mouth and down her neck. Ursula dabbed it off with a cloth then

151

tried again … and again … and again; then, at her fifth attempt she lost her patience.

'*Drink woman, drink! For goodness' sake drink!*'

Yet still the wine wouldn't go down.

She grabbed Pinnosa's hands and started rubbing them hard, desperately trying to break the fever and bring her friend back from the brink.

'Come on Pinnosa, I know you can hear me. Wake up!'

There was no response, so she slapped her across the face.

'In God's name—*wake up woman!*'

She slapped her again harder and then pulled her forward so that she could speak into her ear.

'Pinnosa, I know you can hear me. You have got to wake up and take some drink otherwise … ' She gripped her shoulders and shook her. ' … otherwise—*oh, damn you!*'

She flung Pinnosa back onto the bunk, stood up and glared at her. Pinnosa's head had flopped to her side, and she was barely breathing. She started pacing up and down, wringing her hands in torment and looking wildly about in frustration. After a while, she forced herself to calm down, returned to her stool by the bedside and sat down. She picked up the beaker of medicinal wine and dunked a cloth into it, then forced the dripping cloth in between Pinnosa's lips.

'Come on, old friend,' she said gently. 'It's Ursula here. The others have gone; it's just you and me; and I know you can hear me. You've got to fight this fever as if it were a Hibernian raider. You *must* fight it … please … *ple-eee-ease* … '

Still there was no response. Becoming exasperated, she stood up and once more began pacing the room.

'Dear God! What *is* this life we're leading? Oh, yes; it's an adventurous one, that's for sure, but every bold step we take forward towards achieving victory over our enemies seems to be a step away from the very thing we're fighting for, further away from home.'

She turned to look back at Pinnosa.

'And where is *your* home my friend? The only true home you have these days is when you are riding on Artemis;

152

out on patrol, out on campaign.' She looked away. 'And what of my home? Where is that I wonder?'

She went up to the room's tiny slit of a window and looked down the dark street below. It was a cloudy moonless night and there was little to see outside apart from shadows.

'All I know is that my home is in Contans' eyes,' she murmured. 'In his eyes ... wherever they are.'

She rushed back to the bed and grabbed Pinnosa's hands.

'Only in your eyes, I see hope Pinnosa.' Her lips began to quiver. 'Only in your—*oh, Pinnosa; don't die! Ple-eee-ase don't die!*'

She slumped forward onto Pinnosa's lap, sobbing.

'I can't do this without you. *I can't-I can't-I can't!* You are my strength Pinnosa; you are my— '

'Ugh, what a terrible taste.'

Pinnosa's voice was faint and hoarse.

Ursula sat up in amazement; and as she did so, Pinnosa became racked by a dry hacking cough.

'The – *cough, cough, cough* – Saxons. What's – *cough* – happened to the – *cough* – Saxons?'

'Forget the Saxons; we've taken care of them.'

Ursula pulled herself together.

'You concentrate on getting yourself back on your feet and rebuilding your strength.'

She grabbed the beaker and thrust it at Pinnosa.

'Here, sit up and take some of this medicine that the doctor has prepared; it's good for you.'

'Ugh – *cough, cough* – its foul! I'd rather – *cough* – drink Pictish grog than down that – *cough, cough* – witch's brew.'

IV

Despite Ursula's eagerness for the First Athena to embark on its mission to Arelate, circumstances forced them to postpone it till the following spring. Further Saxon invasions prolonged their operations in the east and it took several weeks for the last of the raiders to be rounded up and deported. By the time the legion returned to Holy Island, there wasn't enough of the campaign

153

season left for them to prepare for and carry out such a large scale and elaborate mission. Their extended campaigning in the east also meant that the recruitment and training of the Athenas fell behind schedule. By the end of the summer, the Second was far from up to the necessary numbers and even the First was below strength. Another reason to delay the expedition was that Pinnosa was still recuperating in Lindum; and embarking on such an important mission without her was simply unthinkable.

In addition to these setbacks, they also discovered there weren't enough sea-worthy galleys to transport all the women across the Oceanus Britannicus. Even after recommissioning several old craft that had not been used for years, including an immense hundred-oar vessel that had been moored at Eboracum for as long as Aurelius could remember, the expedition was still five galleys short. This turned out to be a major problem that would take the entire winter to resolve. Firstly, they had to row three galleys all the way round the coast of Britannia from Maridunum in the far west to the crossing point at Dubris in the southeast; and secondly, they had to wait for two new galleys to be completed at Durobrivae on the River Medway.

'I don't know what the bloody world's bleedin' coming to.'

They all laughed at Martha's caricature of an elderly shipwright. It was the evening before Samhain, the festival to mark the end of the harvest, and the senior officers of both Athenas were assembled on Holy Island to hold their final meeting before the legion disbanded for the winter and the different cohorts returned to their home towns.

Martha had just returned from the ship-building yard at Durobrivae and she was recounting an entertaining conversation she'd had with the old craftsman. He'd been tasked with adding a third position to each of the oar benches and she'd met him whilst inspecting the hulls on their slipways. Martha mimicked his rustic southern accent perfectly.

'I thought "womanising" was what the apprentices did on their bleedin' trips to Londinium! I never thought it'd mean changing bloody galley benches so that three wenches—*er* – 'scuse me Mistress – three "ladies" could work the bleedin' oars! I don't know what the world's bleedin' coming to, honestly I don't!' She mimed him hitting himself on the thumb with his mallet. '*Ow!* Bloody shi—'scuse me Mistress – bloody-bleedin' – I hit me bloody-bleedin'— ' She hopped about, feigning pain; and the others laughed.

'I mean to say Mistress,' she continued. 'An army of women includin' women bleedin' commanders! Excuse me Mistress, but what bleedin' next? Women bloody shipwrights? Do you know something Mistress? My Rachel; she wanted to join your bleedin' lot! What's it called? The First Athletic or some bloody thing. Well, I said "No!" didn't I? "You ain't *not* joining no bleedin' army of women! Your place is right here, looking after your poor mother and your three brothers. There's no bloody way you're leaving us to— "'

Three shrill horn blasts from outside the officers' tent interrupted Martha's tale; and all laughter ceased as they rushed to the entrance. There, on the opposite bank of the river and silhouetted against the sunset, was Pinnosa astride Artemis. She blew her horn again, and the huge mare reared in greeting with her hooves punching the air. A rider with a disabled leg could never have stayed on for such a move.

'It looks like the new Corinium cavalry units will have a full winter training schedule after all,' said Ursula with a smile.

V

The winter of AD 409 turned out to be exceptionally mild, and when Morgan arrived in Londinium shortly before Imbolg, the coming of the spring, he was astonished to find it ablaze with crocuses and primroses. There was fresh fish on the street stalls instead of salted, and he even spotted one trader with several brace of lambs for sale at a premium price.

His unexpected arrival coincided with the first assembly in AD 410 of the commanders of the Legions First and Second Athena. As he entered the great hall in the Imperial Palace, he was expecting an audience with just the three provincial kings and a handful of the Londinium merchant nobility. Instead, he was surprised to find himself addressing a much larger group, including; Ursula, Pinnosa, Brittola, Martha, Saula, Julia and

155

Faustina, as well as several other women in full dress uniform whom he did not know … plus, of course, Cordula.

Morgan wasn't the only one to be surprised. It had been over a year since he'd last been in Britannia and in that time his appearance had changed dramatically.

How different he seems, thought Ursula, noticing his weather worn complexion and darkened skin. *Roasted by the hot southern climes no doubt, or perhaps hardened by the gruelling ordeals he has been through. Goodness, there's no boy left in him!* She glanced at her reflection in a nearby plate of polished bronze. *But then I imagine we've all changed a great deal in the past two years, two long, long years. I wonder how Constans has changed? Would I even recognise him? Would he recognise me?*

'The preparations for the Wedding of the Legions are complete.'

Morgan was forced to pause while they all applauded his opening pronouncement.

'Emperor Constantine has asked me to relay his heartfelt and profound support for the Great Expedition, and to make a point of telling the leaders of not "the First Athena" but of "the Women" that "the Men" eagerly await them. Furthermore, he has sent messages throughout all Rome, both East and West, that his son Constans is about to gain a beautiful royal bride and that the house of Constantine the Third will soon be blessed with heirs!'

The accompanying round of applause was meant for Ursula who smiled in acknowledgement.

'It was I who took Constantine's plans and instructions regarding both the expedition and the wedding to Constans at his secret location in northern Hispania,' continued Morgan, 'where he entrusted me with private letter written by him personally and addressed to our empress-to-be.'

He produced a rolled and sealed parchment from his messenger bag and bowed courteously as he handed it to Ursula, before turning to address the gathering once more.

'Constans urged me to tell you all that he and his men are now doubly eager to complete their mission in Hispania so that they can be ready and waiting for their spring brides in Arelate; and he asked me to issue this proclamation:

"What mountains would we men not traverse; what seas would we not cross; what battles would we not fight, to be at one with our heroic Britannic women ... and to know the warm embrace of home?'"

VI

My Dearest Love, I am writing this in haste as Morgan needs to leave soon if he is to take full advantage of the night in order to avoid our pursuers. I cannot give you details of our mission in case this finds itself in the wrong hands. Similarly, I will not discuss the arrangements for our wedding except to say "Have no fear my love, I will be there!"

I am so proud of you and the work you are doing with the valiant women of the First and Second Athenas to safeguard the province whilst we are distracted by this unfortunate messy business. How I envy the Saxons who have the honour of seeing you all in action!

Take care my love, as you embark on these campaigns. Promise me you will not put your personal safety at risk. Allow Pinnosa to lead the assaults; she is far more formidable in the fray than you. What enemy would not quiver at the knees upon witnessing her terrifying onslaught?

I assure you it is the firm resolve of all the men under my command to relieve the Athenas as soon as possible, not only because we wish to be home with our families and friends, but also because of the shame we feel at not being there to protect Britannia ourselves.

Finally, my love, the thought of being with you again, of looking into your eyes, of listening to your voice, is all I live for. Every day that we are apart is a day away from home, and a day wasted.

All the love in my heart,
Constans.

VII

The day for the First Athena to commence its Great Expedition finally arrived. The legions were up to their required numbers

157

and were all fully trained, armed and equipped; in addition, the necessary arrangements and preparations for their expedition were all complete and they were ready to depart.

Morgan had left several days earlier in order to herald their imminent arrival at the various supply depots and camps they would be using, first at the Oceanus Britannicus ports and then from Gesoriacum through the heart of Gallia to Arelate.

The main farewell speeches had been made the night before at an enormous feast held in the Great Hall of the Imperial Palace. Regulus had paid tribute to the brave women of Britannia and their leaders who he declared "served as a beacon of light in the darkness". He'd then praised the women for their courage and the incredible feats they had already accomplished, but then went on to bemoan the state of the province and decry the need for its womenfolk to fight. He'd ended by wishing his daughter and her companions well on their quest.

All the while Regulus had been talking, Aurelius had looked steadfastly ahead, not engaging anyone, not even his daughter Julia, with his eye; and when he'd eventually risen to speak, his manner had been grave and sombre.

'As these fine women – our daughters, sisters, cousins, friends and loved ones – prepare to depart from our shores, we, of course, fill our hearts with hope that their journey is one that will bring them, and us, great, great happiness. But I am afraid, my friends, that I find myself far from jubilant and my heart is heavy with torment. Where you feel hope and jubilation; I can only feel sorrow; and where you rejoice, I … well, I can only lament. I do not lament for our wonderful beautiful women; nor do I lament for this Great Expedition of theirs; but I *do* lament for Rome. I am sorry to have to say it my friends, but our future seems to be getting more bleak by the day. Rome is becoming like a much-cherished fruit tree that is in danger of withering and perishing. If it isn't tended carefully and nurtured, I don't know what will become of it. I tell you my friends, I fear for us in these dark times and I especially fear for our children. Here in Britannia, it's the Saxons doing their best to burn us off the maps. In Gallia and in Germania, our cousins are being chased from their estates and forced to take refuge in their cities; and it is the same throughout the entire Western Empire. We're all becoming the same – from Britannia to Thracia, Germania to Italia – isolated pockets of civilization in a vast, vast sea of endless barbarism … '

Aurelius had been forced to stop, becoming too choked to continue; and in any case, he knew he had already said too much. Deonotus had then risen and gently eased his old friend back into his seat, before turning to face the gathering and deliver the final address.

'My dear friends, I too lament.' He'd paused to look across at Ursula. 'I lament that I cannot embark on this Great Expedition with my wonderful daughter. I lament I am unable to accompany her on a tour through the western provinces which will be at their finest in their colourful Spring robes. I lament that we shan't be sampling the local wine or learning local songs together … visiting new townships … meeting interesting people like that Helvetian minstrel we met in Lutetia once, remember?' He'd looked at her and smiled. 'Care to join me?'

Ursula had spluttered into a giggle and had waved aside his invitation, blushing.

Deonotus had then *tra-la-la'd* a strange but endearing little ditty that had a high-pitched "yodel" at the end of each chorus which made everybody laugh.

'But my true lament my friends is that I shan't be there for my daughter – my one and only, and very special, daughter – on the day that she is to be wed.'

With a tear in her eye, Ursula had stood up, walked around the feast table, taken her father's hands and bent forward to kiss them. He'd then gently wiped her eyes with the sleeve of his toga before finishing his speech.

'I say to you, my daughter, what I said to your husband-to-be on the day of his departure … "Return home. Return home safe and return home soon." But to this I add from the bottom of my heart … "When you do return home, my daughter, be sure to bring your family with you."'

The streets of Londinium were packed with people; tens of thousands wanted to witness the farewell parade of the First Athena in their full dress uniforms. The legion was due to pass through the heart of the city and over the huge bridge which crossed the Tamesis in front of the Imperial Palace. Then they would commence their march along Watling Street, the road that led eastward to the port of Dubris where over eighty galleys awaited them for their crossing of the Oceanus Britannicus.

The river itself was full of craft of all shapes and sizes, each one crammed with onlookers eager to enjoy the spectacle and hoping for a glimpse of the commanders. The main body of the legion was being led on its grand march through the city and departure down Watling Street by Julia, Faustina and Baetica. Ursula, Pinnosa and the other Corinium officers weren't leaving until the following day with the women of the Vanguard in two new galleys that had just arrived from Durobrivae. They were moored immediately in front of the Imperial Palace beside the bridge where they looked magnificent, being draped from prow to stern in streamers of the legion's colours.

As cohort after cohort paraded past, the noise from the crowd was deafening. The air was full of drum rolls as well as the blasts and toots of countless horns, pipes and whistles. The cacophony was so loud, Ursula and the other commanders, who were with the royal assemblage on the steps to the Basilica, were forced to shout in order to be heard. The march past the palace took almost the entire morning, and by the time Julia and Faustina's standards finally came into view, the commanders' arms were aching from saluting so much. Ursula was just saying to Cordula that she couldn't help feeling relieved at the prospect of the parade coming to an end, when the air was suddenly filled with birds and the sound of flapping wings.

Aurelius and Regulus had arranged for huge flocks of homing pigeons and doves to be released from the buildings surrounding the palace in order to give their daughters a grand farewell. The effect was dramatic, causing the frenzied cheers from the crowd to reach new heights, and was also perfectly timed. At the very moment the birds were released, Julia and Faustina entered the square looking splendid in their full-dress uniforms. They completed their formal salute to the royal party and rode past, waving their helmets to the crowd as they went.

Then, as the commanders of the legion headed off down the short street that led to the great bridge over the Tamesis, the Vanguard commanders and the royal ensemble mounted their horses and followed after them. Once they reached the bridge, the royal escort came to a halt and watched as the commanders make their way across. Just as Julia and Faustina reached the centre point of the great bridge's vast span, at a signal from Deonotus, a hundred horns on the roof of the Imperial Palace sounded a fanfare to herald the legion's departure.

When Julia and Faustina reached the far side, they turned to face the city for their final salute, at which point Aurelius gave the signal for another symbolic farewell gesture. On the southern bank of the river, huge packs of hunting hounds, numbering many hundreds – thousands even – were unmuzzled and allowed to howl. The incredible haunting noise reverberated the entire length of the city's waterfront and could even be heard in the Forum.

The legion's departure, however, was not yet over. Unbeknown to the royal party and the Vanguard commanders, Julia and Faustina had also made arrangements for a special farewell gesture of their own.

As they reached the point in Watling Street where they were about to disappear from view, from specially-built pens hidden amongst the trees, hundreds upon hundreds of swans and geese were released in four waves. As each wave took to the skies everyone could plainly see that the birds had been dyed one of the colours of the First Athena; the first wave was blue, the second red, the third green and the fourth orange.

VIII

'Ursula, my dear?'

It was evening and a private farewell feast held by the kings to honour the remaining commanders was about to begin. Ursula was standing alone on a balcony of the Imperial Palace when her father found her. She was looking down at the two newly-completed galleys moored below which, early the next morning, would be taking her and the others to meet up with the rest of the Grand Fleet.

The colours of the sunset made her white toga look almost purple, and her long blonde hair, unbraided and loose for once, fluttered in the fresh spring evening breeze like a pennant.

As she turned to face her father, he could see that she was crying. Out of uniform, she looked like any other young woman in her prime, albeit an extremely beautiful one with an exceptionally strong will, both qualities she'd inherited from her late mother. In the hectic bustle of recent events, the king had seen plenty of his commander-in-chief, but the father had enjoyed precious few moments alone with his daughter.

'What's the matter my dear? Are you nervous?' he said, putting his arm around her.

'Not nervous Father … terrified.' She forced herself to stop crying and wiped her eyes with the sleeve of her toga. 'I'm terrified of what we're attempting and I'm even more terrified of not succeeding; I'm terrified of whatever the Continent has in store for us; but most of all Father, I'm terrified of not seeing you ever again, and of never returning home!' She grabbed his arm. 'What if we suffer the same curse as all the other Britannic armies that have left the safety of these shores never to return?'

The king did not say anything. He returned her hug and clasped her tight, doing his best to keep his own tears in check; then he held her out at arm's length so he could look at her.

'We haven't been completely honest with each other, have we my dear? We have never discussed the real reason why you're doing all this. You're not Pinnosa; you're not the scourge of all barbarians. And deep in your heart you are not undertaking this 'Great Expedition' for the benefit of Britannia.' He paused to lift her chin and look her in the eye. 'You simply want to be with your Constans.'

She tried to quell her quivering lips … and slowly nodded.

'All that you've suffered these past three years, and all the magnificent things you've achieved, it's *all* been because you want to be back in his arms.'

'Oh, Father. Why couldn't I be happy to remain here and be patient like Mother was while you were away? Why couldn't I be content to stay home and wait … and hope?'

'But you *are* like your mother my dear—exactly like her!' He smiled. 'Like you, she had to be active. Like you, she had to be working her destiny and not having it worked for her by circumstance. Oh, she waited for me all right. But at the same time, she worked with Constantine and many others to shore up the kingdom and make sure I had a secure home to come back to. And you? You're just the same. It's only the circumstances that are different. Her fight was to keep her family and her home ... your fight is to *have* them.'

'But surely my home is here with you.'

'No my dear, your home is somewhere far to the south, somewhere deep in southern Gallia or northern Hispania. When you depart tomorrow, you won't be leaving home ... you'll be heading home.'

'*Oh Father!*' she hugged him once more.

'Come now, the others are waiting.'

He gently released her and led her back inside.

'By the way, how is your Latin? Did you have those extra lessons with Bishop Patroclus?'

She laughed.

'Yes, I did, but I'm not sure how much use "Voluntatem Dei iudicare Diaboli es" – "God's Will is for the Devil to judge" – is going to be in getting us safely to Arelate.'

As they left the balcony arm in arm, a strong gust of wind blew through the moorings below. The furled sails of the two galleys rattled against their masts and the pennants of the First Athena flapped frantically like fish feeding in a stream.

IX

The preparations for the Vanguard's departure commenced soon after dawn.

They began with the horses being taken to the galleys from their stables at the rear of the Imperial Palace. In the stern of each vessel below the main deck were special stalls where up to thirty horses or other beasts could be strapped-in and firmly harnessed. Artemis was the first horse to be led across the ramp onto the deck. She had never been on a vessel before and the unfamiliar noises and smells, plus the gentle rocking of the galley, made her nervous. As she was being put on the loading platform, she flattened her ears and began to resist. Swift, who was following directly behind, stretched forward and nuzzled the

163

great black mare on her back which calmed her down enabling the men to get her into the loading hoist and lower her down.

Once the horses and provisions were all onboard, it became time for the junior officers and the first of the rowing crews to board the galley, the former to make a final check of all the supplies and equipment, the latter to settle into position and prepare the oars. Each galley had fifty oars, twenty-five on each side. The new fittings allowed three women per oar which meant that a rowing crew numbered one hundred and fifty. Each galley had two rowing crews which would rotate at hourly intervals.

By now, the Tamesis was bristling with onlookers eager to see the Vanguard depart on their highly-decorated splendid new galleys. Along both banks of the river and across the great bridge, the pressure of the crowd was so great that some people fell into the water; and one or two unlucky ones who could not swim actually drowned. Fortunately, however, the river was full of craft of every description, from the lavish barges of merchants to the simple skiffs of the local fishermen, and most of those falling in were plucked from the water to safety.

With the rowers in position, the rest of the Vanguard now boarded. Their appearance from the guardhouse in full dress uniform roused a great cheer from the crowd. When they took up their ceremonial positions on the decks of the two vessels, their armour and weapons glistened in the morning light, making the crowds cries even louder.

The cheers eventually died down to be replaced by an expectant hush; everyone could sense that the departure of the commanders was imminent. A great fanfare of trumpets sounded from the roof of the Imperial Palace and a contingent of the royal guard on horseback emerged from the guardhouse to keep the crowds back. It was time for the commanders to make their way to the vessels.

The first to appear was Ursula with King Deonotus by her side; she was in her full-dress uniform and he was wearing his formal robes of court. The crowd roared with excitement as they walked to the leading galley, waving as they went. Behind them, unaccompanied, came Pinnosa. She acknowledged the crowd's cheers by unsheathing her long sword and waving it to-and-fro above her head in great sweeping arcs as she strode up to

164

the second galley to take command. Then, escorted by Regulus and Aurelius, came Cordula and Brittola who were joining Ursula on the first galley. Brittola looked highly embarrassed by the enthusiastic send off, especially when her name was being shouted out by the more frenzied of the onlookers.

The crowd now started chanting '*Mar-tha-aaa!*' and '*Sau-la-aaa!*' in anticipation of the appearance of the final pair. The two old friends didn't disappoint; they emerged from the palace gate together and strolled down to Pinnosa's galley arm-in-arm, waving cheerily with big broad smiles. Then, just before they were about to board, Saula pulled out a pipe from under her cloak to accompany Martha as she danced a little jig performed by West Country sailors for good luck before a voyage. When they finished, they bowed to acknowledge the crowd's rapturous applause and marched up the ramp saluting as they went.

Like the departure of the legion the day before, there were no formal speeches, and this time there were no surprise farewell gestures either. The officers on Ursula's galley simply said their final goodbyes to the kings who then returned to the shore. As Deonotus was about to leave, he took his daughter by the hand one last time and kissed her on both cheeks.

'God goes with you my dear. Remember that I shall be praying to him every day for your safe and speedy return.'

She squeezed his hand tight as she returned his kisses.

'Whatever my personal reasons are for doing this Father, remember that we, the First Athena, are doing it for you, and for all Britannia. So, when you pray, pray for us all ... including yourself.'

He smiled, released her hand and walked down the ramp. As he did so, she felt an overpowering surge of fear. It made her tremble and she had to grab the galley rail, close her eyes and take a couple of deep breaths before she could turn around to face her officers and crew.

The instant she saw Cordula and Brittola looking at her expectantly, Ursula felt better. She gave the orders for the ramps to be removed; and, at that very same moment aboard the other galley, Pinnosa did the same.

The broad green sails of the two craft were unfurled, the mooring ropes were untied and the two magnificent vessels, in all their colourful splendour, pulled away from the waterfront to drift serenely out into the main stream of the river. The raucous noise from the shore drowned out the sounds from below decks of orders being shouted, tempo drums being beaten and the oars creaking; or of the women grunts and groans as they heaved on the specially adapted oars and began the arduous task of getting the huge galleys under way.

Meanwhile, on the decks of both craft the commanders, along with the rest of the Vanguard in their ceremonial dress, remained standing to attention. They maintained their formal positions until they were well downstream from the bridge and the great city of Londinium was receding into the distance.

X

With a full wind in their sails they made good speed and by mid-afternoon they were already well into the broad waters of the river's estuary. On Ursula's galley, they had just completed another change of crew when a lookout on the main mast raised the alarm. As soon as Ursula and Cordula reached the prow, they could see for themselves the reason for the alert … pirates were coming at them from the marshlands off the north shore.

Ever since Constantine's departure and the reduction of regular navy patrols, the number of pirate raids along Britannia's trade routes, of which the estuary of the Tamesis was the busiest, had increased dramatically. The north shore in particular was riddled with shallow inlets that were perfect havens for pirates. They used fast-moving flat-bottomed twenty-oar skiffs that could carry a full gang of fighting men plus plenty of plunder; and their primary targets were the fully-laden trading galleys and barges that constantly plied the great river. They weren't usually active until much later in the year when they knew the vessels carried a bountiful cargo after the harvest season which was why Ursula and her crew were taken by surprise.

'Perhaps this is an instance of the First Athena's reputation and renown acting as a bait for trouble,' she said to Cordula as the alarm horn sounded.

She counted ten of the skiffs emerging from behind a long sand bar. As she looked, Ursula noticed a curious feature on the leading skiffs which gave her cause for serious concern.

'Can you see those faint spirals of smoke on the bows of the ones in front?'

'Yes, I can. I wonder what that could be?' said Cordula, shading her eyes and squinting.

'They sometimes use vats of hot bitumen to make fire-arrows which they shoot at their prey in order to instil panic on board and bring the vessel to a halt.'

She spun round and urgently shouted orders.

'*Bring down the sails and remove all flammables from the deck!*'

Then she rushed to the rear of the galley where Brittola was on watch, and sighed with relief when she saw, five hundred cubits to her stern, Pinnosa's crew were doing the same. She also saw that Saula was signalling with semaphore flags while the galley was starting to alter course.

'Pinnosa wants us to hold our course,' said Brittola. 'But she also wants us to slow down and keep our standards flying so that we draw the attack. She's going to veer around on our right then come tight across our bows and meet them head on.'

'Tell her we'll comply.'

'Wait, Saula hasn't finished; she also says, "This – may – not – be – easy",' said Brittola, smiling.

Ursula frowned.

'Tell Saula to limit her messages to those given to her.'

'But she was only— '

'No "buts" Brittola! We're about to go into battle; the only messages to be transmitted are those essential to ensure survival and victory.'

Brittola looked shocked and hurt.

'Now, do as I say; that's an order!'

XI

Pinnosa's galley was barely in position when the pirate skiffs were upon them. As Ursula predicted, the attack began with flaming arrows. Most of the first volley fell short, plummeting into the water and sending up spumes of steam, but one landed on her galley's deck where it crackled and started to sprout flames. The women rushed to put it out using leather buckets which they filled by throwing them over the side on ropes.

The second volley was aimed at the oar deck and several of the burning and hissing balls of fire hit their target, going in through the oar holes and causing consternation to erupt. With so many women panicking and screaming, Ursula was forced to go below to organise the fire crews; and she barely returned on deck in time to witness Pinnosa's counter attack.

To maximise the element of surprise, Pinnosa cut so close across Ursula's bow that the last couple of oars on her left side were snapped off. In an instant she was amongst the pirate skiffs, meeting them head on at full speed; and her prow rammed hard into the leading one with its large vat of steaming bitumen. The collision lifted the crude craft completely out of the water with men tumbling everywhere, before it snapped in two and fragmented into Pinnosa's wake. A handful of them managed to gain a purchase on the galley's oars and tried to scramble up them, but Martha's archers quickly saw to it that none of them succeeded in reaching the sides.

While all eyes were looking forward, a second skiff came around behind Pinnosa's galley completely unseen. The first Pinnosa's women knew of its presence was when a heavy volley of burning arrows suddenly sizzled through the air onto the rear of the deck immediately followed by two grappling hooks which landed with loud clatters and took hold on the galley's rail.

Pinnosa rushed to the stern and, using her shield to protect herself from a rain of arrows, she desperately started hacking at the grappling lines with her sword. She was still trying to cut the second line when another skiff joined the attack. The barrage of missiles intensified and yet another grappling hook landed on the deck.

'*ARCHERS!*' She ducked to avoid another salvo as she shouted. '*Where are you archers? Hell's teeth, get back here and keep me covered!*'

Martha's women raced to the rear and hastily let fly their reply. In the brief respite their volley created, Pinnosa climbed up onto the rail and – with her sword and shield held high – leapt from the galley side and, for a moment, she filled the air like a fearsome warrior of old with her cloak billowing out behind and her red hair blowing wild and free in the wind.

When she landed on the skiff below, she was next to its steaming vat of bitumen and, before any of the pirates could respond, she kicked the cauldron from its mountings, sending a tongue of fire crackling along its entire length. The only way the men could avoid being burnt was to dive into the water.

She then leapt across onto the prow of the second skiff, leaving the first to drift completely abandoned and ablaze. With no vat of bitumen for her to kick over; her only weapon was her sword. Luckily, the narrowness of the skiff's prow meant that the pirates could only come at her one by one. Six times, in between the volleys of arrows from Martha's archers, a lout leapt up and charged at her, yelping a ferocious war cry and brandishing a huge double-bladed axe or a long vicious-looking sword; and six times she was more than a match for her aggressor with her fast reactions and the skill of her sword-strokes.

Eventually, after she had dispatched the sixth lout, their attacks ceased. Sensing the skiff's crew were beaten, she grabbed a grappling hook rope, wrapped it around her arm and leg, and cut it clean though with a swipe of her sword.

The galley was still moving at speed which meant the moment the rope was severed Pinnosa was yanked off the skiff into the water. She stayed under for what seemed an eternity until Martha and several of her archers, heaving with all their might, eventually managed to pull her to the surface, gasping for breath; they then hauled her back on deck complete with all her uniform intact, including her helmet, her heavy sodden cloak and her body armour.

XII

'How could you; how *dare* you! By what right did you think you could put your life in danger like that! Hmm? Well I'll tell you; by *no* right whatsoever! You had absolutely *no* right to attempt such a—such a stupid, stupid, *stupid* stunt! You could've easily been killed for goodness' sake!'

Ursula was pacing up and down at the end of a long wooden jetty on the southern shore of the Tamesis estuary where the two galleys were safely moored. She was alone with Pinnosa; Martha and Brittola were supervising the camp arrangements a few minutes away beside some salt pans, and both Cordula and Saula had taken the early watch on board their respective vessels. The sun had just set and the evening sky was a rich panoply of colours. A strong southerly breeze was making their cloaks flap and causing the chord of the signal flag at the end of the jetty to rattle against its mast. Ursula stopped pacing and turned to face Pinnosa; her hand was clenching the hilt of her sword so tightly her knuckles were white; her face was flushed with rage and her eyes were wild with anger.

'Under normal circumstances an officer of your rank would be decommissioned and thrown out of the legion for such irresponsible behaviour. Putting your crew, and your vessel, at risk like that, not to mention our mission! What in God's name did you think you were doing?'

'"Under normal circumstances"? What "normal circumstances" might they be pray tell?' Pinnosa looked grim; she was fighting hard to contain her own anger. '*No*, let me tell *you* instead! Under "normal circumstances" you and I would be sitting around a fire somewhere in the West Country eating pheasant and drinking warm winter wine; and *not*—repeat *not* leading twenty thousand young women to the farthest reaches of another province in order to get married and become pregnant!'

'You are right; these are *not* normal circumstances, but they are *our* circumstances. We are the commanding officers of our army and, above all else, we are responsible for our women. What you did out there put the *entire* expedition at risk just for the sake of your-your *idiotic* suicidal pursuit of glory!'

Pinnosa lowered her voice and spoke in slow measured tones through gritted teeth.

'As I have explained, even though we were moving at full speed, they somehow managed to come around behind us and attach grappling hooks; we were in grave peril. If just one boatload of those marauders had boarded, we would've suffered severe casualties. What is more, if hand-to-hand combat had started, we would have in all likelihood slowed down, and they

170

would have been upon us like crows on carrion. The moment those first grappling hooks took hold, I could see the danger— '

Pinnosa had to pause. After they'd left the pirates behind, she'd been surprised to find herself shaking, so much so, she'd had to leave Martha in charge and go to the stern of the galley to be on her own. When she resumed her account, her voice was reduced to a muted growl.

'Things were happening fast; I saw a chance to save the situation and I had to take the risk … fortunately, it worked.'

'The trouble with you Pinnosa is you are *obsessed* with following your father,' snapped Ursula sharply, 'even if it means being maimed for life … or worse!'

'And the trouble with *you* Princess Ursula is you are obsessed with following your Constans!' snapped Pinnosa in reply. 'What's more, you are terrified of where you might be leading the women as you do so!'

Stung by each other's words, they both looked away and stared out over the estuary until, eventually, they calmed down.

'Promise me you will never put yourself in such danger again,' said Ursula, still staring at the view. 'You know full well the Great Expedition would have to be called off without you to lead us.'

'I promise,' said Pinnosa. 'In return, I want you to promise not to use my father against me again. It hurts all the more coming from you.'

'I know.'

They turned to face each other and embraced. Even though the hug was a clumsy one with their cloaks getting in the way and their helmet plumage's becoming entangled, they each held the other close and tight. Hug over, they started walking back to the galleys side-by-side.

'We couldn't believe our eyes when we saw you leap from the galley like that.' Ursula nudged Pinnosa teasingly in the ribs. 'Did you forget you can't swim?'

Pinnosa laughed.

'I honestly don't know why Neptune likes the water so much; it's so cold!'

As they returned to their galleys linked arm-in-arm, their backs were turned against the waning colours of the evening sky. Had they been looking, they would have seen a huge bank of black clouds billow up along the western horizon and smother the final remains of the sunset.

XIII

It was Alban Eiler, the vernal equinox, and the Grand Fleet was assembled out in open water just beyond Dubris, the large sea port that formed the main staging point for crossings of the Oceanus Britannicus. The large natural harbour was flanked on either side by tall white cliffs at the top of which were two giant lighthouses, the twin Pharos's of Dubris. Beneath the great cliffs, the fleet waited patiently to be joined by two vessels coming from Rutupiae in the north containing the two commanders-in-chief who would be leading the legion on its crossing of the Oceanus Britannicus, marking the true commencement of the legion's Great Expedition.

Ursula and Pinnosa had finally arrived in Rutupiae the morning before, giving them just enough time to find replacement oars for the ones Pinnosa had lost in the estuary skirmish, and for both galleys to have some hasty repairs made to the damage the pirates had wrought. The work had been completed overnight and, soon after dawn on Alban Eiler itself, they'd been able to set forth and head out into the open sea as planned.

The sky was clear and conditions were perfect for the galleys to make their crossing, the sea was calm and a gentle breeze blew from the southwest. Soon after they rounded the South Foreland where the coastline turned west toward Dubris, the lookouts spotted a host of green sails.

Ursula smiled. The sails had to be those of the Grand Fleet. They were a little further north than she'd expected, but she soon realised why. Looking up, she could see her own sail starting to billow and bulge; the wind was picking up and that must have caused the vessels to drift northward.

The Grand Fleet was an awe-inspiring sight with fifty full-sized war galleys and over thirty lesser supply craft. Even Ursula was astonished when she saw the accumulated mass of vessels that had assembled on the water. As her and Pinnosa's galleys drew closer, the Oceanus Britannicus seemed to fill with craft. Each one was ablaze with the colour of the unit of the First Athena on board with pennants hanging from the masts and shields strapped over the sides plus the cloaks of the women themselves as they stood to attention in rows on the decks formally saluting their commanders-in-chief.

In order to take up their position at the front alongside Julia and Faustina, Ursula and Pinnosa had to take their galleys through the middle of the fleet. As they passed each vessel, its crew with their freshly burnished armour and weapons glistening in the spring sunshine would let out a great cheer and wave their helmets. Ursula stood on the prow of her galley where she could receive and return their salutes with Cordula and Brittola slightly behind her. She was so moved by the reception the women were giving her, she had her own crew cheer in reply and, far to her rear, she could hear Pinnosa's women doing the same.

By far the most impressive sight out on the water that day was Julia's gigantic one-hundred-oar galley. With its extra-large fore-castle and high masts, it dominated the rest of the vessels like a mother hen with her brood. As Ursula's galley approached, the hundreds of women on deck in their rich-red Eboracum uniforms let out a resounding cheer that could be heard throughout the fleet.

Eventually, by mid-morning Ursula and Pinnosa's galleys were in position and, using semaphores, Ursula issued the order for the fleet to manoeuvre into formation in readiness to commence their crossing of Oceanus Britannicus. During the long winter months in Londinium the commanders had spent many hours with two retired admirals meticulously studying every aspect of naval work, including fleet formations. As a result, it only took a brief exchange of messages for Ursula to establish the formation she'd decided to use.

They were to break into four separate flotillas; Ursula and the Corinium galleys were to form a straight line and take the southernmost flank; Pinnosa and the Londinium flotilla with the largest number of galleys were to form two straight lines and take the centre column; and Faustina with the smaller Lindum flotilla were to form the northern line. Julia in her large one hundred-oar vessel was tasked with escorting the supply galleys and would be following behind the rest of the fleet along with the other Eboracum galleys. Because of the mix of vessels in terms of size and speed, they would form a loose cluster rather than attempt to adopt a regimented line or formation.

It was a good plan, certainly one that the old admirals would have approved of, but it took far longer to execute than Ursula had anticipated. Although extricating the Corinium and Lindum galleys and getting them into formation went quite smoothly, when it came to separating the supply galleys from the war ones and getting the Eboracum and Londinium contingents organised things proved to be much more complicated with some galleys having to double back on themselves in order to get into position. There were even a few near misses with supply vessels almost colliding. As a result, the morning was almost over before the Grand Fleet was finally in formation; and it was at that very moment, just as the sun was approaching its zenith, that the weather began to change.

The wind suddenly picked up and switched direction so that it was coming directly from the south. Ursula knew that in such conditions the galleys' sails would be more of a hindrance than a help, so she had her flotilla take theirs down and signalled for the rest of the fleet to do the same. Her galley was already too far away from the other flotillas to signal directly, and the order had to be relayed down to the rear of her line which was still within semaphore range. Within a few minutes she saw the Londinium vessels lowering their sails. She thought she could see the Eboracum vessels doing the same, but she wasn't certain. The Lindum galleys, however, were already too far away for her to see what they were doing.

By now, the sun was partially hidden and some dark clouds had appeared on the southern horizon. More worryingly, the wind was beginning to blow in stronger and stronger gusts.

174

'Might it not be an idea for us to turn about and head for shelter in Rutupiae Bay?' suggested Cordula, sharing an anxious glance with Brittola.

The two of them were on the prow with Ursula who was staring hard at the distant clouds.

'Rutupiae Bay is only— ' began Brittola.

'I know where Rutupiae Bay is, thank you very much. We spent the night there remember?'

Ursula didn't see the hurt on Brittola's face caused by her rebuke; however, Cordula did and she pulled a funny face as Ursula continued.

'We have just taken the entire morning to position ourselves in formation set for Gesoriacum,' She looked up at a bright patch of sky immediately overhead and squinted. 'It's a little after midday now. We'll be there before sunset as long as this wind doesn't become any stronger. It'd take us another hour at least to turn about and Rutupiae Bay is well over two hours' away.' She looked down at the sea below. 'The swell doesn't seem to be getting any heavier. That means these gusts are just isolated ones, and those … ' she pointed at the ominous dark banks of cloud, 'are harmless, full of rain not storms.'

'Well, I don't think it's worth the risk.' Cordula sounded alarmed. 'Those clouds are moving fast. By my reckoning, we'll be under them in about an hour from now. That means we're going to be out in the middle of the Oceanus Britannicus when we find out what sort of clouds they are; and that's the worst possible place to get caught in a storm. I say we turn back.'

'I agree.' Brittola stepped forward, grabbed Ursula' s arm and pointed at the clouds. 'I think there are storms in those clouds, and there's a message in them too. It's a warning from God and he's saying, "Don't come this way, not today."'

'Messages from God are never so simple.'

Ursula freed herself from Brittola's grasp.

'We could head due east for the northern beaches of Gallia?' suggested Cordula. 'They're only four hours away.'

Just then a junior officer approached them and saluted.

'Message received from Lady Pinnosa, Ma'am.'

'Well, don't just stand there woman,' snapped Ursula. 'What does it say?'

'It says – "Why wait for the wind?" – Ma'am.'

'Thank you. That'll be all.'

Ursula glared at Cordula and Brittola.

'You both know full well what it means for us to have reached this point.' She indicated the Britannic shoreline with a nod of her head. 'The people of Britannia are all praying for the First Athena to succeed in its mission. We are the last hope the province has left. I, for one, cannot—*will not* disappoint them; not *now*, not at this crucial stage, by turning our expedition, *their* expedition – the *Great* Expedition – around; just because of a change in the weather!'

She turned abruptly away from them and scowled at the distant clouds, as if defying them to come any closer.

'The next stage of our appointed mission is to head for Gesoriacum, *not* the northern beaches of Gallia. Gesoriacum is waiting for us with barracks and stables all prepared. If we were to land in an area that wasn't expecting us, we would be risking a hostile reception.'

She turned back to face them.

'I know what Pinnosa is saying. She's saying "We know which way we want to go. Why wait for the wind to make up its mind?" My mind is made up; we shall pray that those clouds pose no real threat and we will proceed as planned.'

Both Brittola and Cordula tried to speak but a fierce look from Ursula forced them to stay quiet.

'Brittola, it is time send the signal "Forward".' She span round to stare once more at the clouds. 'And tell them to make good speed.'

'Yes Ma'am.'

XIV

They made reasonable progress for almost two hours, holding formation and putting quite some distance between themselves and the rapidly receding white cliffs. But then, in the middle of the afternoon, they finally met with the billowing banks of thick black clouds and, as they slipped beneath them, they lost sight of the sun and were plunged into semi-darkness with poor visibility.

In the same instant, the wind intensified and fierce squalls of rain began to lash at their vessels. The swell also worsened, causing the galleys to pitch and roll which made it difficult to send signals. The moment conditions deteriorated, Ursula gave orders for all loose objects to be made secure and then had the order relayed throughout the fleet. Unbeknown to her, it was the last of her orders to reach Faustina whose flotilla had already drifted to the very limit of signalling distance.

Things then got even worse as the full fury of the storm was unleashed. The gusts of wind were so strong they could lift a woman off her feet and throw her across the deck and the driving rain rendered visibility so poor Ursula's women could no longer see the other vessels let alone communicate with them. The sea itself became a tumultuous mass of heaving waves that would rise up to monstrous heights before crashing down onto the deck; and in between the waves, great troughs opened up into which the galley would first yaw and then plummet, hitting the bottom with a terrible terrifying judder.

Soon after a particularly large wave had completely drenched the craft, Brittola battled her way back to the Ursula and Cordula after going below to relay one of Ursula's orders. Completely sodden, she clambered up onto the prow with her hair strewn across her face like streaks of seaweed. She was trying to shout something as she crossed the deck of the fore-castle towards the others, but Ursula and Cordula, who were holding the side rail tight, were struggling to hear her over the wind and the driving rain. At that moment, the galley lurched forward and plummeted down into a huge trough.

The violent judder almost jettisoned Cordula over the side and threw Ursula forward onto her knees; yet somehow, they both managed to keep a hold on the rail. Brittola, however, was standing in the centre of the prow with nothing to hold on to. She toppled forward like a skittle and fell flat on her stomach with her arms and legs splayed-out.

Badly winded, she was momentarily unable to move apart from lifting her head to gasp for breath. Ursula was just reaching forward to help her when the next wave – a truly huge and monstrous one – hit the galley side on and very hard.

XV

Ursula coughed and gagged to clear her throat of the seawater she had swallowed. She needed several deep breaths before she could use her voice, and then all she could manage was a hoarse rasping cackle.

'*Help!*' she screeched. '*Someone—please help!*'

She was hanging over the galley side with her right arm and right leg hooked round two of the rail posts; her left arm was wrapped around Brittola's calf, and it was only her grip on the crook of Brittola's leg that was keeping her from plunging into the raging waters below. Worse still, as the galley pitched and rolled, the dangling and unconscious Brittola was being cruelly smashed against the galley's side.

Cordula suddenly appeared leaning over the galley's side. Seeing what happening, she quickly clambered under the rail and reached down as far as she could, but it was of no use; Brittola's other leg was well beyond her reach.

'*Get a grappling hook!*' cried Ursula. '*Hurry, I can't hold her much longer!*'

Cordula hauled herself back up and disappeared.

Ursula was doing her best to keep hold of Brittola's leg, but the violent jolts of the galley were too strong for her and, with horror, she felt her grip beginning to fail.

Just then, Cordula reappeared with two young officers. Once more she dived beneath the rail, this time throwing her whole body over the side while the officers held her legs tightly. She managed to grab Brittola's other ankle with both hands and the moment she had Brittola in her grasp, the officers tried to pull her up. Barely managing to stay on their feet themselves, by heaving with all their might the two women somehow succeeded in hauling both Cordula and Brittola up onto the prow. They then grabbed hold of Ursula and finally all three of the commanders were back on deck.

With help from Cordula and gripping the rail tight, grimacing with pain and gasping for breath, Ursula managed to stand back up. Brittola, however, remained crumpled in a heap, completely unconscious. Ursula was just reaching forward to tend to her when one of the leaders of the rowing crews came struggling along the deck towards them; her face was wide-eyed with fear and terror.

'*Come quick Ma'am!*' she yelled. '*You must come below quick! Emergency! Emergency!*'

'*What is it?*' cried Ursula.

'*The waves are snapping our oars like firewood!*' She urgently beckoned the officers to follow her. '*We've already lost half of them and we can't get the oar holes shut; the sea is pouring in fast!*'

PART TWO

THE CONTINENT

Chapter Five

COLONIA

I

Report to Augustus Constantine III, Emperor of the West and Grand Commander of all its armies, from Princess Ursula, daughter of King Deonotus of Corinium and Commander-in-Chief of the Legions First and Second Athena. Noviomagus on the Rhenus.

Hail Constantine! I regret to inform you that the First Athena will be delayed in its Great Expedition by a minimum of one full month. A powerful storm of savage ferocity caught us in the middle of the Oceanus Britannicus and scattered our fleet to the four winds. It would seem our galleys were driven eastwards and strewn along the coastline of northern Gallia into Batavian waters. By the grace of God, my galley was spared the depths and is still seaworthy ...

II

Ursula opened her sore swollen eyes and found herself looking at a shimmering yellow light. Squinting at its brightness, she could also make out other hues; golds, reds, greens, blues, oranges and purples, all in a swirl like a whirlpool. All of a sudden, it felt as if the swirling, whirling streaks of colour were about to engulf her and a wave of dizziness made her feel nauseous, forcing her to close her eyes again and roll her head forward. The nausea passed and she looked back up desperate to determine the cause of her torment ... then realised it was the golden glow of dawn.

She suddenly became aware of strange sounds wheeling about her on all sides. Her dizziness returned forcing her to close her eyes once more and, as she did so, she realised the sounds were those made by birds ... birds on water.

Apart from the constant quacking of ducks and honking of geese, she could also hear great crested grebes barking their feeding cries as well as the distinctive bleat of oystercatchers. Over all this the flapping beat of multiple wings accompanied by long sibilant splashes signalled the constant arrival and departure of seabirds and waterfowl. Just then, not far away a very loud bird, a swan maybe or possibly a diver bird, began to yelp with alarm. The sudden sharp sound made the other birds go quiet and the nausea-inducing swirl of bird noise subsided.

As her dizziness faded, Ursula opened her eyes, raised her head and looked around at her surroundings. She was alone and seated upright with her back against the rail on a section of the deck adjacent to the prow. The galley appeared to be deserted and, apart from the occasional slight creak, was eerily silent. The only other women she could see were the two lookouts, one to the fore and one astern. They were both fast asleep at their posts and wrapped in heavy woollen blankets.

She looked down and was horrified to see a body had been placed beside her covered in a blanket with its head resting upon her lap. She peeled back the blanket and gasped as she saw a badly swollen head covered with cuts and bruises. The hair was matted and sticky with blood, but she could tell it had once been loose dark curls. It was Brittola!

'Oh, dear God—look at you!'

Ursula touched her friend's forehead and breathed a sigh of relief … she was warm.

'Don't worry Brittola; the storm is over. We're going home soon. Don't worry.'

The storm had raged into the night with giant monstrous waves constantly attacking them on all sides like demons from Hell with a relentless pounding unforgiving savagery.

To keep the galley from sinking, Ursula's women had formed bailing teams, constantly passing leather buckets to-and-fro. All the while, the crew below had bravely persevered with their rowing, using the few oars that remained intact, and others had tended to the panic-stricken horses who were frantically trying to free themselves from their stalls.

Eventually, the winds had weakened and the waves had died down; but even though the seas had abated, Ursula knew they were still in grave peril. Fearing being smashed on rocks in the darkness, no sooner had the galley steadied, she and Cordula had rallied deck crews and set about dragging the anchors both fore and aft, hoping to bring the crippled vessel to rest. The fore anchor had barely been thrown over the side when it took hold, and within moments the aft line had also gone taut.

Ursula suddenly became aware of a great thirst and tried to call for Oleander, but her voice had been shattered by the seawater and shouting of the night before, and the only noise she could utter was a rasping hiss of a whisper. She gently lifted Brittola's head and lowered it onto a piece of blanket that she'd bunched into a pillow. Groaning and wincing with the sudden pain of her wounds, she grabbed hold of the rail above her head and stood up. As she rose to her feet a fresh surge of dizziness and nausea overcame her and she fell back against the rail, gagging and gasping for breath. A fragmented image of the night before came back to her. Oleander had been on deck, bringing extra blankets and … a leather flagon of water.

Ursula looked to her left and there it was tied to the rail. She fumbled with the stopper, fell to her knees and drank, taking slow deliberate draughts and doing her best not to gulp. The cool water soothed her cracked lips and washed the dryness from her parched throat, bringing the sinews of her drained body back to life. Her thirst quenched, she leaned over Brittola and held the flagon to her cut and swollen mouth. She flinched, but did not wake. Ursula then poured some of the water onto a corner of the blanket and gently squeezed the drips onto Brittola's lips. She responded by licking them which made Ursula smile.

'You'll soon be fine Brittola,' she said in a croaky voice. 'A few days' rest and a good bath, and you'll be— '

Her smile faded and she looked up at the sunrise.

'We'll take you home Brittola, so you can recover. Constans and I will take you home.'

Ursula laid the flagon by Brittola's side and carefully stood back up. Still feeling unsteady and having to hold onto the rail tight, she made her way towards the stair that led below. At the head of the steps, huddled in the duty officer's area, she found Cordula wrapped in a blanket and fast asleep.

'First Brittola and now Cordula. Oleander must be here too somewhere.'

She looked out to sea again, but this time in the opposite direction, peering at the western horizon still shrouded in the last vestiges of night.

'The other galleys can't be far away. We'll probably see them once the sun is up.'

With careful deliberate movements, she grabbed a rail and went below. As she descended, she could hear the gentle sound of waves lapping against the hull. Somewhere a floating piece of debris was rhythmically tapping the vessel's side and the eerie sound echoed throughout the craft like a distant bell.

Suddenly, her foot was in water and she shivered as the cold sharp bite of the Oceanus Britannicus in spring sent a chill throughout her body. It was almost dark on the rowing deck; the only source of light was the odd pale beam seeping in through a damaged oar hole. It took a few moments for her eyes to adjust and when they did, she recoiled with shock.

There before her was row upon row of lifeless bodies huddled in groups upon the oar benches. Shrouded in blankets and staring at her with grey faces and hollow sightless eyes, they looked like a sea of the dead. Three of them were right in front of her, their corpse-like faces looking upward with mouths agape as if begging for food. Ursula stared at them, her eyes wide with horror, but then she spotted they were breathing gently. She sighed with relief – they were sleeping, not dead.

'Why are you here in this hell hole? This is no place for young women like you! How old are you? Sixteen? Eighteen perhaps? Why aren't you at home with your families?'

Just then a faint whinny came from the storage area to her rear. Ursula turned and slowly walked over to the raised platform in the stern. The horse in the first stall was Brittola's Feather; the lively young mare was fully awake and clearly pleased to see a familiar person.

'*Swift!*' she called out. 'Where are you Swift?'

Remembering that Swift was with the others, she took another step toward Feather and reached out to grab hold of her, but then she hesitated.

'What others? Where?'

She shook her head to clear her thoughts; then she put her arms around Feather's neck to give her a hug, and Feather responded by nuzzling her in reply. It was only then she noticed the cuts and grazes across Feather's flanks which she must have gotten from being thrown against the stall posts.

'Poor Feather. You had a bit of a rough ride, didn't you, poor thing?' Her voice was still croaky. 'Poor, poor Feather.'

'"Poor Feather"?'

Oleander's voice made Ursula jump.

'Beggin' your pardon Mistress, but what about the poor First Athena!'

III

The golden beams of morning sunlight grew ever brighter and warmer as they crept their way along the lower deck and, as they progressed, they shone directly into the women's eyes, causing them to stir. Slowly, one by one, they awoke and eased their stiff aching bodies into action like phantasms rising from their tombs.

Miraculously, not a single woman onboard Ursula's galley had been lost in the storm. Brittola being swept over the side had been the most serious incident and her injuries were by far the worst. Many of the crew had cuts and bruises, including some with head wounds caused by falls or being hit by wild oars but, thankfully, no bones had been broken and no amputations were deemed necessary.

Still in shock, Ursula withdrew to the prow where she spent most of the day in solitude wrapped in a blanket. Her hair hung down her back in matted flat streaks. She stared constantly into the distance with a crazed desperate look – fore then aft, starboard then port – scouring the horizon for signs of the rest of the fleet; only pausing to take the occasional swig of water from a flagon. If anyone dared attempt to approach her, even Oleander or Cordula, she waved them away.

Unable to do anything for her mistress, Oleander turned her attention to the other officers which, first and foremost, meant Brittola who remained unconscious throughout most of the morning, eventually waking just before midday and staying awake long enough to take a few sips of water before falling back to sleep.

With both Ursula and Brittola out of action, it fell to Cordula to organise the crew and set about clearing up the mess left by the storm. Those with minor injuries or too exhausted for duty were detailed as bailing out crews and spent the rest of the morning passing buckets to-and-fro. The rest of the women were divided into three work crews; the first was assigned to getting the vessel's contents and provisions back into order; the second attended to the horses and the other livestock; and the third set about clearing away the debris in the rowing deck and doing what they could to reposition the oars. By mid-morning, it was clear that because many were snapped or, more commonly, had broken mountings, only nineteen oars could actually be made usable again; ten on the port side and nine on the starboard.

The recovery of the women owed much to Oleander. As the storm had loomed the previous day, she'd recalled something her husband, an old sea dog, had taught her; and she'd instructed the other attendants to urgently gather all the perishable and dry goods they could find, wrap them in bundles and secure them fast against the beams of the lower deck's ceiling. As a result, once the storm had passed, the women had dry blankets to wrap in and clothes to change into as well as some food that had not been ruined by seawater.

By early afternoon most of the chores were done and the work crews were so exhausted they were ready to drop. Fighting exhaustion, Cordula somehow found the strength to rally them into completing one more task; hoisting the sail to dry it out. The dead weight of the wet cloth was incredibly heavy and it took several of the able-bodied women, including Cordula herself, to heave it to the top of the mast. Eventually, after a great deal of sweat and toil, as well as much chanting, they managed to haul it into place; and the moment had come for them to see whether it had been damaged by the storm.

The damp stays needed several hefty tugs before they let go but, finally, they did and slowly the sail unfurled. The entire crew then cheered as the great green sheet bellied-out in the wind without so much as the slightest rent or tear.

While they were celebrating, Cordula looked across at Ursula who was still on the prow. She remained as she had been, constantly scouring the distant horizon with a fanatical intensity, seemingly oblivious to events on board.

Many of the crew had noticed the strange behaviour of their commander; indeed, it had become the subject of much mumbling and many a comment had been made behind cupped hands in hushed tones. At one point, Cordula had overheard two young women who were working together on an oar mounting.

'She's only a commander when she wants to be,' the first had whispered. 'When there's glory in the offing.'

'That's right,' her companion had replied with a sneer. 'As soon as there's dirty work to be done, she's just a poor little palace princess after all.'

'*That's enough you two!*' Cordula had deliberately raised her voice so others could hear. 'For such insolence, you can go and clean out the horse muck; and if I hear you making any more comments like that, I'll flog you myself. *Now go!*'

Oleander had spotted Cordula looking with concern at Ursula and after she'd finished dressing-down the two women, she quietly went over to whisper in Cordula's ear.

'Excuse me Mistress. I think I know how we can free Princess Ursula from her torment and bring her back here to us.'

186

IV

'The women are ready for inspection Commander.'

Cordula saluted as three nearby horns blew a short fanfare. Ursula jumped at the sudden sharp sound; then she slowly turned around. There, in full dress uniform, was Cordula flanked by two junior officers. Behind them, lining both sides of the deck, was the rest of the crew, including the wounded. They were all standing to attention in their Corinium blue cloaks with their helmets tucked neatly beneath their right arms and their left hands on their sword hilts; all correct and, as Cordula had said, ready for inspection.

'Your cloak, helmet and sword Commander.'

Cordula held out Ursula's uniform correctly folded and arranged for presentation. For moment, Ursula stared at her with a bemused look as if unsure what to do. Unseen by the women behind her, Cordula smiled, prompting Ursula to give a slight smile in return, before perusing the scene on deck.

'Why is the sail unfurled?' she asked with childlike innocence. 'Are we preparing to go somewhere?'

'It's merely drying Commander,' Cordula thrust the cloak forward. 'Now *please* put on your uniform Ma'am. The women are waiting.'

Ursula bent down and carefully placed her flagon on the deck. She allowed the blanket round her shoulders to fall away, exposing her leather tunic and arm bands; then she closed her eyes and took several slow deliberate breaths. Opening her eyes again, she stood up straight, reached for her sword and fastened it around her waist, adjusting the hilt until it rested firmly and correctly against her hip. Then she took hold of her cloak, shook it open and swung it over her shoulders before fixing the clasp neatly in place. Finally, she took her helmet from Cordula and, as she placed it on her head, she looked her cousin in the eye, leaned forward and mouthed "thank you".

Ursula made a point of checking the women's wounds and dressings rather than their uniforms during her inspection.

Before finishing and moving on down the line, she would hold each woman's gaze and smile. Without exception, every woman smiled back. Midway through the circuit, as she was crossing the deck, Ursula stopped and bent down to check on Brittola who was tucked inside the alcove formed by the bulwark at the top of the steps below.

'How are you doing old friend?' She took Brittola by the hand and smiled.

'I hope to God I don't look as bad as you do,' hissed Brittola in a faint whisper, attempting speech for the first time. She then tried to return Ursula's smile, but her swollen face was too sore.

With the inspection complete, Ursula re-joined Cordula by the galley's main mast. Cordula handed her a chord and gave the signal for the horns to blow another fanfare. Realising what was expected of her, Ursula looked upward, then gave the chord a sharp tug.

From the top of the mast two long brightly-coloured pennants unfurled; the rich deep blue of the Corinium cohort and the white, gold and purple of their royal Commander-in-Chief ... and Empress-to-be.

V

'You look tired.' Ursula and Cordula were by themselves on the prow with Oleander seated nearby. 'Go and have a rest. I'll take over from here.'

It was later in the afternoon, the light was dull and grey due to an overcast sky and Cordula just had briefed Ursula on the state of the galley, the crew and the horses.

'Yes,' replied Cordula wearily. 'I think I will go below. It's been a long day.' She saluted and turned to leave.

'One more thing before you go ... ' Ursula grabbed her cousin's arm. 'I ... I want to—I mean, Brittola and I both owe you our lives; and I—well, what I mean to say is, I owe you an apology. You were right about the storm; it was— '

'You don't owe me anything,' Cordula looked Ursula in the eye and smiled. 'You did your duty … and I did mine.'

Ursula pulled Cordula toward her for a long affectionate hug and, as they separated, she whispered into her ear.

'Thank you for everything.'

Cordula saluted again then clambered down the steps, heading for the quiet of the storeroom and some much-needed sleep. The moment she disappeared from view, Ursula clapped her hands with glee and turned to Oleander with a broad smile upon her face.

'Do you know something Oleander?'

'What Mistress?'

'I am well and truly famished; and I'm sure I'm not the only one.'

'I think you might be right Mistress; I've been hearing quite a few rumbling bellies this afternoon.'

'I think some nice freshly-cooked duck is in order, don't you Oleander?'

'That would be very nice Mistress; and a lovely bit of hot goose would go down a treat too, that is *if* it was available.'

Ursula smiled.

'That settles it. I shall lower the boat and take a hunting party over to those wading grounds over there. While I'm away, sharpen your knives and prepare the cooking pots Oleander … we're going to have a feast!'

The women revelled in their feast, eating their fill of duck and goose as well as the odd swan and heron. Once their bellies were full, they broke into song, singing cheery ditties from home with rousing choruses, mixed with the raucous chants and cries of an army on the march. Then, as the sun was about to set, the better singers among them started singing melancholy ballads about lost loves and homes far away. Suddenly, in the middle of one particularly sorrowful lament the lookout on the stern shouted.

'BOAT AHOY!'

Ursula and her officers rushed to the rear, accompanied by Brittola who had recovered enough to be able to walk with some assistance from Oleander. There, heading straight towards them, was a small rowing boat not dissimilar to the one their hunting party had just used. As it drew close, Ursula's crew let out a great cheer; the occupants were wearing Corinium blue.

VI

'Thank goodness we've found you Commander,' shouted the officer in the rowboat. 'I can't come aboard Ma'am; it will soon be dark and we must get back to our galley.'

Ursula recognised her at once as Viventia from Calleva Atrebatum, one of the Corinium cavalry's more capable leaders.

'We will need your help urgently tomorrow Ma'am; we've run aground on a sand bank about a league-and-a-half away.' She pointed towards the north-east. 'And we've lost our commander, Lollia Similina.'

For a moment, Ursula scrutinised where Viventia was pointing; then she called down to the boat below in reply.

'That is grave news indeed about beloved Lollia. How about the rest of your crew? Are many of the women injured? And your galley; is it seriously damaged?'

'Our mast is down; it was the falling mast that killed the commander. No one else was killed, but many were injured. We lost some of our oars and several more have broken mountings, but we are still seaworthy; if only we could get ourselves off the sandbank. I think it should be possible at high tide.'

'We'll be there first thing tomorrow morning.'

'Thank you, Commander. The others will be greatly encouraged to hear that, especially when they know it's you! Thank goodness you lit your fire; if you hadn't, we would never have known you were here.'

Cordula quickly scoured the north-eastern horizon before turning back to Viventia.

'Why can't we see smoke from your fires?'

190

'Everything's too wet: The crew have made camp on the sandbank. We're trying to get everything dry, but without any fire it's very difficult.'

'You said many were injured. Do you have any who are seriously wounded?' asked Ursula.

'Not really Commander. No amputations thank goodness. Our biggest problem is the cold.'

'Stay where you are for a moment.' Ursula turned to Cordula. 'Do you feel up to it?'

Cordula looked down at the shivering women on the boat below them, then back at her cousin.

'Yes, I do.'

'Good. Take the five best women we have and follow them back to their galley. Be sure to return here at first light though.'

Cordula nodded and set off to round up her crew.

Ursula turned to Oleander.

'I want you to gather all the dry clothes and blankets we can spare as well as any uneaten hot food; then load everything onto the two boats, theirs and ours.'

As Oleander bustled off to obey her mistress, she muttered under her breath.

'Oh, she's back to her old self all right, barking her orders and giving us plenty of work: "fix the fire", "prepare some food", "see to the horses", "do this; do that".'

Ursula overhead the old attendant's mumblings and smiled to herself, then she returned her attention to Viventia.

'We're going to send our boat with you,' she shouted. 'We have some spare provisions you can take.'

'Thank you, Commander; but we must make haste. It will soon be dark.'

'Have no fear; they'll be with you in just a moment. Tell me, have you spotted any signals from other galleys?'

'As we were preparing to come here, one of our lookouts thought she saw a wisp of smoke further north, but we couldn't confirm it; the light was too poor.'

'How about inland? Any signs of civilization?'

'Nothing Commander, not even a sheep.'

Just then, Cordula reappeared along with her crew and they clambered down into their galley's rowboat. Oleander and the other attendants then lowered several brace of cooked birds plus some bundles of clothes and blankets down into the waiting boats. The instant they were loaded, both craft set off with their crews rowing as hard as they could in order to beat the night. As they disappeared into the gathering dusk, Brittola tapped Ursula on the shoulder and spoke into her ear with a hoarse whisper.

'You do realise that if all the other galleys are spread out leagues apart like our two, that means the First Athena could be scattered along hundreds of miles of coastline.'

'Ah, but you're forgetting that we were the southernmost flotilla and we took the brunt of the storm,' replied Ursula, doing her best to sound reassuring. 'I'm sure Pinnosa has managed to rally the others; they're probably moored in a cluster somewhere just up the coast. I wouldn't be surprised if we made contact with them sometime tomorrow.'

VII

The following day, most of the crew were fit for duty; apart from Brittola, only a handful of women were still too weak to work. By the time Cordula returned soon after dawn, the galley was already bustling with activity and a chorus of 'Praise the Lord' could be heard coming from below.

It took Ursula's crew most of the morning to row to the beached galley. It wasn't just the loss of over half their oars that slowed them down; it was also having to proceed slowly in order to avoid running aground themselves. Several times they thought they were in open water and were about to row faster, when the pilot boat's plumb line alerted them to a hidden sandbar which they would then have to circumnavigate. The last such diversion was the most frustrating. They were barely half a mile from the other women who they could hear cheering, when the plumb line struck bottom. This final sandbar was actually the same one the other galley was aground on, and it seemed to be endless. It took Cordula in the pilot boat an hour to find a channel deep enough for them to use, and Ursula's galley had to execute several tight turns in order to follow her. When they eventually broke through into the right channel, they rowed as fast as they could to join their comrades; and as they drew close, the stranded crew greeted them with wild cries of joy.

The bow of the stricken galley was grounded squarely upon a spit of sand, shingle and mud that sloped dramatically downward, leaving the stern in clear water. The tide was already at its zenith, so they lost no time in making preparations for its refloating. Ursula began by manoeuvring her galley into position so the two vessels were stern to stern. Cordula and Viventia in the two small boats, quickly set about connecting the craft with a pair of long ropes, one on each side. When Cordula gave the 'all clear' signal, the women on the spit waded as far as they could into the freezing water, carrying their oars to use as levers and push-poles. As soon as they were in position, on Ursula's order three rapid horn blasts sounded out.

The moment they heard the signal, all of the women – rowers and pushers alike – began to heave as hard as they could. Ursula's rowing crew did their best to build up as much speed as possible before the slack in the ropes was taken up. At the same time, the women in the water pushed and levered with all their might. There was a tremendous jolt as the two ropes pulled tight, bringing Ursula's galley to an abrupt halt and causing the horses in both vessels to whinny with fear. A loud cheer went up from the women in the water because the other galley had moved a little. It had shifted, but not enough; the bow was still stuck fast.

Ursula's second rowing crew took over the oars and hastily rowed their galley back into position for another tug. In order to maximise the rowing distance, Ursula manoeuvred her galley so close the two craft scraped together. She then raised her hand for the horn to give three more short sharp blasts.

The second oar crew was determined to outdo the first; and, with the help of the extra slack Ursula had given them, they succeeded. The resulting jolt, however, was too strong for one of

193

the ropes; it snapped with a loud '*crack*' and the severed ends whipped through the air. One of the ends almost hit some of the crew in the shallows, forcing them to bob down into the bitter cold water like ducks. Meanwhile, the remaining rope served to pull Ursula's galley around to starboard, enabling the women on deck to witness the results of their efforts; and, as they watched, the other galley seemed to take on a life of its own.

Slowly at first, but then building up speed, it began to pivot on its port side. Suddenly, it shifted and the women in the water screamed as they felt the sand and mud moving beneath their feet. Their screams quickly turned to cries of fear as the currents created by the sliding hulk started to suck them under.

Ursula and her crew could only look on helplessly as their comrades struggled to avoid being overcome; and several of them were sucked into the depths as the galley slid sideways off the sandbar. Miraculously, and much to Ursula's relief, one-by-one, they each managed to escape the churn and scramble back to safety exhausted and shivering with cold.

Finally, the huge craft, with a chorus of creaks and groans, broke free from the clutches of the sandbar and drifted sideways out into the deep channel. Once afloat, it rocked to a standstill, and the echoing neighs of the horses in its stern filled the air with an eerie sound like the forlorn wails and cries of a siren in torment.

VIII

'*It's no use!*' shouted Cordula from the pilot boat. '*We have to go about! Make a tight turn to port!*'

Ursula thumped the rail in exasperation and turned to Brittola who was standing beside her on the prow.

'I'm certain we've explored this channel before. I recognise that sandbank.'

'How can you be so sure? They all look alike to me,' replied Brittola.

194

Her voice was back to full strength and the swelling on her face had diminished considerably. It was mid-afternoon of their third day with the other galley and progress was proving to be frustratingly elusive. The pilot boats were doing their best, indeed Cordula and Viventia were becoming quite adept at their task, but the endless maze of channels, sandbanks, shallows and spits was proving to be a seemingly insurmountable obstacle as well as a never-ending nightmare.

Their main problem was navigation. Persistent thick clouds were keeping the sun hidden during the day as well as masking the moon at night along with any pilot stars. To make matters worse, there were no landmarks whatsoever. The vista didn't change from one day to the next; they were totally lost in a seemingly endless landscape of mudflats and sandbars.

After two days, the officers could sense tension and frustration building within the women which was being made worse by the incessant noise of the countless hundreds of birds that surrounded the galleys, driving many of them to the point of distraction, including Ursula herself.

But then, on the morning of their third day, a southerly wind started to blow; it quickly scattered the heavy grey clouds, allowing the sun to shine for the first time in days which lifted everyone's spirits.

'It looks like our prayers have been answered,' said Ursula, giving Brittola a cheery hug. 'What we really need now is to find some sign of land. Just one sheep or a goat would— '

'*BOAT AHOY!*' cried a lookout.

Ursula and Brittola rushed to the stern and there to their rear – heading directly towards them – was the unmistakable sight of a small white sail. It was about three leagues distant and moving rapidly.

'*Full dress uniforms!*' Ursula had to shout her order for it to be heard over the women's cheers. '*Tell the other galley to do the same; and get Cordula and Viventia back on board as a precaution!*'

As soon as she was on deck, Cordula rushed to join Ursula and Brittola in scrutinising the approaching vessel and speculating who the occupants might be. It was a strange-looking craft with not one but two sails, one main and another to the fore. It was moving rapidly and appeared to be big enough for a crew of five or six. It also moved in a curious fashion, appearing to zigzag a great deal. From this evidence, Ursula and the others concluded they were most probably Batavians who were known to inhabit such waters and had built special vessels for use in them. They studied it carefully as it made its final approach and Ursula commented to the others that such a craft might be put to good use in the wetlands south of Lindum.

As the craft drew near, they could see that the crew consisted of a man and two teenage boys who looked to be his sons; and they were wearing attire that Ursula and the others had never seen before. Their white cloaks were shorter than Britannic ones and their clasps were more elongated. On their heads, they wore curious leather skullcaps with a fur trim and side-flaps for their ears. Their garb reinforced Ursula's suspicions that the visitors were indeed Batavians and not from Gallia.

'*Salvete, amici – greetings, friends!*' she cried as they came alongside. '*Pacis amantes sumus – we come in peace!*'

The man shouted his reply in a booming voice that was plain to hear; however, the words he spoke were unintelligible.

'*Sal-ve-te … a-mi-ci,*' she repeated slowly and deliberately. '*We come in peace! We are from Britannia!*'

He repeated his reply equally as deliberately, adding at the end a sentence which seemed to include "Britannia", but his accented was too strong and his message still eluded them.

Ursula and Cordula were still trying to piece together what they thought he might be saying, when he unexpectedly reached for the galley's boarding ladder.

'*GUARDS!*'

At Ursula's command, three women at the top of the rope ladder drew their swords and thrust their shields to the fore. He paused and stared hard at the women as if sizing them up, then he shrugged his shoulders and stepped back into his boat where he grabbed an oar and started pushing at the galley's side.

196

As he moved away, he shouted a new message up to Ursula, this time with an obvious note of annoyance in his voice.

'*Pacis amantes sumus – we come in peace!*' Ursula called out once more. '*But we will not allow unidentified personnel on board. This is a military vessel on a mission!*'

She turned to Cordula in frustration.

'It's no use; he doesn't speak Latin or Britannic. Are there any women on board who speak Batavian?'

'No, I'm sure there aren't.'

'Quickly, send a message to Viventia and ask her,' she ordered. 'I'll do my best to keep him talking.'

While Cordula rushed to the stern, Ursula once more tried to communicate with him, stressing each syllable just in case it was her accent that was causing the problem.

'*Pa-cis a-man-tes su-mus – we come in peace! Ba-ta-vi es? – are you Batavians?*'

He did not reply. It was clear from his manner that he failed to even realise she had asked him a question; furthermore, he was obviously tiring of the situation.

'*We need to get to Gesoriacum, I repeat, Ges-or-i-a-cum. Can you help us navigate out of these*—oh "shallows" … '

Ursula turned and muttered to Brittola, glaring fiercely at the deck in frustration.

'What *is* blasted Latin for "shallows"?'

'I don't think it matters,' replied Brittola, pointing. 'He's leaving.'

Ursula looked up and saw the two teenagers using small paddles to turn the craft around. At the same time, the man was positioning his main sail to catch the breeze.

'*WAIT! Please don't go! We're checking to see whether there's someone on board who can speak Batavian,*' she cried—

—but it was too late.

The craft completed its turn and moved way. As it picked up speed, the man turned to face them and, using hand signals, indicated in no uncertain terms that they should stay where they were, and that he would return.

Ursula grabbed Brittola and hugged her tight.

'He'll be back, he'll be back! I know it—*I know it!*'

She held Brittola out at arm's length and laughed so loud in her jubilation everyone on deck could hear her.

'*Ha-aaa – ha-ha-HA-AAA!* He's gone to fetch someone who can speak Latin.'

IX

... We were rescued from the treacherous sandbanks of the Batavian coast by the good people of a small fishing village called Veere. It was their mayor, Udo, and his two sons who found us and, with the assistance of the village priest, Maxian, he guided us through the endless maze of shallows to the safety of their harbour.

They informed us that their people and other Batavians had encountered more of our galleys out in the shallows and that some of them were still seaworthy. Since then, we have been making good use of the Batavian light craft to relay messages to the other crews. They are to muster here in Noviomagus, which has adequate facilities to repair our damaged fleet, barrack the women and hospitalise our wounded.

Since Noviomagus is the first major military base on the Rhenus after the river's many mouths have converged, it is also a convenient rallying point which should prove easy for the other galley crews to find. Indeed, when we arrived here yesterday, there were already six of our vessels in the harbour waiting for us. From their reports, we have now accounted for twenty-seven galleys, over eight thousand women and approximately three hundred horses.

The death toll from the storm so far is thirty-seven. Among those lost are Lollia Similina, daughter of Titinius Similina of Deva, and Magunna of Luguvalium. We have nearly three hundred serious casualties receiving treatment in hospital. Only seven amputations have been necessary so far and the rest of the wounded should be fit for duty within a fortnight.

Cordula and Brittola are with me, and are well, plus a highly competent officer, Viventia Martius from Calleva Atrebatum. There is no news yet of Julia, Faustina, Pinnosa, Martha or Saula, but we do know that Baetica is safe. Her galley is aground on a sandbar which is connected to land about half a day's march from here. Because she has valuable supplies, she won't abandon it until another vessel comes to relieve her; and I will shortly be sending Cordula and Viventia to accomplish this.

Along with this message, I am also sending a light vessel to Britannia in case any of our fleet was forced back by the storm. I dispatched riders to Gesoriacum to inform them of our situation. It would seem that no further messages are necessary since the Batavians have remarkably efficient communications! Not only was Noviomagus expecting us, Colonia, Mogontiacum and Treveris have all been informed of the arrival and plight of the First Athena; and Colonia has even replied.

I have a brief, and rather curt, message before me from a certain Rusticus who claims to be your good friend. It says that if the "highly esteemed" women of Britannia are unable to endure the prospect of the long and arduous journey to Arelate, they can be assured of an even warmer embrace in Colonia! He sounds like a crude sort and I cannot say I shall be sorry not to accept his offer.

I estimate we need a further three weeks for the First Athena to complete its muster and be ready to recommence the Great Expedition. The Batavians have already promised to replace our lost horses. They have huge stables here and plenty of stock (and yet they tell me the Noviomagus facilities are small compared to those in Colonia!).

Finally, when you relay our news to Constans, please be sure to add that the storm has strengthened our resolve. Once the Great Expedition is resumed, nothing more will prevent the First Athena from fulfilling its duty.

You are both constantly in my prayers,
Ursula.

X

My dearest daughter. It was with great relief that I received your report. For the sake of Aurelius and Regulus, please send more dispatches as soon as either Julia or Faustina are sighted or accounted for.

We first knew of the storm when a messenger arrived from Gesoriacum, telling us that no vessels from the Great Expedition had arrived or been sighted. The moment we received the report, Aurelius, Regulus and I rode in haste to Rutupiae in order to organise the search for galleys, but to no avail. Not one vessel from your fleet has been sighted this side of the Oceanus Britannicus. Regulus, who spent many years on naval patrols in Batavian waters, says the galleys could be scattered as far as the land of the Frisians many miles to the north of the Rhenus.

You did not mention in your report the exact nature or extent of the damage to your vessels, but we presume the main problems you have are broken or lost oars and perhaps fallen masts. If this is the case, please limit the repairs to the oars only. Do not ask the shipwrights at Noviomagus to replace masts or repair damaged hulls. That would be too costly as well as time consuming. There is no shortage of vessels on your side of the Oceanus Britannicus that you can commission to bring the First Athena safely back.

I have one piece of good news which should bring you some cheer. We received a report two days ago that the Second Athena under the capable leadership of Claudia Marcia who, along with her fearsome charioteers from the eastern flatlands, proved more than a match for a fifty-boat Hibernian invasion along the West Coast, putting over a hundred of the murderous swine to the sword and sending the rest back in leg irons, and minus their thumbs as you instructed. Only twelve of the infantry and three of the cavalry were killed and less than thirty women were wounded. It would seem that the rigorous training you and the others put them through is proving to be highly effective.

That is all for now my dear. I hope all goes well with the muster, especially your search for your fellow commanders. You

*are constantly in our thoughts and the whole of Britannia is
praying for the successful re-commencement of the Great
Expedition.*

> *Your loving father,*
> *Deonotus.*

XI

*From Augustus Constantine III, Emperor of the West and Grand
Commander of all its armies, to Princess Ursula, Commander-
in-Chief of the Legions First and Second Athena. Arelate.*

> *Hail great princess and commander! I hope this finds
you fully reunited with the brave women of the First Athena and
that you have recovered from your adventure upon the high seas.
The Oceanus Britannicus can be surprisingly treacherous for
such a narrow stretch of water.*

> *More importantly, I hope this reaches you before you
embark on your long march south; for I fear I must order you to
postpone the Great Expedition.*

> *You have not been alone in suffering setbacks in recent
weeks. While you were having your ordeal at sea, an unholy
alliance consisting of armies from Hispania plus a large band of
Suebi tribesmen sneaked through the mountains and laid siege to
Arelate. They are ostensibly under the leadership of our old
'friend' Gerontius and a certain Maximus who claims the title
"Emperor". However, these two fellows are but mere puppets.
Pulling the strings are busy hands, hands governorial and ex-
governorial ... as well as hands imperial, I suspect.*

> *Normally, I could crush such a rabble in one swift and
decisive attack. But I recently had to send twelve thousand of my
best men to the Rhenus to deal with yet more Burgundians who
seem to be intent upon ravaging eastern Gallia. I have sent
urgent messages ordering their recall and I am awaiting their
return as I write. It is also entirely possible that Constans might
come to my aid. He was on his way here for the 'Wedding of the
Legions'. He should have received my message which I sent by*

trusty Morgan a few days ago; and I am optimistic that he will arrive very soon.

In the meantime, I reluctantly have to order you and the entire First Athena to stay where you are. I know Noviomagus well. It is a safe place. The people are warm-spirited and kind, and it is a good distance from the troubled areas of Germania, northern Gallia and the frontier. I am sending a dispatch to the mayor, Dagvalda, whom I have known many years, instructing him to make the necessary arrangements for yourself, your fellow officers and the rest of your women. He is a trusted friend and I have every confidence he will ensure you are well treated.

So, you have heard from that old rascal Rusticus. Have no fear of him unless you fear hospitality itself! I won't attempt to describe him; he defies description. Suffice to say he is one of those all too rare people who are a welcome counterbalance to the world and its troubles.

His letter does raise one very serious and important point, however. There are forces 'on the other side of the Alps' that count me as their enemy. This means they most assuredly see you and the First Athena as a threat too. For this very reason, for your own personal safety, and for the safety of the legion, I therefore order you not to go to Colonia under any circumstances. From Noviomagus Colonia is the first step to Roma; and the nearer you get to Roma the greater the dangers become, both physical and political.

From where you are now stationed, there are only two possible routes for you to follow. The first, head directly south across central Gallia to Arelate as planned. The second, go back to Britannia. Any other route, especially the route to Roma, is most certainly a route to ruin and disaster.

Do not go to Colonia. Do not send a patrol there. Do not even send a dispatch via the city. The risks are far too high in each case. Instead, you, all your officers, and the entire First Athena, must stay in the relative safety of Noviomagus. Complete your muster, let your wounded women heal, keep up your training and enjoy Batavian hospitality.

I shall send for you when the time is right which should
be soon. I know how disappointed you will be to receive this
news and these orders, but you have persevered well these past
three years. I know you have the discipline to be patient for just
a few weeks more while Constans and I finally put a stop to
Gerontius and his antics.

I'll leave you with this happy thought: Arelate is at its
best in high summer, perfect for weddings and young couples!

Until then, may God be with you,
Constantine.

XII

The galley was back to its full splendour and the commanders
were assembled on deck enjoying the cloudless bright blue day.
A warm summer breeze filled their sail as they made their way
along the crystal-clear waters of a gentle meandering river …
heading for home.

They all smiled as they ate their pheasant. Oleander was
busy readying the grate for the next course and as she worked,
she sang a lively summer singalong song called 'Off we go!'.

Off we go!
A-sailing, a-sailing
Off we go!
A-sailing along

Take damsons and raisins -
and all things nice
Take bully beef and salt it -
salt it thrice
Take the best wine and cork it -
adding some spice
And off we go sailing
A-sailing along

Suddenly, Pinnosa spotted a lone stag on a nearby hilltop, looking very much the master of all it surveyed.

'*Come on everybody!*' she cried. '*Let's go hunting!*'

Oleander kept up her song and the women all joined in as they rode their horses hard across the river and up the hill, giving the stag the chase of its life.

Off we go!
A-hunting, a-hunting
Off we go!
A-hunting along

Take arrows and daggers -
and all things keen
Take the high ground and low ground -
but don't be seen
Take your meat as you find it -
but keep it clean
And off we go hunting
A-hunting along

When she reached the point where the stag had been standing, Ursula stopped and let the others ride on without her. The sound of their singing mingled with the pounding of their horses' hooves and faded into the distance as she took in the magnificent view.

There before her was a vivid panorama of hills and valleys richly coated with the deep vibrant green of luscious woodland growth; here and there she could see a waterfall beneath a full crescent rainbow; a nearby valley poured forth a trickling stream which ran over moss-covered boulders into the river where the galley was moored; and she could hear the sound of birdsong in the trees as they chirped and chirruped their way through the long summer's day.

Just then, from way on high somewhere near the heart of the sun, came the haunting cry of a hawk. Upon hearing the bird, Ursula suddenly realised that even though she had never been to this magnificent place before, it had the unmistakable feeling of 'home' about it.

'You are home.'

Pinnosa's voice made her jump.

She turned to face her and they were standing so close she could feel the heat of her friend's breath.

'Remember? Only in your eyes, I see home,' said a voice behind her. 'And only in your voice, I hear family.'

She turned and found herself looking into Constans' deep brown eyes. She could see his pink tongue flickering behind his perfect white teeth as he spoke.

'Oh, Constans.'

She leaned forward to kiss him, yearning with all her being to feel the warm touch of his soft sweet lips.

'*There's no time for that!*' bellowed Constantine. '*Come! We must save the townsfolk from the great black bear!*'

Ursula started to run as fast as she could because she knew the great black bear was the most dangerous beast on God's earth; people everywhere had to be saved from it, and from the terror that it wrought.

She and Constans were running together; as they ran, she could feel his hand holding hers tightly. Even though they were running as hard as they could, Pinnosa and Constantine were somehow always in front, just beyond reach and running harder than anyone else.

Looking back, she saw Martha, Saula, Julia, Faustina and Brittola – but curiously not Cordula – all running faster and faster, and leaping over rocks and fallen branches. Some of the branches were crossed, perhaps to make a signal. Behind them, she could see her father and the other kings in their full regalia, all running like the wind; and she even caught a glimpse of her mother bringing up the rear with a lumbering Bishop Patroclus.

Ursula stopped running and looked all around. She was in a huge cavernous dark space and she couldn't see a thing, but she knew at once she was inside the black bear's lair. Suddenly, in the heart of the darkness she lost hold of Constans' hand.

The shock of losing contact with him filled her with a fear more horrifying than any she had ever felt; and she tried to scream, but couldn't.

A strange murmuring noise started and she stopped trying to scream in order to listen. It was the sound of voices, a multitude of clamorous voices. She turned to face the source of the sound and there in front of her, emerging from the darkness, was the First Athena. Thousands upon thousands of women, all of them wet and cold, all wrapped in grey blankets. They were pointing their fingers at her in accusation … and Brittola was their leader.

'*There it is!*' she cried. '*There's the great black bear! There's the monster that's killing us all!*'

They started to approach her intent on revenge. As they drew nearer and nearer, Ursula realised the only way she could survive was by becoming one of them and pointing her own accusatory finger; but she knew that the only way she could point it … was toward Constans and Constantine.

'*I will not!*' she cried. '*I cannot!*'

A voice from somewhere deep, deep within whispered in her ear.

'You must. You have no choice. They have betrayed you, just as you betrayed the First Athena.'

The voice was her own, but it was also Pinnosa's.

'*No-ooo-ooo!*'

Ursula spun round so violently, she felt nauseous.

And then … she too pointed.

She became part of the multitude clamouring for retribution, and the act of pointing her finger gave her a joyous feeling of relief.

As Ursula and the rest of the women closed in on the two men, much to Ursula's shame and disgust, Constans started to cower in fear.

'*No! Not me! It wasn't me!*' he whined like a small boy as he fell in a pathetic heap at his father's feet.

Constantine stood firm and defiant, his feet firmly planted and his cloak thrown back over his shoulder with his hand upon his hilt. With a fierce resolve, he drew his sword and pointed it threateningly at the women.

'*Stop! Do not come a step closer! I am ordering you to stay right there! Stay where you are!*'

The women paused, but only with great difficulty, for they were filled with a momentum that had an awesome power of its own; and, like all the other women, Ursula knew they had to move forward.

'*Leave me be I say!*' Constantine looked fearful. 'I am not the great black bear that you seek; but I am sworn to protect you from it. *Stand back – stand back I say!*'

As the mass of women moved relentlessly forward, Ursula – with her finger still pointing and about to touch the tip of Constantine's sword – was barely able to contain the ranks upon ranks behind her. A tremendous force was being unleashed; a force that could not, would not, be denied. To Ursula it felt as if a constant relentless pressure was both pushing from without and pulling from within.

'*Stand back I say!* Seek not the great black bear! For if you seek it, in turn, it will seek you; and it will seek to destroy you! Mark my words … *it will kill you all!*'

The sea of women moved closer still, their hands reaching for his arms, his body, his face, forcing Constantine to cower and reel as he tried to fend them away and fight against being engulfed.

'Come no further in this direction,' he cried, dodging and ducking in his desperate attempts to avoid the clinging and clutching hands with their pointing accusatory fingers. '*Beyond me lies the great black bear!*'

Then, just as he was about to be smothered by the indomitable force of women, Constantine also turned and pointed with his sword into the darkest depths of the cavern. With the final obstacle overcome, the fearsome power of the women was unleashed and wave after wave surged over the precipice to plunge into the darkness, not one of them knowing what lay ahead.

As she fell, Ursula wasn't frightened. She knew that the women's force was an all-conquering power that could never be contained; an invisible and inevitable force like Spring. Now that she was part of the body, the darkness held no fear for her ... only freedom.

She was beginning to enjoy the sensation of flying through the darkness when, suddenly, there seemed to come from everywhere at once, a hideous loud roar; the awful sound was so loud it filled her ears, causing physical pain. The roar then changed to become a deep reverberant voice, a laughing mocking voice, hacking the air with cruel hideous laughter that filled her with a quivering fear of its chilling and evil intent.

'Is that the great black bear?' said Brittola flying by her side.

'Yes. And I think the great black bear is really the emperor.'

'I don't,' said Pinnosa from her other side. 'I think it's God!'

At that moment, a small silver light appeared in the centre of the darkness and began to grow. Ursula felt as if her heart would burst with excitement because she knew they were about to find the answer. The hideous laughter began to fade and the ever-brightening light started to engulf the cavern, leaving her free to fly wherever she wished, and—

—someone was pulling at her cloak, impeding her flight.

'*Let me go!*' she cried. 'Can't you see we're about to find the truth? We're about to find out the cause of all our suffering. *Let me go I say!*'

She looked behind her and saw the sky was full of the women of the First Athena. There were countless, endless ranks of them, all wearing long white cloaks, all riding beautiful white horses and all galloping forward at full speed into the wonderful welcoming silver light.

'*The white riders!*'

Ursula leapt up from her chair, knocking Oleander to the floor. As she fell, Oleander let go of Ursula's cloak which she'd been gently tugging.

They were alone in Ursula's private chamber in the Officers' Hall. Cordula was away with Viventia searching for the missing vessels and Brittola was down at the waterfront getting the newly-repaired galleys ready for inspection.

'Were you having those dreams again Mistress?' Oleander looked concerned as she picked herself up. 'If you don't mind me saying Mistress, you shouldn't let yourself fall asleep like that. It's not healthy for a young woman like you to doze during the day.'

Oleander bent down and picked up a parchment that had fallen from Ursula's lap which they both knew was the cause of her torment, the order from Constantine to wait in Noviomagus indefinitely.

'Anyway Mistress, it's almost evening bells. You should get yourself down to the galleys for your inspection; Mistress Brittola will be waiting for you.'

Ursula nodded then, with some effort, began to ready herself. She tidied her cloak which had slipped off her shoulder and straightened the clasp; she then buckled her sword round her waist, grabbed her helmet and made to leave; but, as she reached for the door handle, she paused and stood still, staring vacantly at the floor.

Oleander had seen her like this as a child; the bemused expression she used whenever her parents had left her on her own, an utterly lost and bewildered look. She walked over and took Ursula by the hand just as she'd done all those years ago.

'I'm sure all the others are safe and well; Martha, Saula and especially Pinnosa are very capable women. Moreover, I would bet my donkey Toby that you receive the order from Constantine to resume the Great Expedition any day now.'

Ursula snapped out of her daze, returned Oleander's reassuring smile and squeezed her hand ... then opened the door, put her helmet on and left the room.

XIV

Ten craft were still unaccounted for of which six were supply vessels and four were war galleys, including Pinnosa's and Faustina's.

Julia's huge one-hundred-oar galley had been a very splendid one but also very old, and it had broken to pieces as soon as it grounded on a sandbar to the far west of the Rhenus delta. Miraculously, only three women had died, but they had lost all of their horses as well as most of their supplies when the cold water of the Oceanus Britannicus had claimed the stern. Her women had managed to survive for ten whole days, scavenging amongst the floating wreckage until one of the Batavian skiffs had eventually spotted them. Julia had suffered terribly from the ordeal and, even now seven days later, Ursula could still not persuade her to leave her room, let alone talk about the horrors she and her crew experienced.

The death toll from the storm now stood at almost four hundred. A hundred and sixty were from two of the old supply craft which had been seen to sink taking with them their crews. This did not bode well for the missing supply vessels that were of a similar type. In all, nearly seventeen hundred women of the First Athena were still unaccounted for, plus four hundred horses. Forty-three vessels were known to be wrecked, most of them beached, including a few that had completely broken up like Julia's. Several of the older craft had sprung leaks and sank in the shallows. Their crews had been forced to swim ashore, abandoning their horses to the water. Only twenty-six vessels, seventeen of which were war galleys, had survived the storm intact and were still seaworthy. These were now safely moored in Noviomagus' naval harbour, well-guarded by sentry towers and floating port booms to keep unwanted craft away.

As Deonotus suggested, Ursula only commissioned the shipwrights to repair the damage to the oars and their mountings. Accompanied by Brittola, she had just completed her inspection of these repairs when they heard a familiar voice boom out from the quayside.

'*Ahoy there!* Are any of these galleys heading for Gesoriacum? I have an urgent appointment to keep!'

'*Pinnosa! It's Pinnosa!*' cried Brittola. '*Pinnosa, you're safe!*'

'Why, oh why, does my Christian conscience always have to state the obvious?'

Laughing heartily, Pinnosa held her arms out for a hug. Brittola and Ursula ran down the ramp towards her and the three old friends embraced each other tight, until they heard awkward shuffling noises behind them and remembered the guards.

'Where are Martha and Saula?' asked Ursula as they pulled apart. 'Are they all right? Are they here?'

'They're fine but they won't be here until late tomorrow. They're with Faustina, leading our galley crews here from the north. I thought you two might be a little worried, so I came on ahead to let you know we're all safe.'

'Martha and Saula will be here tomorrow?' Brittola reached up to touch Pinnosa's face as if checking she was real. 'And Faustina too?'

'Must you keep repeating everything I say Brittola?' She playfully ruffled Brittola's hair before turning to Ursula. 'Oh, I almost forgot. I brought two others with me who I thought you might be pleased to see.'

Pinnosa let out a shrill whistle and, from behind a nearby workman's hut two loud neighs could be heard in reply as two mares, one black and one grey, came into view.

'*It's Artemis and Swift!*' cried Brittola.

'You're doing it again Brittola!'

Pinnosa gave Brittola a playful nudge in the ribs and the two of them started to mock-wrestle. While they were jostling each other, Ursula stepped off the jetty onto the dockside to greet the two great horses, both of which looked in good condition.

For a moment, the pair stood still and simply returned her gaze as if they too were finding it hard to believe what they were seeing. Swift then shook her head, gave a little whinny and trotted over, obviously pleased to be back with her mistress. Ursula greeted her with a hug almost as big as the one she gave Pinnosa; to which Swift snorted and nuzzled her in reply.

While Ursula and Swift were happily reuniting, Artemis walked quietly up behind Ursula, took her officer's cloak in her teeth and gave it a sharp pull. Ursula span round with a face like thunder to chastise whoever had had the temerity to tug her uniform and, upon seeing Artemis, burst into laughter. Brittola and Pinnosa laughed too and all three women made a fuss over the frolicsome black mare.

'Come on you two,' said Ursula after their reunion was complete. 'Let's return to the Officers' Hall and have a simple meal. We'll have a proper welcome feast when others arrive tomorrow.'

'"Simple" is fine,' said Pinnosa. 'But can we please have some red meat? I've eaten enough waterfowl recently to last me till the moon turns blue!'

XV

Later that evening, while they ate in Ursula's private chamber, the three of them exchanged accounts of their adventures.

Stripped of their mast and with few oars left in working order, Pinnosa's women had drifted for three days before they'd sighted land. When they'd eventually made it ashore, they'd sent forth scouting parties to seek out crews from other vessels. Two days later, one of Martha's patrols had heard horns blowing and round a headland had appeared ten of Faustina's women on horseback. With so many serious injuries to deal with and urgent supplies to be secured, it had taken over a week for Pinnosa and Faustina's women to combine forces, but eventually they'd been able to form a contingent six-hundred-strong and commence a proper search for the rest of the legion.

Because they'd assumed they were on the coast of northern Gallia, they had initially headed north, thinking they were heading towards the Rhenus. Eventually, they'd met up with some German hunters who'd told them they were heading the wrong way. The storm had actually blown them much further to the north than they'd thought and they had been marching *away* from the Rhenus rather than towards it, heading deeper into the lands of the dangerous and unpredictable Frisians.

Even though they'd turned around immediately upon realising their error, it had taken them a full week to reach their wrecked galleys. A few days later, they'd come across a scouting party from a third galley and the following day they'd arrived at the vessel itself to be warmly greeted by three hundred women from Lindum. This galley had also lost most of its oars, but it had kept its mast and hoist which had enabled them to unload their horses. The craft had been beached but, unlike Pinnosa and Faustina's, it had been refloatable and could still have been used.

Saula had offered to stay behind with a detachment of women and guard the craft until it could be recovered; however, Faustina had insisted that because they were in enemy territory the women's safety had to come first and she'd reluctantly given the order for the seaworthy galley to be scuttled. It had been an emotional moment for the Lindum cohort when their galley was floated out into deep water and had its hull stoppers removed. Pinnosa had led a prayer, in which she'd pleaded with God to spare the First Athena's grand fleet such a fate as the proud vessel had disappeared beneath the waves.

Three days later one of Martha's scouting patrols had met a band of Batavian merchants heading north. The men had told them of the muster of the First Athena around "the most beautiful commander-in-chief in the entire Roman army" at Noviomagus and had given them directions how to get there. Soon after that, they'd found the road that led inland from the coast and headed straight for Noviomagus. Pinnosa had ridden ahead, not only to let Ursula and the others know they were safe, but also to make arrangements for the nine hundred women, their horses and their attendants.

'They are moving slowly because they still have the burden of many wounded, but they should be here sometime tomorrow and we need to be ready for them; they are completely exhausted,' said Pinnosa, completing her story.

She took a final bite out of the haunch of venison that she'd been eating, burped a long loud and lingering burp, then took another swig from her goblet of wine, before settling back on her couch and rounding off her simple meal with a handful of juicy plum-purple grapes.

'They will all need a long hot bath when they get here as well as a good hearty meal and, at long, long last, a well-earned and much-needed rest.'

XVI

'Good evening ladies! Your Highnesses! Allow me to introduce myself. I am Decimius Rusticus Amorius Pantheus Maximus; though my friends – and I know we will soon be very good friends – usually call me Rusticus.

'I come from the greatest city north of the Alps, glorious Colonia, where I am not only the Praetorian Prefect appointed by a very dear mutual friend of ours, the Emperor Constantine the Third, but I am also one of the most well-known, respected and, dare I say, "beloved" of its denizens.'

He laughed a rich hearty laugh full of the baritone boom of his voice, before adjusting the sleeve of his toga, straightening himself up and striking a theatrical pose.

'As you can hear, I speak perfect Britannic like a native. This is because I come from a huge family and one of my many aunts, my beloved Aunt Phoebe, was Britannic. I loved her dearly, and she taught me well.'

He took several steps further into the room and, with a flicker of his mischievous eyes and a broadening of his white-toothed grin that flashed from beneath his dark curly beard and moustache, he attempted a gracious bow which his ample frame limited to little more than a courteous nod.

214

He quickly surveyed the gathering of officers in the commanders' room and his eyes settled upon Brittola who was standing immediately in front of him, causing her to blush.

'So, here we have the mighty Britannic women who have formed a great army, beaten off the murderous Hibernians, kept those hideous wild Picts at bay and even defeated powerful Saxon armies. Now, you have managed to survive a terrifying ordeal at sea only to find yourselves here in this quaint Batavian backwater we like to call "Noviomagus"; a little out of your way perhaps, but basically on course for your intended rendezvous with Constantine in Arelate; however, you are forced to wait until he has joined forces with Constans and driven the evil Gerontius into the ground where he belongs. Am I right?'

He cast a questioning eye around the room but was met by a stunned silence. They had all gone quiet the instant he'd made his entrance, and were staring at him intensely not only because his arrival was both unannounced and unexpected, he was also the only man present. Eventually, after a long awkward pause, Ursula put down the roll of parchment she was holding and spoke.

'You are remarkably well informed Rusticus,' she said.

He turned, slowly and deliberately, to look at her.

'And *you*, Your Highness—for I take it I am addressing Princess Ursula, daughter of King Deonotus of Corinium?' She nodded graciously; and so did he. '*Ahem!* As I was saying, Your Highness, *you* are every bit as beautiful as your much-lamented mother, Queen Daria.'

Pinnosa laughed.

'He caught you there Ursula! A compliment traded for a compliment, eh Rusticus? Well, if you are so well-informed … pray tell, who am I?'

He turned his large round face toward Pinnosa and his grin grew even broader.

'You, fearsome lady with the bright red hair, you must be the legendary Pinnosa; horsewoman supreme and scourge of the enemies of Britannia. Am I right?'

She smiled and nodded.

'*Ha!* I knew it, I knew it! They say the only man who can tame you is to be found on Mount Olympus! And as for you my dear,' his voice softened as he lowered his gaze once more to Brittola, 'the youngest and sweetest of the bunch; you must be the one and only Brittola I've heard so much about.'

She instinctively grasped her cross and, without saying a word, bowed forward with great decorum. He acknowledged her formal bow, then raised his head to address the entire gathering in his rich baritone voice.

'As for the rest of you lovely ladies ... I'm afraid you'll have to introduce yourselves.'

'Introductions can wait until later Rusticus,' said Ursula politely but firmly. 'First, I think we would all like to know what brings you here.'

He reeled as if from shock at her words and raised the back of his chubby hand to his receding hairline.

'Ah, but Your Highness, it has been a tiring journey for me to come and see you today. Would you deny a humble guest some refreshment before taxing his weary mind with difficult questions? I have brought with me amphorae full of excellent wine from the cellars of the Imperial Palace at Colonia. May I suggest we dine first and get to know each other a little better before we discuss ... shall we say ... "matters"?'

His smile broadened once more as he cast his eye around the group.

Ursula looked across at Pinnosa, Julia and Faustina; and they each gave surreptitious nods.

'Very well. Please forgive our rudeness Rusticus. Even though I'm sure you can appreciate our need for caution; we wouldn't wish you to think us officers of the Legion First Athena lacking in basic civilities. You are, of course, welcome to join us as an honoured guest ... '

She paused as if inviting him to respond, but before he could say anything she added curtly and pointedly.

'Even if you *do* arrive unexpected, uninvited, unheralded and unannounced. Now please excuse me while I attend to some pressing matters.'

She turned to address the others.

'Ladies! Please introduce yourselves to our new friend, the honourable Rusticus of Colonia, and indulge him for a short time until our feast is ready. Remember our Emperor praises him greatly as a host, so do your very best to entertain him with true Britannic hospitality.'

She gave Rusticus a cursory bow and headed for the door to her chamber. As she left, he called out after her.

'To dine with you and your fellow commanders, Your Highness, will not be a matter of receiving mere hospitality, it will be to dine in the highest heaven above!'

XVII

It had been two weeks since Pinnosa's arrival in Noviomagus. Earlier that day, Baetica had entered the town's large river port with the final "missing" galley from the London Flotilla which meant the entire Grand Fleet was now fully accounted for and the muster of the Legion First Athena was deemed complete. To celebrate the achievement, Ursula and the other commanders had decided to hold a 'Grand Feast' for all the legion's officers, both senior and junior, numbering over one hundred women in total.

After the commanders and officers had all left the commanders room in the Officers' Hall and returned to their quarters to get ready for the banquet, it didn't take long for the slaves and attendants to transform it from being the centre of the legion's operations to a room fit for a feast. Maps – along with all their measuring instruments, piles of parchments and much other military paraphernalia – were cleared away; and in their place were brought tableware, eating utensils, drinking vessels and general dining accoutrements.

The attendants and kitchen slaves had spent the whole day preparing the food, and when the officers and their surprise guest returned to the room after bathing and changing into dining robes, the sumptuous spread before them was truly magnificent.

The elaborately decorated tables were piled high with hot food of every description; great mounds of steaming cooked vegetables on bronze platters; piles of fruit, fish and eels on huge silver salvers, and large copper bowls of freshly-cooked shellfish as well as dozens of smaller dishes with sauces and dainties.

As the women and Rusticus settled into their positions, an endless stream of attendants and slaves emerged from the kitchen carrying various meats for them to savour and enjoy. Haunches of mutton, pork and venison followed by whole hares, boars and calves on spits, even a couple of stags.

As if the plethora of rich smells wasn't enough to excite their taste buds, the full-bodied aromatic red wine from Colonia warmed the palate perfectly and created an anticipation in the mouth that turned the faintest appetite into a ravenous hunger.

While they feasted, Ursula was fascinated by Rusticus and kept looking at him out of the corner of her eye. He seemed not to 'eat' so much as 'graze'. Bishop Patroclus was the only other 'ample-bodied' man Ursula had ever dined with and like most Britannic men he either ate, talked or sang, but only one at a time and to the exclusion of the others. Rusticus, on the other hand, would gnaw distractedly on a bone while talking or singing, or interrupt a sentence to pop a dainty into his mouth. Pausing only to strip the meat from a wing, he would continue chewing whilst conversing, stabbing the air with the bones to emphasise his point. All this was punctuated with so much wine, she began to think he was Bacchus incarnate.

He was obviously in his element at a feast. His repartee had the whole company laughing raucously, especially after he discovered they were nearly all chaste; and he began making quips about women and marriage. At one point, he leaned over toward Ursula who was reclining on the couch next to his and pinched her on the arm.

'*Ow!*' she cried, 'What was that for?'

'That's what the first bite of marriage feels like. Simple wasn't it? Just a delicate little pinch. But suddenly you're no longer a virgin, you're a woman.' He looked her in the eye and winked. 'Hopefully a married one! *Ha ha ha!*'

Long after the women had finished eating, his appetite eventually began to wane. As he learned back on his couch, rearranging his toga and changing his position to one where he could continue quaffing his beloved Colonia wine, Ursula felt the moment had finally come for questions.

'Well, Rusticus,' she said, as she too adjusted her toga and adopted a more comfortable drinking position, 'I think it's time you told us the *real* reason why you are here.'

'Yes, of course, Your Highness; quite right you are ... '

His jovial smile suddenly disappeared and his forehead furrowed with a frown; the change in his mood was so stark the women fell completely silent as he prepared to speak.

'It is with a heavy heart, Your Highness, that I fear I must distract us from our merriment and pleasure.' He raised his voice to address the gathering. 'Ladies! I'm afraid it falls upon me to be the reluctant bearer of unfortunate news.'

He paused to hold his goblet out for more wine and waited for it to be filled before continuing.

'Three weeks ago, a large tribe of Burgundians came down the River Moenus and broke through the frontier defences near Mogontiacum intent on heading south to join their fellow tribes folk who are causing Constantine so many problems. When news of this reached us in Colonia, we sent five thousand men, including nearly two thousand cavalry, to help the much-depleted garrison at Mogontiacum attend to the matter.

'Unfortunately, since their departure, we have received reports that yet another tribe – the Franks – have gathered along the frontier defences just beyond the Taunus Hills; and they seem intent on heading toward Colonia itself. They could be upon us any day now, yet we are down to less than a thousand men in our garrison, with no reserves and hardly any cavalry, to protect us.' He paused for another swig of wine. 'I have come here today, Your Highness, to ask for your help. Will the First Athena, as the only sizeable field army in the area with its highly-esteemed cavalry, come to Colonia's aid in one of our great city's most miserable and darkest hours?'

Rusticus looked questioningly around the room at the other commanders before fixing his gaze firmly upon Ursula.

'I'm afraid we can't respond to your request Rusticus,' she said quietly but firmly. 'Our orders are to remain here in Noviomagus until it is safe for us to proceed south.'

'With all due respect, Your Highness, your orders are over a month old, and events have now overtaken circumstances. I'm sure if Constantine were here and could see for himself the desperate situation Colonia is facing, he would authorise your deployment immediately.'

Before Ursula could reply, Pinnosa beat her to it.

'It is only by luck—bad luck that we are here Rusticus. What would Colonia do if there was no First Athena?'

He returned her fierce stare before replying.

'Close its gates and pray.'

Pinnosa huffed incredulously.

'I simply cannot believe the great city of Colonia is so defenceless. Surely you can round up enough retired legionaries to mount a credible deterrent? Can't you even muster a thousand or so cavalry to rein these Franks in and turn them around?'

'Please do not forget Commander, that the people of Colonia, like those of Mogontiacum and Treveris, are well experienced in handling Germanic tribes. Why, most of us are of German origin ourselves. We understand their thinking and we know what it would take to stop them. To "rein these Franks in and turn them around" as you put it would require much more than a thousand cavalry. Even with your recent unfortunate losses, the First Athena can not only match that number, it can more than double it.'

He returned his attention to Ursula. Her expression was grave and she was staring into her wine goblet deep in thought.

'The expedition would only take a month,' he insisted. 'You could still be in Arelate well before Lughnasadh.'

Ursula continued to stare into her goblet before eventually looking up at him and replying.

'There is sense in what you say Rusticus. The First Athena is ready for action and I'm sure we have the numbers to achieve what you ask. However, Pinnosa is also right; we are here only by coincidence and circumstance, by ill fortune to be precise. Our mission is not to reinforce the Rhenus frontier; our mission is to go to Arelate and then return to Britannia which is also in desperate need of reinforcement against invading tribes.'

She looked across to the others before continuing.

'And anyway, I will not disobey the orders of our emperor no matter what the circumstances.'

'"Our Emperor"—*PAH!* He's only wearing the purple because he needs to control the mints!' He took an angry swig of wine, obviously embarrassed at his loss of discretion. '*Bah!*'

Ursula and Pinnosa exchanged a look. He saw this and leaned forward, intent on pressing his case.

'I'm sorry, Your Highness. I don't mean to offend you; but surely you can see that Britannia doesn't stand a chance on its own if the frontier is allowed to crumble. Constantine knows that better than anyone. If the frontier falls, Germania and Gallia will fall. If Germania and Gallia fall, Hispania will fall. And, if Hispania falls, Britannia will be surrounded by hostile tribes on all sides. Furthermore, if the Germans combine forces with the Hibernians and the Picts, how long do you think your little island province could resist the onslaught? A year maybe? Two?'

Ursula looked at their drunken guest with pity as he held out his goblet for yet more wine to drown his sorrows. She could see that in better times he would shun such serious talk in favour of fun and merriment.

While she was staring at Rusticus, his face suddenly brightened. He looked up from his goblet, sat up straight and returned her gaze.

'Please accept my apologies, Your Highness. I have just realised that I have been sadly remiss. I've been concentrating so much upon my mission I have completely forgotten another, entirely separate, matter. Prince Jovinus of Colonia asked me to convey his greetings to our royal visitors: the Princesses Ursula, Julia and Faustina and relay his personal invitation for the three of you to come and visit him. The hunting in the Taunus Hills is excellent at this time of the year and the prince is most eager to return some of the generous hospitality shown to him when he and his father toured Britannia several years ago.'

Ursula looked at Julia and Faustina, and they shared an expression of pleasant surprise. Rusticus' manner had been so convincing, for a brief moment their commanders' roles were completely forgotten and the three princesses found themselves warming to the royal invitation; then Ursula snapped them back to reality.

'Would you kindly thank Prince Jovinus for his most generous invitation and tell him that under normal circumstances we would be delighted to accept. Unfortunately, however— '

'Just a moment,' interrupted Pinnosa. 'May I have a quiet word with you, Your Highness?' She turned to Julia and Faustina. 'And with you too, Your Highnesses?'

The four women withdrew to an antechamber where Pinnosa immediately huddled them into a corner and spoke in a hushed whisper.

'I think it would be a very good idea if all three of you accepted this royal invitation.'

'*What!*' exclaimed all three in disbelief.

Pinnosa shushed them quiet as they were still within earshot of the head table.

'You know what Constantine said about Colonia in his orders,' said Faustina.

'Yes, but think for a moment.'

Pinnosa leaned forward and drew the others closer to make doubly sure they weren't overheard; then continued speaking in muted tones.

'We didn't study any maps of the defences along the Rhenus before we left and we didn't bring any with us. It's an ideal opportunity to explore the area and become familiar with the terrain. You'll also be able to make your own assessment of possible manpower strengths and deployments.'

'But we can rely on the Batavians and others for such information,' objected Faustina.

Ursula and Julia, however, were nodding.

'I disagree,' replied Pinnosa. 'I don't think we can rely on anyone. Our "friend" has proven that to me beyond doubt this evening with his display of "loyalty" to Constantine. I wouldn't trust him any more than I would trust a Pict with a baby. The only information we would ever get from Rusticus would be that which he deemed important, and that which he thought would bend *our* means to *his* ends.'

She paused and looked at them one by one.

'We've all discovered recently what it's like to be completely lost with no first-hand knowledge of the area.' Julia shuddered. 'I for one would feel much more at ease with our current predicament if we had our own reliable information on things like the fortifications along the Rhenus further upstream and possible crossing points, including Colonia itself, its defences and the surrounding lay of the land. You could even take up this offer of a hunting trip and see for yourselves what the frontier lands look like on the other side of the river. We could then make our own assessment of how quickly a German tribe can travel across such terrain.'

She paused to let her suggestion take root.

'The more I think about it, the more value I see in you going. I only wish I could go with you, but one of us needs to stay here. Anyway, I think you ought to go as the invitation intended, as princesses without a military escort. Leave your uniforms and weapons here; just take your hunting kits.'

'What if orders come through from Constantine while we're away?' said Ursula.

'You know as well as I do that we won't hear from Constantine until sometime next month. But, even if orders *do* come through, by all accounts, Colonia is just a short ride away. I'm sure you could be back here well before our preparations were complete and we were ready to depart.'

A few moments later, the four commanders returned to the feast and Ursula made an announcement.

'Rusticus. Julia, Faustina and I have decided to accept Prince Jovinus' kind invitation. We will leave with you first thing tomorrow morning ... and head straight for Colonia.'

XVIII

'*Pro iucundissima omnium in orbe urbium!* Here's to the most exhilarating city in the world!' Ursula raised her glass to lead yet another toast. 'Long may she be the greatest jewel in Rome's crown north of the Alps!'

She was pleasantly intoxicated on the finest wine that she had ever tasted. Mixed with the clean air of the Taunus Hills, it made her feel wonderfully light-headed and joyously free.

It was the third day of their hunting trip and the three princesses were enjoying themselves enormously with all the worries of the world left far behind then and, for the moment at least, completely forgotten. Apart from themselves, their hunting group consisted of Rusticus, Bishop Clematius and, of course, their host Prince Jovinus. There was also a small contingent of the Colonia Royal Guard accompanying them, performing the duties of attendants and generally enabling the royal party to enjoy their pursuit of the Taunus Hills' abundant prey.

A few days earlier, Ursula's initial impression of Colonia had been one of wonder. The great walled city was at least as big as Londinium but, because of its strategic position on the frontier of Rome, it also had a vast military complex, one that rivalled that of Eboracum. Indeed, "Londinium and Eboracum combined" was Faustina's apt description of it.

Ursula had been particularly struck by the stark contrast between the military and civilian areas. As the royal party had ridden through the outer districts, Rusticus had made a point of taking them through the huge barrack complexes on either side of the river. The harsh reality of row after row of empty and deserted buildings had immediately made her realise how weak and defenceless the city really was.

Then, as they had entered the city through its main gate, they'd witnessed a dramatic transformation. The haunting eerie stillness of the empty military complex had given way to a hectic and bustling cosmopolitan metropolis that could have easily been confused with Mother Roma itself. Its streets had been crammed with people, goods and beasts from every corner of the empire; and so many languages were being spoken, they'd struggled to tell which of them was the local German dialect.

While riding through the streets on their way to the Royal Palace, they'd witnessed some astonishing sights. There was a troupe of performing creatures that they'd heard of but never encountered before called "apes". Each one was dressed in a mock uniform and performing tricks. The apes' owners were dark-skinned men from Africa wearing exotic clothes in hues they'd never seen before; and they'd sung strange songs while the apes were performing. They'd also come across a curious machine powered by a donkey on a treadmill which played a kind of music. A tall man speaking a most peculiar form of Latin had approached them and enthusiastically explained in detail how the contraption actually worked. As they'd ridden away and its inharmonious sounds had receded into the distance, Julia had commented to Ursula and Faustina that it had been the machine itself rather than the irksome music it produced that had been the real attraction.

Elsewhere in the great city's streets, they'd come across vendors selling goods that none of them had ever seen before. Of special interest had been the exquisite very expensive glassware for which Colonia was justly renowned. Being surrounded by so much exotica, the princesses had dismounted and, accompanied by their escort who kept the crowds at bay, slowly made their way to the Royal Palace where they'd been officially received by Prince Jovinus.

He'd been a mere boy of twelve when Ursula had last seen him. She'd barely remembered him, having only been eight at the time. When he'd appeared from behind a column, walking with Bishop Clematius, she'd been pleasantly surprised to find herself exchanging greetings with a rather handsome red-haired

225

young man. Moreover, it had been clear from the outset that he took great pleasure from the company of the three princesses, especially Ursula.

That had all been three days ago. It was Jovinus who now responded to Ursula's toast.

'And here's to Britannia! Long may she continue to produce such remarkable women!'

The references to Britannia and its remarkable women jolted Ursula's memory, filling her mind with thoughts of the First Athena and home. She downed her wine and stood up.

'I'm just going to check on Swift,' she announced then broke from the group to head for the nearby woodland glade where the horses were grazing.

'Wait! I'll come with you.' Jovinus leapt to his feet. 'We're in bear country and you shouldn't go off alone.'

Before she could stop him, he had taken her by the arm and was leading her toward the trees. As she went, she looked back at Julia and Faustina and noticed their exchange of smirks. She poked her tongue out at them over her shoulder which made them giggle.

'When do you think the First Athena will commence its long march south?' he asked as they entered the trees and lost sight of the others.

'Hmm?' she replied distractedly.

She'd been enjoying walking arm in arm with him through the dappled pools of sunlight that filtered through the canopy of leaves and had drifted into a soporific daze.

'All right, I'll be more direct … '

He stopped walking and pulled her round to face him.

'When will you be leaving?'

'I … I'm not sure. We really ought to get back to Noviomagus as soon as possible.'

'Why don't you let Julia and Faustina return to Noviomagus, and you stay here for a while longer … '

He grabbed her by the shoulders and pulled her close.

' … with me?'

She tried to step back but there was a tree behind her and all she succeeded in doing was allow him to pin her against it.

'But … but I couldn't,' she said clumsily, her mind racing.

'Why not?'

He put his hand under her chin and lifted her mouth toward his.

'You know you want to, just as I want you to.'

She tried to turn away, but his grip tightened; all she could do was press herself tight against the tree trunk.

'I want you to stay here in Colonia and— '

His lips were almost upon hers; she could feel the heat of his breath.

'*Stop it!*' she shouted. 'Say no more, and *do* no more!'

He looked nervously over his shoulder in case anyone had heard her.

'Now, will you *please*, let me go,' she said through gritted teeth, her eyes ablaze.

Turning back to face her, he saw her fierce expression and immediately released his grip.

'Thank you,' she said stiffly. 'I am now going to check on the horses. I suggest you go back to the others and tell them to get ready to leave. Tell them also we are going to head to that high vantage point you've been telling us about an hour's ride from here.' She glared at him. 'Is that all right?'

He tried to say something.

'*All right?*' she snapped.

He nodded, turned and walked sheepishly away.

Ursula closed her eyes and as she did, she began to tremble.

XIX

'*What a magnificent view!*' shouted Faustina over the roar of the wind.

227

The highest point in the east of the Taunus Hills was akin to a small mountain and at its top was a lookout tower.

All six of the hunting party were standing on its upper platform with a strong northerly wind blowing their hair and lifting their cloaks out behind them.

Acting as guide, Jovinus started pointing things out to them. Most importantly, to the north they were looking directly into German frontier territory. They could even see stretches of the River Moenus in the far distance glistening softly in the haze between the hills. He then indicated a wide break in the forest about five miles distant that extended from one horizon to the other and told them it was the *Limes*, the line of fortifications over two-hundred-and-fifty-miles long that ran from Confluentes on the Rhenus to Castra Regina on the Danuvius and marked the northern frontier of Rome ... and was the bane of Constantine.

Rusticus was just beginning a humorous tale about his last visit to Castra Regina, when Ursula abruptly cut him short.

'*Look!*' she cried, pointing immediately below them. 'What do you think is causing that?'

The woodland immediately in front of them was alive with movement. Birds were shooting out of the trees and the few clearings that could be seen were full of creatures – deer, boars even foxes – all running as if trying to get away from something. As they scoured the scene, they realised the entire forest between themselves and the *Limes* was in a similar state of 'agitation'.

Then they spotted the first of them ... Germans.

Faustina pointed to a clearing barely a mile from the base of the hill they were on that was full of people on the move with carts. Behind the wagons came a small herd of cattle driven by figures on horseback. The whole group was moving slowly and heading directly toward them.

Ursula then spotted another clearing beside a river a little further away from their hill which was also full of many people on the move; she could even make out a large group of children playing in the water.

'Great God!' she murmured to herself. 'Look how much of the woodland is being disturbed. There must be thousands of these people on the move, tens of thousands even.' She looked back up at the *Limes* in the far distance. 'They're already well inside the frontier with nothing now between them and Colonia. Even if only a fraction of these people reach the city, the guards don't stand a chance of defending themselves against such large numbers!'

Just then the leader of the Royal Guard appeared at the top of the ladder.

'*It's the Franks! We are in grave peril here! Their advanced scouts travel in large bands and they always head for high land. We must leave at once Your Highness!*'

'*WAIT!*'

Ursula dashed the top of the steps and blocked the others from going down.

'*I have an announcement to make before we go!*'

She looked Julia and Faustina firmly in the eye.

'*As soon as we get back, I shall order the First Athena's deployment to Colonia, so that we can help the city contain and control these Franks!*'

Even Rusticus gasped at her sudden decision.

'*Oh, and one more thing …* '

Ursula glared pointedly at Jovinus.

'*Having experienced the delights and distractions of "the greatest city north of the Alps" the women shall be confined to barracks …* ' she shifted her gaze to Julia and Faustina, before adding ' *… including ALL the officers!*'

Chapter Six

MUNDZUK

I

Scouts from the Mogontiacum and Colonia garrisons disguised as woodland folk monitored the progress of the Franks as they made their way through the Taunus Hills towards Colonia led by their king Sunno who had a reputation as a fierce warrior.

From their reports, Ursula and the other commanders determined that the tribe was guarded by five groups of fighting men; four appeared to be loose ragtag groups of undisciplined louts, each a couple of hundred in number and led by a band of elders; the fifth, however, was a well-trained, well-armed and much better organised military unit – Sunno's hand-picked personal guards –who were several hundred in strength.

They decided to lay their trap in an area of hills that were a day's ride to the east of the Rhenus where the great river ran through a long twisting gorge on its way from Mogontiacum to Confluentes. Rusticus had strongly advised that the operation should take place early in the morning when most of the tribe's fighting men, especially the younger ones, would still be sober, making them easier to deal with than later in the day when they would be filled with 'liquid courage'.

So it was that, soon after dawn on the third day after their arrival in the Colonia area, Ursula gave the orders for the operation to commence; and for the Legion First Athena to go into action for the first time outside of Britannia.

It began with four 'decoy' cavalry units led by Saula, Brittola, Faustina and Viventia, galloping their way through the outer fringes of the tribe's sprawling camp area at four carefully selected separate points in order to draw away the large bands of disorganised rabble. In each case, the elders in charge fell for the bait and gave chase on horseback only to find themselves led into clearings where they were surrounded by ranks of archers and a large force of cavalry. By the time the rest of the men arrived on foot the leaders were already disarmed and held captive under guard, giving the foot soldiers no choice other than to surrender and relinquish their weapons, including their fearsome throwing axes.

All four of the 'rabble' groups readily surrendered apart from a small gang of teenagers on the most northern flank of the tribe's camp area who were still full of 'ale bravado' from the previous night's carousing, and who attacked one of Viventia's infantry units. The instant they realised they were encountering the famous First Athena; they began yelling their wild war cries and rushed at the women. They managed to hurl several of their large and vicious spiked axes before being felled by a volley of arrows. Several of the women were hit, including four who were killed outright.

Meanwhile, at the heart of the tribe's sprawling camp area, Martha and Baetica with their units of cavalry emerged from their place of hiding up a small gully into the valley where the Frankish king and his elite bodyguards had spent the night. The royal party, including Sunno and his children along with several tribal elders, were just having their morning wash in the valley stream when the women's horns sounded. Sunno's guards were still scrambling for their weapons and horses when Martha and Baetica's cavalry thundered out of the trees and pressed home a flying attack with arrows and spears before racing off down the valley towards the Rhenus, leaving behind several dead and many wounded. Looking back over her shoulder as they galloped away, Martha was pleased to see their plan working. Almost the entire unit of bodyguards, led by Sunno himself, had mounted and were already giving chase.

Not far away, from in amongst the crags that overlooked the same river valley, Ursula, Pinnosa and Julia, accompanied by Rusticus, led another much larger division of the First Athena cavalry, along with a cohort of men from the Colonia garrison, and galloped hard down through the dense forest in order to take full advantage of the opportunity that Martha's and Baetica's skirmish had created.

By following a hunter's track that led straight to the Frankish royal party's camp site, Ursula and her cavalry were able to emerge from the trees at the opposite end of the clearing the royals had been bathing in to find the rest of the Frankish nobility and what remained of their guards in complete disarray.

Led by Ursula, with Pinnosa at her side, the Roman cavalry then galloped hard across the clearing and made a ferocious attacking pass, felling more of the Frankish men with their arrows and spears, before regrouping and taking up position by the First Athena standard on the high ground along the edge of the clearing away from the river.

Lined up in their disciplined ranks, in full battle armour with the sun's rays shining through the trees behind them, and being over three hundred in number, they made an impressive show of force. With no cavalry of their own in support, the few remaining Frankish royal guards realised they were defeated and reluctantly surrendered, allowing themselves to be disarmed by the men from the Colonia garrison without any real resistance.

The Colonia men had barely finished tying-up their captives and removing their weapons when they heard the sound of galloping hooves approaching fast; they knew at once that it was Sunno with his main force of bodyguards returning from their futile pursuit of Martha and Baetica's women.

When the Frankish king and his cavalry arrived back at the royal encampment, they were confronted by the sight of disciplined Roman ranks in formation across the centre of the clearing, and were aghast to see their fellow warriors corralled beside the river with their hands and legs firmly bound. There was no sign of his tribe's nobles and elders, however; and Sunno rightly assumed they were being held behind the Roman line.

Sunno hastily reined his horse to a halt and shouted for his men to do the same, but he was unable to prevent a handful of his enraged warriors from shouting frenzied war cries and charging towards the Roman ranks where they let fly several battle-axes as well as a loose volley of arrows.

The Roman shields deflected most of the Frankish missiles, but some did hit home, including an axe that felled a horse not far from Julia's position and an arrow that impaled the leg of a woman stationed close to Pinnosa.

Incensed to the point of rage by their senseless attack, Pinnosa leapt from Artemis and disappeared behind the Roman line; she reappeared almost immediately, dragging with her an old woman from the royal party who Rusticus had determined to be Sunno's mother.

The old woman yelled in protest as Pinnosa took her to the back of an abandoned cart that was lying in the open ground between the two armies, then forced her to place her hand on the cart's backboard and spread it open. She then drew her short sword and, with deft precision, sliced off her little finger.

'*AIYEE-EEE!*' shrieked the woman, her face grimacing with the sudden fierce pain.

Pinnosa then called out in a loud voice.

'*Rusticus! I want you here—NOW!*'

Rusticus looked nervously at Ursula who indicated he should go to help Pinnosa.

Earlier, back in Colonia, they had insisted on him accompanying them because he could speak fluent Frankish.

'One of my many aunts, Aunt Aiga, was a Frank,' he had boasted. 'I loved her dearly, and she taught me well.'

It had also been his idea to capture the womenfolk of the Frankish leaders and use them as bargaining tools in the hope of avoiding bloodshed.

Ursula intensified her glare, urging him to go to Pinnosa's aid.

Realising he had no choice, Rusticus reluctantly nodded then gee'd his horse to step out from the Roman ranks.

'I want you to inform him that his family are being held by the Legion First Athena!' she said as soon as he was close by. 'Then please tell him I'm going to count to three and, if they don't drop their weapons, I'll slit her throat!'

Mopping his sweaty brow with a brightly-coloured cloth, Rusticus delivered her ultimatum in Frankish, his baritone voice rich and clear despite his obvious nerves.

Upon hearing Pinnosa's ultimatum, Sunno's bodyguards began shouting war cries and chanting '*Pinnosa Bloodhair! We want Pinnosa blood!*' in Britannic; but Sunno quickly raised his hand for them to be silent.

The king – a big man with a braided dark beard and long hair tied back in a ponytail – then signalled that his men should stay put; and he slowly rode out alone into the clearing toward

Pinnosa and the old woman who had by now collapsed onto her knees and was whimpering.

When he was just a few cubits away from the cart, Sunno stopped and scrutinised Pinnosa, who glared defiantly back, her sword still drawn and poised. She, in turn, scrutinised him and noted with interest he was wearing leather and chain body armour with a brace of throwing axes tied to his waist.

Eventually, after a brief glance down at the old woman, he shouted out his response in a deep gruff voice for the Roman commanders to hear.

Rusticus was obviously highly agitated by what Sunno had said and started to mop his brow even more frantically. Sensing Rusticus' hesitation, Sunno glared at him then repeated his message word by word in a dark menacing growl, forcing him to give the translation.

'He – *er-r-r-r* – he says he'd heard that the women from Britannia were brave and fought like men, b-b-but now he can see for himself that – *um* – that they—well, what he said is, they – *um* – they are just gutless and devious wenches who deserve to be trodden into the ground beneath his feet like the vile vermin that they are.'

'*ÜNUS!*' shouted Pinnosa.

Sunno went for one of his axes. Pinnosa grabbed the old woman by the hair, pulled back her head and exposed her throat.

'*DUO!*' she cried, raising her sword. 'Tell him this is his last chance to order his men to drop their weapons.'

Rusticus hastily repeated her words; but Sunno remained poised to grab his axe.

'Tell him it'll be the children next,' she snapped.

Rusticus hesitated.

'*Go on, tell him!* Say he'll be losing both his past *and* his future if he goes for that axe!'

Rusticus urgently translated, his voice trembling.

Sunno carefully surveyed the scene. He could just make out the rest of his family behind the commanders under armed guard; down by the river's edge, his men were bound and closely guarded by Roman horsemen; and there behind him was his own cavalry, weapons drawn and ready to charge.

'*TRËS!*' shouted Pinnosa, placing the edge of her blade against the old woman's neck—ready to cut.

Returning Pinnosa's fierce glare, Sunno called out an order over his shoulder.

His men glanced at each other with suspicion and not a little confusion.

He repeated his order, shouting even louder to make sure his men heard him correctly and, reluctantly, one-by-one, they dropped their weapons.

II

Surrounded by a ring of guards on horseback, Ursula and the other Roman commanders held their meeting with Sunno and a handful of his close aids, including his son Clothar, in the centre of the clearing not far from the abandoned cart. They were seated in a circle, using their bedrolls as improvised seating; and before them was a modest assortment of dainties that had been hastily prepared by the Roman attendants.

Rusticus, once again, was there to act as translator. He'd refreshed his voice with a few swigs from his ever-present flagon of wine which had the additional benefit of easing his nerves.

Sunno began the meeting by explaining that the reason his tribe was heading for Colonia was because they were seeking refuge in Roman territory. They'd been forced to leave their homelands in the east by a massive invading horde comprised of many different peoples from further east. They, in turn, were fleeing from an even greater terror—the Huns.

The various eastern tribes that comprised the horde had previously been rivals, sworn enemies even, but they'd formed into a loose federation called the "Alemanni" in order to unite against the threat that the murderous Huns posed with their relentless and merciless pursuit of plunder. It was clear Sunno thought the Huns to be the root cause of all the ill fortune that had befallen his people. He told how he'd heard from some of the Frankish merchants that these Huns weren't human. They were hideous creatures that looked like they had emerged from the underworld with long square heads and small lifeless eyes. According to Sunno's soothsayers, evil forces, demons that

craved suffering and thrived on hatred and war, had set the Huns
– who were the spawn of the Devil – loose upon the world.

Sunno paused at that point and, while Rusticus was
translating, a strange faraway look, a mix of fear and hatred,
clouded his face.

'I have even learned of their leader's name,' he said
darkly once Rusticus was ready to continue.

Ursula felt the hairs on her arms rise. Even before Sunno
spoke, she somehow knew what he was going to say.

'"Mundzuk"!'

The sound of the word as it was emitted from Sunno's
horrible brown-toothed mouth made Ursula break out in a cold
sweat. She had to reach for Rusticus' flagon of wine and take a
sizeable swig to prevent herself from fainting. While she fought
to retain her composure, Sunno continued.

'The Alemanni tribes that follow behind us are also
seeking refuge in Roman lands, because only Rome is powerful
enough to protect us from this Hun menace.

'When do you think this horde of Alemanni will reach
here?' she asked.

'They will cross the River Moenus and break through
those puny defences you call the *Limes* sometime before two
more cycles of the moon are complete.'

Ursula politely thanked Sunno for his information; then,
solemnly and sombrely, she announced she was about to inform
the king of his status in the eyes of the Roman authorities as well
as explain his options.

She then nodded at Rusticus who clapped his hands.

At this signal, one of the nearby attendants scurried
away and quickly returned carrying a bejewelled casket. With
due solemnity, Rusticus ceremonially opened the casket and
produced from within a roll of parchment with an imperial seal
which he then handed to Ursula with a genteel bow. She then
carefully, and with due decorum, broke the seal of the roll and
began reading out loud the articles that it contained in formal
Latin, pausing after each one to allow Rusticus to translate.

'This decree is hereby made by His Imperial Majesty,
Augustus Constantine the Third. It is concerning the Frankish

people and their legal status according to the laws of Rome; and is addressed to His Royal Highness, King Sunno.

'His Imperial Majesty, Augustus Constantine the Third hereby decrees that the Frankish people are denied permission to cross the Rhenus.

'His Imperial Majesty further decrees, however, that the Frankish people and their leaders have the option of taking on Roman federate status on the condition that they agree to settle in the frontier lands between the Rivers Rhenus and Moenus and the *Limes*.

'Should His Royal Highness, King Sunno, wish to take this option, he personally, along with his fellow leaders of the Frankish people, will be required to swear a solemn Oath of Allegiance to Rome.

'Upon pledging their loyalty to Rome, the Frankish people will then assume as their primary duty the defence of the *Limes* between Confluentes and the River Moenus. In the exercise of this duty, the Frankish people will be subject to the authority of the senior commanders of both the Mogontiacum and Colonia garrisons.

'Finally, should His Royal Highness, King Sunno, agree to these terms, as federate allies of Rome, his army will be allowed to carry weapons, including their Frankish axes. They will also be given training in the Roman Arts of War and granted access to military materiel from the garrisons at Mogontiacum and Colonia.'

After Rusticus completed translating the final sentence, they all looked to Sunno for his response.

At first, the Frankish King simply returned their gaze without any expression. Then he lowered his eyes to the ground and slowly began to nod and smile …

—then, suddenly, he stood up.

Ursula, Pinnosa and Julia leapt to their feet and drew their swords. The sight of the three of them caused Sunno to burst into horrible snorting bellicose laughter.

'*Ha-aaa ha ha* – do you – *ha ha-aaa ha* – take me for a – *ha ha ha* – a *fool?*' he cried, and Rusticus rapidly translated.

'Look at you; a "Roman army" of women and an "imperial agent" with more wine in his body than blood!'

237

He leered into their faces.

'Is this the "majesty and might" of Rome that we are now "entitled" to become a part of?'

They looked at him impassively in silence.

'Your so-called "Emperor" Constantine and whoever *really* wrote that so-called "decree" can continue making as many pretty pieces of parchment as he – *or she* – wants.'

He hawked his throat loudly and spat a huge globule of phlegm into the grass at Ursula's feet.

'It's all Roman *spit* that's all it is! And like you and your precious First Athena … ' he waved his hand dismissively at the nearby ranks, 'it will mean *nothing* to the likes of the Alemanni when they come here—or to the Huns when they follow! The Burgundians have proven how feeble you Romans have become. The Suebi too, and yes, the Goths who are knocking on Roma's door, just as the Saxons are knocking on Londinium's.'

'I take it then that you reject the emperor's offer.'

Ursula's voice sounded resolute, but while her words were being translated, she could feel the strain of her facade as she struggled to disguise her fears; deep down inside, she knew that what Sunno had said was true.

Rusticus, obviously feeling uncomfortable, hesitantly translated the Frankish king's reply in hushed tones.

'You – *um* – you may take it – *um* – pretty girl, that the Franks, like their other German cousins, will do exactly as they please. There is nothing the likes of you can do to stand in our way; we won't be caught off guard again and allow you to nibble away at a few fingers!'

Both Ursula and Pinnosa made to reply, but Sunno held his hand up for silence. Deliberately ignoring them, he turned to address his son.

'As I see it Clothar we have a simple choice. Either we join the Alemanni and pick the bones clean of the fine feast that once was Rome,' he turned back to face Ursula, 'or we work with this Roman "army" to defend what is left of the crumbling empire *against* the Alemanni. Who would you rather fight my son, the fierce tribesmen of the Alemanni or these women pretending to be—*AAA-AHH!*'

Sunno was so intent upon aiming his verbal attack at Ursula and Pinnosa, he'd failed to notice Julia deftly slip round behind him.

As he'd leaned forward to leer into their faces with his taunting tirade, Julia had lunged forward, thrust her hand beneath his leather tunic and grabbed hold of his testicles.

His eyes watering with pain, he tried to twist around to grab his attacker; but she squeezed even tighter, making him realise that to move at all meant excruciating agony.

Clothar tried to leap to his father's aid, but Pinnosa was upon him in an instant, knocking him to the ground and pinning him there with her sword; its tip pricking his neck and saying in no uncertain terms 'Don't move a muscle!'

'Please tell our esteemed visitor,' said Ursula calmly to Rusticus, 'that he seems to have forgotten something—no, better still, ask him *whether* he has forgotten something.'

Rusticus once again began to mop the sweat from his brow as he hastily translated; and Sunno equally hastily nodded in reply.

'Good. Now ask him if he knows what it is that he has forgotten.'

After the translation, Sunno grunted, but did not reply.

Ursula nodded to Julia who squeezed even tighter.

Sunno started to gag, his face becoming pale and his eyes bulging.

'Ask him if he would like us to remind him.'

Sunno nodded frantically well before Rusticus had finished his translation.

'Would you please point out in plain and simple terms Rusticus that this humble army of Roman women has got his tribe, and its leader, by the balls. He was right about one thing; they do, indeed, have two choices. They can remain barbarians, in which case they won't be protected by Rome's laws and there will be nothing to stop us killing them all right here and now; *or* they can take their solemn oath and become federate citizens of Rome; they will then be protected by Roman law and granted a measure of citizen rights, as long as they uphold their duties as outlined in the emperor's offer. Oh, and Rusticus … '

'Y-y-yes, Commander?'

'After you've translated all that, please finish with just one simple question.'

'What is that, Commander?'

'Will he accept the emperor's terms? Yes or no?'

III

From Augustus Constantine III, Emperor of the West and Grand Commander of all its armies, to Princess Ursula, Commander-in-Chief of the Legions First and Second Athena.

Hail great princess and commander! Your report on the situation along the Limes *saddened me greatly and added much to my burdens. It would seem that all our hard work of three years ago has proven futile and fruitless. The* Limes *seems to be acting more as a lure than a deterrent to these German tribes and would appear to be more porous than it is resistant!*

First of all, I exonerate you and the First Athena from disobeying my orders. I have also received reports from Rusticus and Jovinus and it is now clear that the Franks posed a great threat to Colonia which the city could not have resisted without your help. I was wrong to think we could afford to keep nineteen thousand seasoned veterans, including some of the best cavalry units in the Roman army, out of the thick of things. Indeed, you and your women deserve full credit for the way you handled the campaign. I don't think we men could have achieved what you achieved with so few casualties. As Rusticus says, 'These incredible women remind us all that there is much more to fighting than missiles and blades!'

Secondly, I now order you to deploy the First Athena to Mogontiacum. This is for two important reasons. Firstly, you need to supervise your new 'friend' Sunno very closely; not only because he is himself untrustworthy, but also because his loyalty, if he knows such a concept, may be elsewhere (read on). The other reason is that this approaching body of Alemanni is a very serious threat indeed. If they break through into Germania and Gallia, it will be no exaggeration to say that the West is lost!

I therefore want you in Mogontiacum where you will be in a much better position to deal with the problem as it develops. You and the others as well as Rusticus (I'm encouraged to hear you work well together) need to think very carefully about your tactics with the Alemanni when they appear. You can be sure that the techniques you used so effectively with the Franks will now be known to them and they will be taking measures such as disguising their noblewomen as peasant folk and replacing them with substitutes.

Your biggest problem with the Alemanni will be the sheer number of armed men, especially the large cavalry units from some of their more eastern tribes. I suggest you look for an opportunity to make a massive show of force. In my experience, it is the only way to halt their advance. If you had four times your actual number of cavalry this would pose no problem!

My third and final message in this report is a cautionary warning. Now that you are caught up in continental events, you must exercise even greater caution and be less trusting than ever before. The Franks and your 'friend' Sunno are a case in point. They may very well be in the pay of one of the Emperors from the House of Theodosius. Honorius is still holed up in Ravenna. His half-nephew, Theodosius, has now returned to Constantinopolis after his lengthy campaign into Parthia. Either of them could be planning with Sunno for the Franks to turn on you as so many 'federate' tribes have done recently.

We now know, for example, that the Burgundians, who are the bane of eastern Gallia and have been tying up most of my men, have been 'encouraged' in their endeavours by one or the other of our Theodosian friends, quite possibly both! More than that, I now have conclusive proof that the House of Theodosius is behind this Hispanian insurrection, which still has us penned in by Gerontius' and Maximus' incessant siege.

Most serious of all, Constans has had problems with treachery from most, if not all, of his auxiliary Suebi units. Their true loyalty would seem to stretch back over the Alps. In fact, he has been so caught up with overcoming the rebellious units, he has yet to emerge from the mountains to come to my aid; though I am expecting him to do so any day now.

Even these Huns now wreaking havoc beyond Rome's borders are probably working for Theodosius the Second. He has a strong interest in keeping the West weak and preoccupied. We now know for example that this monster, Mundzuk, seems to have assembled the nucleus of his force more than two years ago along the northern shore of the Black Sea within easy reach of Constantinopolis.

Incidentally, do not succumb to this hysteria and wild panic that precedes these Huns. It is their most potent weapon. Apart from their gruesome appearance (they place their babies' heads in block clamps during their formative years which gives them their horrifying looks), they are no more fearsome than any other barbarian tribe and just as vulnerable to attack from a well-disciplined Roman army.

Hopefully, we will soon crush all these pests that are currently bothering us so that your Great Expedition can be resumed. Arelate is just as beautiful in the autumn as it is in the summer. As the campaign season will be almost over, it should be possible for the 'army of newly-weds' to winter together and keep each other warm!

Until then, may God be with you,
Constantine

IV

'I suggest you look for an opportunity to make a massive show of force. In my experience, it is the only way to halt their advance. If you had four times your actual number of cavalry this would pose no problem!'

The words from Constantine's letter kept repeating in Ursula's mind as she sat in the commanders' room in Colonia, poring over maps and reports, trying to think of a strategy for dealing with the Alemanni. The first tribes were reported to be less than five days' ride from the *Limes*. They were moving very slowly, however, which meant the First Athena still had some time to formulate a plan and implement it.

She was interrupted from her thoughts by the sound of approaching footsteps which made her look up and smile.

'Good day to you, Your Highness,' said Rusticus as he joined her for their routine daily exchange of news. 'The weather is perfect for hunting. You should be outside on Swift gathering game, not imprisoned with your charts gathering far too much information for such a beautiful young head!'

He handed his hunting cloak and riding hat with its extended plume of feathers to Oleander and, as was his habit, strolled across the large room to the table by the fireplace with its selection of refreshments.

'Good day to you.' Ursula smiled at the sight of him adjusting the riding belt round his ample girth and trying to get comfortable. 'Rusticus. I'd like to ask you something.'

He breathed a sigh of relief as he settled on his seat and his bodily bulges assumed their natural positions.

'Hmm?'

'How many women are there in the First Athena?'

Rusticus grabbed a platter and started filling it with bread and cheese before reaching for the wine.

'What a curious question coming from you.' He looked at her askance as he selected the largest of the goblets and started to pour. 'You might as well ask me how many angels there are in Heaven.'

'I am curious to hear your answer. To your knowledge, what are the exact numbers of the First Athena; infantry and cavalry?'

He took a swig of wine before replying.

'You *are* serious, aren't you?'

She nodded. 'Have you ever known me not to be?'

'Well then, in that case let me see … '

He took another swig from his goblet and looked up at the ceiling, twirling the whiskers of his beard as he gave the matter some thought.

'I would estimate you have around—oh, I don't know, it must be at least … fifteen thousand infantry … '

He looked at her out of the corner of his eye; but she retained her inscrutable expression.

' … and about … three thousand cavalry?'

'How many people in Colonia would share those estimates, besides you?'

'Apart from myself? Well, there's Jovinus of course; the commander of the garrison; the ordnance official of the barracks maybe, although you do your own purveyance … ' He seemed to run out of possibilities. 'Bishop Clematius, perhaps … that is assuming all you good Christian women go to confession!'

He quaffed more of his beloved wine.

'Oh, I don't know. It's difficult to say. You've kept the security around the barracks and stables so tight.'

'*Exactly!*'

She thumped the table, startling Rusticus and making him spill wine down his front.

'What about Mogontiacum? How many of the First Athena are they expecting?'

She placed her hands on the table and leaned forward in earnest.

'I don't really know.' He shrugged. 'Mogontiacum's barracks and stables are bigger than ours—*and* emptier. The fact that we've accommodated you without any problem would be sufficient for their preparations; but to answer your question, they are probably expecting no less than ten thousand and no more than thirty.'

'*Ha!* Perfect!' She pummelled the table with her fists in excitement. 'Last question, Rusticus, and the most important one: How about the Alemanni?'

'How big do they think the First Athena is?'

'Yes.'

'Well, they probably think of you simply as "big enough to crush the Franks and the Saxons." If they have a number in mind at all, it will be even vaguer than the one the people of Mogontiacum have.'

'That's *it* Rusticus!' She rushed round the table and threw her arms around his shoulders, making him spill even more of his wine. 'I know how we can contain the Alemanni!'

'That's *what?*' His bemusement turned to exasperation as he wiped his chest. '*What's* it? *How?*'

'By making the Alemanni believe the First Athena is much bigger than it really is.'

Rusticus laughed and took another swig of wine in celebration.

'By the way,' he asked, feigning a casual air. 'How big is the First Athena exactly?'

She playfully tweaked his bulbous nose.

'How many angels are there in Heaven?'

V

Ursula's women were initially prevented from redeploying to Mogontiacum by a severe lack of horses resulting from their heavy losses at sea. Even after they'd commandeered all those available from both the Noviomagus and Colonia stables, they were still a few hundred short. Fortunately, thanks to the efforts of Cordula and Rusticus, they were able to secure a sufficient number in time for the legion to commence their march south just ten days after receiving Constantine's order.

Eventually, the Legion First Athena was ready to implement Ursula's plan for dealing with the Alemanni which she'd dubbed the "Grand Deception". The basic ploy was to create the impression that their cavalry was four times its actual size. To achieve this, Pinnosa and the cavalry commanders set about training three thousand of the infantry, ensuring they had sufficient horse handling skills to be able to parade convincingly on horseback and act as an escort for a marching army; and by the time the extra horses were ready, so were they.

Instead of having the whole legion parade through the city as they'd done earlier when leaving Londinium, Ursula dispatched the women in six separate contingents, each an hour apart, starting at dawn and continuing till mid-afternoon. Each contingent comprised of a cavalry vanguard followed by a cohort of infantry, with a further corps of cavalry bringing up the rear. The infantry ranks varied in composition from contingent to contingent, but each cavalry unit was conspicuously the same in number; one thousand per contingent; all in neat ranks five wide and twenty deep, and each one very easy for prying eyes to count as they departed Colonia heading south.

Less than half a day's march from Colonia, the entire legion crossed back over the Rhenus, using a rickety old bridge rumoured to have been built by Julius Caesar himself at a small garrison town called Bonna, and returned to Colonia's barracks along the opposite bank of the river under the cover of darkness, led by Rusticus' hand-picked scouts along lesser roads and forest tracks that were usually only used by the local woodland folk.

The legion then departed a second time the following day, once again in six separate detachments, thereby creating the impression that the First Athena was significantly larger than it really was, crucially including a cavalry four times its actual size; a full twelve thousand in strength rather than just three.

Once the women were assembled many miles south of Colonia, beyond Bonna and safely away from prying eyes, they finally set off and commenced their long march along the broad military road, heading south to Mogontiacum.

The following day, the stark blue silhouette of the Taunus Hills started to loom large on the opposite side of the Rhenus from where they were marching. The Taunus marked the end of Roman territory, the limit of Roman rule and, just beyond, the beginning of the never-ending sea of Germanic barbarianism.

Later that day, just as evening bells were sounding, they crested the last hill on their route and there immediately before them was the largest and most powerful fortified city north of the Alps, Mogontiacum. Its massive yellow and red stone ramparts were catching the rays of the setting sun, causing the magnificent edifice to glow as it bathed in the golden twilight, making the entire spectacle look like a fine tapestry or a wall painting, depicting a mythical city of old.

Ursula and the rest of the commanders paused on a promontory and looked in awe at the extensive and immense garrison fortifications. There was nothing like it in all Britannia, not even the fortifications at Deva or Eboracum came close to the scale of those before them.

Mogontiacum lay at a strategically important point on the River Rhenus where the great river joined with the River Moenus just before completing a great sweeping curve to head northwest toward Colonia from whence they had just come.

The actual city itself, with its Royal Palace, Basilica and Forum, was dwarfed by the vast fortifications that surrounded it, being nestled along the water's edge beneath a long natural ridge of jutting bedrock that enveloped it on all sides and formed the foundation of the great fortress' battlements and towers.

The gigantic fortress complex was orientated northward, against the ever-present threat of Germanic barbarism; and it was an intimidating presence on the landscape like an indomitable sentry on eternal watch, forever warning would-be invaders:

'*Halt!* You are now approaching Roman territory. You may not enter without due permission from the Roman authorities, and you will not proceed any further unless you abide by Roman laws, follow Roman customs and obey Roman orders.'

The First Athena marched into Mogontiacum early the following morning; Ursula then replicated the deceptive ploy they had used in Colonia and repeated their arrival in the afternoon, though this time, the manoeuvre somehow felt a rather futile gesture when set against the backdrop of the city's imposing fortifications.

The legion did not actually enter the main fortress itself. Instead, the women circuited the city walls along the waterfront and crossed the Rhenus on the city's great bridge to the northern shore where there was a secondary much less spectacular and more inconspicuous, though no less well-equipped and perfectly functional, military complex and barracks.

A number of reports were waiting for Ursula when they arrived; one informing them that the first of the Alemanni tribes would be reaching the *Limes* within a week to ten days; and another more recent one alerting them that Roman patrols had already encountered several Alemanni scouting parties less than a day's ride from the frontier.

Ursula, Pinnosa and the other commanders set to work immediately with the praetorian prefect of Mogontiacum, as well as the 'spy networks' of local woodland folk, to gather as much first-hand intelligence regarding the approaching menace as possible. At the same time, reconnaissance units of the First Athena's Vanguard, accompanied by guides from Mogontiacum headed off into the un-tamed lands beyond the *Limes* to gain a good understanding of the terrain they were about to operate in.

The reconnaissance patrols had barely reported back when Rusticus arrived by boat from Colonia, joining them once again to act as translator. Even though the Alemanni peoples spoke a wide variety of languages, only two tongues were used when their leaders held meetings; and it just so happened that Rusticus could speak both of them fluently.

'My dear late aunts, Uta and Gorda, were both from Alemanni tribes,' he'd said forlornly over a glass of wine as they'd formulated their plans back in Colonia. 'I loved them

247

dearly, and they taught me well.' He'd then wiped away a tear and blown his nose into his toga.

The day after Rusticus' arrival, they received reports that the foremost tribes of the Alemanni were starting to make camp in the military zone adjacent to the *Limes*. Ursula wasted no time and issued the order for the next, much more ambitious and dangerous, stage of the Grand Deception to begin.

Official Roman delegations were sent to each of the tribes where they formally greeted their leaders with an appropriate welcome. They politely informed each leader that the Commander-in-Chief of the Legion First Athena, Princess Ursula of Britannia, official representative of the Emperor, Augustus Constantine the Third, would like to convene a meeting to discuss their approach of Roman territory. The meeting was to be held at a special point where three rivers met just north of the *Limes*. The chieftains all readily agreed; and each of the official delegations returned safely without incident.

As the tribal chieftains and their entourages, including escorts of heavily armed guards, made their way along the three valleys that converged upon the designated place of assembly, each one caught sight of a number of contingents of the First Athena cavalry monitoring their movements from various key vantage points. A patrol might briefly appear riding along an adjacent hill crest with their Londinium colours plain to see as their bright orange cloaks caught the wind; and then, soon after, another patrol might be spotted in a clearing on a nearby hillside in their unmistakable Corinium royal blue livery.

Once the Alemanni reached the clearing where the meeting was to take place, and while they were waiting for the imperial delegation to arrive, the chieftains began to exchange reports of their various encounters with the extraordinary 'army of Roman women'. They quickly determined that each of the three valleys they had come down had been patrolled by at least four cavalry units in a variety of different liveries: sometimes blue, sometimes red, sometimes green and sometimes orange. This all tallied with the intelligence they'd received from their spies in Colonia, and appeared to confirm the rumours that this remarkable 'legion of women' really was of a considerable size.

Furthermore, they concluded the reports that the legion had a cavalry at least ten thousand strong, and perhaps numbering as many as twelve thousand, might just be true.

By the time Ursula and the imperial delegation finally arrived, the chieftains had decided that the information they'd received from the Franks, suggesting that Mogontiacum and Colonia were defenceless and ripe for plucking apart from a few feeble women had been misleading at best, and might have been deliberately false in order to act as a lure, possibly even a trap.

The assembly, involving fifteen tribal chieftains and their entourages, took place in a huge ornate tent complete with decorative tapestries and long trestles for an elaborate spread of fine Roman food, all of which had been prepared in the centre of a large clearing by a special ordnance crew from Mogontiacum.

After formal ceremonial greetings and a ritual exchange of gifts, the chieftains took their places in a large circle, each seated upon a lavish cushion beside a table containing wine in golden jewel-encrusted vessels as well as a tantalising selection of delicacies. When they were all settled, Ursula, along with Rusticus as translator, began the official proceedings.

Once again reading from an ornate roll of parchment, Ursula laid out the terms of the Imperial Decree which offered federal status plus special rights and incentives, as long as the Alemanni agreed to settle in the Taunus Hills beyond the *Limes* and act in concert with the Roman garrisons of Colonia and Mogontiacum to keep further invading tribes at bay.

The chieftains made a token show of resistance which Ursula could see through, but after a modest amount of haggling, and some equally token concessions on the part of Ursula and the praetorian prefect from Mogontiacum, they unanimously, and unconditionally, accepted the emperor's offer ... much to Ursula's relief.

The Grand Deception had worked; Ursula's plan had actually succeeded and the fierce warlike tribes of the notorious Alemanni had been beaten into submission by an emphatic and impressive, if exaggerated, show of force.

Sharing discreet looks of triumph with Pinnosa and the others, Ursula declared the meeting closed, stood up and called for her cloak in preparation for her departure and, following her lead, the rest of the imperial delegation did the same.

Pinnosa and the rest of the commanders had remained fully garbed in their uniforms throughout the proceedings; it had only been Rusticus and the princesses Ursula, Julia and Faustina who, following Roman tradition as hosts, had disrobed and discarded their riding accoutrements.

It was while the royal party was being dressed by their attendants and prepared for their journey back to Mogontiacum, that one of the tribal chieftains, a very tall man called Luethari, suddenly leapt to his feet and demanded to see a demonstration of the renowned prowess of the women of the First Athena in what he called 'the arts of men'.

'What better way to strengthen our new allegiance to Rome,' he declared, and Rusticus hastily translated, 'than by a "challenge"; the best of the young Roman Amazons in a contest with the best of our men ... champions against champions!'

The rest of the chieftains roared their approval of the idea and, one by one, they each stood up to add their voices to Luethari's call for a demonstration of Roman prowess.

Smiling politely, Ursula whispered urgently in Britannic to Rusticus.

'We can't agree to this. What are we going to do? What, in God's name, are we going to do?'

'Keep smiling and pretend to laugh with enthusiasm at the suggestion.'

Rusticus demonstrated, forcing a broad smile and a hearty chuckle as if relishing the prospect of what was being suggested.

'The longer we stay here,' said Julia, also adopting a gamely smile and a false light-hearted tone, 'the greater the risk of the truth being exposed.' She feigned a jocular laugh. '*Ha ha ha* – I say we leave right now.'

'*Ha ha-aaa ha ha ha*' Rusticus guffawed loudly to add to the charade. 'We can't decline their invitation; to do so would be a serious insult; it would put our alliance with them in utter peril, not to mention our lives. *Ha-aaa ha ha ha!*'

Ursula joined in the pretend joke and added her own 'ha ha's' to the round of false laughter.

'Very well – *ha ha ha* – Rusticus,' she said, 'We'll agree to a contest, but do your best to keep it short – *ha ha ha* – and, whatever you do, be sure to – *ha-aaa ha ha* – keep our women well away from their men.'

Ursula smiled graciously at the chieftains and nodded her consent; and, the instant she did so, preparations for the contest commenced. One side of the vast field tent was opened up to give the royal dignitaries and imperial nobles a view of the clearing, while the entourages and guards both Roman and tribal, withdrew to opposite sides, thereby creating a suitable arena for the contest. Within less than an hour of Luethari issuing his invitation, the dignitaries and nobles were all seated, the two opposing crowds of supporters were starting to cheer and the arena was ready for the 'challenge' to start.

Rusticus began the proceedings by announcing that Viventia, Baetica and Pinnosa would perform a display of Roman horse-riding skills.

Viventia went first, doing circuits of the arena standing on her horse's back, then sitting sideways and firing arrows into stationary targets while riding past – all at a full gallop. Baetica then made a similar show of expertise in horsewomanship except she rode backwards instead of sideways as she her fired arrows. Like Viventia, she drew an enormous roar of cheers from the Alemanni tribesmen as well as the ranks of her fellow Roman women opposite.

The cheers and cries from both halves of the crowd were still ongoing when Pinnosa appeared alone and on foot at the far end of the clearing; and there she stood completely still – a lone solitary figure, out of her uniform for once and wearing a plain and simple tunic, without any weapons – waiting patiently for the raucous noise to cease.

The cheering quickly died down to be replaced by an expectant silence at which point she stepped forward into the arena. Her hands were cupped together before her and appeared to be carrying something delicate and fragile. Upon reaching the centre, she whistled a sharp high note. The moment she did so a neigh sounded and Artemis appeared without any trappings. At a second whistle the great horse reared; at another she started to trot around the clearing; and, at the next, she broke into a gallop. A final shrill note then brought her to her mistress.

The Alemanni shouted, banged their shields with their swords and cracked their whips in the air in appreciation of such horse tricks. While they were still applauding, Pinnosa carefully placed whatever she'd been carrying in Artemis' mouth. Then she leapt up onto Artemis' bare back and rode over to the tribal leaders who were sitting with Ursula. Guiding Artemis with pressure from her knees and leaning forward so that she could whisper simple commands, Pinnosa then directed the great black mare to place a bird's egg, a single and completely intact bird's egg, into five of the chieftain's outstretched hands ... delicately ... one by one.

Once the trick was complete, Pinnosa then had Artemis back-step the length of the arena to the edge of the clearing where she reared several times with dramatic air-punches of her hooves – each one accompanied by a great roar from the crowd – before finally departing.

Her exit marked the end of the First Athena's display. Next, it was the turn of the Alemanni who fielded a group of over twenty riders. To demonstrate their skills in battle, they performed a bewildering array of tricks; standing on a horse's back at a full gallop, firing missiles and hitting targets also at a full gallop, leaping from their horse to dismount attacking foes; riding while leaning to the side of their mount to avoid missiles that were fired or hurled at them; and many, many more.

Eventually, after almost a whole hour, the riding demonstrations were complete and it became time for the true contest to begin. The first round of games was to be a test of marksmanship. While the preparations were underway for the arrow and spear competitions, Rusticus, resuming his fake jocularity, leaned over to speak with Ursula, Julia and Pinnosa who had re-joined the delegation and was once again wearing her uniform. Laughing merrily, he spoke in Britannic.

'I hope you realise – *ha ha ha* – that we are all in grave peril!' He pointed surreptitiously at a ferocious looking chieftain who was leering salaciously at an extremely nervous-looking Brittola. Pinnosa pretended to enjoy his joke.

'Yes, I know – *ha ha ha* – any moment now one of their guards is going to get near enough to our patrols to realise what they are wearing,' she said, referring to the women's cloaks with reversible colours. 'They may have fooled the Alemanni from a distance – *ha ha ha* – but they won't deceive them up close.'

'Not only that – *ha ha ha*' Rusticus' laughter began to sound tense and false. 'The next round of the contest will be – *ha ha ha* – man-to-woman combat.'

'We'll simply *refuse* to participate!' blurted Julia, momentarily breaking her façade with a flash of anger.

'*Ha ha-aaa ha ha ha* – It's not as simple as that,' said Rusticus, laughing loudly to mask Julia's outburst. 'It would be a great insult to them and place the whole alliance in jeopardy.'

'But if we go ahead and participate, the alliance will also be undermined,' said Ursula. 'Look at the size of some of those men. They'd be more than a match for even our biggest and best women. That would make us beatable in their minds.'

'It depends what kind of hand to hand they have in mind,' suggested Pinnosa.

'Don't even *think* about it,' hissed Ursula, dropping her smile. 'We must find a way to disengage from the rest of the contest without insulting them Rusticus. It's the only answer.'

'Yes, you are right – *ha ha ha*' replied Rusticus. 'But, *ha-ha*-how?

Throughout the marksmanship bouts, Ursula and the others racked their brains for a way to end the contest without either side losing face; and all the while they could see the Alemanni fighters and wrestlers limbering up beneath the nearby trees and having their bodies oiled; some of them were huge men with thick bulging arms and legs; others were thin and lean and bristling with ominous-looking weaponry.

Both marksmanship teams performed well and were in the main equally-matched, though the men were slightly better with spears and throwing-knives and the women were more accurate with arrows. Eventually, after an hour or so, the contest drew to a close and the incessant roars from the crowd started to diminish. One-to-one combat was about to commence; and still Ursula and the others had yet to come up with a plan.

253

Then, just as Ursula was racking her brains, desperately trying to think of something they could do to avert disaster, in the middle of the final round of archery, gusts of wind began to blow from the west; the sky filled with dark clouds and large raindrops began to fall.

Undeterred by the weather, a group of Alemanni fighters ran into the arena to get the combat session underway. They had just arranged themselves in a row in the arena's centre and were flexing their muscles when the heavens opened and a torrential downpour made it impossible for the contest to continue.

Ursula and her commanders plus the rest of the imperial delegation were able to depart with their dignity and their newly-formed alliance with the Alemanni chieftains – as well as their Grand Deception – intact and secure … at least for time being.

VI

Upon their return to Mogontiacum, Ursula declared a day of rest for the legion; and at Rusticus' suggestion the commanders left the barracks early the following morning to visit a large open-air bathing spa not far from the garrison complex in the foothills of the Taunus Hills called Aquae Mattiacorum.

There, set in a glade surrounded by tall and ancient trees, was a special grotto reserved for senior officers and others of high rank, the centrepiece of which was a large open-air bathing pool, a *natatio*, decorated with dark blue, red and gold mosaics. Behind the *natatio* and slightly above it were the *caldarium* and *tepidarium*, the hot and tepid baths. They lay beneath the dense dark canopy of leaves from the overhanging trees that trapped the steam, causing it to linger in great voluptuous clouds. The source of the hot spa water was a natural spring that oozed from a large crevice in the rocks between the roots of two towering chestnut trees and was a rusty red in colour. Wisps of the steam drifted out across the *natatio* to the more exposed cold-water pools, or *frigidaria*, which were fed by mountain streams.

To the side of the *natatio* was the massage area, as well as the way out to the stables and the narrow track that led to the Mogontiacum Road; and it was here that Ursula and Brittola had retired to, leaving the others in the pool with Rusticus who was in his element, languishing naked in the bathing water, drinking his beloved wine and enjoying the antics of his fellow bathers, twenty nubile young women.

Brittola and Ursula were laying side-by-side and face-down on adjacent wooden trestle-tables while their attendants kneaded warm aromatic herbal oils into their necks, backs and shoulders. They smiled as they listened to the sound of their old friends playing in the water; they could hear Martha, Saula and Cordula's giggles as they swooshed each other with spray; then there was the occasional loud splash, followed by Pinnosa's hearty laugh.

'This place would be perfect,' said Brittola after a while, 'if only it had a chapel.'

'Hmmm? What did you say Brittola?' Ursula's eyes were drooping as she started to drift into slumber.

'I said this place would be perfect if it had a chapel, a place where we could praise God and thank him for all that he has blessed us with; his wisdom, the beauty of nature, the— '

'It would be even more perfect,' said Ursula, drowsily interrupting, 'if it was back in the West Country.'

'Mistress?'

Oleander's voice had a strange edge to it.

'What is it?'

'I think you should sit up Mistress. There's someone here to see you.' Oleander's unease was palpable, causing both Ursula and Brittola to lift themselves up so that they could see the visitor. The instant Ursula saw the familiar silhouette framed in the bright sunlight beyond the great chestnut tree—she froze.

There, standing in the entrance to the bathing complex and casting a long shadow, was Morgan; he had paused to allow his eyes to adjust after coming into the dappled shade from the strong afternoon sunshine. There was a tension about him which was instantly apparent and spoke of unwelcome news.

Spotting Ursula, he made his way towards her and, as he did so, Ursula shivered. In a daze, she got off the massage table, donned her robe and readied herself to receive him. Behind her, Brittola also put on her robe and ordered the attendants to fetch the others; but Ursula didn't hear her, because at that moment Morgan came to a halt and bowed.

Ursula already knew what he had come to tell her. It was as if Morgan's arrival and the message he bore was an event that repeated itself endlessly throughout the whole of eternity; and this, the mere enactment, was some kind of perpetual ritual.

He said nothing at first; instead he simply looked at her, his gaze conveying far more than mere words. It was to be his sorrowful expression more than anything else that Ursula would relive again and again in thoughts and dreams.

Still without speaking, Morgan reached out, gently took hold of her hand, turned it palm upwards and delicately placed within it a small object.

She didn't need to look down to know what it was.

With the crowd still chanting "More!" *she pulled back and handed him the small trinket she had been working on.*

'*What is it?*' *he was forced to shout.*

'*It's a tiny portrait of me that Brittola painted. I had it set in a silver frame and encased in wood. I decorated it myself. It's something for you to remember me by.*'

While she was speaking, she placed it around his neck. For a moment, it dangled awkwardly against his breastplate on its black cord. She smiled and tucked it inside against his chest.

'*I shall never take it off even when I'm bathing.*'

He took her firmly by the shoulders and looked deep into her eyes.

'*Always remember this. Only in your voice ... I hear family. Only in your eyes ... I see home.*'

'There was a great battle, Your Highness.'

Morgan's voice finally pierced the heavy silence.

'Constans was down to just a thousand men, his trusted Vanguard and a loyal detachment of Batavian cavalry. The others had deserted him, believing the rumours that Constantine was about to be ousted. It was said that a huge force from Italia was coming, possibly led by Honorius himself, but certainly sent in his name, and only those loyal to the House of Theodosius would be rewarded, or even spared.

'Constans was determined to come to his father's aid and join forces with him in order to crush Gerontius and his puny

256

army, but the defectors knew too many of his secrets – mountain paths, caves and camps – and Gerontius was able to set a trap. Constans and his men were using a narrow pass to slip past the enemy when they rounded a bend in the ravine and suddenly found themselves facing a fierce array of chariots blocking their path with many hundreds of cavalry rapidly approaching to their rear. Even though— '

'*No-no! It can't be true!*' shrieked one of the younger officers and several of the women began to cry.

'Even though they were outnumbered five-to-one and at a complete disadvantage, the enemy lost over half their number before the fighting was over. Constans himself was one of the last to succumb; they found his body still kneeling in the midst of many slain enemy warriors all of whom had perished by his sword. The standard of the First Horse was tucked under his right arm, for he'd used it as a crutch after he received his first wounds. His hand was so tightly clasped around … ' he nodded to indicate the object in Ursula's grasp, 'those who found him had to cut it free.'

'Was there any … ' Ursula paused to quell her tears, then began again. 'I mean, did he send a final message?'

Morgan shook his head and looked downward as if to say 'you have it in your hand.'

He then turned to face the others and address them in a much louder voice.

'As if this tragedy wasn't enough of a burden to convey, I'm afraid I bring yet more grave news that affects us all; indeed, the entire world.'

'Go on,' said Pinnosa, walking over to Ursula and putting an arm around her.

'Soon after I arrived in Mogontiacum earlier today, another urgent, and most terrible, report also reached the city from beyond the Alps.'

He looked upward to the heavens and took a long deep breath, steeling himself for a proclamation he clearly did not wish to deliver.

'The Eternal City has been assailed, ransacked and pillaged by that curse of the West, Alaric and his Visigoths!'

'You don't mean— ' gasped Rusticus with shock as several of the women wailed in anguish.

'Yes, I fear Mother Roma herself has been razed to the ground; the greatest of all cities smoulders still – like a sacrificial pyre – as we speak.'

VII

Ursula was pacing up and down in the small chapel attached to the Officers' Hall at the barracks in Colonia. In the weeks since Morgan had delivered his news, it had become her custom to shut herself away in the quiet barely-lit and plainly-decorated room, leaving strict orders not to be disturbed.

After a while, she sat cross-legged on the floor and stared blankly at the altar, her eyes devoid of expression; then she rose to her feet and resumed her pacing, this time tugging at her hair and plucking at her robe. The tugging quickly intensified until she was pulling out great tufts of hair and at the same time her robe began to tear and fray; suddenly, she stopped pacing and cried out loud.

'Dear God! Dear merciful God! Where *are* you? Where is your light? Please, *please* let me see your light, Lord, so that I might know you are there, Lord, and know your Will; for I am withering in this accursed darkness, Lord; I am drowning in these shadows, these horrid, *horrid* shadows!'

She collapsed at the base of the altar, heaving with sobs, her tears flowing freely and staining the cold stone.

'I know now that my great sin has been selfishness, Lord. All that I did, I did for my own ends. I formed the First Athena, taking twenty thousand of Britannia's best from their homes and families and denying them natural lives. I brought them on this-this *accursed* mission, all because I wanted to secure a home and a family for myself. You've seen fit to punish me for my sins, Lord, and deny me that which I craved. All I ask, dear Lord, is that you punish *only* me; punish *me*, Lord, and spare the others.'

'*Amen!*'

Startled, Ursula span round to see Brittola standing in the doorway, looking unsure whether to enter.

'Why are you bothering me? What do you want?'

'May I join you in prayer?'

Brittola smiled and took a tentative step forward.

Ursula stared at her blankly for the longest of moments, then slowly nodded and turned away, returning her sightless gaze to the altar.

Brittola gently knelt down beside Ursula and produced her cross from inside her tunic; then she closed her eyes tight and began praying in a quiet voice that was almost a whisper.

'Dear Lord. Her Highness, Princess Ursula of Corinium, dutiful daughter of King Deonotus, founder and commander-in-chief of the Legion First Athena, is feeling completely lost and bewildered. She thinks, Lord, that it was *she* who created our legion of women and set them on their mission. Please find it in your mercy, Lord, to make her realise that in all that she has done she has been *your* instrument, working in *your* service. Please enable her to understand, Lord, that it was *your* Will that plucked us from our homes and families; and it was *your* Will that sent us on this mission. Most importantly, Dear Lord, please make her see that without her at its head, without her as your instrument, Lord, the First Athena cannot continue on its Great Expedition which the people of Britannia, and of all Rome, now need to succeed more than ever.'

Brittola opened her eyes and turned to look at Ursula who continued to stare impassively into space. She then leaned forward determined to catch Ursula's eye. Ursula groaned and turned to face her, eyes glaring.

'Oh dear,' said Brittola. 'You're giving me that look.'

'What look?'

'The look you used to give me when we were children, especially when you wanted me to keep quiet, remember?'

Ursula frowned for a moment, then smiled a faint smile.

'I could certainly be noisy in those days, couldn't I?'

Brittola gave a slight chuckle. 'If I didn't get what I wanted; I used to whine and— '

'*Ha!* "Whine" you say? Squeal like a scared cat, more like. It was most annoying.'

Ursula stood up, wandered over to the tiny window behind the altar and stared out of it.

'I wasn't the only one with annoying traits in those days,' continued Brittola. 'You weren't perfect yourself you know; you could be just as annoying in your own way.'

'How do you mean?'

'You used to hate being distracted. When you were fully engrossed in something, you used to make a terrible fuss if anyone dared to interrupt you.'

'No, that's not true.'

'Oh? What about that time you were arguing with Bishop Patroclus about the preachings of that wily old fox Pelagius; something about the mortal duties of Man versus the immortal duties of God? You were determined to go through the reasoning meticulously, point by point, pulling apart the logic. It was around the time of my grandfather's birthday. I came in to ask you about the preparations for the feast and I interrupted you, remember? You shouted at me in a voice so loud, I swear the angels must have heard in Heaven! You said "Don't *distract* me so Brittola; can't you see— "'

'"Can't you see I'm busy?"' Ursula's voice overlapped with Brittola's. 'Then you said "But it's important Ursula; I need your help." to which I said "No-no-no please don't distract me so, not now; I will *not* suffer such distraction when I'm busy with something important; do you hear? I will *not* be distracted; never, never, not *ever*, again!"'

'Heavens—yes, that is exactly what you said, word for word!'

Ursula spun around, her eyes blazing.

'Brittola, you've been a great help! I can see now where I went wrong; I allowed myself to be distracted … distracted from performing God's will.' She smiled. 'Well, I most certainly will not be distracted again!'

'I'm not sure I understand Ursula. What are you saying?'

'I thought it was the storm and our unplanned diversion into Germania that was the distraction, distracting us from our task; from the Great Expedition. But I was wrong Brittola, I was completely wrong. Don't you see?' Brittola shook her head. 'Our *true* task – God's task – was to come to these ravaged lands and do what the First Athena was originally created to do; what the

260

First Athena does best; what God *intended* the First Athena to do ... *frontier patrols!'*

Returning to the altar, Ursula once more knelt down by Brittola's side.

'Our being blown off course and our fleet scattered as far as the land of the Friesians wasn't a *"distraction"* from our mission, it *was* our mission; God's mission, and our Destiny! As you have always said old friend, our true mission in life is to do the work that God sets before us; and I can see now that if I'm to complete our mission, I need to serve Him ... exclusively.'

'What do you mean?'

'I'll not be distracted from my calling to God or to the First Athena ever again; and there is only one way I can prevent any further distractions ... '

She looked up at the altar's plain wooden cross.

' ... and that is to wear the White.'

Brittola gasped.

'I'll never be distracted from my mission again Brittola by the whims of men and the clammy hands of-of-princes and-and would-be emperors! Tomorrow morning, I will go to Bishop Clematius and ask him to administer a Vow of Chastity.'

Brittola stared at Ursula aghast then leapt to her feet.

'Oh Ursula, that is truly wonderful news! I have long wished to take the Vow and wear the White,' she cried, her lips trembling. 'Can I take it with you? Can I ... *ple-eee-ease?'*

For a long moment they locked eyes then Ursula slowly nodded which made Brittola smile; but then, almost immediately her smile faltered and she looked anxious—vexed even.

'There's something else, something you need to know. It's the reason I came here to see you ... '

Brittola fiddled with her cross uneasily.

'What is it?'

'Ursula ... Cordula will also be with Bishop Clematius tomorrow; but she won't be taking any vows ... she'll be seeking forgiveness and mercy.'

'Oh? Why's that?'

'She is with child.'

VIII

From Augustus Constantine III, Emperor of the West and Grand Commander of all its armies, to Princess Ursula, Commander-in-Chief of the Legions First and Second Athena.

Hail great princess and commander! Please accept my apologies for not writing sooner. I will refrain from expressing my grief, for in Constans' death I know we both share a loss of similar magnitude. Suffice to say I hope the time will come soon when we can console each other in person and alleviate some of the pain. Unfortunately, we must not only mourn his death, we must also grieve his defeat which was a major setback in terms of our fight against Gerontius and his horde (his undisciplined rabble does not merit the title "army").

As Morgan's reports will have informed you, I took full advantage of the winter months to slip out of Arelate undetected and survey the situation with our nemeses, the Burgundians. No less than twelve separate tribes are now wandering throughout the upper Rhenus and Rhodanus valleys, keeping the main force of my army fully preoccupied! I have just returned to Arelate to make preparations for the forthcoming campaign season which I don't mind admitting I now dread.

Our situation here in southern Gallia is becoming more and more perilous. When I returned from my surveillance of the Burgundians, I discovered that a further five hundred of my imperial guard had deserted to Gerontius' ranks, apparently believing they will be better rewarded there. With the complete loss of Constans' division and the depletion of my main force due to the near constant run-ins with Burgundians, I can now only count twelve thousand men loyal to me, of which less than five thousand are cavalry.

My greatest fear is what might now come at us from across the Alps. After their victory at Roma, the Goths are now emboldened and might even be contemplating an expansion into Gallia. More worryingly, instead of doing as he should and join forces with me in order to rid Italia of its nemeses, Honorius has instead sent for reinforcements from Constantinopolis which he may then decide to use against me.

Oh, the tragedy of Rome and the absurdities wrought by our thirst for power! When will we realise that ultimately our fellow Romans are more than our greatest rivals? They are also our greatest allies!

On to matters concerning you and the First Athena.

Firstly, I discovered in the course of my surveillance mission that the "Grand Deception" plan you used so effectively with the Alemanni may now be working against you. Several of our informers told me that the Burgundian tribes are convinced a great army of over thirty thousand women is patrolling the Limes. I have also received reports from Italia that suggest the same beliefs are held there. Beware! You can be certain that Honorius and Theodosius the Second are following your feats up there in frontier country very closely. If they perceive you to be a formidable force loyal to me, you can expect them to be plotting your downfall, probably working in league together.

I think the greatest potential threat you must be on constant alert against is Mundzuk and his ever-growing horde. The Huns are now wintering on the banks of the Danuvius just west of Vindobona. Theodosius positioned them there to keep Honorius's forces divided. All the while the Goths are keeping Honorius fully preoccupied, the Huns will no longer have a part to play in Theodosius' grand scheme. Mundzuk and his warlords may be feeling restless and spoiling for a fight, in which case the prospect of taking on a large mobile force of Roman women may be too tempting to resist!

This brings me to a sensitive topic: whether or not the Legion First Athena should stay on the Continent. I am no longer optimistic that the Great Expedition can proceed. I do not think at this stage that the First Athena should continue to be deployed along the Rhenus or for that matter anywhere on the Continent where you are at risk from hostile forces such as Mundzuk's horde. I shall refrain from ordering your return to Britannia in this dispatch, but I would like your comments on the matter in your next report so that I can make a final decision before the campaign season gets properly under way.

Finally, a personal comment on your decision to take a Vow of Chastity. I have to confess that in my mind's eye you are still a young teenager full of joy, hope and happiness. You used to play such games with your friends and family when I saw you at feasts. I sometimes find it difficult to reconcile that image of you with the highly resourceful and respected commander of legions that I now know.

But then I remember a stalwart young nineteen-year-old woman who stood up to me behind the Officers' Hall in Corinium. Then, two mornings later, you held yourself with such dignity and grace as your beloved and betrothed Constans made what was to be his final farewell. It was always clear to me that you have all the warmth and compassion of your father as well as the fierce determination of your late mother (indeed these were the qualities I welcomed in my son's choice for his bride).

I now realise there is something special in you that was put there by God to equip you for the great challenges that you were to face. Whatever this quality is in you, I know that it is something I cannot fully fathom, having never encountered anything quite like it before in a woman. Perhaps it is this quality that has guided you to your momentous decision.

As your commander, I fully respect your decision. Your Vow of Chastity does not compromise your effectiveness as an officer in any way; indeed, it may even enhance it! As the father of Constans, I would like to say to you that a love such as yours was made in Heaven, and I believe that he took your soul there with him when he died. Without your soul, no other relationship would ever hold meaning for you. This explains why you have chosen to forego other men in what is left of this, your mortal life. Constans, I know, is with you in this, as he will always be with you. Moreover, he is the only one who can truly appreciate what it means to you.

May God be with you.
Augustus Constantine III.

PS I wasn't surprised to hear of Brittola's decision to wear the White with you, but I'm curious to know why Martha has taken the Vow, and even more curious to know why Saula didn't. I thought those two always did everything together!

264

IX

Report to Emperor Augustus Constantine III, Grand Commander of all the armies of the West, from Princess Ursula, daughter of King Deonotus of Corinium, Commander-in-Chief of the Legions First and Second Athena.

    Hail Constantine! Thank you for your generous words about Constans. I too look forward to the day we can mourn him together which is why I was so saddened by your suggestion that the First Athena should leave the lands of the Rhenus and return to Britannia. I do not share your pessimism concerning your position or ours or, indeed, the prospect of our recommencing the Great Expedition. Your numbers might be down to twelve thousand, the Burgundians may be keeping you embroiled in the provincial matters of Gallia more than you had anticipated, and Gerontius may be proving more tenacious than anyone expected, but I am positive the tide will turn in our favour soon.

    Allow me to refresh your memory concerning the more positive aspects of our situation. Firstly, the frontier along the Rhenus is secure with the Alemanni and the Franks now proving themselves to be credible allies in keeping other tribes at bay. Secondly, Jovinus, after much prompting by Bishop Clematius, Rusticus and myself, is finally making use of the new-found security of the frontier to entice several cities in northern Gallia to release their standing guards in order to march south to reinforce you. He is making the rounds personally and should have accumulated at least seven thousand men, including three thousand cavalry, by the time he sets forth in July. Thirdly, all the reports we receive here from Italia suggest that the Goths and Honorius are keeping each other so busy, there is little or no possibility of either of them being capable of crossing the Alps to strike at you, certainly not before Jovinus arrives with his reinforcements. Finally, now that the frontier is holding and no further tribes are breaking through, the Burgundians should settle down on the lands you have allocated them in the Rhenus and Rhodanus valleys and your main force should be free to assist you in breaking Gerontius' siege around the same time as Jovinus heads south. My optimism is possible because the First Athena is making good use of the improved military roads you built four years ago on the Limes. We are able to maintain cavalry and infantry patrols that represent a credible Roman presence. This in turn keeps the Franks and Alemanni in check.

I would now like to relay to you our recommendations concerning the legion's deployment which we have discussed at length here. Firstly, now that your numbers are down to under twelve thousand we don't see the need to maintain more women on the Continent than would be needed for a reduced Great Expedition, so we recommend that around six thousand infantry and five hundred cavalry return to Britannia to reinforce the Second Athena. The Second may well become stretched this year if the rumours of a Grand Alliance between the Hibernians, Picts and Saxons are true. Julia has volunteered to lead the force; and I strongly recommend we appoint her to the task and make her acting commander-in-chief of both armies; the Second will benefit greatly from her experience and skill as a leader. I would also like to send Baetica back as head of the cavalry; apart from Pinnosa, she and Viventia are the only commanders who could command the necessary respect from the Second.

Another reason why we think it would be good to send some of the women back is that it would give a much-needed boost to the morale of those left behind. A minority, about a third, of the women are finding their task here difficult and the conditions hard to bear. I can't help feeling that if we allowed them to return to Britannia, the morale of the remaining two thirds, who are still fully intent on the Great Expedition, would improve dramatically.

My second recommendation concerns the duties of the remaining eleven thousand of the First Athena. I propose to continue our patrols of the frontier, sending a deployment of two thousand cavalry per month down the full length of the Limes as a show of force. In addition, I will send two smaller detachments of a thousand infantry plus five hundred cavalry per month into northern Gallia to reassure the cities and towns of our presence. We will implement these plans twenty days from this date unless we receive orders to the contrary.

Thank you for your kind words concerning my Vow of Chastity. It's a great shame that you as a man cannot make the same choice; I would heartily recommend it!

Incidentally, your messenger's wife is doing well; the baby is due in July. She has discharged herself from the legion, but refuses to be separated from her friends despite Morgan's pleas for her to return to Britannia. We have made a special home for her in the messengers' courtyard from where she supervises all our ordnance crews. A few of Rusticus' many aunts visit her there and fuss over her like an empress!

You are always in my prayers.
Your ever faithful
Ursula.

PS Finally, a note to explain something that we shouldn't expect a busy emperor to be aware of: Martha's young man, Blussus of Glevum, was killed with Constans, whereas Saula's young man, Lucius Brigionis, is still with you in your imperial guard.

X

'It is said that their leaders take cruel pleasure in skinning and burning their victims alive.'

The speaker was a lean man named Gunderic who was Chief of the Vandals, a nomadic and particularly warlike people who were looking to the Roman authorities to protect them from the Huns. He paused momentarily to allow his statement to be translated throughout the assembly; then he continued to address the gathering in his distinctive thick dark voice.

'Then, while the wretched souls still breathe, they tear their victims' innards out with their bare hands and eat the offal raw before their dying eyes.'

Upon hearing this, one of the younger Alemanni princes had to withdraw from the chamber and could be heard retching outside.

It was Ursula's third meeting with the Alemanni chiefs and leaders in Mogontiacum, and the first since taking her Vow. She chose to hold it in the grandiose Augustus Room with its colonnade of pillars, statues of past Roman emperors and huge circular table made of oak because not only was it the most imperious, imposing and impressive meeting space in all

Mogontiacum, it was also the most appropriate for her new guise as a confirmed virgin dedicated to Christ, having several sacred wall hangings and tapestries that were Christian.

Whether it was the décor or Ursula's dominating and intimidating presence – a full imperial Roman commander-in-chief's uniform all in pure white – the setting certainly had the desired effect on the Alemanni chieftains; they were on their best behaviour for their meeting with the Roman delegation which on this occasion included just Pinnosa and Rusticus from Colonia plus the garrison commander and some high-ranking officials from Mogontiacum.

At each successive meeting that Ursula held with the Alemanni or their fellow Roman federates the Franks, the reports about Mundzuk and his approaching Hun horde were becoming more and more worrying as well as increasingly gruesome. This was the first time the chieftain of the Vandals had been invited to join them; he'd been invited because his people roamed farther to the east than any of the other tribes and as a result had more contact with victims of the Huns.

'We hear many stories about these Huns, concerning their prowess as fighters, but we don't know what to believe,' said the Alemanni chief, Luethari. 'For instance, I have heard they can fire arrows round corners and have special spears that can fly wherever the thrower wills them to fly, defying the laws of nature. Is there any truth in these rumours?'

Gunderic shook his head vigorously and frowned.

'These are the fanciful myths of children Luethari; you must not believe all that you hear! The truth is these Huns are no better fighters than any of us. I have met men who have fought them in battle and I can tell you it is not their skills with weapons that you need to fear—it is their skill with horses! It is said that on the battlefield their ability to get into one formation then change tactics and regroup is second to none. One man told me it is like fighting a swarm of hornets, ever shifting, ever regrouping and ever on the attack.'

'Yes, I have heard that,' said Luethari. 'I've also heard that just when you think they have scattered to the four winds, they are able to regroup out of nowhere and charge at you while your own cavalry is still giving chase; and when they attack, they attack as one, completely overwhelming you like a rampaging bull. It is said if the Hun charges at you, *he* cannot miss … and *you* cannot hide.'

Rusticus' translation was followed by a long ominous silence. Neither Ursula nor Pinnosa could think of anything to say to counteract the sense of gloom and dismay that enveloped the gathering and, just for once, not even Rusticus could find words to raise their mood. Eventually, Gunderic spoke again.

'As you know, we have scouts patrolling the *Limes*—'

'*Hah!* Do you take us for fools Gunderic?' exclaimed Pinnosa in a loud mocking voice. 'Please don't insult us so; "patrolling the Limes"—*pah!* "looking for opportunities to mount a raid" more like.'

Gunderic glared at her, then continued.

'It is clear to us what Mundzuk and his horde are doing; they are following the line of the abandoned *Limes* and using it as if it were a "road", a road they know will lead them directly to the Rhenus. And why are they doing this? Well, isn't it obvious? They cannot resist the tantalising prospect, the irresistible lure, of an encounter with the legendary Britannic fighting women … and their leader, the Virgin Princess.'

He stared fiercely at Ursula and all eyes followed, as the delegates turned to hear her response. Slowly, she cast her gaze around the table, deliberately looking each one of the Alemanni chieftains in the eye, attempting to gauge their mood. They were much more nervous than usual but, more worryingly, there was little sign of the deference they had previously shown her, all of which made her feel distinctly uncomfortable.

She'd come to the meeting intending to inform them about the reduction in numbers and redeployment of the First Athena as well as the departure of the remaining detachments of men from the Colonia and Mogontiacum garrisons to Arelate in support of Constantine, but now she realised that she needed to choose her words extra carefully.

'Friends, allies and esteemed guests; I have come here today to inform you that we have temporarily had to curtail some of our routine patrols along the *Limes* and re-deploy units of the First Athena and the Colonia garrison elsewhere.'

There were exclamations of surprise and cries of protest at her announcement. The chieftains began talking animatedly amongst themselves with many beginning to sound angry; the mood in the large hall had suddenly, and palpably, darkened.

Pinnosa thumped her fist on the table for quiet; then nodded for Ursula to continue.

'Throughout the summer months you, the Alemanni, along with the Franks, will have to take on a larger share of the frontier responsibilities. This includes the border patrols who will be— '

' —*the first to run into Mundzuk!*'

It was Botilin, a burly broad-chested man with a thick beard and a face like gnarled wood who had spoken in Britannic. He leapt to his feet and cracked his whip across the table at the Roman delegation.

'We the Alemanni are the world's *greatest* fighters, but even we will struggle to defeat such a powerful foe!' He glared at the far end of the table where Ursula and Pinnosa were seated side by side. 'How do you suggest we stop this horde which, so I've heard, is thirty thousand strong and still growing? How do we stop this rampaging murderous beast with thirty thousand heads that can swipe whole armies away as a bear might do a troublesome gnat, especially if they are feeble women be they Roman or— '

Pinnosa threw back her chair with a loud clatter and leapt to her feet, muttering in Ursula's ear 'I'm nipping this in the bud right now!'

'*That's enough!*' she cried and drew her sword.

Then, with a swift downward swipe, she severed the lash of Botilin's whip before he could snatch it back.

The meeting erupted into shouts, threats and counter-shouts; weapons were drawn and even a spear was thrown at the royal delegation, passing close to Rusticus' head before impaling itself in a tapestry of the three Magi bearing gifts for baby Jesus.

'*I will have silence!*' shouted Pinnosa. '*I will have* … *SILENCE!*'

She leapt onto the table with both swords drawn and rotated in a full circle, pointing her blades at each chieftain.

Slowly, one-by-one, they all sat back down.

'You do not attack a beast with thirty thousand heads,' she continued in a calmer more measured voice, but still circling with her swords pointing. 'You watch it carefully; you study its habits; and you continue studying its habits relentlessly until you discover its weak point. Then, and only then, once you know its weakness, will you be in a position to know how to defeat it.'

While Rusticus translated, she continued to circle with her blades poised, gauging their response; and she saw them begin to sneer at her suggestion. Realising she needed to do more, she jumped off the table and landed in front of Botilin; then she immediately flipped her long officer's sword over end-to-end so that she was holding it by the point, and knelt down to offer him the hilt.

'We, the women of the First Athena, will help you study this Mundzuk and his horde; we will work with you to devise a plan to defeat them and capture Mundzuk himself; and when we *do* find him, whether we kill him there and then or put him on trial first to humiliate him before killing him, it would give us no greater honour than if you, great chief Botilin, were to deliver the killing blow.'

Her speech over, she thrust the hilt toward Botilin and smiled at him. The swarthy old chieftain was utterly confused, not knowing what to do. As he listened to Rusticus' translation, he kept nervously looking this way and that; then, with a clumsy attempt at a gracious bow, he smiled a broad toothless smile and awkwardly accepted her gift, tentatively at first but then firmly, gripping the much-prized Roman sword tight and thrusting it high in triumph.

From that moment on, the rest of the meeting was calm and constructive.

Afterwards, as the Roman delegation made its way back across the Rhenus bridge, heading for the barracks on the opposite shore, Ursula, Pinnosa and Rusticus exchanged thoughts on the meeting while riding side-by-side.

'There is one thing you must understand about these Germanic tribes,' said Rusticus, taking a much-needed swig of his beloved wine. 'They can take up the life of wandering and roaming just as easily as they gave it up. When they agreed to fight for Rome, they thought it would simply mean keeping out more of their own kind. When these horrendous Huns and their horde arrive, you'd be foolish to count on them standing by your side. If the Huns are after Roman prey, as far as the Germans are concerned, that is a Roman problem.'

He looked at them both before continuing.

'Should events turn out that way, I advise you to move the First Athena inside the fortress if you're at Mogontiacum or inside the city walls if you're at Colonia. From there, you should be able to look on in safety as you hope and pray for the monster with thirty thousand heads to get bored of toying with the caged birds that it can't get its claws on and move on elsewhere in a search for easier pickings.'

'Thank you for your kind advice Rusticus,' said Ursula with a wry smile and a wink at Pinnosa, 'but please don't forget we "caged birds" have claws of our own!'

XI

The following morning, Rusticus rose early for his departure to Treveris where he was to rendezvous with Jovinus. It had been decided he would accompany the new army the prince had raised on their long march south to relieve Constantine whose need for a skilled interpreter was now even greater than Ursula's.

When he emerged from the barracks, he was dressed more for a hunt than a military campaign, with a long red riding cloak and a bright green hunting hat which had an even brighter plume of orange feathers. Ursula and the others looked on sadly as he and his attendant commenced their usual struggle to heave his full frame onto his mount, then stood in line beside his horse, taking it in turn to kiss his heavily bejewelled hand as they said their farewells.

'Take care of yourself Rusticus!' said Ursula. 'Be sure to give our regards to Jovinus; and tell him to have courage.'

'And if by chance you meet up with Gerontius on your travels,' said Pinnosa, 'kindly slash his throat for me! But before you do, please remember to say a few short words first.'

'What are they?'

'"This is a thorn from a young Britannic rose".'

272

'Will that mean something to him?'

'Oh yes, it will mean something all right! It'll remind him of something he'd rather leave forgotten; and hopefully add to his torment in Hell!'

'When you see Constantine,' said Saula, 'please impress upon him that the First Athena is ready to recommence the Great Expedition at a moment's notice? All we need is his word.'

'Don't worry. We'll get you young Britannic people together for your Grand Wedding as soon as we can.'

Rusticus smiled and looked over toward the assembled ranks of the Vanguard who had especially turned out in their full dress uniforms for his send-off; then he returned his gaze to the commanders who were all huddled about his horse like a bunch of adoring children.

'Ladies! It has been an honour and a privilege to work with you this past year-and-a-half. You have not only shown me what women are truly capable of, but you have also made me realise it is wrong to despair even when it seems all hope is lost.'

He looked at them one-by-one, ending with Ursula.

'You have taught me well ... and I love you dearly.'

Upon seeing that the women were all close to tears, even Pinnosa; he grinned a mischievous grin.

'I want you all to promise me that one day, when this dreadful turmoil is over, we'll get together and return to the hot springs at Aquae Mattiacorum to resume our all-too-brief respite from our duties that was so rudely interrupted.'

'We will, dear Rusticus; we surely will,' said Ursula. 'On behalf of the entire First Athena, I hereby promise. Now go; and fare well in Arelate!'

He nudged his horse and moved off towards the bridge that would take back him to Mogontiacum, After a few steps he turned to call out over his shoulder.

'Oh, by the way, there is no need for you to worry about me; my Aunt Thebis is from Arelate and— '

'*We know, we know!*' shouted Ursula as she and the others all joined in chorus. '*You loved her dearly, and she taught you well!*'

XII

'*Oooh*—just look at those dinky fingers,' Saula teased Cordula's baby boy with a gentle tickle, 'and that handsome dark hair!'

'He's such a cutie-pie!' Martha chuckled.

The six old friends from Corinium, along with Faustina and Viventia and a few junior officers, were huddled around the wickerwork crib that Cordula had placed beside the window in the commanders' room at the barracks in Colonia so that they could admire him. Ursula, Martha and Brittola were dressed in their whites along with one of Viventia's junior officers.

'We all know who *your* father is, don't we you little fidget midget?' Martha tickled the baby's tummy making him giggle which, in turn, made the women laugh.

While they were laughing, Ursula pulled Pinnosa away, leaving the others to their fun. Despite it being mid-August, the July frontier patrols had barely been completed; indeed, Pinnosa had only just returned that morning and this was Ursula's first chance to speak to her alone.

'I am so pleased to see you,' she said in hushed tones once they were away from the others. 'I was beginning to get worried.'

'We had a bit of trouble with a rogue unit of Vandals which took us further east along the *Limes* than we usually— '

'"East"? "Along the Limes"? Any sign of— '

'No nothing! If there is a horde, it's a horde of rumours. Anyway, I understand we weren't the only ones to be waylaid. What's this I hear about you having to make a special trip to Mogontiacum?'

'Tongues talk fast around here, don't they?' Ursula lowered her voice to a hushed whisper. 'It's the Alemanni. The closer you-know-who gets, the more restless they become. Once again, they threatened to cross the frontier and head into Gallia; and they insisted on meeting with me personally. Reassurance, reassurance, reassurance; they *crave* reassurance!'

'At least they still acknowledge your authority.'

'That is small comfort. It's not just the Alemanni or the delays to our patrols that are troubling me. While you've been away, I had to send Martha and Faustina to Treveris to bolster the standing guards; it turned out the entire garrison was about to disband following the departure of Jovinus.'

She looked anxiously at Pinnosa.

'Do you think we are in danger of becoming stretched too thin? We are being asked and expected to cover ever more duties, ever more ground.'

'I still think our main problems lay with the Alemanni. Constantine was right in his misgivings; I sometimes think our duties would be easier without them.'

'And what exactly are our "duties" these days? I'm not sure I know anymore. I sometimes think— '

Suddenly noticing that the room had gone conspicuously quiet, Ursula and Pinnosa turned around to find all eyes fixated upon them and all ears listening to what they were saying. There was a quiet cough and Brittola stepped out from the huddle to break the awkward silence that ensued.

'Well, I think our duty is most definitely to protect this area and all its peoples, be they Christian or barbarian, from the scourge of the Huns. Mundzuk and his minions are the biggest monsters on God's earth; there is nothing they wouldn't do to satisfy their lust for plunder.'

'That is true and Brittola is right,' said Faustina. 'The *Limes* is theirs to wander – and plunder – as they wish. I hear they spent the spring laying waste to many of the estates in Noricum, an area neither Honorius nor Constantine have the resources to patrol. There is no-one who can stand up to them down in the south; but there is someone here … *US!*'

'You say "laying waste" Faustina as if it was nothing, a mere trifle!' Brittola's voice was shrill with emotion. 'Have you heard what they actually *do* to people? It is said they— '

'Come, come now!' Ursula strode over and put her arm around Brittola's shoulder. 'Not in front of the baby, please!'

She turned to address Cordula, clearly determined to change the subject.

'What will you call him?' she asked, clasping Cordula's hand. 'Will you give him Morgan's father's name?'

'No-no, we've already decided against that.'

Cordula looked magnificent in motherhood, like a rose in full bloom even though she was no longer in uniform and dressed in a plain brown tunic.

'We both feel we'd like a name which stands for a completely new start, the beginning of a new world.'

Cordula led Ursula back to her baby and picked him up; his eyes were open wide and he appeared to grin at the sight of the white lady before him which made them all laugh.

'Anyway, his father hasn't seen him yet. How can he name a child he doesn't know? When he does— '

'Your Highness, ladies; I bring you grave news!'

They all spun around to where the familiar male voice had come from and were astonished to see Morgan standing in the doorway, looking horribly pale. He was holding on tight to a pillar to steady himself and he was dressed in what looked to be a monk's garb, though it was hard to tell; his robes were so tattered and smothered in road dust.

Ursula stepped forward.

'Morgan. We were just admiring your new-born son.' She gestured for the others to move aside. 'Cordula?'

Cordula emerged from the cluster of women to stand before him, holding her baby in her arms. Morgan's face filled with wonder and he took several wobbly steps toward his wife and child with his arms outstretched; but then his smile faded and his arms drooped; and he staggered sideways to a nearby bench where he collapsed, the last vestige of his energy spent. The magical moment was shattered, leaving Cordula to stare at her husband wide-eyed with shock.

'Constantine is dead!' he cried out in anguish. 'They're *all* dead or worse than dead ... many have turned traitor!'

XIII

Having ridden Hermes hard almost non-stop, day upon day, to deliver his terrible news, Morgan was so utterly exhausted he was unable to move from the bench where he had collapsed. Even so, after Oleander had wiped him down and given him some refreshment, he forced himself to summon the strength to tell the gathering what had happened.

While he was speaking, most of the women remained seated around him, listening intently, but Ursula moved away to stand by the window, preferring to stare out at the parade ground and watch a late-summer squall sprinkle the dry grey dust as she listened to his heart-wrenching words.

'Things started to go wrong for us with the surprise death of Alaric. Honorius was once again back in control of northern Italia with a full force of over ten thousand well-armed and fully-trained Roman legionaries at his disposal. Half of them were on loan from Constantinopolis and under the leadership of a certain Constantius of Moesia – a ruthless and highly capable commander known as "Iron Fist" – and this Iron Fist was more than ready to crush his master's enemies which, first and foremost, meant Constantine.

'With Alaric gone, the Visioths no longer posed a threat to Honorius and, in any case, they were safely out of his way far to the south. We, on the other hand, were just over the Alps and, although we were considerably weakened by the web of intrigue that he and Stilicho had engineered, to him we were still looking dangerously poised to muster our forces and make a foray into Italia. Indeed, we now know that Honorius was even concerned we might be joined at any moment by our incredibly resourceful women on the Rhenus.

'So it was that the moment the marching season started, Honorius sent Iron Fist across the Alps to retake Gallia. He and his army emerged from the Alps without any warning soon after Ostara, the vernal equinox, and marched straight for Arelate. We had just managed to assemble a sizeable force ourselves and were in the process of chasing down Gerontius when Iron Fist's army suddenly arrived from Italia, catching us all completely off-guard. Gerontius, in his dim-witted confusion, presumed Iron Fist was reinforcing us and took flight, returning to Hispania and leaving behind his "federate" German tribesmen who, by now, were completely confused as to where their allegiance should lie.

'In the midst of all the mayhem and confusion, Iron Fist caught up with Gerontius and pinned him down in a fortress in northern Hispania. Apparently, the sad debauched old dog tried to fend them off with a few arrows that he fired from the rooftop before committing suicide rather than face justice. The remaining

Hispanic men from Gerontius' army then joined forces with the Italians and marched back with them to Arelate to confront us.

'This was to prove the final, and fatal, turning point in Constantine's fortunes. While we'd been out in the field dealing with yet another Germanic invasion down the Rhodanus valley, the imperial court in Arelate took heart in the surprise presence of a considerable force coming from Italia and, in a show of allegiance to "the true emperor Honorius", they closed the city gates on "Constantine the usurper", denying us entry.

'We suddenly found ourselves with no base, out in the open and exposed to attack; a brave but weary army of just five thousand pitted against a force of ten thousand fresh legionaries from Italia reinforced by three thousand seasoned federate traitors and another three thousand Hispanic allies.

'The battle lasted barely an hour; and I'm ashamed to say only a few of the Britannic divisions actually fought. I was standing beside Constantine when at one point we saw a whole cohort throw down their standard and run to join the opposing ranks—*so blatant was their treachery!*'

Overcome with emotion, Morgan was forced to pause and take several deep breaths before he could continue.

'The spirit of the men had been waning ever since the fateful decision to head south and support the court at Arelate; but it was the defeat of Constans last year that placed so much doubt in their hearts.

'As soon as Constantine saw which way the wind was blowing, he gave his last order. I was standing right next to him, so I can repeat it word for word.

"Brave and loyal men of Britannia, we must concede that the day is lost. All we have fought hard for and tried to achieve these past few years is about to be destroyed. Our only chance now is to flee this field of shattered dreams and meet again in a long-lost land that we once proudly called home.

"I have no other choice on this godforsaken day but to issue the most cowardly of orders ... *FLEE I SAY—FLEE NOW! Flee as fast as you can and as far as you can; make good your escape! Head for home; head for Britannia!* With the good lord on our side, months from now, we will regroup on home soil and begin to rebuild, perhaps with the help of our valiant women. *NOW, GO! ... ALL OF YOU—GO!*"'

Morgan sobbed with the pain of his memories; and Cordula wiped away his tears, coaxing him to finish.

'We had left it too late. We were the victims of our own foolish pride. The decision to withdraw should have been made much earlier; the enemy was too near and we ... we were too weak. Most of the officers were caught before they could leave the battlefield and were immediately beheaded. Those few that did manage to escape didn't get far, and were soon dead too.

'Constantine and I were fortunate; in the midst of all the confusion we managed to escape from the battlefield. We were alone together just the two of us; and it was then that we had a small stroke of luck which gave us some brief respite. With a cohort of Iron Fist's Italian riders almost upon us, we ducked into a densely wooded valley and stumbled upon a tiny out-of-the-way monastery where we were able to disguise ourselves as priests. In fact ... Your Highness?'

'Yes?'

Ursula turned towards him; her face seemed to have aged ten years and her white uniform, silhouetted against the light of the window, made her look more like a temple priestess than a commander-in-chief.

'Even though the enemy was so close that we could hear them searching for us in the surrounding trees, Constantine made a point of kneeling before the altar in the chapel and saying a short prayer.

"Oh, Holy Father. Some will say it was my misplaced faith that brought me to this place and others will say it was fate, but you know as well as I, Father, that it was neither that led me here; it was one thing, and one thing only ... duty. Apart from you, Holy Father, and my beloved Constans, only Ursula will understand what that truly means".'

He stared at Ursula.

'Do you know what he meant, Your Highness?'

'Yes ... yes, I do.' They all looked at her expectantly, but she simply added quietly, 'Thank you for conveying his words so faithfully; now please continue.'

'There isn't much more to tell, Your Highness. The following morning, still in the guise of priests, we were riding along a narrow road and heading north when suddenly we heard the horns of our pursuers approaching from behind.

"Go!" he shouted to me. "Let Hermes fly and make sure Ursula and the others hear of our demise! *Go, for heaven's sake. Go now!*"'

'Reluctantly, I obeyed him, but then I stopped when I reached the first ridge to look back. The problem was, of course, our horses; priests don't ride such steeds. The search party didn't even bother to check whether or not he was a real priest; they just rode down hard upon him with their swords drawn. He let out a spirited yell and raised his great blade in reply.'

Morgan paused, struggling to retain his composure.

'He died as he had lived; fighting with all his strength!'

XIV

'Ursula?'

Pinnosa appeared in the doorway.

'There's a young Alemanni girl here who I think you should see. Apparently, she was found outside the gate to the barracks a few days ago; she was so badly injured and weak, she was close to death. Cordula took pity on her and admitted her to our hospital where she has responded well to food and medical treatment; and today she spoke for the very first time. When Cordula heard what she had to say, she thought you and I ought to hear it too.'

The commanders' room at the Colonia barracks was almost empty. Ursula and Brittola were seated at the planning table and Oleander was on a stall by the window, sewing. It was the middle of the afternoon on the day after Morgan's awful news. The rest of the commanders and officers were in the bath houses, cleansing themselves as part of their respect for the 'Day of Mourning' that Ursula had declared.

Ursula looked up from her maps and shared a brief look with Brittola.

'Very well,' she said. 'Show her in.'

280

Into the room came a short young teenage girl with her hair bunched on the top of her head in a fashion favoured by the eastern Alemanni tribes. She was accompanied by a legionary from the Londinium cohort, a talented linguist called Cunoarda who was to act as translator.

The Alemanni girl was clearly uncomfortable in the presence of such senior Roman officers; and she was also in obvious physical pain. As she walked toward them, there was a stiffness to her steps and she grimaced as she bowed. Seeing her discomfort, Brittola dragged over a bench and indicated that she should be seated.

The girl's name was impossible to pronounce, but it translated into "Amber" which was what they decided to call her. Her people had been camped near the *Limes* by a tributary of the Moenus about three days' ride from Mogontiacum, when they'd been ambushed by a scouting party from Mundzuk's horde. Most of her people were killed, but a number of the women, including Amber's mother and her two sisters, had been captured and taken back to the Hun's camp for the leaders' as "playthings".

Amber still found it very difficult to talk about the horrors she'd experienced in their camp. Several times she began to sob uncontrollably as she recalled some particularly abhorrent or violent memory at which point Brittola would console her and coax her to continue.

She and her sisters had been forced to watch her mother being raped, not once but many times by the "long head" chiefs. It had then been the turn of Amber and her sisters; and the vile drunkards had tortured them when they tried to resist. At this point, Amber drew up her tunic to show her appalling wounds. There were terrible gouges on her legs and open sores on her abdomen and back; the worst was a long and deep sore across her upper right thigh where the flesh had been completely stripped off.

Amber went on to tell them how she and her younger sister, being especially "sweet and delicate", had been deemed good enough for the chief of the long-heads, Mundzuk himself. He'd joined the orgy later than the others; and Amber guessed who he was by the fear that he generated with his wicked and evil aura.

The evillest part of Mundzuk was his strange heavily-lidded dark eyes; and they seemed to exert a controlling power over his fellow Hun warlords. He had stayed with the others just long enough to eat some of their foul-smelling dried-pressed meat and drink some plundered Alemanni ale, before grabbing Amber and her sister and carrying them, one under each arm, back to his tent. Once inside, he'd thrown her sister aside, obviously saving her for later, and had concentrated on 'enjoying' Amber first. Laughing with relish, he'd gone to the camp fire and returned with a bowl of boiling hot liquid, some sort of oil. Then, with a wicked expression she would never forget, he'd pinned Amber down, leered over her and poured the hot oil directly into her open wounds. She vividly remembered screaming out in agony; but then the pain had become so intense she'd passed out.

When she awoke, she'd found herself lying in a heap of women's bodies, including those of her dead mother and sisters. The camp was deserted and the Huns were nowhere to be seen; the long heads had had their sport and simply discarded the dead bodies like scraps from a feast.

In great pain, Amber had managed to crawl to a nearby river where she'd found an old-but-usable boat hidden amongst some reeds. Believing that the craft had been put there by one of the gods, the God of Revenge perhaps, Amber had just enough strength to climb on board the boat and push it out into mid-stream where it caught the flowing current … before fainting.

The next thing she knew, she was being woken by a fisherman from Mogontiacum and his young son who'd taken her to their home and tended to her wounds. A few days later, as soon as she'd been able to walk, she'd set out for Colonia intent on finding the only people that could help get her revenge; the fighting women of the First Athena. Her hope was that by being in the one army that could stand up to Huns, the same god that had given her the small boat would also give her an opportunity to plunge a dagger deep into Mundzuk's innards.

She finished by swearing an oath to kill Mundzuk, saying only his death would cause the horde to fall apart and the evil menace that was perpetrating such horrors day-after-day in its relentless pursuit of plunder to finally go away.

When Amber finished her story, Ursula called Oleander over and sent her out on an errand before addressing the young Alemanni girl.

'Please tell her that there is very little the First Athena can do to help her because ... ' she glanced at Pinnosa, 'because we are about to depart for our homeland in the west.'

'*What?*' exclaimed Pinnosa, glaring at Ursula.

Ursula raised her hand for silence, forcing Pinnosa to curb her outburst while the message was being translated. Once Cunoarda had finished, she continued.

'Now please tell her— '

Amber threw herself on the floor at Ursula's feet, screaming and wailing.

'She says we can't leave, Commander,' Cunoarda hastily translated as Brittola pulled the hysterical Alemanni girl back up onto the bench. 'She says we must stay here and fight, otherwise all the women in the lands of the rivers Rhenus and Moenus will have to go through what she and her sisters went through; and all the men will die!'

'I thought that was what she might be saying.' Ursula sounded more than a little tense as she did her best to avoid Pinnosa's fierce gaze. 'Please inform her firstly, that she cannot join the First Athena, secondly that her audience is now over and thirdly that she can continue to receive treatment for her wounds in our hospital.'

'But, Commander!' Cunoarda sounded almost as shocked and upset as Amber. 'Surely we can— '

'You have performed your duty well,' snapped Ursula curtly, once more holding up her hand for silence. 'Now, you are dismissed.'

Badly shaken by her commander's sharp rebuke, Cunoarda grabbed Amber by the arm and led her away. They were halfway to the door when Oleander reappeared carrying Ursula's old Corinium blue cloak. The old attendant presented it to Amber who fell silent as she took hold of the neatly-folded cloth in her arms, staring at it wide-eyed with wonder.

Visibly trembling, Cunoarda spun on her heels and shouted at Ursula:

'Just because the men are gone and the Great Expedition is off, doesn't mean there's nothing for us women to do! All the homesick cowards have gone home; and those of us that stayed behind want to *fight* this evil menace— ' she pointed at Amber's wounds, ' —not run away from it! Surely you can believe what you see before you with your own eyes? Why can't you— '

Amber interrupted Cunoarda, calling across the room to Ursula, her voice full of emotion. Cunoarda needed a moment before translating, having to fight hard to regain her composure.

'She – *um* – she says thank you for the present Ma'am. She says it'll give her something to remember us by and prove that we weren't a just a dream after all.'

Without waiting to be dismissed again, Cunoarda saluted and led Amber briskly out. As their footsteps receded down the corridor, both women could be heard sobbing.

Still avoiding eye contact with Pinnosa, Ursula went over to join Oleander by the window and stared unseeingly at the view outside with a stern and sullen demeaner intended to stifle any discussion.

'Beggin' your pardon, Mistress,' said Oleander, without looking up from her sewing, 'but, if we are going to be leaving before these horrible Huns get here, shouldn't we begin making preparations soon?'

Ursula span on her heels and glared at the old attendant.

'Hold your tongue!' she snapped.

'Yes, Oleander,' said Pinnosa, finally breaking her silence, 'you are right, we should; but first, perhaps we could start by making the *decision* to leave!'

Ursula turned to face Pinnosa and for the longest of moments they glowered fiercely at each other, their eyes boring deep. Eventually, it was Brittola who spoke.

'What made you say we were going back to Britannia Ursula?' she asked. 'Is *that* God's Will now?'

'It's not a question of God's Will Brittola.' Ursula broke free from Pinnosa's fierce gaze and moved across the room to stand by the fire. 'It's a question of facing up to reality. These Huns are not the enemy of Britannia nor of the First Athena. If we leave this area, so will they; and I can promise you they will not pursue us over the Oceanus Britannicus. I say we let our true enemy, the House of Theodosius, who brought these Huns out of the wilderness to become the bane of Rome's borderlands in the first place, deal with them.'

'If we leave now,' snarled Pinnosa through gritted teeth, 'everyone will say that we ran away from this Hun rabble like cowards; and that we failed in our sworn duty to defend Rome against all barbarians. If we leave now, and we abandon the good people of the lands of the Rhenus to this merciless Mundzuk and his murderous horde, we will leave in shame and the House of Theodosius will have secured complete victory over the armies of Britannia. If we leave now and shy away from our duty; all that we have achieved … all that we have worked hard for … will amount to *NOTHING!*'

Pinnosa smashed her clenched fist down on the table, causing a bowl of fruit to topple, scattering apples, pears and oranges everywhere.

'"All that we have worked for"? "All that we have achieved"?' Ursula too raised her voice and thumped the table hard. 'Everything we were working for is *gone*; and *NOTHING* is precisely what we have "achieved"—*NOTHING AT ALL!*'

The two of them were now both leaning across the table, barely an arm's reach apart, glaring at each other hard.

'But, that's not true Ursula,' cried Brittola, leaping to her feet. 'That's simply not true. We've created a magnificent army of women who fight for order and who stand for peace.'

Ursula and Pinnosa turned to face her; and she looked pleadingly at them with her cross clasped tight in her grip.

'Now, as the senior commanders of that army, may I suggest you think calmly and carefully about how best it should be deployed? You have no higher authority to refer to now, apart from God; so, may I further suggest you pray very hard before you make any decisions?'

Ursula and Pinnosa both sighed and they each started pacing the room; Ursula by the window, Pinnosa by the fire. Ursula was the first to speak.

'I … I admit that we could be seen to have a duty to stay here and protect these people, maybe even fight this evil that is drawing closer by the day. But I also feel that we have a greater duty to the women now that Cons—I mean, the men are— '

'Forget the men!'

Pinnosa stopped pacing, span round and strode briskly up to Ursula.

'They are all dead!'

Ursula visibly flinched as if Pinnosa's words were stab wounds to her heart. Seeing this, she deliberately repeated them.

'They are all dead!'

She grabbed Ursula by the shoulders.

'Even before they died, you knew the Great Expedition would never take place, didn't you?'

'No, I ... I ... '

Ursula tried to pull herself free from Pinnosa but she tightened her grip, pinning Ursula's arms to her side.

'You *knew* the First Athena had found its true mission, God's mission, to defend the frontier lands, didn't you?'

'Well, I— '

'Didn't you?'

Ursula strained hard to free herself from Pinnosa's iron grip, looking first to Brittola then to Oleander for help, then back at Pinnosa again ... before eventually lowering her gaze.

'Yes,' she said in the faintest of whispers.

Pinnosa shook Ursula hard, forcing her to lift her head back up.

'And, you know in your heart that enforcing the frontier is what the First Athena should be doing now.'

Ursula once more tried to wrestle free from Pinnosa's grasp, but once more her old friend tightened her grasp.

'Am I right?'

Ursula glared at her.

'Am I right?'

Slowly ... Ursula nodded.

'Well, that's all right then, isn't it?' Pinnosa let Ursula go and walked to the door. 'Now, let's get the others in here and start making some *real* plans!'

'No, wait!' cried Ursula. *'Wait-wait-wait!'*

Pinnosa halted and reluctantly turned back to face her.

Ursula took a deep breath to regain her composure.

'It's not that simple,' she said. 'You might think it's obvious what we should do; and I ... '

She took a tentative step toward Pinnosa.

'I might agree with you.'

She took a second step.

'Under normal circumstances, if you and I agree that something should be done, it *is* done; but not this time.'

Pinnosa tried to speak, but Ursula cut her off.

'This isn't a decision that we alone can make; not you, not me, not even all the officers together. I will not lead a single woman against the Huns who would rather return to Britannia and her home. You know as well as I do Pinnosa that these Huns are a truly formidable foe the likes of which no Roman army has ever encountered before; and I don't mind admitting that I am frightened of them, truly, truly terrified. Yes, the First Athena can attempt to overcome them, but there is a very real chance that—well, that *this* time … we might not succeed.'

She paused and glanced at Brittola before adding.

'I only want to lead an army – even an army of peace – that is following me willingly and knows full well where I am leading them.'

She returned her gaze to the empty parade ground outside.

'I'm going to give the women the choice on this mission. Each and every one of them, officer or legionary, will have the freedom to choose their fate. We shall see if that Londinium lass was right about what the women want to do … I'm going to ask for volunteers.'

Surprised at what Ursula had said, Pinnosa and Brittola looked at each other; then, slowly, they both began to nod.

Ursula, meanwhile, continued in a quiet voice, speaking more to herself than the others.

'And for those that do volunteer to take on this Mundzuk and his vile murderous horde, I think I may have a plan that might … just … work.'

Satisfied that nothing more needed to be said – and with a purposeful gleam in her eye – Pinnosa quietly led Brittola out of the commanders' room to hunt down the others.

XV

After discussing the approach of Mundzuk's horde with the rest of the senior commanders, Ursula expressed her intention to ask for volunteers herself personally and concluded their hastily-convened meeting by giving orders for the legion to muster immediately after morning bells the following day so that she could address the women directly.

The following morning, soon after dawn, Martha found Ursula in the commanders' room and informed her that several cavalry units had already departed on escort duty which meant a complete assembly of the legion wouldn't be possible until after evening bells. Slightly disgruntled, Ursula resigned herself to the situation and spent the morning with Brittola, composing reports to Britannia, as well as to Jovinus, regarding Iron Fist and his army from Italia. In the afternoon, they were joined by Cordula and they went over various contingency plans for their ordnance requirements, depending on what the will of the legion might be. Then, just before evening bells, Martha finally returned to the commanders' room to report that the entire First Athena was assembled and ready for Ursula's address.

'At last,' muttered Ursula to Brittola as she headed down the long corridor toward the entrance. 'Now, I have to hope that God will give me the words I need to help each woman make her choice.'

She was still talking to Brittola and adjusting her helmet when they exited the Officers' Hall through its main doorway and walked out of the grandiose stone building. The sight that met her eyes made her gasp with astonishment; indeed, she was so surprised, Brittola had to gently nudge her forward.

The grand entrance with its bronze-studded heavy oak door opened onto a broad portico with an ornately-carved pillar either side and a steep set of steps that led down to the parade ground a full horse's height below. As Ursula emerged from between the pillars, she finally had a clear view of the entire legion standing to attention before her. Every single woman, both infantry and cavalry, was dressed in a new white uniform that mirrored Ursula's own; and in the bright evening sunlight they glistened and shone like freshly fallen snow.

Ursula stood still on the portico for a moment to take in the wondrous sight and, as she did so, a shrill fanfare of horns sounded which was the signal for the entire legion to salute and cry out "*HAIL COMMANDER!*".

All the infantry cohorts were lined up neatly in their ranks; behind each cohort were the cavalry divisions and to the fore were its standard bearers and officers. To Ursula's left and facing the rest of the legion was the Vanguard, all mounted and in full ceremonial uniform with ornately-plumed helmets and highly-polished breastplates. In front of the Vanguard were the senior officers in a line which Brittola and Martha now slipped away down the side of the portico steps to join.

The only member of the Legion First Athena missing was the commander of the cavalry. Ursula peered around the parade ground looking for her, and she was about to call for Oleander when a second fanfare of horns sounded.

The whole parade ground fell absolutely silent; even the attendants gathered to one side made not a sound. Then, from the far corner of the square, there came the distinct '*clip-crunch*' of approaching horse's hooves and Pinnosa emerged through the gateway that led to the stables. She was riding Artemis and leading Swift who was walking alongside her stablemate; and, like the rest of the women, she was also dressed in a uniform of the purest white.

Pinnosa then brought Artemis and Swift slowly through the assembled ranks to the entrance of the Officers' Hall. When they reached the base of the steps, Pinnosa leaned forward and whispered in Artemis' ear. At her bidding, the great black mare pranced up the large stone steps to where Ursula was waiting; and Swift did the same.

As Ursula prepared to mount Swift, she looked at Pinnosa and gave her a wry smile. Pinnosa smiled back then pretended to notice an imaginary speck of dirt on her cloak and made a great show of removing it daintily with her little finger which forced Ursula to stifle a giggle as she hoisted herself up.

The front of the Officers' Hall faced west and when the two commanders-in chief turned their horses in order to address the legion at the top of the steps between the two great pillars they were caught by a ray of golden light from the evening sun.

'Women of the First Athena ... I SALUTE YOU!'

When Ursula spoke, her voice was amplified by the portico and could be heard throughout the parade ground.

'Legion First Athena; you are truly the most magnificent of all Rome's armies! You are also Britannia's finest; and that is beyond doubt! Today, as I look at you in your splendour, I see you shining forth like a burning beacon in these dark times. You are truly a wondrous light, dazzling all our enemies with your brilliance! You are ... you ... '

Suddenly overcome by emotion, she had to pause.

Pinnosa leaned toward Ursula and spoke quietly.

'May I address the legion? I believe I might be able to save us some time.'

Ursula looked at her old friend and nodded.

'Women of the First Athena! You all know that you have been called here today because your commander-in-chief wishes to share with you a difficult dilemma. Now I call upon you to let her know your faith in her judgment.'

She glanced at Ursula and gave her a reassuring smile.

'All of you who wish to return to Britannia with your honour intact, stand down and assemble here to my left. All of you who wish to risk your lives and attempt to turn back this murderous horde of Huns that is wreaking a path of devastation ... *raise your swords!'*

Ursula was about to protest: that Pinnosa had not given the women a full description of their predicament; that facing the Huns meant risking the real prospect of death; that choosing to return home was not cowardice and they could do so without shame. But, before she could say anything, the entire Vanguard, who already had their swords drawn in salute, raised them high, pointing to the sky.

In an instant, from across the parade ground could be heard the clatter and rattle of blades being drawn. The air was then filled with a sea of flashing metal burning bright like the flames of torches as burnished blades caught the last rays of the setting sun. Not one woman went to stand at Pinnosa's left; the 'vote' was unanimous.

Ursula carefully surveyed the scene then once more called out across the parade ground; her voice now steady.

'*Women of the First Athena—I salute you!* You have yet again shown your incredibly courageous strength which comes from your discipline and honour. You have also demonstrated your willingness to stand up and fight for what is right … even though it is not you who are wronged!'

She paused to enjoy the spectacle one last time.

'I will now go to formulate our plans with your other commanders. Rest assured we will do our utmost to ensure your lives are not placed in unnecessary jeopardy as we manoeuvre to wrestle these lands from the Huns' tyrannical grip!'

She glanced again at Pinnosa.

'Women of the First Athena, I am proud of you all! And I say to you now … *salute yourselves!*'

In one voice, the entire legion gave three almighty cheers. Eleven thousand women's voices filled the military complex and resounded far afield. Their cries were so loud, people on the other side of the Rhenus could hear them; they were even heard inside the mighty walls of Colonia itself.

XVI

As the autumn equinox approached, so did Mundzuk. His horde reached the River Moenus around the time of the harvest moon and, once they'd crossed the river, they abandoned the *Limes*, preferring instead to roam the dense forest of the Taunus Hills to the east of Confluentes with its rich wildlife and the prospect of bounteous hunting.

With the horde drawing ever closer to Colonia, Ursula began to receive more frequent and detailed reports about their activities; and it soon became abundantly clear that Mundzuk and his fellow chieftains were rather fond of the hunt, so much so they would often take off on their own, heading up into the hills for their sport, and taking with them just a small group of their elite cavalry as escort.

Ursula quickly realised that this habit of the Hun leaders gave her the chance she was looking for; and she wasted no time in putting her plan into action.

So it was that one bright autumn morning, Ursula and Pinnosa watched as Mundzuk, following the lead of local scouts, came riding hard and fast into a highland clearing in hot pursuit of a clutch of deer led by a particularly nimble buck.

As they reached the crest in the centre of the clearing, Mundzuk and his fellow chieftains pulled up short; and Ursula could see them urgently signalling for the accompanying cohort of around a hundred or so men to quickly get into formation.

Ursula shared a smile with Pinnosa; their little "surprise" had worked perfectly.

The First Athena Vanguard were neatly lined-up along the edge of the clearing, with Ursula seated upon Swift in the centre of their line beneath the legion's standards, including the original one her father had given her back in Corinium. The women, including the officers, were all dressed in their white uniforms and were absolutely still apart from the gentle flap of their cloaks in the breeze and the odd shuffle of their horses.

Within moments, the Huns had also formed into a line, and for a while the two opposing cavalries remained motionless, scrutinising each other from a distance like two great bears, one brown, one white, preparing to wrestle.

Ursula eventually nodded to Pinnosa who then moved forward away from the women's line accompanied by Viventia and flanked on either side by two Alemanni tribeswomen each carrying a white flag of truce; one of whom was Amber. She then watched as Pinnosa's delegation rode out into the middle ground between the two lines of cavalry. Across the clearing on the Hun line she saw Mundzuk select a man with a horrendous scar on his face to act as his representative. She knew at once who he was, Mundzuk's half-brother Rugila. By all accounts, he was one of the more able and intelligent – and no doubt cunning – of the Hun warlords who could count amongst his skills an ability to speak basic Latin; and, as Ursula looked on, she saw him break from the Hun line and head out to meet with Pinnosa along with an escort of three men.

While the two delegations were approaching each other, Ursula narrowed her eyes and peered hard at the figure of Mundzuk, knowing full well that he would, in turn, be staring back at her.

Even from afar, she could make out his hideously deformed and elongated head; a feature he appeared to share in common with some of the others, including Rugila.

'So, this is the terrifying monster; he's here at last,' she said quietly to herself. 'He is, indeed, an ugly repugnant beast of a man; but a man nevertheless.'

Suddenly, a young boy from the Hun ranks gave a loud yell and whipped his mount forward. He then galloped across the clearing, past the two delegations and over toward the ranks of the First Athena. The women looked on anxiously as he boldly rode the length of the women's line well within spear-throwing distance and came to a halt directly in front of Ursula.

He stared at her with obvious contempt then called out in fluent Latin.

'Are you Princess Ursula, the leader of the Legion First Athena?'

His voice had not yet broken and Ursula was amused by his youthful brashness; though at the same time, she was also startled by his strange alien appearance. She studied his shaven head which seemed cruelly deformed and stared into his strange unhuman eyes, before giving her reply in Latin.

'It is customary for an uninvited visitor to introduce himself first. Whom do I have the honour of addressing?'

'I am Prince Attila, son of the great Mundzuk, ruler of all the lands beyond your Roman Empire! Soon he will cross the Alps, crush the puny Goths and add the great sow Mother Roma herself to the beasts that are under his control!'

He lifted his head with great pomposity.

'One day, I shall be King of the Huns; and I will rule over all of my father's minions from the Black Sea to Hispania. And, after today, that will include you Princess Ursula, assuming you do the sensible thing and surrender.'

He pulled out a vicious-looking hunting knife and brandished it threateningly in a throwing position, prompting Martha and the rest of Ursula's guard to draw their bows; but Ursula held up her hand to signal restraint.

'Be not so hasty to make enemies young prince,' she snapped. 'We Romans are of far greater value to you as friends.'

He returned his knife to its sheath and Ursula smiled. She then continued in a more gentle tone.

'Please tell me, Prince Attila, how did you come to speak such fluent Latin?'

'We have one of your Roman priests among us who teaches us many things about your strange ways, including your god Christ who preferred to suffer rather than fight.'

'So he did; that is true, but I think there is another way to view that. You could say he preferred to "win" rather than fight.'

'In the same way that you do?'

Ursula did not answer. Instead she gazed at him intently. She could sense a keen, if alien, intelligence behind his eyes.

'You don't intend to fight my father, do you Princess Ursula? What do you intend to do?'

Ursula laughed out loud at his impudence. His nostrils flared with a surprisingly hostile anger and he reached for his knife again, but then he remembered the guards and their bows, and his hand moved away from the sheath.

She stopped laughing and glared at the boy.

'Such big questions from one so small. Now go back to your father quickly, before he thinks I've taken you prisoner! You'll find out soon enough the intentions of the First Athena.'

Attila turned his horse around and made it rear up on its hind legs in a defiant gesture, before breaking into a gallop. The moment he departed, Martha's women breathed an audible sigh of relief and Ursula returned her attention to the meeting of the delegations just in time to see them break apart and start heading back to their respective ranks.

Ursula cursed under her breath for missing the exchange; she'd been hoping to study the Huns' manner as they'd held their discussion, but the distraction of the pugnacious little prince had denied her the opportunity. Indeed, Attila still hadn't finished his audacious display for, as she looked on, he deliberately rode close by Pinnosa's returning delegation, showing off his riding skills by standing on his mount's back and using his free hand to wave at the passing women. He reached the Hun ranks at the same time as Rugila; and Ursula expected to see Mundzuk give his son a severe tongue-lashing for such brash behaviour.

She was therefore surprised when Mundzuk appeared to completely ignore the boy, concentrating instead on listening to what his brother had to say. She watched as Rugila delivered his report, relaying Pinnosa's message; and, even at a distance, she could plainly see Mundzuk's expression change from brooding dark menace to plain astonishment which gave her cause her to smile … her plan was beginning to work.

She knew that what Rugila was reporting would be utterly unforeseen and completely unexpected by Mundzuk; and, once again, she went over in her mind the message that she had carefully crafted with Faustina, and Pinnosa had then practised a hundred times.

"Princess Ursula of the Britons, Commander-in-Chief of the Legion First Athena, comes here today not to fight but to see for herself whether the Huns are worthy of breaking her Vow to God, so that she may marry their renowned leader, the great Mundzuk, master of all lands north of the Empire. She therefore hereby challenges the Huns to put on a display of their prowess so that she can assess their worthiness as aspirants to having a Britannic queen."

Without uttering a word, Mundzuk rode out alone into the middle ground so that he could study her across the clearing. Although she couldn't quite make out his eyes in the sun's glare, she could feel their cold penetrating gaze and, as his silent stare continued, she began to feel more and more uncomfortable.

Then, suddenly without warning, Mundzuk smiled. He veered his horse round and galloped back to speak with Rugila; then sent his brother back out to the centre of the clearing with his reply. Rugila make his pronouncement in a loud guttural voice, speaking in crude broken Latin.

'It would give the Lord Mundzuk great pleasure to give the esteemed Princess Ursula and her ladies a demonstration of Hun horse-riding and fighting skills. Before he agrees, however, he asks whether the renowned Britannic women would favour us with a similar display in return.'

Ursula smiled politely at Rugila and nodded her acknowledgement; she then feigned a brief discussion with Pinnosa who then rode forth to deliver their reply.

'The women of the First Athena will be honoured to show Lord Mundzuk what we are made of.'

Within a few moments, the Huns commenced their display. The horsemanship skills they demonstrated first were not dissimilar to those displayed by the Alemanni; and Ursula speculated with Pinnosa about who might have learnt what from whom; but then they produced the weapons Ursula and the others had heard so much about, the lariats and whips that they were renowned for using with deadly effect in battle. The women then looked on in amazement as, with seemingly effortless ease, the Hun riders demonstrated how, using their lariats, they could ensnare another horse and its rider at full gallop and bring them to the ground.

The second, and final, part of the Huns' display was given by Rugila himself. He had five of his men line up in a row about ten paces apart, each with a bird's egg placed upon their heads. He then rode to the far end of the clearing before charging towards them at full gallop with his whip drawn. There were five loud whip cracks and all five eggs splattered profusely, without a single man being hit.

As soon as he had finished, Pinnosa once more rode out to the centre of the clearing to deliver Ursula's message.

'Princess Ursula congratulates the Lord Mundzuk and his remarkable men on such an impressive display! It will now be the First Athena's great honour to demonstrate to eminently worthy Lord Mundzuk and his men what we women can do.'

Mundzuk and the other Hun leaders leaned forward in their saddles, eager with anticipation of the forthcoming display. Ursula could see them sharing salacious looks at the prospect of seeing some young Britannic women cavorting on horseback.

There was then a long pause throughout which the line of the First Athena remained completely motionless. The pause continued, becoming more and more prolonged; and all the while there was no sign of activity anywhere along the women's line.

Mundzuk and the rest of the Huns were just starting to become restless, sharing glances of impatience, shouting jeers of frustration and even the odd outburst of indignant anger when, all of a sudden, a wondrous thing happened.

The entire First Athena Vanguard was engulfed in a swirling mass of white birds – mostly doves, geese and ducks, but also swans and egrets – which filled the far side of the clearing like a shimmering haze before flying up into the clear bright blue autumnal sky and completely disappearing from view, leaving behind an empty and deserted space where the women had just been.

It appeared to Mundzuk and his men as if the Britannic women, dressed in the purest of whites, had magically turned into white birds and flown away … free from their grasp.

XVII

Three weeks later, Ursula and the legion's other senior officers were vexed to the point of distraction, because ever since the First Athena's 'disappearance' in front of Mundzuk and his fellow warlords, the Huns had also completely vanished.

Not knowing the Huns' whereabouts had at first been a cause for much frenzied speculation, and the entire legion had taken to trying to guess where the first sightings would be made; indeed, some Londinium women had even started taking wagers. But now, three weeks later, the relentless absence of any news was beginning to weigh heavily on their minds. Every night, in officers' quarters and general barracks alike, conversations revolved around the same questions: 'Where are the Huns?' 'What should we do now?' 'How much longer should we wait for Mundzuk?' 'Is the horde heading for Colonia, or another direction; or has it split up and the menace dissipated?' 'Should we depart for Britannia and leave Colonia undefended?' 'Can we at last – at long, long last – leave for home?'

It was into this mood of unease and growing despair that one of the night guards entered the commanders' room to deliver an urgent message to the commander-in-chief. After speaking for some time into Ursula's ear, the guardswoman stood to attention; then, slowly, with a sombre expression, Ursula rose to address the gathering.

'Ladies, I'm pleased to announce that our long wait is over. Our "groom" has not rejected the offer of a Britannic "bride" and taken flight after all, nor has he mysteriously disappeared into the night; instead he has taken our bait and accepted our "invitation" along with all thirty thousand of his "wedding guests".'

'Is he here in Colonia?' Brittola leapt to her feet. 'Is Mundzuk here?'

'Don't be silly Brittola,' said Pinnosa. 'We have half our women out looking for him and his horde, trying to track them down; we'd know about it if they were anywhere near Colonia.'

She looked at Ursula.

'I'm curious; whereabouts has our "monster with thirty thousand heads" been hiding these past few weeks? I bet they've been out beyond the *Limes* in wild frontier country.'

'According to his emissary ... ' Ursula glanced at the guardswoman who nodded. ' ... he's just three days away.'

'*What!*' exclaimed Faustina. 'That cannot be true!'

'The intriguing thing is ... ' Ursula looked pointedly at Pinnosa and Faustina before continuing. 'He's not coming from the south; he's coming from the north.'

'How can that be?' cried Brittola. 'That's just not possible!'

'I agree with Brittola,' said Martha, 'It's impossible for thirty thousand men to pass down river to the north of Colonia, especially with so many patrols out looking for them both east and west; as well as all the local people on the alert; why, there's the woodland folk, the Colonia guards, the river people, the— '

'Yes, that is all very true,' interrupted Ursula, 'we *have*, indeed, had many eyes and ears scouring the lands both east and west of the Rhenus these recent few weeks, but if you think for a moment, all that activity, all that searching, both east and west ... has been in the south!'

For a moment they were all dumfounded and the room fell silent until, eventually, Ursula put on a brave smile and spoke again.

'It would appear that my "husband-to-be" would like to impress upon me I am not the only one capable of performing a "disappearing trick"!'

XVIII

In contrast to the long drawn out weeks of waiting for news of Mundzuk, the next three days were extremely hectic with Ursula and the other senior commanders constantly busy amid a flurry of frenetic activity.

First and foremost, there were the preparations for the wedding itself which had to be convincing if Ursula's plan was going to work. Messengers came and went endlessly to-and-fro the commanders' room; and ordnance crews a-plenty were to be found bustling about the military complex, as well as inside the city of Colonia, purchasing this, preparing that and storing everything in readiness for the big day.

At the same time, the commanders were also making preparations for the legion's return to Britannia. Reports were arriving almost daily from Gesoriacum and Noviomagus on the availability of seaworthy ships, including some warnings that the weather was likely to worsen in the coming weeks with the onset of winter, including storms that might render a crossing of the Oceanus Britannicus impossible.

In the midst of all this, Ursula felt a strong need to write reports to Jovinus and Rusticus in Gallia, as well as to Julia and her father back in Britannia; keeping them fully informed; but she realised that her dealings with Mundzuk had to be resolved before she would have anything significant to tell them, so her pen remained dry and her stylus unsharpened.

Then, in the middle of the afternoon on the second day after Mundzuk's emissary was dispatched with instructions for the wedding, a flurry of reports reached the commanders saying that the 'lost' horde had finally been spotted. They'd apparently emerged from the flat marshlands a day's march to the north of the city and were beginning to cross the broad flat plains, heading straight for Colonia.

Sure enough, that evening, the northern horizon glowed blood-red with their fires; and Ursula knew with certainty that the day she'd carefully planned for was finally about to dawn.

Late that evening, long after their meals were over and the women had retired to their bed rolls, Ursula pushed open the heavy wooden door to the Officers' Hall and strolled out onto the portico where, weeks before, Pinnosa had addressed the legion and asked for volunteers.

She was still in her white uniform but she, untypically, had her hair clipped back in a bunch which exposed her slender neck and made her look much younger.

As she stared at the red streak across the northern horizon a sudden noise to her left startled her, the sound of approaching footsteps.

'Halt, whoever you are! Who's there?' she called out, reaching for her sword.

'It's only us Ursula,' came a familiar voice; and out of the night, at the bottom of the steps and into the light from the open door, emerged Martha, Saula, Cordula and Brittola.

Ursula sighed with relief.

'You should all be in bed,' she said. 'It's going to be a long hard day tomorrow.'

'*You're* the one who should be in bed.'

Pinnosa's voice came from behind the large pillar on the opposite side of the portico as she too moved into the light.

'After all you *are* the bride!'

'I'm glad you're here Ursula and not in bed,' said Martha, stepping up beside Ursula and taking hold of her arm. 'There's something bothering us, something that only you can help us with.'

'Oh, what's that?'

'We-eee-ell, we were just talking about the plans for tomorrow and we realised there's one thing you haven't told us, one tiny detail that you have kept to yourself and haven't shared with any of us ... ' She looked deeply into Ursula's eyes. 'How exactly are you going to kill him?'

Ursula smiled.

'Do you know something Pinnosa?' she said cheerily without taking her eyes from Martha's. 'You're right. I should go to bed early before my wedding day, but I can't; my mind is still racing this way and that and I—do you know something, I've just realised that I feel a little hungry—*Oleander!*'

The old attendant promptly appeared in the doorway.

'I want something quick and easy to eat, but what shall I have? Oh, I know Oleander, fetch me the most appropriate food for a bride-to-be before her wedding; fetch me an apple!'

As Oleander hurried off, the old friends from Corinium sat down on the cool stone steps, and for a long while they all stared at the distant red glow.

'Ursula?' said Brittola, breaking the silence.

'Yes?'

'Please answer Martha's question. Apart from putting that wounded Hibernian out of his misery back at Pinnosa's villa, you've never actually killed a person before, have you? At least not— '

'Why should that affect what she'll be doing tomorrow?' interrupted Pinnosa. 'This is a foul Hun we're talking about, not a Roman citizen!'

'No Pinnosa,' said Ursula firmly. 'Brittola's right; we should talk about it. I have never killed an able-bodied foe close-up, eye-to-eye and hand-to-hand before; all my kills have been at a distance using an arrow or a spear; I've never actually used a blade on a living breathing, strong and healthy, body; but you have Pinnosa. In fact, you're the only one of us who has. Tell me; I'm curious. What is it like? How does it feel to cut open another's living body?'

'Can we please talk about something else?'

Pinnosa turned to look pleadingly at the others, but they all continued to stare at her, waiting for her reply. She sighed and looked back at the glow of the distant fires.

'It feels just like cutting meat, except it's warm instead of hot or cold,' she said in a matter-of-fact manner, then added in a quieter voice, 'and it's more wet than oily.'

Brittola began to cry.

'Oh, God! Why must we live in a world full of death and killing?' She looked up and started to sob. 'Wh-when w-w-will all the k-killing and dying sto-o-o-op?'

Pinnosa put her arms around her.

'There, there now; there's no need for that.'

As she comforted her old friend, the others could see a lone tear rolling down her cheek.

'Ursula.' Cordula sounded tense. 'I'm not going to be with you – with any of you – tomorrow, and I … '

Ursula turned to look at her cousin.

'What is it?'

'Well, I-I'm just not ready to say "goodnight" just yet.'

She too started to cry, and this time it was Saula who did the comforting.

Ursula turned to Martha whose grip on her arm had suddenly tightened and saw that she was also on the verge of tears. Just then, Oleander returned with the apple.

'Ah! Thank you, Oleander.'

Ursula placed the apple in her lap, reached up to unclip her hair and then picked up the apple again.

'Would anyone like to share this with me?'

The others were all too upset to answer.

'Come on Brittola. You look like you could do with something to take your mind off things. Have a piece,' she said holding out the fruit.

Brittola shook her head.

'Cordula? How about you? A nice juicy slice perhaps?'

Ursula offered her the apple, but she too shook her head.

'Oh, do *stop* it Ursula!' exclaimed Saula. 'Can't you see that no one apart from you is in the slightest bit interested in that blasted apple!'

'I'll have a piece,' said Pinnosa, suddenly looking up.

'Good, that's settled then.'

Brittola also looked up with curiosity at Ursula's strange behaviour and now they were all staring at her; she had their full attention.

Holding the apple up before her, so that they could all see it clearly, Ursula squeezed it tight and, instantaneously, it fell apart into two pieces, neatly sliced in half.

They all gasped, and Brittola broke away from Pinnosa in amazement.

'How did you do that? Was it already cut for you by Oleander?'

Ursula didn't reply. Instead, she picked up one of the halves and once more closed her hand tightly around it. Again, it separated into two cleanly cut pieces.

'Perhaps we should all have a slice each?' she suggested and started to laugh.

She flipped her hand over and exposed the fine crescent-shaped blade that was cupped across her palm; it was being held in place by what looked like a kind of open ring that stretched across her two middle fingers.

'And *that* by the way … ' she looked pointedly at Martha, ' … is the answer to your question.'

She produced the rest of the elaborate 'hairpin' that Nugget had made especially for her back in Corinium and allowed them to examine it.

'I'm very pleased to see that it works. Not one of you had any idea I had a blade in my hand, did you?' They shook their heads. 'If five senior Roman officers could be fooled, I think I may just have a chance with a Hun warlord.'

She looked at Pinnosa.

'The only thing that troubles me is that the first cut has to be the killing cut; and I'm not sure which is the most lethal.'

She motioned across her neck.

'To cut here … ' She nodded toward her lap, to the region of the genitalia. '… or there? What do you think?'

XIX

It was the latter half of October AD 411 and the weather was autumnal but pleasant. Soon after dawn, trumpets sounded from the four walls of Colonia, warning those outside that the city's main gates would soon be closed and secured. By morning bells, the outer city beyond the walls was completely deserted; not a soul was to be found in the artisans' workshops or scholars' colleges; the apprentices and slaves who were usually busy doing errands had vanished; and the myriad of brothels that catered to every taste were abandoned. Not even a stray dog wandered the streets.

All the preparations in both the city and the military complex across the river were complete; and the entire area settled into an uneasy silence as it waited … and waited.

Ursula and the other senior officers were gathered on the roof of the Officers' Hall from where they could see that the city's battlements on the opposite shore of the Rhenus were already crowded with people, from the highest nobles and officials to the lowliest sewer slave, all scrambling for the best view and waiting for something to happen. They were closely watching the flagpoles over the city's east gate, as they waited for the series of prearranged signals that would inform them of the enemy's approach. The rest of the legion was resting in their barracks and the parade ground was deserted, apart from the occasional slave or attendant going about her tasks.

Then, just before midday ... it began.

The first indication of the horde's approach was felt more through the feet than heard through the air; a deep, deep rumble as if a large four-oxen cart fully laden with rock from a quarry was drawing near. Everyone could feel it, whether on the city walls or the roof to the Officers' Hall, and within moments the first black flag went up over the city's east gate.

Shortly afterwards, the rumble became something that you could actually hear, a deep dark noise that filled your ears with sound and your heart with dread; the relentless pounding *baroom—baroom—baroom-boom-boom* of a thousand drums. There was no doubt now, everybody knew it ... the Huns were coming.

A little later, a second black flag was hoisted which meant the horde was in plain view. Soon afterwards a single white flag meant they were, as the Alemanni chiefs had foretold, moving as one body thirty thousand strong and not divided into separate units of any kind.

'I can't see any sign of burning,' said Pinnosa as she scoured the northern horizon. 'I'm surprised! I thought they laid waste to everything in their path.'

'They must be on their best behaviour,' quipped Martha, giving Pinnosa a playful nudge. 'A sign of respect perhaps for their master's bride!'

They all laughed nervously.

A short while later, a third black flag signalled that the Huns were entering the city's outer perimeters which meant the scouts would soon find the strings of white bunting that would lead them to where the wedding ceremony was due to take place.

This was the key signal the commanders had been waiting for and Ursula gave the order for the First Athena to assemble.

Within a few moments the parade ground was full; eleven thousand white-clad women, standing to attention with the Vanguard in formation nearest the gate already in position to lead the women out. Pinnosa on Artemis and Ursula on Swift once more rode up onto the portico outside the entrance of the Officers' Hall to address the legion; and this time Ursula didn't need any help from Pinnosa.

'*Women of the First Athena—I SALUTE YOU!*'

She drew her sword and raised it on high.

'You are truly the most magnificent and splendid legion in all of Rome's armies! I am proud of each and every one of you! You have served Britannia well and Rome better than she deserves! You have also served yourselves with great valour and great honour, proving beyond doubt you are worthy of living the rest of your lives with pride in your hearts and dignity in your manner! For when you are old, and all that we have been through together is but a dim and distant memory, you will be able to hold your head up high and say "I was once in the great First Athena; *I was once in the triumphant First Athena!*"'

A rousing cheer went up from the ranks, forcing her to pause; and she glanced round at Pinnosa who smiled.

'Now, before we embark upon the most dangerous mission we have ever faced together, I ask you all to join me in prayer.'

She lifted the hilt of her sword up before her like a cross; and as she did so, Pinnosa bellowed an order.

'*First Athena! Swords out and … KNEEL!*'

The infantry bent down on one knee before their swords, and the cavalry did the same as Ursula, all holding their sword hilts out before them with their heads bowed forward. Brittola was the only exception; keeping her sword sheathed, she reached inside her cloak for her personal cross and clasped it tight against her chest while Ursula said a prayer.

'Dear merciful everlasting God. We, the humble women of the First Athena, are here today to counter a terrible wicked evil that has been sent to plague these lands by dark forces that would seek to be the undoing of Rome and all that we stand for!

We pray with all our hearts, Lord, that you give us not only the strength to face this terror, but also the power to defeat it! For this day, Lord, we fight not for Rome, not for Britannia, not even for ourselves! We fight so that your divine rule can prevail in this troubled world; and that peace in your name, Lord, can finally reign … Amen.'

The legion's *"AMEN!"* filled the parade ground and, while it was still reverberating, Pinnosa shouted her next order.

'First Athena—ATTENTION! First Athena—FACE RIGHT!'

Ursula and Pinnosa rode down the steps from the portico then crossed the parade ground to join the other commanders at the rear of the Vanguard. The instant they were in position, a fanfare of horns sounded to announce the legion's departure and the heavy oak gates to the military complex opened.

'First Athena—FORWARD!'

Following Pinnosa's order, led by the Vanguard, the ranks of the First Athena began to march out through the gates, leaving behind the huge barracks that had become their home.

The moment the Vanguard in their ceremonial white uniforms emerged from the military complex, a resounding cheer went up from the top of the city walls. It was the first time the women had been seen in formal uniform since they'd all taken their Vows with Bishop Clematius and started to wear the White; and the sight of the whole legion – cavalry first; infantry behind – parading over the bridge toward the city was a truly wondrous spectacle, the likes of which had never been seen by any of the city folk.

When the commanders at the rear of the Vanguard reached the opposite shore of the Rhenus and started to pass beneath the huge buttresses and high battlements of the city's imposing and indomitable walls, they could hear people far up above their heads calling down to them in a mixture of Latin, German, and even Britannic:

'Kill the Long heads!'
'God goes with you Ursula!'
'Pinnosa Bloodhair! Bathe in Hun blood tonight!'

Following Ursula's lead, all the commanders took off their helmets with their long white plumages and waved them in reply to the cheers.

'If only there were just cause for such celebrations!' shouted Saula to Martha over the din as she waved and waved, and waved yet again.

'Oh, we'll give them something to celebrate;' cried Martha in reply, 'of that, you need have no fear!'

XX

To the north of the city outside its Northern Gate was a broad area of open grassland known as Shepherds' Meadow. It was an elongated natural hollow extending the length of the city walls in a gentle slope that led down to the shore of the Rhenus. It was where farm folk and stockmen bringing their stock to market would leave their animals be they sheep, cattle, goats, geese or oxen, to graze before being slaughtered and turned into meat.

Around the far side of the meadow away from the city walls and roughly following the rim of the hollow was Colonia's main graveyard where old Roman legionaries and their families were buried. In amongst the countless tombs and graves were a number of temples and shrines mostly small in scale though a few were of quite a size, including a modest Christian chapel that was set slightly forward from the cemetery and encroached upon the edge of the meadow.

On this particular day the chapel was looking all the more conspicuous because it had been freshly painted in white limewash in preparation for the wedding and it glistened in the bright midday sun. Eye-catching though the freshly-painted chapel may have been, it was only a small part of the special preparations for Ursula's wedding day. Immediately outside the city's main gate a large wooden edifice had been erected with a raised dais as its centrepiece surrounded by tall panels to its rear and sides that were intended to amplify a speaker's voice as well as provide an ornamental backdrop. The stage was adorned in a profusion of white flowers in large free-hanging garlands that were strung in voluptuous interweaved loops.

307

In addition to the chapel and the speaker's dais a sizeable white tent had been erected in the very centre of the clearing which was also ornately decorated in white flowers arranged in wreath-like bunches and tied firmly to each of its eight sides.

Finally, and most spectacularly, the whole of Shepherds' Meadow, from the city walls to the edge of the cemetery and extending its entire length, was covered by a scattering of loose and delicate white flower petals that lay ankle deep.

As soon as Ursula rounded the corner and caught sight of the prepared ground she smiled and her eyes filled with tears. It was all exactly as she'd ordered, precisely as she'd planned ... and just as she'd dreamed.

She brought Swift to a halt on the edge of the field of petals at a midpoint along the river shoreline and then waited patiently for the rest of the First Athena to assemble behind her. Quietly and sombrely, cohort after cohort of the women emerged from the shadow of the city's walls and took up their position until they had formed a continuous and unbroken white line of disciplined ranks flanking the water's edge.

The last of the women were just falling into line when the first Hun made his appearance. On the far rim of the hollow, from between two prominent mausoleums each with Greek-style frontages, a tribesman on horseback suddenly burst into view; the women could see him reining his horse in as he beheld the spectacle before him. Almost immediately, another appeared further along the rim; then another, and another, all in quick succession.

For a moment, it looked as if the dead themselves were rising from their tombs as from behind grave after grave and shrine after shrine, all along the crest of the rise that surrounded the clearing, countless horsemen appeared; and their scrawny dark forms were in stark contrast to the glistening pure white field before them.

The Hun horsemen picked their way through the graves and came to a halt in a loose line along the edge of the petal-strewn clearing. Then, as the women of the First Athena – plus the many hundreds of city folk that were crowded atop the city's walls – looked on the rest of the horde appeared, streaming through the graves like ants and filling the spaces between the outriders, thickening the Hun line until it became a concentrated mass of menace, bristling with weaponry of every description along with a gruesome blend of skulls – some human, others animal – effigies and grubby brown-stained pennants all weatherworn, torn and frayed.

Very quickly the graveyard was completely smothered and the gathering was complete: a loose rabble of thirty thousand ruthless warriors who had travelled far from distant lands faced eleven thousand women dressed in white and assembled in a neat row of disciplined Roman ranks with their backs to the mighty river Rhenus. Both sides were fully-armed and the only thing separating them was a long gentle slope strewn with a carpet of white petals.

The drumming suddenly stopped and an eerie silence fell. All that could be heard was the rattling harnesses of restless horses and from somewhere high above the piercing cry of a lone hawk.

Ursula and the other commanders scoured the ranks of the Huns for some sign of Mundzuk or the other chieftains, but in vain.

'Is he here?'

Ursula put her hand up to shade her eyes.

'Oh, he's here all right,' snarled Pinnosa, 'as sure as there's a snake in grass.'

They exchanged a look and Pinnosa nodded signalling it was time for proceedings to commence. Ursula returned her nod then promptly raised her hand. A shrill fanfare of horns sounded and Ursula, Pinnosa and Faustina set off towards the imposing structure that had been erected outside the city gate. As they moved away from the rest of the commanders, Brittola cried out after them.

'God goes with you!'

As Ursula drew near the dais a cacophony of sounds erupted from the Hun ranks; there were horns, whistles and strange vocal cries like cats mewing or dogs whining as well as drum rolls, cymbal clashes and the loud din of a host of foreign percussion instruments that the Romans had never heard before. Then, from the very centre of the Hun ranks, a gap opened up forming a kind of passage, or corridor, lined with battle-scarred shields and over-arched by long pike staffs with vicious-looking spikes and blades.

Then, down the passage, riding a huge black stallion and dressed completely in black fur, came Mundzuk accompanied by three others of his kind in identical dress, including his brother Rugila; though, curiously, there was no sign of his son Attila.

The two delegations were now side by side, providing Ursula with her first clear view of the Hun warlords. She could see immediately that Mundzuk was exceptionally tall for a Hun, though only of average height compared to a Roman man. Like his fellow Hun lords, his chief and most striking characteristic was the distorted shape of his head which appeared to have been stretched or elongated, giving prominence to his other distinctive feature; his alien-looking eyes.

He caught Ursula staring at him and returned her gaze with a cold heartless penetrating stare before suddenly breaking into a smile which exposed a surprisingly white array of teeth. This unexpected burst of conviviality took her completely by surprise and she quickly averted her eyes, taking a sudden keen interest in the garlands that adorned the platform before them; and, as she did so, she could feel herself blushing. She was spared any further embarrassment by Rugila who rode forward to position himself immediately below the dais; then he turned to face the horde and raised his hand. The drumming and clattering clashes ceased and Rugila addressed the gathering in his heavily accented and faltering Latin.

'*The Great Mundzuk, King of all lands north of Rome, bids greetings to the valiant women of Britannia and welcomes his bride-to-be, the beautiful Princess Ursula! And the Great Mundzuk says to all here present ... HAPPY WEDDING!*'

Once more the cacophony of musical sounds erupted and the horde began to cheer and shout. While they were celebrating, Ursula nodded to Pinnosa who moved forward on Artemis to deliver the reply. Once in position beside Rugila she too raised her hand and again the horde fell silent.

'*Princess Ursula of Britannia welcomes Mundzuk and his worthy Hun lords! We are truly honoured by your presence here today! Princess Ursula and the women of the First Athena say … HAIL GREAT MUNDZUK! HAIL THE HUNS!'*

The Hun horde filled Shepherds' Meadow with their wild cheers and irksome musical sounds; and Mundzuk lifted his head up to emit a long loud howl, obviously enjoying himself.

Pinnosa patiently waited for Mundzuk's howl to finish then politely smiled at him as she once again raised her hand to command silence.

'Let the Royal Marriage commence!'

The door to the little Christian chapel opened and Bishop Clematius emerged in ceremonial regalia accompanied by six women dressed in plain white togas; they were the Astraeans, Colonia's Celestial Virgins; the city's counterparts of Roma's Vestal Virgins. The Huns became so excited by the sight of the women with their extra-long hair flowing loose and free they gave their loudest chorus of war cries yet; indeed, the women were extremely lucky to depart their ranks unmolested; though the last one in their line did get her toga tugged as one of the thugs cut off a remnant to keep as a souvenir.

Clematius and the virgins cleared the Hun ranks and walked slowly in solemn formal procession across the field of petals toward the dais. The bishop carried an ornate scroll of parchment that contained the Holy Scriptures; three of the women each held a sacred object; and the other three bore incense burners which they swayed to-and-fro on long ornate brass chains.

Mundzuk and his fellow lords watched the procession pass by with great interest; but then, as they climbed the steps to the dais, he muttered something to Rugila and the two of them sniggered and smirked. This caused Ursula to cast them both a scowl of disapproval which Mundzuk acknowledged and duly resumed his regal pose, indicating to his brother that he should do the same.

After the Celestial Virgins had taken their positions at the rear of the platform, the bishop stepped sombrely up to the dais and commenced the proceedings. With studied ceremonial deliberation he carefully untied the scroll and with due deference slowly unrolled it. Once it was fully extended, he straightening his back and cleared his throat in readiness to speak; and—

—at that moment, a loud scream was heard from the ranks of the First Athena at the far end of the clearing down near the water's edge.

Everyone, including Ursula and Pinnosa, Mundzuk and Rugila, as well as Bishop Clematius, looked round to see what the cause of the commotion was. Suddenly, from out of the women's ranks a rider burst forth wearing a Corinium blue cloak. It was Amber, the young Alemanni girl, and she was yelling fierce war cries as she galloped headlong towards the royal delegations, sending up a great spume of petals. Halfway across the clearing, she unsheathed a long sword and raised it in readiness to strike. The moment she did so, Mundzuk broke from the wedding delegations in order to intercept her. As he urged his powerful steed forward, from under his billowing fur cloak he produced a vicious-looking blade twice as long as the one Amber was brandishing.

He was just about to clash with the Alemanni girl, when a throwing knife whooshed past his ear and sank into Amber's shoulder, causing her to cry out in pain and drop her sword.

Mundzuk reined his horse in and looked round to see where the knife had come from. Realising it was Pinnosa, he threw back his head and laughed—a horrible shrieking sound that reverberated throughout the hollow, unnerving all the women and making Ursula suddenly feel physically sick.

Then, with all eyes upon him, Mundzuk once more urged his horse forward, rode up to Amber and, using a single perfectly-aimed swipe of his long blade, neatly scythed through her exposed neck, completely beheading her in an instant.

Miraculously, Amber's body remained seated upon her horse with her hand still holding the reins tight. Mundzuk went over to where the head had fallen and leaned forward to skewer it with his sword; he then rode up to Ursula and held it out for her to peruse before flinging the gruesome object at the dais, forcing Bishop Clematius to duck. With a loud thud it slammed into one of the back panels where it become stuck, having gotten entangled in one of the large garlands of flowers.

The Huns fell ominously silent; all their eyes were upon their leader and it was obvious to Ursula they had no idea what he was going to do.

Holding his blood-stained sword at Ursula's throat, Mundzuk surveyed the scene, obviously assessing the situation and considering his next move.

She opened her mouth and was about to say something, but his gaze snapped back to her and his eyes – malevolent eyes full of malice – blazed with a silent but emphatic order '*No!* Do not say anything; keep quiet!'

Ursula obeyed, shutting her mouth and keeping it firmly closed.

Mundzuk put his finger to his lips and shook his head, reinforcing his message even though there was no need. He then lowered his sword to her abdomen and used the blade to lift her heavy white cloak, exposing her white under-tunic and bare legs.

A sudden rustle and a rattling sound made Mundzuk and Ursula spin round. Pinnosa had just flicked back her cloak and was unsheathing her sword.

'*No, don't!*' cried Ursula. 'There's no need.'

The three of them exchanged looks; then, with a slight nod to Ursula, Pinnosa slowly slipped her sword back into its scabbard. As she did so, Mundzuk smiled.

Satisfied that Ursula was unarmed, he carefully placed her white cloak back in its original position and withdrew his sword, leaving behind a long red smear. He then did exactly the same to Faustina, lifting her cloak to check what weapons she might have hidden. Content she too was weaponless, he moved on to Pinnosa who was still in position beside Rugila slightly away from the two princesses.

He pulled up in front of her and raised his sword as if preparing to strike all the while glaring at her with his alien eyes, daring her to make a move.

Pinnosa returned his gaze and remained motionless, frozen like a statue. Her tension communicated itself to Artemis who also stood completely still despite the presence close by of a virile black stallion. With no warning, Mundzuk let go of his sword and it dropped to the ground where it was instantly, and silently, swallowed-up by the carpet of flower petals.

Rugila then produced his sword, as well as his lariat and whip, and threw all three to the ground; and, following his lead, the other two members of the Hun delegation did the same.

Now knowing what was expected, Pinnosa too removed her sword and threw it to the ground. She also lifted up her cloak so that Mundzuk and the other Huns could see she carried no further weaponry.

Just at that moment, there was a loud double-thump followed by a horse's neigh. They all looked round and saw that Amber's body had toppled off her horse which had spooked it, causing it to scamper back to the ranks of the First Athena.

Mundzuk threw back his head and laughed again; his cackling laughter was still hideous and shrill as it hacked the air; but this time, for Ursula, it was the most welcome of sounds and she allowed herself a deep sigh of relief.

The wedding was still on.

XXI

Bishop Clematius conducted the service well with convincing conviction as he read the Holy Scriptures then proceeded to orchestrate the Exchange of Vows. He was even gracious in his patience as Rugila completed each translation and the ceremony had to be put on hold while the Huns cheered every time.

Eventually, the ceremony reached its conclusion and the bishop closed the proceedings by anointing the bride and groom with holy water and giving their marriage a holy blessing, using both Christian and ancient Roman ritual prayers.

As the bishop and the Astraeans once more braved the horde and slowly made their way back in procession to the small Christian chapel, Pinnosa raised her hand for silence.

'*My Lord, King Mundzuk, and your fellow Hun warrior lords, the greatest warriors north of Rome; tonight the great city of Colonia will freely open its doors to you and invite you in as honoured visitors and esteemed guests!*'

Another roar of cheers forced Pinnosa to pause and she exchanged a quick glance with Ursula which, for once, went unnoticed by Mundzuk who was busy swigging some Alemanni ale that had been thrown by one of his men. In their exchange of looks, Pinnosa asked one last time 'Are you certain you want to proceed with this?' and Ursula replied with an emphatic 'Yes; now will you please get on with it?'

With a quick glance at Faustina who had witnessed the exchange, Pinnosa raised her hand again.

'Before the festivities commence, Princess Ursula would like some time alone with her new husband ... '

While she waited for yet another roar – the loudest yet – to abate, she indicated with her arm the large octagonal tent in the centre of the clearing.

'Princess Ursula invites King Mundzuk to join her ... in private!'

For once, instead of shouting his translation to the horde, Rugila whispered into Mundzuk's ear and the brothers shared a private joke, prompting Mundzuk to laugh heartily ... and as before his loud hacking laughter caused Ursula to feel sick.

Mundzuk caught sight of Ursula grimacing and holding her stomach and, with a look of husbandly concern, he began to ride toward her with the intention of helping her off her horse. Pinnosa just managed to manoeuvre Artemis in time to block him, then looked keenly at Rugila, urging him to translate.

'Princess Ursula would like a few moments to herself in order to be sure she receives her new husband properly.'

Both Hun lords had visibly bristled at Pinnosa's move; and when Rugila translated his voice was grim with suspicion.

Mundzuk looked first at Rugila then at Ursula; then he slowly turned to face Pinnosa and once again burst into raucous laughter. He shouted something back to Rugila which caused Rugila to laugh too, as well as those of their men who were within ear shot. The humorous quip was obviously something to do with newly-wed brides or women in general; whatever it was, it was quickly relayed throughout the horde and the crude raucous laughter spread.

Pleased at the success of his little joke, Mundzuk nodded to Pinnosa then wheeled his horse round to return to his brother for another swig of ale.

The time had finally come for Ursula to be left on her own. Pinnosa and Faustina led her away from Mundzuk and his men; when they were a safe distance, they came to a halt in order to say their parting comments. Reaching out to clench forearms, it was Faustina who spoke first.

'What you are doing here today Ursula will never be forgotten. Not only will your father be proud of you, the whole of Britannia – the whole of Rome – will also be proud!' She lowered her voice to a hushed whisper. 'I know you don't need my advice, but I will give it anyway; get this thing over with as quickly as possible; the quicker you act, the greater the effect it will have—you mark my words.'

'Those are wise words Faustina for which I thank you. Now please go back to the women. Remind them to stand firm; they must not make a move, especially when … well you know.'

Faustina nodded then bowed and urged her horse on, leaving Pinnosa and Ursula completely alone.

They stared at each other in silence for the longest of moments, neither knowing what to say. Eventually Pinnosa bent forward to pat Artemis and spoke quietly.

'You know I said to forget the men because they were dead?'

'Hmmm?'

'Well, I was wrong about that. They're here; Constans, Constantine and the others, they're all here with us … I can feel their presence. They are willing us on, willing us to succeed.'

Ursula also leaned forward to pat Swift and spoke equally as quietly, but with a firm emphasis.

'No, they are not; they are gone. They're not here with us; they're not anywhere any more. It's just us here now, just you and me … as it has always been.'

They both looked back at Mundzuk and Rugila who were still swigging ale from their flagons and making jokes, but Mundzuk kept glancing over towards them and towards the tent, obviously revelling in anticipation.

'You'd better go inside. I don't think he's going to give you very long.'

'Yes, you are right … it's time.'

Pinnosa wheeled Artemis around to head back to the legion and, as she did so, they exchanged one last look. There was so much they wanted to say, so much they had to say; but there was no more time. As she rode away and Artemis broke into a canter she called out over her shoulder.

'*Good luck Princess!*'

Ursula gave a little wave and even managed to force a cheery smile as she muttered to herself.

'Good luck Pinnosa; good luck Brittola … and good luck all the rest of you.'

She then gave Swift a nudge and rode slowly across the petals toward the ornate octagonal tent at its centre bestrewn with garlands of white flowers. Once there, she dismounted and discretely attached Swift's harness to a strong chord made from the same rope used to hoist galley sails that was hidden under the carpet of petals.

While she was doing this, she glanced back at the First Athena. They all looked so beautiful, calm and peaceful in the afternoon sun, standing silent and still in their disciplined ranks like a picture painted on a chapel wall.

Suddenly, Ursula was filled with an overwhelming urge to leap back on Swift and ride far away, taking the legion with her. For a fleeting moment, she imagined she was together with the others out in the sunshine, hunting, fishing, singing songs and drinking wine. Then her fear returned like a knot tightening in the pit of her stomach, making her gag and struggle for breath. She had to swallow hard to prevent herself from vomiting.

'*Mistress!*' Oleander's head peeped out from the tent opening. '*Come inside, quick!*'

Ursula took deep breaths as she fought to quell her churning stomach, but still she couldn't move.

Oleander dashed out from the tent and grabbed her by the arm; then, smiling nervously at Mundzuk's delegation, she led Ursula back to the tent.

'Come on; let's get inside; you've got to be brave now.'

Once they were inside the tent, Ursula couldn't stop talking.

'He's almost here—*he's almost here!* And I'm not ready—I am *not* ready! My hair! We have to prepare my hair Oleander—*quick!* We have to prepare my hair. Now, where's that hairpin? Oh Oleander, where is it?'

'It's here Mistress. Now please stand still while I put it in for you.'

The old attendant carefully removed Ursula's helmet and plumage then began brushing out Ursula's hair and arranging it in the style they'd practised.

'Make sure it's in the right way, will you?'

'Yes, Mistress.'

A sudden cheer from the Huns signalled that Mundzuk was making his way over to the tent.

'Oh God! He'll be here soon! Have the tent ropes been done properly?'

'Yes Mistress, everything is ready. Now will you please keep still!'

'I can't do this! *I can't!*'

'*Yes you can!*'

Oleander gave Ursula's hair a tug just like she used to when the young princess was having a tantrum as a child.

'You can, and you will! The others are all depending on you.'

Ursula took a deep breath, clenched her teeth and closed her eyes; and Oleander assumed a gentler tone.

'That's better Mistress.'

For a moment both were silent while Oleander finished her work.

'There, that's got it.'

Ursula reached back to check the hairpin was correctly in place ... and nodded.

'I'd best be going Mistress. The sooner I leave, the sooner it'll all be over.'

Oleander walked to the tent opening and turned to look back at Ursula standing in the middle of the tent; a lonely figure with an expression of fear and horror on her face.

'Oh, what have we come to Mistress? You are such a lovely young woman with such soft blonde hair and beautiful blue eyes that can command a room. Look at you; you're in the prime of your life and absolutely ripe for a *real* marriage.'

She ran over and flung her arms round Ursula who returned the embrace then stepped back to look deeply into Oleander's tear-filled eyes.

'Thank you Oleander. You have been like a second mother to me.'

'I love you Mistress … ever so much.'

Ursula nodded, then indicated the tent opening; it was time for her to leave. Oleander wiped her tears and, with a final squeeze of her mistress' hands, moved away; then she opened the flap, looked back with a tearful smile and left.

Ursula was finally alone.

She looked around, scrutinising the tent's interior; everything was just as she'd planned. In the centre, well away from the tent's sides, was a large raised bed adorned with the finest embroidered silks and a large pile of cushions to make it welcoming and comfortable.

A wave of calmness overcame her and there in the soft light of the tent, lying on the wedding bed, was Constans. It was a sunny October morning somewhere in another lifetime; he was lying on his back with a barley stalk between his teeth, looking up at the sky. They were seventeen again and alone together in their favourite spot, the Maidens' Meadow beside a small stream that flowed in a lazy meander just outside Corinium's city walls.

'Come here,' he said, 'and kiss me.'

As they kissed, she could feel the familiar tingling sensations she always felt whenever he ran his fingers through her hair and gently touched her neck and shoulders. She looked into his eyes, his deep blue eyes that were so close, so big … and so real.

Suddenly, they were saying 'goodbye' in the forum. She was kissing him and the crowd roared; she saw again the little trinket she'd fashioned for him; and there was the tear rolling down his cheek during the speeches. She could hear her father's powerful parting words; and she could feel her heart pounding as she watched his plumage disappear into the distance, heading down the long road to Londinium.

There now, in the hazy light of the tent, was Pinnosa's face and her grim expression as they planned how to tackle the Saxons. Even with her terrible injuries, she scraped her blade on the stones, sending up a great rain of sparks as she prepared to lunge forward. The rain fell down on the battlefield and there was Brittola desperately trying to shield her from the relentless Saxon blows. There too was Cordula's face as she stood to attention on the deck of the galley and said 'The women are ready for inspection, Commander.'

She smiled as she thought about Rusticus and his aunts; and there were Martha and Saula dancing a jig before marching proudly up the gang plank. The sound of pipes filled her mind and forced it into such a whirl that she felt nauseous and dizzy.

Fleeting images flashed before her: drunk Hibernians asleep in a courtyard; a disembowelled boy on a rope; tattooed Picts; Saxon war cries; the Franks and Julia holding their king by the balls; Alemanni and Huns doing tricks on horses; cavalry galloping hard through trees; six young women flying through the twilight deep into frontier lands, heading for Magnis; the white riders—

A shrill neigh sounded from outside the tent.

'Was that Swift? Mundzuk must be here. I can't do this!'

Wringing her hands, she bent up double all crunched up as if in pain.

'I can't,' she sobbed. 'I can't, I can't—*I can't!*'

Just then, as if from the very air itself, she could hear Brittola's voice singing 'Praise the Lord'. The sound was sweet like honey mixed with wine and it soothed Ursula's fears like a balm. There too was Pinnosa's fuller tones, singing out loud and clear; and as she listened, she could also make out Martha and Saula joining in; and the tent filled with the sound of the old hymn as the entire First Athena began to sing.

Suddenly, there before her was Amber accompanied by the young Londinium woman Cunoarda who was translating.

"She swears by all that is holy that one day she will find a way to kill the evil Mundzuk. She says there is only way to stop all the killing, and all the raping and pillaging; and that is to cut off the snake's head. With Mundzuk dead, the horde will break up; then, and only then, will we have peace."

Ursula stood up straight ... she was ready.

The tent flap opened and Mundzuk entered. He looked at her and grunted something in his native tongue which, to her, sounded like a dog growling. Deciding not to bother with any more words, he walked straight up to her with a broad grin on his hideous face and grabbed her by the arm.

'*No!*'

She snatched her arm free and stepped away. This clearly displeased him; his anger was tangible, so she forced a coy smile and hastily indicated the bed, nodding as invitingly and enticingly as she could manage.

Slowly and guardedly, he turned his other-worldly eyes toward the bed; then he snapped them back to glare at her, his expression full of suspicion.

For a fleeting moment her heart filled with fear that he was going to spurn her and walk away. She returned his gaze, feeling as she did so that she was staring into the eyes of hell; and once more she forced a smile.

Mundzuk then said something in his gruff alien tongue and burst into a surprisingly high-pitched giggle. Abruptly and without warning, he tore off his furs and stood before her completely naked. His scarred torso was surprisingly hairless, apart from his groin which, much to her relief, had a profusion of hair that hid most of what she did not wish to see; the little she could see filled her with revulsion.

With a playful grin, Mundzuk then leapt up onto the bed with so much force it almost broke; and, lying on his back with his arms outstretched, he beckoned her to join him.

Ursula gave Mundzuk what she hoped was the nervous look of a shy bride and turned away, feigning embarrassment. With her back to him, she smiled to herself because now she knew for certain that he was completely unarmed. She loosened her cloak and let it fall; then she turned to face him, deliberately flaunting her naked body seductively in order to distract him while she reached up to unclip her hair.

Suddenly, Constans filled her mind again.

'I'm coming home now my love … ' she said out loud in her native Britannic as she approached him, smiling reassuringly at her prey. ' … I'm coming home.'

Chapter 7

THE PETAL FIELD

'*Cordula! Cordula!* Where are you Cordula?'

High up in the lookout tower adjacent to the north gate which was reserved for the city's nobility, Bishop Clematius pushed his way through the crowded assemblage of nobles and Roman officials, desperately seeking the Britannic woman he had grown rather fond of; the mother and baby he had willingly sworn to protect when asked personally and in private by the child's father, Morgan.

'*I'm here!* Who is it that wants me?'

'It is I, Clematius,' he said as he finally reached her. She had taught him Britannic and he had taught her Germanic; and they were both good learners.

'But that's impossible. How can that be? I thought you were down there.'

'Aha, don't forget I'm a native of this city; I know my way around here far better than any stranger.'

Cordula looked him up and down and noticed the dust, plus the odd spider's web, on his ornate bishop's raiment. She suspected there was a tunnel involved and she was about to say as such when, suddenly, there was a loud scream from the city wall immediately below them, followed by wails of anguish. Clematius dashed to the parapet's edge and, along with several nobles, leaned over to see what had caused the commotion.

Cordula couldn't do the same because she had her baby in her arms. Although she was unable to see what was happening directly below, she still had a good view of the rest of the 'petal field' as the people of Colonia had dubbed it. To her right by the water's edge was the First Athena in their disciplined ranks; to her left was the horde; and immediately in front of her was the octagonal tent where Ursula and Mundzuk were together.

'It looks like another poor soul has fallen from the city ramparts,' said a nearby city official. 'It's terrible the crush down there; the rabble are constantly pushing and shoving each other; it's no wonder people are falling off.'

322

'There are far too many on that parapet,' said another man, 'I fear many more will die before the day is done. Who allowed so many up there? Where are the guards? There aren't enough guards these days to— '

'*They* are your guards for goodness' sake; they are your *true* guards!' Cordula pointed at the ranks of the First Athena. 'And it is *they* who might die before the day is done. Why can't you idiots— '

'How dare you call me an "id— '

'Hush, hush; ignore them!'

Clematius hastily positioned himself between Cordula and the two men then turned to chastise them.

'Can't you see you're frightening this woman's baby!'

He turned back to Cordula and smiled.

'I must say, he looks very well—all wrapped up in his fine white linen. Do you remember when we had to bleach all that cloth in time for the parade after the mass Vow of Chastity?'

Cordula nodded, her anger spent.

'Yes, I do remember Bishop; the bleaching yards worked all through the night. It was a good thing Ursula didn't inspect Faustina's women too carefully; they'd not had their final rinse and the smell was— '

A cry went up and people started pointing.

Cordula and Clematius returned their attention to events below where movement had just been spotted at the tent.

'Oh, where *is* my Morgan?' she muttered out loud to herself. 'He should be here for this; he was due yesterday; why isn't he here?'

Far below, Ursula emerged from the tent. She was dressed in her full pure white commander's uniform; and it was smothered all over with blood stains; even the fine feathered plumage of her helmet was flecked with red.

The entire gathering; Hun, Roman, Britannic, Germanic – man, woman and child – fell silent as she moved clear from the tent and stood completely still for the longest of moments as if catching her breath. Then, letting out a loud cry of victory, she thrust her hand aloft and punched the air in triumph; all present could instantly see that her entire arm was soaked in blood; and that in her clenched fist, she was holding something.

Upon seeing her gesture, the entire First Athena let out a great cheer.

'*She's done it!*'

Cordula thumped the wall with her fist.

'Yes-yes-yes, she's done it; she's *actually* done it!'

'Done what?' asked Clematius.

'Wait; you'll see!' she replied, then started cheering. '*Well done Ursula! You did it—you did it!*'

Her excitement prompted those around her to start cheering and their cries were, in turn, picked up by the people below. Very quickly, everyone in the crowd was shouting even though they didn't know yet why.

Back down in the petal field, Ursula leapt upon Swift and urged the strong mare forward. The rope connected to her harness instantly sprung into the air and started tugging at the animal skins that formed the tent sides, causing them to come loose. One last peg held briefly, stretching the skins out like a bat's wing before it too let go and the whole tent broke free. As it came away, a sight was revealed that caused the citizenry of Colonia to gasp with amazement and the Huns to let out an ominous guttural cry.

There for all to see was the naked body of Mundzuk, lying on his back upon a raised bed. His head and one arm were dangling over the side, his throat was cut from ear to ear and a large pool of blood spread out from his groin. It was now plain to everyone what it was that Ursula was holding up; the scourge of Rome's northern provinces was dead, and had been emasculated.

Ursula rode Swift over toward the First Athena, back to Pinnosa and the other commanders, with the remnants of the tent flapping wildly behind her, rapidly losing anything that remained of the neatly-arranged wreaths of white flowers.

As Cordula watched, she yearned with all her heart to be down there with her old friends, standing beneath the legion's standards, enjoying Ursula's moment of triumph and sharing in their jubilant embraces.

But then, Ursula did something which was totally unexpected. She was almost back with the legion and already close enough for the commanders to be showering her with praise when, with a wild yell, she veered Swift round and broke into a full gallop, heading straight towards Rugila and the Hun delegation, still brandishing Mundzuk's genitalia on high and screaming a furious and powerful war cry.

Cordula quickly glanced to her left; Rugila was hastily withdrawing to the safety of their ranks and the open 'corridor' was closing tight behind him. She looked back at Ursula and saw her redouble her efforts to pursue him; urging Swift forward.

'*NO!*' she cried. '*Please Ursula; NO-OOO-OOO!*'

This time the crowd knew exactly why Cordula had cried out and were quick to echo her.

'*No! No! Don't!*'

Ursula was now getting dangerously close to the horde, still aiming for the point where Rugila had disappeared; and the crowd's pleas for her to stop intensified. Then, as they all looked on helplessly, their fears were realised as from out of the Hun ranks flew a single well-aimed spear which plunged into her leg just above her knee and impaled her to Swift's flank, penetrating deep into the mare's side.

The great horse neighed as she reared in distress, and Ursula's face was a mask of agony as she dropped her trophy and tried desperately to pull the weapon out. Struggling with her sudden pain, Swift started kicking wildly and turned to face the horde sideways, presenting a clear target. A volley of arrows instantly flew toward them; two embedded themselves in Swift's rear, while another caught Ursula's unprotected shoulder and went in deep.

'*NO-OOO! PLEASE GOD! NO-OOO!*'

Pinnosa's powerful cry could be heard throughout the petal field.

'*URSULA-AAA-AAA!*'

She urged Artemis forward and the great black mare broke into a full gallop.

'*No! Pinnosa, don't!*' shouted Cordula.

Then, Brittola too shouted '*Ursula!*' and Feather also set off as fast as she could go.

'*No! Brittola! No, you mustn't!*' cried Cordula.

She then saw Martha break ranks to chase after Brittola with Saula close behind; and now all four of her old friends were galloping hard across the petal field with their shields raised high to fend off the hail of arrows and missiles that assailed them.

Meanwhile, Ursula and Swift had come to a complete halt; the pain was too much for them both. Ursula was making no further attempt to extract the spear pinning her to Swift's side; instead, she was leaning forward and speaking into Swift's ear as if she was trying to comfort her. Just then, another flurry of arrows flew; one penetrated Ursula's arm which she was using to shield her face, and another sank deep into Swift's neck just beneath her flowing mane.

'*URSULA!*'

Pinnosa's cry caused Ursula to look back and she saw her friends closing in fast. She waved feebly as if shooing them away, then turned Swift to face the horde once more; and urged her to move forward.

Rider and mount mustered all of their remaining strength and, with their heads held high, entered the Hun ranks at the very point where Rugila and the delegation had disappeared. Large pikes, spears and other blades of every imaginable description closed in upon them and they disappeared from sight, engulfed by a seething mass of metal and men.

At that moment, three loud horn blasts sounded from the opposite end of the petal field. Cordula looked round and saw Faustina and Viventia leading the Vanguard in a furious charge to save their senior commanders. As they raced forward, their freshly-burnished armour gleamed bright beneath their billowing white cloaks, making them truly awe-inspiring and magnificent; however, Cordula was far from buoyed by the sight; for she had just seen something very worrying happening behind the cavalry; the rest of the First Athena, cohort upon cohort, was beginning to advance.

Realising what was about to happen, Cordula lifted her baby up and placed his head beside hers, so they could witness the events below together.

'Look on my son and remember well; for you will never see the likes of these fine women in white again.'

By now, the Huns were yelling their fierce war cries, filling the petal field with a screaming and screeching roar that crescendo'd as they worked themselves into a frenzy. Suddenly, the vast mass of men began to fragment and move; groups here and there were letting loose a hail of missiles before breaking into a wild undisciplined charge, waving their weapons and running headlong towards the women.

The next to fall was Pinnosa. Yelling her furious war cry and wielding both her swords, she momentarily forced the horde to scatter as she urged Artemis to follow after Swift in the hope of coming to Ursula's rescue. Artemis managed to make several strides through their ranks toward where Ursula had disappeared, before a huge pike caught her square in the centre of her chest. The great black mare collapsed instantly, falling to her knees; and Pinnosa had to leap from her back to avoid being crushed as she toppled to her side, dead.

Things were now happening so quickly, Cordula didn't know where to look next. In the same instant that Pinnosa fell, not far away Brittola was urging Feather on, desperately trying to come to her friends' aid despite having an arrow in her leg; close behind her, Saula was slashing away with her long sword at a group of tribesmen carrying long pikes and nearby Martha was struggling to avoid a second group of pikemen in order to break through to Pinnosa.

Brittola was first to succumb. She was so intent on going straight for Pinnosa she forgot to watch her left unshielded side; and a pikeman found himself in the perfect position for a deadly thrust. The cacophony of noise was far too much for any one scream to be distinguished, but Cordula was certain she heard Brittola cry 'Dear Lord, have mercy!' as she went down.

Now Saula was completely surrounded by pikemen; and just as she was fending them off, something hit her in the neck. Cordula caught a glimpse of her clasping at her blood-soaked throat before she too toppled out of sight. It was at this point that Faustina, Viventia and the rest of the Vanguard joined the fray.

For a few brief moments, as they charged into the Hun ranks with their swords flashing left and right, Cordula dared to hope that the enemy might actually be forced back and at least one of her old friends could be saved; but then she surveyed the broader scene and saw the thousands upon thousands of battle-thirsty men swarming forward; and her heart sank.

Something caught her eye to her left. She looked down and spotted a close-knit group following the Hun standard; they were withdrawing from the petal field and disappearing around the corner of the city wall. She realised it was Rugila departing along with the other Hun lords who, like many a true huntsman, were leaving their pack to its kill.

Suddenly, amidst the terrible cacophony of sounds that were assaulting her ears, Cordula plainly heard Martha shouting orders which snapped her attention back to the bloodshed. She quickly spotted her not far from where Saula had fallen. She was desperately trying to communicate something to Viventia, but before she could finish her message, her horse was felled from beneath her; and, still brandishing her sword, she was engulfed by a mass of spikes and blades.

Cordula scoured the carnage, looking for any hopeful sign, and was astonished to see that Pinnosa was still standing. Having lost her shield, she was using Artemis' dead body to protect her back. She was holding her ground with both swords drawn; and the bodies of many dead Huns were scattered about her feet. Screaming her defiance, she was daring the tribesmen who had formed a loose semicircle around her, to attack.

As Cordula looked on, a young Hun with a dagger leapt over Artemis and came at Pinnosa from behind. She spun around and made short shrift of him with her long sword, but while she was doing so, a massive pike was launched from the rabble. It hit home right between her shoulders and went in deep. She fell to the ground instantly; and Cordula was certain that she was dead before the mob was upon her.

By the time of evening bells, it was all over. Faustina, Viventia and the Vanguard had fought valiantly and had killed many of the horde before they were overrun. With the cavalry all gone, the infantry had then been easy prey, mere fodder for more carnage and slaughter.

Cordula had been so overwhelmed by the sheer scale of the massacre, she'd became immune to witnessing death after death; the sights before her eyes simply left her numb, incapable of feeling. She'd nevertheless watched the entire bloody tragedy unfold and throughout it all she'd held her son up in front of her, hoping that somehow the images would sear themselves into his youthful mind even though he was far too young to comprehend what was happening.

Below her on one of the ramparts, she could hear Bishop Clematius and the Astraeans chanting in Latin. Whenever she recognised one of the verses, she would join in as she continued to stare in sadness and despair at the awful place, the battlefield where her friends had perished.

To her distraught mind, a white radiant light, that had burned bright for so long like a beacon in the darkness, had been extinguished right before her eyes by a smothering, and stifling, black cloud.

The white petals strewn upon the field had briefly turned red with blood, before being trampled into the mud; pure white cloaks ripped from their wearers' necks were now nothing but bloody and muddy shreds; and countless mutilated bodies lay across Shepherds' Meadow like discarded cuts of meat.

Cordula continued to watch until long after the sun had set, keeping her vigil, wishing, hoping and praying for the Huns to depart; yet still they remained long after the fateful event had ended, poring over the dead, both horses and women, in the twilight; and helping themselves to anything of value.

The once proud and magnificent First Athena was no more, just lifeless bodies scattered like discarded chaff across a bloodied field … rich pickings for the scavengers of the night.

EPILOGUE

The following morning, the horde had departed and there wasn't a Hun to be seen.

Morgan arrived at Colonia around mid-morning. The day before, he'd been travelling at a steady pace in order to give Hermes a well-earned rest; but late in the afternoon he'd met a merchant who'd told him of the imminent approach of the Huns so he'd ridden Hermes hard through the night, determined to reach Colonia, and Cordula, as soon as possible.

When he eventually found her, she was rocking her baby boy in her arms and wandering through Shepherds' Meadow in a daze, completely oblivious to the activity all around her. A large contingent of the city's guards were digging a vast series of deep holes to act as mass graves and the city folk were busy loading cart after cart with dismembered corpses, both horse and human; and making preparations for a mass burial.

He called out her name, but she didn't answer at first, being obsessed with trying to find one solitary object, anything, no matter how insignificant, that would remind her of her old friends; but there was nothing to be found; between them, the Huns and other night scavengers had taken everything. When, eventually, she heard her husband's call, she looked up and saw him, then ran into his arms as fast as she could.

'It's time for us to leave,' he said eventually after their embrace. 'I've made arrangements for a galley to be prepared at Gesoriacum to take all the attendants back to Britannia and— '

'You mean— '

'Yes, we're going home my dear—oh, and we'll be taking our own new attendant with us.'

'"Our new attendant"? What are you talking about?' Cordula looked at him quizzically. '*Who* are you talking about?'

Morgan looked across at Hermes who was standing nearby, put his fingers to his lips and whistled. Hermes moved aside, exposing Oleander who was waiting quietly behind with her belongings. As she walked up to them, she looked a little awkward; and as she drew near, she hesitated.

'I-I don't want to appear ungrateful, Master, but a father doesn't have the final say when it comes to looking after a child;

it's a mother's decision.' She looked at Cordula and asked politely. 'Will you have me, Mistress?'

'What a question Oleander! You may as well ask "Will Rusticus have his wine?"'

Oleander didn't just smile, she laughed; then she darted forward and kissed Cordula's hand.

'Do you know, Mistress, I always wanted to care for a boy.' She looked up at Morgan. 'Don't you think it's about time this boy of yours had a name? He needs a strong brave name like "Arthur" or "Victor" or something.'

Morgan and Cordula both nodded then spoke as one.

'"Arthur" it is!'

Oleander reached for the baby, took him into her arms and gently rocked him to-and-fro.

'So, you're Arthur eh? Hello, little Arthur. Your parents have given you a very good name you know, a very good name indeed. It means "great bear" and it's a very special name for boys just like "Ursula" is a special name for—sorry, Mistress.'

Cordula could contain herself no longer; she collapsed into her husband's arms and sobbed her heart out. Morgan held her tight and waited patiently until her sorrow was spent; then he gently turned her away from the battlefield and led her past the scorched stage that had lost its dais back toward the city gate which was once again open wide. As they walked through the tall arch arm in arm, they began to talk.

'Before we depart for Britannia,' said Cordula, 'do you think we could ask Bishop Clematius to christen Arthur? It would mean an awful lot to me.'

'I think that is a very good idea.' Morgan looked at his wife and smiled. 'Do you know something; I have a feeling the bishop will soon be getting many such requests. There will be many more Arthurs and Ursulas, of that you can be certain; and so there should be! We should fill the world with such names in memory of the greatest "little bear" of all, and of the glorious women who followed her; our own truly unique … Ursula.'

THE END

Historical Note

In Cologne Germany, to the rear of the Hauptbahnhof just off Ursula Strasse and tucked away in a quiet unassuming cobbled square named Ursula Platz, is the Basilica church of St. Ursula; a pleasant reconstructed sixteenth century church well worth a visit should you ever be in the vicinity.

What should interest you more, however, and give you cause to pause and linger in the Platz, is the events that took place there over 1500 years ago a thousand years before the modern-day church was built; for on that very ground beneath the anonymous cobbles which in Antiquity lay immediately outside one of the main gates to Colonia – 'the jewel of Rome north of the Alps' – something truly terrible took place.

Whatever did happen there most probably transpired sometime around the fourth or fifth centuries. This was the time of the collapse of Rome; the time of the Germanic invasions; the time of the chaos that led the whole of Western Europe into the Dark Ages. Many terrible things were happening in many places and all at once, but only some were properly recorded. History's front page was full and this story simply did not make it into the record.

Turn sharp right as you enter the church and go into the Golden Chamber. See the bones of victims stacked high, literally floor to ceiling. See the skulls of women brutally murdered who were later wrapped in medieval packaging to be sold as religious reliquaries; indeed, there were so many bodies in the mass grave beside this church, it became a veritable factory of relics with more than enough raw material to sustain a thriving industry. For hundreds of years, bits of Ursuline bone were what brought most visitors to Cologne; indeed, as icons go, Ursula and her 'virgin-martyrs' were the fourteenth century equivalent of Elvis!

Back in the main chamber of the modern church, set in the wall and about the size of a large TV screen, is the enigmatic Clematius stone. Its difficult-to-decipher and rather ambiguous Latin inscription* carved soon after the appalling event provides us with the only 'historical' evidence for the atrocity that once occurred here. Apart from giving us the sole name we have that is associated with the real-life episode, 'Clematius', it simply alludes in vague terms to the martyrdom of many virgins and fails to enlighten us about who they were or why they were there. But that in itself is surely enough! It is testament that something *did* happen; something involving the death of many hundreds of women.

It may not have been written down and recorded, but such a powerful story about some undoubtedly incredible women simply *had* to be told; and so, it was! The Romanised Germans of the Rhineland made it their own. As bear-worshipping folk, they most probably changed the name of the women's leader to Ursula, 'Little Bear'; and they passed it orally down through the generations, no doubt elaborating here and embroidering there; and the truth, as well as the distortions, became preserved in the ageless aspic of myth and legend.

Then, several hundred years later, Latin scholars, hagiographers sent from the Vatican, came to the Rhineland on an important task: they sought pagan heroes they could turn into saints, thereby achieving the church's ambition to expand by becoming truly 'Catholic', truly all-embracing. The papal clerics concocted their own interpretation of the stories they heard from the Rhineland folk and 'Saint Ursula' was created, the forlorn fateful woman who led eleven thousand 'virgins' to their death whilst on an ill-fated and unfortunate 'pilgrimage'.

But the German scholars accompanying the papal officials noted a different story, recording references to the women as being "armour-clad", "weapon-bearing" horse riders who were "well-versed in the arts of war". These descriptions were so potent, even the priests themselves could not resist the iconic image of Ursula being depicted with her clutching an arrow, or even a brace of them. Let there be no mistake, all agreed, Ursula's 'virgins' were no strangers to weaponry, but what the Church preferred to ignore was that the women were not on a 'pilgrimage' of some kind, they were women of war, they had formed an army and they were on a mission!

The truth is … the truth is lost. The actual story of whoever the real women were, and whatever really happened, is something we shall never know. I have, nevertheless, attempted to piece together the sparse fragments of the real story that have come down to us and incorporated these, plus the main elements of the Ursuline legend, into this fictional account, including very importantly the great storm at sea which scattered their whole fleet. There almost certainly was a real Pinnosa as well as a real Brittola, Martha, Saula and Cordula; these names survived in the oral tradition and were recorded by both the papal hagiographers and their accompanying German scholars; and who knows, maybe amongst their number there really was a truly unique and remarkable princess from Britannia; one who formed an army of women and led them on a campaign to the Continent where they met a horrific death at the merciless hands of the terrifying Huns right outside the gates to the heavily-fortified Roman city of Cologne.

* The Latin inscription on the Clematius Stone reads as follows:

DIVINIS FLAMMEIS VISIONIB. FREQVENTER ADMONIT. ET VIRTVTIS MAGNÆ MAI IESTATIS MARTYRII CAELESTIVM VIRGIN IMMINENTIVM EX PARTIB. ORIENTIS EXSIBITVS PRO VOTO CLEMATIVS V. C. DE PROPRIO IN LOCO SVO HANC BASILICA VOTO QVOD DEBEBAT A FVNDAMENTIS RESTITVIT SI QVIS AVTEM SVPER TANTAM MAIIESTATEM HVIIVS BASILICÆ VBI SANC TAE VIRGINES PRO NOMINE. XPI. SAN GVINEM SVVM FVDERVNT CORPVS ALICVIIVS DEPOSVERIT EXCEPTIS VIRCINIB. SCIAT SE SEMPITERNIS TARTARI IGNIB. PVNIENDVM

(A certain Clematius, a man of senatorial rank, who seems to have lived in the Orient before going to Cologne, was led by frequent visions to rebuild in this city, on land belonging to him, a basilica which had fallen into ruins, in honour of virgins who had suffered martyrdom on that spot.**)

** English translation courtesy of: *The Catholic Encyclopaedia, Volume XV* Copyright © 1912 by Robert Appleton Company

Appendix

Roman place names and their modern equivalents:

Aquae Mattiacorum	Wiesbaden
Arelate	Arles
Ariconium	Bury Hill, Weston-under-Penyard
Argentorate	Strasbourg
Batavia	Holland*
Bonna	Bonn
Britannia	Britain*
Calleva Atrebatum	Silchester
Causennae	Ancaster
Castra Regina	Regensburg
Cesaraugusta	Zaragoza
Cilurnum	Walwick Chesters
Colonia	Cologne
Confluentes	Koblenz
Constantinopolis	Istanbul
Corinium	Cirencester
Danuvius	Danube
Deva	Chester
Dubris	Dover
Durobrivae	Rochester
Eboracum	York
Emerita Augusta	Merida
Germania	Germany*
Gallia	France, Belgium, Switzerland*
Gesoriacum	Boulogne
Glevum	Gloucester
Hibernia	Ireland*
Hispania	Spain & Portugal*
Italia	Italy*
Liger	River Loire
Lindinis	Ilchester
Lindum	Lincoln
Londinium	London
Luguvalium	Carlisle
Lutetia	Paris

Magnis	Kenchester
Moenus	River Main
Mogontiacum	Mainz
Maridunum	Carmarthen
Moesia	Serbia, Macedonia, Bulgaria*
Noviomagus	Nijmegen
Oceanus Britannicus	English Channel*
Oceanus Germanicus	North Sea*
Parthia	Iran*
Rhenus	Rhine River
Rhodanus	Rhone River
Roma	Rome (the city)
Rutupiae	Richborough
Sabrina	River Severn
Segedunum	Wallsend
Sequana	River Seine
Tamesis	River Thames
Thracia	Bulgaria, Greece, Turkey*
Treveris	Trier
Vaga River	River Wye
Vedra River	River North Tyne
Venta Belgarum	Winchester
Vindobona	Vienna
Viroconium	Wroxeter

(*approximate equivalent)

341

Printed in Great Britain
by Amazon